AMMON

AMMON

a novel

H.B. MOORE

Covenant Communications, Inc.

Cover image: *Filled with the Spirit of God* © Gary Kapp.

Cover design copyright © 2011 by Covenant Communications, Inc.

Published by Covenant Communications, Inc.
American Fork, Utah

Printed in the United States of America
First Printing: June 2011

17 16 15 14 13 12 11   10 9 8 7 6 5 4 3 2 1

ISBN-13: 978-1-60861-238-3

PRAISE FOR
H.B. MOORE'S BOOKS

"The teeming world that H.B. Moore has created in her series on notable Book of Mormon leaders is as real as morning dew on roses. Believable events and social currents pour out of her pages [in *Alma the Younger*], flowing through the lives and ambitions of her heroes and heroines. Palaces and huts, forests and cities, rogues and gentlefolk all form bright threads in her rich narrative. Just as Moore's other works, this volume offers a superb read."

—S. Kent Brown
Emeritus Professor of Ancient Scripture, BYU

"The artistry behind [*Alma the Younger*] gives us great insight into how the adversary works—how he can take someone as noble as the son of the high priest and place the cord of discontent around his neck and then use small, even true things, to make that discontent grow until the cord becomes a chain. This is a masterful, beautifully written novel."

—G.G. Vandagriff
Whitney Award–Winning Author

"[In *Alma the Younger*], Moore's genius is her handling of Alma the Younger himself. As this young man turns from truth and discovers how his natural charisma and talents can be employed in what feels to him like a righteous cause, I was dismayed to find myself actually sympathizing with him. I've read Mosiah 27 dozens of times, but only while reading *Alma the Younger* did I actually understand how someone can arrive at that dark place called anti-Christ. The scary thing is that the rationalizing that leads to it sometimes makes all too much sense. Even without the gripping story and strong characters, that insight alone is worth this book's price."

—Michael Knudsen
Author and Reviewer

"Reading [*Women of the Book of Mormon*], I was edified by my role in the lives of my family. A lot of what I do is background and foundational—but it matters. Both for their growth and mine. I can't wait until my daughters ask why there is so little mention of women in the Book of Mormon. This book is a powerful witness to the fact that life is hard for everyone—that is how we become strong, it is how we learn to carry the yoke of being a daughter of God."

—Josi S. Kilpack
Whitney Award–Winning Author

"*Women of the Book of Mormon* is a book I will return to read again during my scripture study or when I need a moment to ponder how blessed I am in my own life trials. . . . The information is well researched and documented, yet easy to read and interesting."

—Lu Ann Staheli
Best of [Utah] State Author

"*Alma* has it all: vibrant characters, danger, spiritual challenges, and bittersweet joy. Moore has created an epic tale that's simply impossible to put down."

—Jason F. Wright
New York Times Bestselling Author

"An exciting and faith-promoting tale—the Book of Mormon in 3D and technicolor."

—Richard Cracroft
BYU Magazine

"[In *Alma*], H.B.Moore brings the remarkable characters to life through well-researched detail, a hard-to-put-down story line, and scripturally accurate counsel that reflects the author's own deep understanding of the scriptures. I have thoroughly enjoyed this series and the way in which the books cause you to ponder the scriptural accounts."

—Al Rounds
Artist

"[*Alma*] is an exciting and interesting exploration of the followers and enemies of Alma and how they might have been involved in and affected by what happened. Not only do the characters struggle to survive, but they also love and mourn and laugh and misunderstand and grow together, or apart, as the case may be. Moore is true to what is known about that time and place, and this book offers worthy speculations of what surrounded those events."

—Kathleen Dalton-Woodbury
Mormon Times

"H.B.Moore takes the reader on an incredible journey of a man who makes the ultimate sacrifice. *Abinadi* is a historically rich, well-researched, poignant account of one of the most influential prophets in the Book of Mormon. Moore's creativity, mixed with the heart of Mesoamerican culture, brings new insights to the influence that the prophet Abinadi had on generations to come."

—Dian Thomas
#1 New York Times Bestselling Author

"[In *Abinadi*], Moore once again establishes herself as the best Book of Mormon fiction writer in the business. She has created a flesh-and-blood Abinadi that will forever change my perception of this remarkable man, his influence on Alma, and the importance of his mission in Book of Mormon history."

—Charlene Hirschi
The Herald Journal

"[*Abinadi*] is a delightful combination of careful research and of getting inside an inspiring character. Although H.B.Moore disclaims being a scholar, her Abinadi not only lives and breathes but is authentic to the time and place in which he lived. While she paints a fuller picture of a fascinating Book of Mormon character, she stays close to the facts, as presented in that book."

—Ann Madsen
Ancient Scripture Department, BYU

"In the first three volumes of her [*Out of Jerusalem*] series, H.B.Moore showed that she could create a view of an ancient world that combines the best scholarship with a lively imagination. She does a fine job of walking the tricky line between faithfulness to the scripture and creative storytelling. She opened up the hearts of her characters in ways both remarkably touching and authentic. In this fourth and final volume, [*Land of Inheritance*], she does all of that, as well as writes one of the most exciting adventure tales I have read in a while."

—Andrew Hall
Association of Mormon Letters

In loving memory of Marjorie Newbold Sjoblom,
who taught the gospel her whole life and now
continues on the other side.

MESOAMERICA
The Late Preclassic Era
300 B.C. — A.D. 250

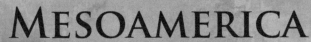

GULF OF MEXICO

Bay of Campeche

M E X I C O

Narrow Neck of Land

Wilderness of Hermounts

Valley of Gideon

Chiapa de Corzo ●

▲ Hill Amnih

Land of Zarahemla

R. Sidon

GULF OF TEHUANTEPEC

● Iza

Sali

UNITED STATES

MEXICO

SOUTH AMERICA

N

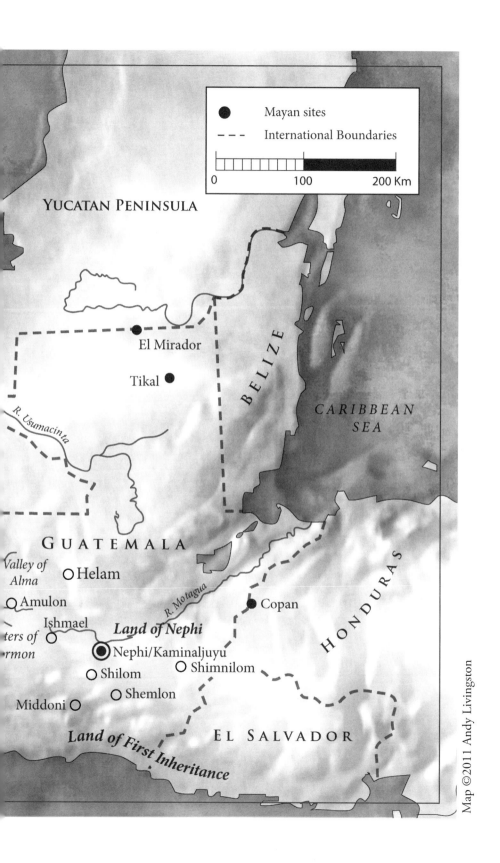

Map ©2011 Andy Livingston

ACKNOWLEDGMENTS

Writing about Ammon was like a breath of fresh air after writing the previous volume, *Alma the Younger*. I had already set up Ammon's character in *Alma the Younger* and chose alpha readers who were familiar with that book.

Part of the challenge in writing this book was fully developing Ammon's character beyond the Primary stories of the missionary who cut off the Lamanites' arms at the waters of Sebus. I'm indebted to those who helped me with the development and fine-tuning of this manuscript, specifically Lu Ann Staheli, Robison Wells, Jeff Savage, Michele Holmes, and Sarah Eden. In addition, Annette Lyon, Josi Kilpack, and Julie Wright read the entire manuscript on a tight deadline, each offering their own specialties in editing. All of these people are extraordinary writers, and I have to pinch myself from time to time to remind myself that they are such great friends.

A special thanks goes to Kristina Boler, Marie Waldvogel, and Alex Buckley. They offered valuable insights and have been a great support. Many thanks also go to excellent map designer Andy Livingston and website designer Phill Babbitt.

I appreciate my father, S. Kent Brown, who is always willing to answer my many questions about the smallest of details. Also, my mother, Gayle Brown, and my father-in-law, Lester Moore, have been champions of my work for many years, purchasing and giving away many copies to family and friends.

I'm so grateful to all those at my publishing house, Covenant Communications, who've put in many hours in order to deliver the final product into your hands: editor Eliza Nevin, with whom I had many insightful discussions preproduction; editor Samantha Van Walraven, who waded through the manuscript and offered many helpful suggestions to make it shine; managing editor Kathy Jenkins, who was enthusiastic about this project and gave me the green light on this story; designer Margaret Weber, who is always too modest but deserves tons of praise for delivering beautiful covers; Robby Nichols in marketing who keeps my career moving upward; and Kelly Smurthwaite, who goes above and beyond in publicity. Thank you!

I also belong to a few writing communities—the LDStorymakers, League of Utah Writers, and ANWA—that have been excellent sources of inspiration, discussion, and support.

Finally, endless thanks to my husband, Chris, who takes over the household when the deadlines are looming, and thanks to my children who make living a good life all the more worth it.

PREFACE

This volume covers the journey and teachings of Ammon, as outlined in Alma 17:6–Alma 20, in addition to Alma 21:18–23. Chronologically, it is a sequel to my other historical novel, *Alma the Younger*, but can be read as a stand-alone. Writing about Ammon was a completely different experience than writing about Alma the Younger's descent into wickedness and his eventual change of heart and emergence back into the light of Christ. Ammon was an incredible man, one who gave up his inheritance of the throne of Zarahemla, where he could have lived out his days in relative comfort. Instead, he dedicated his life—in fact, the next fourteen years—to missionary work in a foreign land among his enemies.

In the previous volume, *Alma the Younger*, Ammon is a close friend and co-conspirator with Alma the Younger when they set about destroying the Lord's Church in Zarahemla. When they are visited by an angel, both have a mighty change of heart.

In this volume, *Ammon*, Alma the Younger remains in Zarahemla to continue preaching repentance, and Ammon ventures into Lamanite territory with his brethren, determined to change the hearts of his enemies.

One of the most incredible events in the Book of Mormon takes place between Ammon and the wife of King Lamoni. Ammon arrives in the land of Ishmael to serve the Lamanite king and ultimately gains a chance to teach the Savior's message to the Lamanites.

When Ammon is given the opportunity to deliver the Lord's message, King Lamoni collapses and is consumed with a vision. After two days and two nights pass with no change, his queen decides to consult with Ammon—a Nephite and an intruder into her court. Although her husband has approved Ammon to live among the people, this does not mean the queen has such a conviction. Nevertheless, she exercises faith and asks for Ammon's advice.

Ammon promptly tells the queen that the king is not dead. "Believest thou this?" he adds (Alma 19:9).

The queen replies, "I have no witness save thy word . . . nevertheless I believe that it shall be according as thou hast said" (v. 9).

Before we learn Ammon's answer, let's remember who he is and where he came from. Ammon is the son of King Mosiah and the grandson of King Benjamin. His childhood friend is Alma the Younger. He has given up everything—his claim to the throne and his home in Zarahemla—to teach his enemy. Yet, to a Lamanite queen, he says, "Blessed art thou because of thy exceeding faith; I say unto thee, woman, there has not been such great faith among all the people of the Nephites" (v. 10).

I find this passage remarkable in more ways than one. First, a "heathen" queen is touched enough by the Spirit to recognize truth and respond with pure faith—faith that, according to Ammon, exceeds all the Nephites' he's been associated with. Second, the Lord truly is all-powerful and His spirit can touch the hearts of even the most "stiffnecked . . . whose hearts delight in the shedding of blood; whose days have been spent in the grossest iniquity" (Alma 26:24).

An exciting change is in effect among the royal family of the land of Ishmael, and Ammon's actions are at the heart of it. The sacrifice on Ammon's part is immense.

We might think of our own modern-day missionaries when studying the life of Ammon. Sending out missionaries into the world for eighteen months to two years is daunting enough for parents. Think of Mosiah and what led up to his final consent to allow not only one son but four to leave the relative safety of home life to travel into enemy territory.

King Mosiah has no idea how long his sons would be gone, if they'd ever return, what their successes would be, or who would succeed his throne. Ammon and his brethren "did plead with their father many days" (Mosiah 28:5) until Mosiah finally inquired of the Lord and received a revelation in which he is promised that his sons will have eternal life and be delivered "out of the hands of the Lamanites" (v. 7). Of course, this doesn't guarantee they'd see each other again, but a parent's ultimate wish for his or her children is eternal life—a promise, that in this case, softens the blow of saying good-bye.

There is no doubt that with careful study of the Book of Mormon events, especially those verses that chronicle Ammon's missionary work, we find that we have a loving Heavenly Father who truly cares about all of His children.

CHARACTER CHART

Ammon—eldest son of King Mosiah

Aaron—son of King Mosiah

Omner—son of King Mosiah

Himni—son of King Mosiah

Muloki and Ammah—missionary companions

Lamoni—king of the land of Ishmael

      Son: Pacal*

      Daughters: Meztli* and Romie*

Moriah*—King Lamoni's clothier

      Son: Zaman*

      Daughter: Elena*

Abish—servant to the queen

Gad*—blacksmith

Loki*—brother of Gad

Dedan*—border guard

Pahrun*—King Lamoni's head guard and chief advisor

Kumen*—servant

Corien*—brother to Kumen* and servant

Antiomno*—king of the land of Middoni

* Denotes fictional names/characters created by author

CHAPTER 1

Go ye into all the world, and preach the gospel to every creature.
—Mark 16:15

94 BC

"Watch out!" Ammon shouted as he tore through the brush, the bleeding tapir racing after him.

He leapt over a small stream and landed on the edge of the camp he and the other missionaries had set up the night before. As the animal screeched behind him, Ammon imagined he felt its hot angry breath at his heels.

"Why did you try to kill a tapir?" someone yelled.

But Ammon didn't have time to explain. He sprinted through the camp, scattering the other missionaries and narrowly avoiding the cooking fire. Scrambling up the rocky ledge on the other side, he grabbed several stones and turned, ready to hurl rocks at the beast.

His twenty-one-year-old brother, Aaron, who had lunged for his bow, now stood in the middle of camp, the bow pulled taut as he faced the charging beast.

"It's too fast," Ammon called out. "Run!"

Aaron didn't flinch. The arrow released and deftly hit its target in the neck, stopping the tapir almost instantly.

Everyone was silent as they turned to look at Ammon.

He let the rocks fall from his hands as he straightened and wiped the perspiration from his face. "I—uh—" He stared at the black creature with its long snout.

Omner and Himni started laughing. Ammon stared at his two youngest brothers—if any of the missionaries got into a scrape, it was usually one of them. He couldn't count how many times he'd prevented disaster when it came to those two. Now he was the disaster.

Just the night before, Ammon had successfully prevented Omner from falling into an animal trap, likely set by a Lamanite. Ammon looked around at the group of men, relief surging through him. It had been a long time since they'd laughed together. They had been traveling for weeks, surviving off the land, and constantly looking out for the Lamanites, who considered them bitter enemies.

Aaron shook his head in exasperation, but there was a smile on his face.

As the laughter settled, Ammon raised his hands. "All right," he said, catching his breath. "I'll admit to my mistake. I thought it was a small deer."

The men looked from Ammon to the black carcass. Out in the open, Ammon realized it was difficult to understand how he could have mixed up the two animals. The tapir had a thick body with short legs. Its long snout and large ears bore little resemblance to the elegant lines of a deer.

Ammon wiped his brow again, regret running through him. He'd wasted both time and energy killing a beast with cloven hooves—something they were forbidden to eat according to the law of Moses.

"What should we do with it?" Aaron asked, walking to the beast and pulling out the two protruding arrows—his precise one and Ammon's misdirected one.

"Let's drag the tapir over to that animal trap we discovered last night," Ammon said. "A Lamanite should check it soon enough."

"Won't that look suspicious?" Omner asked, his voice betraying his nervousness. At seventeen, he was the second to youngest but tended to be more hesitant than Himni, the youngest. "The Lamanites will know something happened when they see how the animal died. They'll know Nephites were here."

"It's a risk, but I don't see another choice," Ammon said. "The meat will go to waste if we leave it here."

"I'll help," Muloki said, stepping forward. He was the best hunter of the group and wouldn't have made the same mistake. Predictably, his brother Ammah followed. The two helped Ammon drag the beast through the trees toward the trap. Muloki looked like a Lamanite, with his tanned skin, thick arms, and black hair that hung to his shoulders, whereas Ammah was thin but strong and kept his curly hair short. The brothers had joined with the sons of Mosiah after converting to the true gospel of the Lord.

Ammon's forearms and neck were also dark from spending so much time in the sun, but he wouldn't be mistaken as a Lamanite. His brown hair had lightened in the sun and was cut as short as a dagger would allow. He knew his clothing would give him and the other men away from the start since Lamanite men rarely wore tunics.

As they continued to drag the tapir, staying as quiet as possible, Ammon's mind flashed back to his friend Alma, who'd remained behind in the Nephite city of Zarahemla. Alma had wanted to travel with the brothers, but King Mosiah had asked him to stay and take over for Alma the Elder as head of the Church.

It had been a bittersweet parting, and Ammon found that when he was the most tired or frustrated, he missed the things of home more.

"How far is it?" Ammah asked, interrupting Ammon's thoughts.

He glanced about the trees and vines. "We're at least halfway there." The men traded positions and started dragging again.

His thoughts returned to his upbringing. Yes, he'd grown up in a palace and, as the oldest prince, had been educated and trained to take over the kingship. But it wasn't the royal responsibility he was missing. It was the small things, like his sister's cooking and his mother's encouragement, such as when he'd shown her his first handmade dagger. He thought warmly of the renewed relationship with his father—when Ammon had found forgiveness for his wrongdoings through repentance. He remembered the compassion in his father's eyes and only hoped that by sharing the message of the Lord with the Lamanites, he could begin to redeem himself of the wrongs he'd caused among his own people.

Ammah grunted, the strain of the tapir's weight starting to slow him down.

"We're almost there," Ammon said. This jungle was thicker here than those surrounding Zarahemla, and he hadn't quite adapted to the increased humidity. A few more paces and they dumped the tapir into the pit dug for the trap.

Ammon paused, catching his breath with the others. Then he froze. Something didn't feel right: the jungle was too quiet. The usual call and chatter of birds and monkeys was missing. It was as if the trees held their breath, watching.

He brought a finger to his lips, motioning for the brothers to be quiet and follow him. They picked their way through the trees, staying as silent as possible, when they heard a harsh cry. Then another. They sounded like a mixture between a warning and a battle cry, but they were definitely human.

A flash of movement caught Ammon's attention. There was no doubt—at least one Lamanite had spotted them.

"Run!" Ammon called out. No longer careful about making noise, the missionaries tore through the jungle toward their camp.

The noise they made was nothing compared to the hollering that rose behind them. Ammon cast a glance behind. The Lamanite was chasing after them. And he was fast.

Although Ammon knew he could sprint ahead of Ammah and Muloki, he stayed at the rear. He pulled both his daggers from his waistband pouch, ready to turn and defend if needed. "To the left—we'll try to throw him off."

Muloki kept looking behind. "I can only see one chasing us—we can best him."

Ammon didn't want to risk stopping to fight. More Lamanites could be on their way. "It's too much of a risk. We need to shake him off. Go left; lead him away from the camp so he can't track us later."

But the man was gaining. Something struck Ammon's shoulder, and he moved slightly, thinking it was a branch. One glance told him he'd been grazed by an arrow.

"Get down!" Ammon said.

In front of him, Ammah and Muloki dove toward some bushes, Ammon following as another arrow sailed through the air.

"You're hit," Muloki said.

Ammon ignored him and crawled toward a thick tree. Everything was quiet again. He slowly rose to his feet, keeping his body concealed from the original direction from which the arrow had come. No Lamanite in sight now.

He tried to keep his breathing quiet as his heart hammered in his ears.

He wished he'd carried his bow with him, or at least his obsidian sword. The daggers in his hands were only good for close combat. He reached for the sling he used to hit small animals, and while trying to keep one eye on his surroundings, he picked up a rock.

Looking over at Muloki and Ammah, he motioned for them to stay down.

Then he took a step back from the tree and swung the sling twice. As he released the rock, he wondered if he'd made a mistake. The Lamanite could have plenty of help by now.

The rock embedded itself into a tree two dozen paces away. Ammon was surprised it had made it that far with all the vines.

The sound sent a quetzal flying but no return arrow from the Lamanite.

"He's left to get help," Muloki whispered.

"Let's get out of here and warn the others," Ammon said.

"How's your shoulder?" Ammah asked as they stood from their hiding place.

"It will have to wait," Ammon said. The three men raced toward camp.

When they entered the campsite, Aaron and his other brothers looked up from their tasks.

Ammon burst out, "There's someone—back there—he might be following us."

"Slow down," Aaron said as he crossed to them. His gaze went from Ammon's bleeding shoulder to his eyes. "Lamanites?"

"One spotted us," Ammon said, his breath coming in gasps. He removed the cloth belt from his tunic and pressed the belt against his shoulder. It ached like a burning torch was being held against it. "After shooting a couple of arrows, he disappeared."

"Everyone stay armed as we pack," Aaron called out to the others. Muloki and Ammah each grabbed a spear, keeping wary eyes on the surrounding foliage. Aaron looked at Ammon. "What about your shoulder?"

"We'll clean it after we get out of here. We need to move now," Ammon said. "We may only have minutes until more arrive."

***

The moon was high in the sky and the howler monkey cries had fallen silent when Ammon picked a location for their next camp. They'd traveled all day, making their way carefully around outlying settlements and hunting preserves—more evidence of civilization as they approached the borders. Ammon knew it was nearly time for them to start preaching. According to his map, they were closing in on the border of the land of Nephi.

He surveyed the moonlit terrain, just south of a set of hills. They were in a small valley. His shoulder ached fiercely, but he didn't want to stop unless he was sure they'd be safe for the night. They hadn't seen traps that would indicate hunters might show up at dawn to check on them for quite a while. "This will do for the night," he told the others. It didn't take long to organize the camp, since they used no tents but slept out in the open.

Ammon and Aaron worked together to get a fire going, striking chert together to create a spark then lighting several sides of the mound of wood. Omner and Himni scavenged for additional wood and anything that appeared edible to go along with the small game Aaron had captured along the way. They'd become quite sufficient in digging up roots and hunting for berries or other fruit over the past several weeks.

Muloki took up his usual position as guard, his brother guarding the opposite side of the camp.

Ammon spread out several of the weapons the group carried with them, checking the strength and sharpness of the spears and swords. In Zarahemla, he'd been trained in military combat and had taught himself in the craftsmanship of daggers and other weapons, but that hadn't translated into superior hunting skills. He'd brought along several more knives than the other men, just in case they lost or somehow damaged one. When he had completed the weapons check, Ammon unwrapped the animal skin map he kept protected in a square of cloth. With the light the fire provided, his gaze traveled over the familiar sketch that Gideon, a military commander in Zarahemla, had drawn for them. Aaron settled next to Ammon. "Where are we now?" Aaron asked.

Ammon pointed at a jagged line that was about a finger's length from the border of Zarahemla. "Here, just past the grouping of hills Gideon told us about. We're near the border of the land of Nephi." He looked past the fire, as if he could see the landscape in the darkness.

Aaron followed his gaze. "Will we split up?"

"I think we have to," Ammon said, although the last thing he wanted to do was say good-bye to his brothers. He'd already left his parents and sister behind in Zarahemla. "If we arrive as a group, we'll be seen as more of a threat."

The two lapsed into silence for a moment. "You're right," Aaron said. "But how will we find each other again?"

"Through the Lord's guidance," Ammon said in a quiet voice. "It would be easier to form companionships and to have each other's support. But if we arrive in various lands as single missionaries, we'll likely be listened to more. And we can spread out and teach more people."

Himni entered the camp and dumped several long pieces of wood onto the fire. "How close are we?" he asked, crouching next to Ammon. During the journey, Himni had lost a good deal of weight from his youth. His once round middle had grown lean and hard. The tunics he'd brought dwarfed him now.

"Less than an hour's walk," Ammon said.

"Who am I going with?" Himni asked.

Ammon glanced at Aaron, who nodded.

"We're all going our separate ways, Himni. Each man alone."

Himni's eyes widened. "How will we protect ourselves? You said yourself that we needed to stay together as a group, to always be armed and ready."

Ammon let a sigh escape. "That was before we were chased by the Lamanite this morning. We might be seen as a greater threat if we stay together as a group. The Lamanites must be convinced of our good intentions right from the start." Another glance at Aaron. "*Before* they attack."

A shuffle of feet drew Ammon's attention, and he looked up. Omner, Muloki, and Ammah stood listening at the edge of the circle.

Omner's expression was riddled with fear. Muloki looked as if he expected it, and Ammah glanced furtively between his brother and the other men.

"Ammon's right," Aaron said. He'd spent more time studying their people's history and the nature of the Lamanites than the others. "If the Lamanites capture . . . or discover us as lone men . . . we'll seem much less of a threat."

"And be more teachable," Ammah finished in a hushed voice, clearly understanding.

"Exactly," Ammon said. Ammah was quiet and never did anything without his brother—causing Ammon to worry about him the most. But Ammah had seemed determined to come on the mission and had professed his faith on more than one occasion.

Omner folded his arms. "How long do we teach among the Lamanites before trying to reunite again?"

Ammon remained silent for a moment then said, "At the close of our harvest, whenever that might be."

Himni rose to his feet and stepped toward the fire, stretching out his hands as if for warmth. "When do we separate?"

The words wrenched through Ammon, and a myriad of emotions rocked through him. Separating from his brethren would be the hardest part. "Tomorrow morning," he said in a low voice. "We will each travel to our own destination according to the will of God."

All eyes riveted on him as he continued. "I've been fasting today so that I may administer to each of you before we go our different ways. We've been protected by the Lord in the wilderness." Ammon met the gaze of each man in turn. "If we continue to fast and pray, the Lord will grant us His Spirit so we may be an instrument in His hands."

As he spoke, he spread his palms up as if to emphasize his hands would become the Lord's hands. He winced slightly at the still prominent scar across his right palm. All of the missionaries in the group had a similar scar on their right hands—a reminder of a terrible blood oath they'd made together in Zarahemla, one that preceded an evil plot to overthrow the true Church.

But tonight, these men came together, scarred, yes, but united in a completely different cause. They would not forget their past, yet they would use their hard-earned lessons to drum up the deepest compassion for the Lamanites.

Ammon bowed his head for a few moments, praying that he'd know the right words to say as he administered to his brethren. A whisper came, strong yet soft: *Be comforted.*

Warmth spread through him as he lifted his head. The other men looked at him in wonder. They'd heard it too.

The same voice, barely above a whisper, spoke again: *Go forth among the Lamanites, thy brethren, and establish my word.*

Ammon stepped forward, putting one hand on Aaron's shoulder and his other hand on Himni's. The men drew together, each with a hand on a shoulder or across a back until they formed a united circle around the fire.

Heart pounding, Ammon's eyes pricked with tears as the voice continued, *Yet ye shall be patient in long-suffering and afflictions, that ye may show forth good examples unto them in me, and I will make an instrument of thee in my hands unto the salvation of many souls.*

The silence that followed was pure, sweet, and comforting. No one spoke for several moments as they stood together in the circle. "Amen," Aaron whispered after awhile. The others' murmured amens followed.

Ammon turned and embraced his brother then the other men in the group, one by one.

"And now," he said in a trembling voice as he looked into the faces of his fellow missionaries, "I will give each of you a blessing according to your station."

CHAPTER 2

A wise man is strong; yea, a man of knowledge increaseth strength.
—Proverb 24:5

Land of Ishmael

"You ornery boy," Elena murmured to the quetzal she was trying to feed. The bird hopped on one foot in its bamboo cage as Elena nudged a small avocado forward with a stick. She'd been too close to hostile quetzals before. Thin scars from numerous beak and claw marks lined her fair skin. She wouldn't make that mistake again.

"Come on, boy," she urged in a musical voice. "Tomorrow you'll be set free, right after the plucking. You'll be back in the wild and can grow back your beautiful feathers."

Still, the bird backed away, its wary eyes flitting around its cage. Elena sat down with a sigh as she watched the bird ruffle its blue and red feathers on its haughty breast. This was a mature male, with feathers nearly as long as her arm.

Out of habit, she pulled down her sleeves, completely covering her arms. Elena had been born with Nephite skin—not surprising because both of her parents were former Nephites. They'd fled the city of Zarahemla when her father's brother had cheated him out of his inheritance. The two brothers had been at odds since their youth, and her father had finally declared he'd rather "live among the filthy Lamanites" than be subservient to his own greedy brother. Her father's pride had quickly crumbled when they were captured by a group of Lamanite guards just outside the land of Nephi.

Brought before High King Laman, her father had pledged his loyalty, in spite of the color of his skin. They'd served as near-slaves to the Lamanite court until her father had created a beautiful and intricate coat of quetzal feathers as a gift to the newly ordained King Lamoni, who had just been commissioned to rule over the land of Ishmael.

Lamoni had fallen in love with her father's work and ordered the family to join him there. From the time Elena was ten, her family had lived on a small homestead not far from Lamoni's palace. Her father was commissioned to create all ceremonial clothing for the new royal family, in addition to being allowed to make ceremonial attire for local customers and clothing for the aristocracy.

It was a quiet, peaceful life, for the most part. For the past eight years, Elena had followed her brother around, learning to hunt birds and, in turn, designing capes and headdresses. She loved it and only broke away when it was time to prepare supper. Her mother hadn't lived to see the day of their prosperity but had died young, just after moving to the land of Ishmael and suffering from an infection.

"He's still not eating?" a voice said behind Elena.

She turned to see her brother. Zaman strode across the courtyard. His fair skin didn't seem to bother him one bit. Being outdoors so much and wearing nothing but a loin cloth and a sling across his torso made his skin nearly as dark as a Lamanite's.

He stopped and peered into the cage. "I want him full and lazy before the plucking, or we'll have a hard time."

Elena nodded. Both her brother and father had significant scars on their arms, even though they wore leather arm wraps while handling the birds. "When does Father return?"

"Tonight. New merchants have come to the market with furs and cloth. He'll be haggling over them until they've bled every last bit of silver from him."

Elena laughed, imagining her father arguing over every hand span of fur or cloth, determining whether it was fine enough for the king. Her father might have skin the color of a Nephite, but over the years, he'd commanded respect from the Lamanite aristocracy. He dressed in fine clothing and wore his trademark multicolored cape.

"He'll stay as long as it takes," Zaman said. "Abish is coming tomorrow to place an order for the royal family." A small smile played on his face.

Elena watched the emotions on his face with interest. Abish and Zaman had been recently betrothed, though it was not official since Abish was waiting for the queen's approval. Since she was an orphan and had been under the queen's care, working as a servant for the past several years, it was as if the queen were her guardian.

"Is that where you were this morning? Visiting Abish?" she asked.

His face reddened, and he stopped smiling. "It was business only."

Elena knew it was more than that, but she let her brother continue.

"The great feast is in less than a month, and the court wants to impress the high king," he said, rushing through an explanation. "I was simply discussing with her the preparation of the design samples we will present to the queen."

She smiled but didn't say anything.

"Father says he wants to show Abish the designs you made for the queen and princesses. They might be desirable for the upcoming Maize Festival."

Elena perked up at the mention of the opportunity to show some of her designs. "The festival is in two weeks; I'd have to hurry if they order the costumes."

Her brother nodded absently, his thoughts already elsewhere. Elena could easily guess he was thinking of Abish. Elena was eager for the queen's approval of the marriage. If all went well, Zaman and Abish would marry in two months' time. Although the woman was Lamanite, she seemed very interested in their Nephite roots. Elena enjoyed talking to her about them too. With the loss of Elena's mother, Abish had become a comfort to her. Abish had asked about Zarahemla, the government, and even the main religious practices, which were so different from the Lamanites' various gods and goddesses of nature. As a people, the Lamanites rarely questioned religion and went along with the beliefs of the current king.

Elena didn't remember too much about her Nephite life, but when she'd offered to get more details from her father or brother, Abish had quickly told her not to. Elena was surprised that Abish didn't just ask Zaman.

Her brother crouched in front of the cage; the quetzal seemed to be more relaxed now. With a stick, he pushed the avocado slowly toward the bird then backed away. He motioned for Elena to move away, and she rose to creep back. After a few minutes of silence, the bird snatched the fruit, swallowing it whole.

Zaman grinned but put a finger to his lips and motioned for her to move away. She walked to the shade of a guava tree, and from there, she watched as Zaman spoke quietly to the bird.

The quetzal relaxed and even let Zaman reach in and touch one of its tail feathers. Zaman left the cage and joined Elena beneath the tree.

"Well done!" she whispered.

He smiled. "We need to feed him again before sunset. He should be ready after that." He patted Elena's shoulder then turned away.

"Where are you going?"

"I need at least two more birds to fill the royal order for Abish."

Elena scrambled after him. "Can I come with you?"

"No," he said, turning back. "Father will be expecting supper when he comes home."

"I just need to check on the beans I had soaking overnight then set the pot over the coals. If it gets too late, I'll come back on my own."

Zaman hesitated, but Elena could already see acceptance in his eyes.

"All right," he said, his tone amused. "Bring your bow, and we can do some target shooting as well."

Elena held back a squeal but couldn't resist kissing her brother's cheek. He swatted her away, and she ran past him with a laugh. Inside their home, she hurried to the cooking room and poured more water over the soaking beans. She pinched one as a test—they would be good and soft by suppertime. She lifted the pot and set it over the coals that were still warm from the morning's fire. She checked the maize basket, discovering plenty of ground maize left to make several cakes when she returned. Her meals were simple, and she knew her father often ate at his clients' houses, providing him with more variety. But he never complained about her cooking when he did eat it.

She grabbed a carrying sling in case she found some cherries along the way. Her father loved anything with cherries, and they would be a delicious addition to the maize cakes, making them moist and sweet. Then she left the cooking room and walked down the narrow hallway to her bedchamber. She pulled her bow and quiver of three arrows from beneath her platform bed. Her brother had fashioned the bow and arrow set two years before. In that time, she'd become a decent shot but had yet to aim at anything living.

She hurried outside to find Zaman, who was waiting for her.

She followed behind her brother as he strode along the short path that led from their property. As they joined the main road, Elena pulled up her scarf to cover her sand-colored hair. "Let's stick to the side path," Elena said.

"No," Zaman said. "It's time you spend more time in public."

"According to who?" Elena said, her face growing hot.

"Me," Zaman said. "I don't want my sister to be an old spinster."

Elena had no choice but to follow her brother. For a moment, she envied his ease. Zaman was so confident in his appearance—comments or jeers from the Lamanites never seemed to bother him. He had plenty of friends and more than enough girls eyeing him. But Elena didn't like to stand out. Although the neighbors and the regulars at the marketplace knew her identity and didn't bother her, she'd been given plenty of curious gazes and had even overheard disdainful comments about her appearance when she crossed paths with traveling merchants or Lamanites who weren't familiar with her family.

Her scarf gave her the security she needed when she did go out on rare occasions, and it made her feel more comfortable knowing her fair skin was somewhat covered.

"Greetings, Zaman!" a man called out to her brother.

"Good morning, Gad," her brother said. "You look well."

Elena looked over at the man who had crossed the road to greet them. The man seemed to straighten up as their eyes met briefly. His dark skin and thick arms were accentuated by a brilliant red cape across his shoulders—a cape her father had made. She knew him by name but hadn't seen him for a while. Gad was a successful blacksmith by trade, and having earned favor by the king, he employed a horde of the king's servants in his smith shop. The servants were free labor to Gad, securing his wealth all the more and ensuring his position as a member of the aristocracy. "And you look like a man on an important errand," Gad said to Zaman, his gaze straying back to her brother.

She lowered her eyes as the men spoke.

"Off to meet your father?" Gad prodded.

"No," Zaman said. "We need to capture more quetzals."

She felt Gad's eyes on her again. He was close to her father's age, widowed as well, with a brood of young children still at home.

"And your sister is accompanying you?" Gad's voice barely contained his surprise.

She glanced up then looked away as her cheeks heated.

"She's a good tracker and a decent aim." Zaman laughed then whispered loudly, "Should it be necessary."

Gad offered a mischievous grin, displaying his gapped front teeth. "I guess your sister is a woman with *many* talents. She has grown up since I last saw her."

Shifting from one foot to another, Elena prickled at the way Gad spoke as if she weren't there. But she was reluctant to interrupt or contribute to the conversation.

"Yes, she's eighteen now," Zaman said, placing a hand on her shoulder and guiding her ahead. "We need to hurry so she'll have time to fix supper for our father."

"It's nice to see a young woman with a variety of skills." Gad stepped aside, the grin still on his face.

"Thank you," Zaman said.

"Give your father my greetings," Gad called out after them. Zaman waved, but Elena kept her eyes averted.

"Let's take the back roads next time," Elena muttered as she elbowed her brother.

He dodged her blow and chuckled. "You'll never capture a husband with that sour face of yours."

"Rather, this *pale* face of mine." Was an older man, a widowed man, the only chance she had for marriage?

"Plenty of men wouldn't mind a fair-skinned woman as a *second* wife," Zaman said.

Elena punched Zaman in the arm, and this time she didn't miss. He just laughed and continued walking, calling out greetings to various friends as he passed. Inwardly, Elena seethed. To encourage Gad about her abilities was wrong of Zaman. Gad was a widow, on the market for marriage—the thought of his age and his brood of children made her shudder.

When they left the main road, her temper cooled, and she exhaled a silent sigh of relief. She was much more comfortable in the seclusion of the jungle or in privacy of her home. She had never had friends or spent time with other girls her age. She was just too different. Even when she collected water at the well, she was rarely acknowledged or spoken to. Because of that, she usually went very early, before any other girls arrived.

The sun was plenty warm, and Elena was grateful for the cooling shade. Removing the scarf from her head, she relished in the light breeze that lifted the damp pieces of hair away from her face.

Zaman maintained a brisk pace, but Elena kept up easily, used to these frequent sojourns. *Gad might add* endurance *to my "list of skills,"* she thought ironically.

They spent nearly an hour walking, and Elena finally asked, "How far are we going?"

"Near the northern border, by the guard post. Dedan said a family of quetzals were spotted near there."

"How would Dedan know?" Elena stared at her brother's back as she followed him up an incline.

"He was just assigned as a border guard."

Nerves tightened Elena's stomach. The country by the borders was known to be dangerous, with beasts, such as leopards and wild tapirs, lurking about. Hunters who came out this far did so in groups, carrying spears and swords made from obsidian. She and her brother had a couple of bows and a few arrows between them.

At the top of the rise, Zaman stopped and brought his finger to his lips. After a moment of near silence, he whispered, "Can you hear it?"

Elena strained to listen, then, sure enough, a bird call sounded. Then another. "How many do you think there are?"

"That whole family Dedan told me about, if we're lucky," Zaman said. "I need your help capturing the birds this time. We'll need to strike at the same time to get two of them. The rest will be scared off."

"But I thought I'd be doing the distracting like I usually do."

Zaman pulled out two nets from his pack and handed one to her. "When we get close enough, I'll shoot an arrow to the opposite side. Hopefully, they'll fly in our direction."

The two of them crept toward the bird calls until they reached a thick bush. Zaman stopped and crouched. Elena did the same. Zaman pointed upward at a tree several paces away. Her eyes widened at the sight before them. A mother bird was feeding a trio of babies. Their tiny cries could barely be heard above the commotion of jungle sounds of other birds and chattering monkeys. On the ground in front of the tree, a male quetzal stalked back and forth. After a few seconds, he flew up to the nest then back down again.

"We can't take the female," Elena whispered.

Zaman rolled his eyes. "I knew you were going to say that. The babies will be *fine*."

"Come on," Elena said, tugging his arm. "Let's leave the male too. They're a family."

Zaman looked at her with disdain. "We need the feathers by tomorrow. The male can find his way back." He turned from her, ignoring her pleading eyes. Quietly, he nocked an arrow. "Get ready with the net," he whispered. "I'm going to aim right over its head."

Elena opened the net, her hands trembling slightly. Usually she was the distraction and her brother did all the capturing. Zaman released the arrow, and it zinged through the air, striking the tree.

The male quetzal flew straight at Elena's head. She lifted up the net then ducked at the last second. The bird sailed above her, squawking in alarm.

Zaman was on his feet, running after it. Elena darted after her brother, but by the time she caught up, he'd lost the bird.

He turned to her, his face red. "Why did you duck?"

She opened her mouth, but the words stuck in her throat.

Zaman shook his head. "Stay here—near the female. The male won't go far. I'm going to flush him back here. *Be ready!*"

Elena nodded, chagrined that she'd missed the bird.

With Zaman gone, she moved toward the tree, careful not to alarm the female. She found a shaded spot to sit and wait for the male's return. She spread the net in front of her so she could retrieve it quickly and it wouldn't tangle. Then she listened.

She heard nothing above an occasional monkey howl or the chattering of quail. The gentle sounds and soft breeze lulled her into a catatonic state. She sat up straighter and focused on the female bird that had finished feeding her babies and now contentedly perched next to them.

A dark shape moved just behind the tree, and Elena froze. She didn't dare call out to Zaman for fear of thwarting whatever plan he had. Then the shape rose higher, and Elena stared in terror. It was a man—but not her brother. Not a Lamanite either. Two things were plain: the man's fair skin and his strange clothing. He wore a red-dyed leather band around his head, and he dressed like a woman, covered in a tunic from shoulder to knees. One shoulder was wrapped with a clumsy bandage that looked stained with blood.

The man's eyes were on her, staring at her intently.

A rush of fear moved through Elena. She could scream, but what if her brother was too far away? She hadn't seen any border guards nearby. There was no one to hear her. The man had a long sword strapped to his back, and his broad shoulders indicated that he was no stranger to using it.

Keeping her gaze locked on the man, Elena stood and reached for her bow and arrows. If he moved, she'd probably drop everything and run screaming, but until then she had to be rational.

The man watched her as she nocked an arrow. Her hands trembled as she took aim. This man was built like a warrior and could easily best her. Slowly, he raised a hand as if he could stop the arrow.

"Who are you?" Her voice quavered as she leveled the arrow at his chest. One slight movement on her part or his and she'd probably miss, but he didn't have to know that.

She willed her shaking hands to be still. He simply stared. She knew he was a foreigner, so maybe he didn't speak the language.

"Wait," he said in almost a whisper. His eyes didn't show fear, but his expression was anxious—drawn and tight.

The man did speak their language. *Where is he from?* She lowered the bow and relaxed her grip.

"Thank you," the man said, gratitude reflecting in his eyes.

A loud sound came from Elena's right, and she turned her head slightly. Zaman came crashing through the brush, followed by three Lamanite guards. "Elena! There's a man—"

Zaman stopped, his mouth open as he noticed the Nephite. But before Elena could explain anything, two of the Lamanites leapt toward the man. Within seconds, they had him pinned to the ground. The third Lamanite tied the stranger's hands behind his back.

The man groaned but didn't complain or fight back.

Did he *want* to be captured? Who was this fool? By the looks of him, he could have bested at least two guards. He must be starving or wounded to risk capture by the guards. Or maybe he was after *her.* She shuddered as they tied the stranger up. Lamanite women had been abducted before by foreigners. But she didn't look like a Lamanite. Maybe that's what confused him.

Zaman was at her side, speaking, and she tore her gaze from the stranger to hear him.

"Did he touch you?"

"No," Elena said, her voice suddenly losing its strength. "He just stood there. Don't hurt him."

Zaman pried the bow and arrow from her grip. "You did well to keep him here until we arrived."

The two guards dragged the man away. Elena met her brother's gaze. There was an unspoken understanding between the two of them—remembering the moment of their own capture when they were fleeing their Nephite home.

Although Elena had been a girl of only eight, she remembered how frightened she'd been when her family had been arrested and brought before the high king. Had that king been merciful because they had come as a family? Would King Lamoni be as compassionate toward this lone man? Surely he had a story, a reason to be in Lamanite land alone. He'd told her to "wait"; was he going to offer an explanation? He could have easily fled her presence or even tried to attack despite her drawn bow and arrow.

Dedan, the Lamanite guard, had remained behind. He peered closely at Elena. "You're sure he didn't harm you? The king will want to know a list of his crimes."

"No . . . he didn't come near me—just stared as if he were as surprised as I."

Dedan gazed past her, a thoughtful look on his face. He was short for a man, about Elena's height, but his brawn made up for his height, and she could see why the king chose him as a guard. "He didn't even struggle or protest."

"Was he the only Nephite you spotted?" Zaman asked.

"So far," Dedan said. "The others think it might be a trap—that there might be more Nephites." He spat on the ground in disgust then looked a little sheepish. "Sorry, I despise the Nephites, but you two are like us."

"We understand, Dedan." Zaman looked at Elena, his expression worried. "I need to get you home."

A mixture of relief and anxiety flooded through her. What started out as a promising adventure had left her shaken and troubled. She wanted to go home, yet she was fearful for the Nephite.

"I should get back to the others at the border," Dedan said. "We'll be conducting a full hunt for any more Nephites. I doubt he's traveling alone."

After Dedan left, Elena turned to her brother. "What about the quetzals?"

"I'll come back after I take you home." He held up his hand as if anticipating her protest. "I won't come this direction." He glanced at the tree where the nest still lay, but the female was nowhere in sight. "I think the male will stay away from here for a while."

Elena followed her brother as they hurried back through the jungle toward the city. Seeing the Nephite made her wonder even more about her former home. Although her brother had integrated into the Lamanite society quite successfully, Elena still felt confused about where she belonged. Which city had the Nephite come from and why? Her heart pounded, not only because of their haste but also because she wondered if a young Nephite man was meeting his fate at that very moment.

CHAPTER 3

Deliver me, O Lord, from the evil man: preserve me from the violent man.
—Psalm 140:1

Ammon groaned as the Lamanite kicked him in the side. He'd been dumped in a shaded courtyard, a small mercy after the harsh journey through the jungle where he was forced to practically run the entire way. Not even a sip of water had been offered.

"Who are you?" yelled one of the guards who'd dragged him through the jungle.

"I told you—I come in peace. I'm here to serve the king," he said through gritted teeth. Even though he was bound, he knew he could inflict some injury on the man. But he was here to teach, not to fight. He tugged against the bands about his wrists—testing their strength. Hot pain seared through his arms at the effort, and his shoulder started bleeding again. He exhaled slowly, reining in the instinct to fight back.

"Where are the others?" came another question.

Ammon took a deep breath, wincing at the new bruise on his side. "There's no one with me."

"Liar!" the Lamanite shouted, spitting in the dust next to him.

He flinched at the insult then raised his head as much as possible to look at his accuser. The guard was barely clothed, wearing only a loincloth, his lean muscles well defined from obvious hard work.

Two other guards stood nearby, dark eyes narrow and suspicious as they weighed Ammon carefully. They seemed to be waiting—but for what?

His throat was parched, and he felt dizzy from lack of water. He was about to ask for a drink when the guards' attention was diverted.

"What is this?" a deep voice said.

Ammon craned his head and saw a large man approach, thick around
his torso with broad shoulders. He wore a cape of feathers, combined with
pieces of fur. Ammon had never seen anything so extravagant. He might
have laughed at the man's excessiveness if he weren't worried about being
kicked again. The kilt about the man's waist was a brilliant turquoise color,
and in his hand, he gripped a sizable dagger. Ammon studied the thin
blade—the craftsmanship was exquisite. Was it just a decoration, or did
this man know how to use the dagger?

"Pahrun," one of the guards greeted. "We've captured a trespasser—a
Nephite who dared to cross our borders."

"Ah," Pahrun said with a calm expression beneath his thick brow, not
seeming overly concerned. He squatted and looked Ammon in the eye as
he held his fine weapon close to Ammon's face, making an obvious display.
"And where are you from, my man?"

Keeping his tone patient, Ammon said, "I've come to serve the king."

Pahrun arched a thick brow. "Displeased with your Nephite home, are
you? A deserter?"

"No. I plan to return someday." Ammon relaxed his head against the
ground as he looked up and spoke. "But I'll dwell here as long as the king
can use my service."

Pahrun nodded to the guards as if he'd heard the excuse before. "Where
are the Nephite's things?"

One of the guards handed over Ammon's pack and the various weapons
they'd taken from him. Pahrun first sorted through the pack, finding only
some dried meat and an extra cape. But then he pulled out several scrolls
of vellum. He opened them and scanned through the contents.

Ammon held his breath, hoping that Pahrun wouldn't confiscate the
scriptural scrolls. But Pahrun only said, "Nephite jibberish," as he replaced
the scrolls. He looked more interested when he examined the weapons—a
bow and quiver of arrows, a sword, and half a dozen daggers. Pahrun
held up the sword then scrutinized the daggers. "Fine workmanship. The
Nephites have some improvements to make, but I'm impressed."

"Those weren't made by a blacksmith," Ammon couldn't help answering.
"I made them."

Pahrun's brow lifted. "Very nice. But why so many? A man couldn't
use more than one, perhaps two, at once. Are you smuggling in weapons?"

"No." Ammon's face heated. He always carried plenty of daggers. His
brothers liked to tease him about it.

Pahrun placed one of the daggers in his own belt then commanded the guards, "Stand him up!"

They hoisted Ammon to his feet, creating more bruises on his arms. He clenched his hands into fists, aching to clout one of the guards. Instead, he regained his balance and straightened to face Pahrun.

The man walked around Ammon, surveying him from every angle. "What village do you come from?"

Ammon's tongue felt thick as he spoke. "It doesn't matter now. This is my new home." He craned his neck to look at the man. "On my life, I come in peace."

Pahrun kept moving until he was standing directly behind him.

A breath of frustration escaped Ammon.

"What's this?" Pahrun pulled up Ammon's tied hands.

Pain shot through Ammon's shoulder, and he groaned. The bindings dug deeper into his flesh at the movement. Then he groaned for another reason. His ring. He'd been wearing it for so long that he didn't even realize he had it on anymore.

As Pahrun twisted the heavy ring from Ammon's swollen finger, shooting pain reached up into his arms.

Pahrun had walked around him again and now faced him eye to eye. "Who'd you steal this ring from?"

"I didn't steal it." Ammon swallowed futilely against his dry throat.

Pahrun's face moved into a lopsided, knowing smile. "Who *gave* it to you then?"

For a moment, Ammon considered making up a story, but how would he explain later when he preached to these people? How would they trust him? "My father gave it to me."

Pahrun's gaze flickered from Ammon back to the ring. He lifted it up and held it against the sky as if the added light could make the design more readable. "This ring contains the royal symbol of Zarahemla."

The guards crowded closer to see the ring for themselves. Pahrun wouldn't let them handle it but allowed each to get a good look. Then his attention was back on Ammon.

"What did you say your name was?" Pahrun asked.

"I didn't."

Pahrun blinked once. "Now would be a good time to state it." In his other hand, he raised his dagger and touched it to Ammon's chest.

Ammon closed his eyes for an instant then said, "Ammon."

"And who is your father?" Pahrun said, his gaze unmoving, his dagger pressing harder against Ammon's chest.

"Mosiah, son of Benjamin."

The dagger's prick loosened just a bit, but Pahrun's dark eyes bore into him. "*King* Mosiah?"

Ammon's face grew hot. Why hadn't he taken off his ring? He should have left it in Zarahemla.

"King Mosiah has four sons. You say you are . . . *Ammon?*" Pahrun's eyes narrowed. "That's the name of the prince regent."

Ammon gave a short nod, causing a deep ache to shoot through his neck. "I have denounced my birthright as the next king of Zarahemla. My father gave me his blessing to live among the Lamanites." He held his breath.

Pahrun's expression changed from suspicion to astonishment, and then he barked out a laugh. "Well, my friend, if that's the case, our king will be *very* interested in meeting you." Doubt shone on his face, but he lowered the dagger and threw a look at the guards. "Bring him inside!"

The guards shoved Ammon forward, and he nearly lost his balance. He walked up the steps to the nearest building, where the interior was cool and welcoming, allowing him just enough time to catch his breath. They entered a large hall that interconnected with the palace. Pushed forward by the guards, Ammon stumbled ahead, barely able to catch a glimpse of the servants who bowed as Pahrun barreled through the hallway.

Ammon sensed the difference in atmosphere when they entered the palace. The stone floors here were polished and gleamed as if some sort of oil had been rubbed into them. Someone stopped Pahrun and handed him a scroll. He took it and read it as he walked, then he rolled it back up and tucked it inside his waistband. They walked until they reached a set of tall wooden doors that stood open, leading to the throne room.

The room seemed familiar yet not so familiar, causing a pang of nostalgia in Ammon as he lifted his eyes to gaze at the assembled court.

Musicians sat in one corner of the room, quietly playing a rhythmic tune, though the court members largely ignored the beautiful music. A low table spanned the other side, piled with food that looked half eaten. Three women who hovered near the table turned to gaze openly at Ammon.

He quickly noted their colorful, sleeveless tunics contrasting with their dark skin then looked away as a hush moved through the room. Everyone stared at him. Men, dressed in flamboyant finery comparable to Pahrun's, turned to gawk. A petite woman, who could only be the queen, stood below the dais. Her tunic was bright saffron with an elaborate beaded belt, and across her shoulders was a cape made of hundreds of tiny blue feathers. Her arms and neck dripped with silver and jade. Two men rushed to her side in protection—as if the king's guards who surrounded Ammon weren't enough.

Then Ammon's gaze found the king's. The king was seated on the dais upon a throne made of a rich, dark wood, inlaid with jewels. Carvings of snakes decorated the wood, and two stone statues flanked the throne, one of the maize god, the other of the jaguar god. Incense burned in front of each, smoldering on small platters. He rose, staring at Ammon. His youth was a surprise. He was perhaps in his thirtieth year, but he had an intelligent face, a wise face.

The curiosity in the king's eyes didn't hurry his actions. He motioned for his wife to join him on the dais and then looked at Pahrun.

"A Nephite?"

"Found trespassing on our border, Your Highness." Pahrun bowed deeply.

"Why is he in my court and not in prison?" the king said.

"He claims to be no ordinary Nephite." Pahrun had fully captured the attention of everyone in the room. He held up the ring for all to see. After he spun around slowly, displaying it to the confused crowd, he handed it to the king.

The king examined it then looked up at Pahrun, confusion in his eyes.

"His says his name is *Ammon*," Pahrun continued, his voice authoritative. "He claims to be the oldest son of King Mosiah—out of the land of Zarahemla."

The king quirked a brow, turning over the ring. "And you believe him? Because he was wearing this ring?" He scoffed. "I don't have time for this. The high priest of the Maize Temple is on his way to approve our sacrifice selection."

"There's only one ring like that in all the land," Pahrun said.

The king paused. Ammon held his breath, gauging the king's reaction. He didn't look convinced. The king folded his arms across his chest. "Continue."

Everyone in the room was silent as Pahrun spoke. "When King Mosiah the First took over the northern lands from King Zarahemla, he had this ring made. He passed it to his son, Benjamin, who passed it to his son, Mosiah . . . who then passed it to his eldest son, Ammon." He waved the ring in Ammon's direction. "There has been no news from our . . . ambassadors . . . that another heir is to inherit the throne."

"What if this man stole it from Mosiah's son?" the king asked.

Ammon was about to say he was no thief, but Pahrun cut in. "Possible, but unlikely. On the way here, I received a message from our ambassador who reports the goings-on in Zarahemla. I have it with me now, Your Highness."

"What does it say?" the king asked.

Pahrun made a great ceremony of opening the scroll. He cleared his throat. "It is reported that King Mosiah has called upon his people to elect twelve judges who will reign upon his death. The king's four sons—Ammon, Aaron, Himni, and Omner—have left Zarahemla. All have denounced the throne."

Exhaling, Ammon said a silent prayer of gratitude. The king now had verification.

"Why would all four sons denounce the throne?" the king asked, his voice incredulous. He left the queen's side and stepped down from the dais, turning his gaze on Ammon. "Are you truly the son of King Mosiah?"

"I am." Ammon hoped the scroll was enough evidence for the king.

The monarch shook his head with disbelief. "All four sons giving up the throne. I can hardly believe it." His looked at Pahrun. "And why has this man traveled here? For trade? He doesn't travel like a prince."

All eyes seemed to scrutinize Ammon's dusty clothing and his lack of decoration—nothing he wore indicated his position.

Pahrun answered, "He says he's denounced his throne because he'd rather become your servant."

The king's mouth twitched, and he smiled then laughed. The rest of those in the room followed suit and laughed until the king stopped. As soon as he stopped, the room quieted abruptly.

"Perhaps you should ask the advice of your father, the high king," Pahrun said to Lamoni.

A scowl crossed the king's face. "I already know what his advice would be. He'd never allow a Nephite prince to deceive him." His voice deepened. "Nor will I."

"Nevertheless, this man's arrival should be reported to your father immediately," Pahrun said.

Lamoni's face flushed as he pointedly ignored Pahrun's suggestion.

This king must be subservient to the high king. Interesting. Ammon straightened his shoulders and met the king's gaze. He may have been bound like a prisoner, but he wanted the king to understand that he was here to serve—truly serve.

A group of men entered the throne room dressed in long robes the color of dried maize stalks. They kept their heads lowered until the king acknowledged them.

"Ah, the high priest has arrived." The king looked at Pahrun. "Move our prisoner aside; we have business to attend to. Then I'll make my decision about the Nephite."

The guards pulled Ammon to the far wall as the group of priests stepped forward. One of the priests, apparently the high priest, wore an embroidered cape over his shoulders. His arms had dark, snakelike designs twisting up his arms.

"We come here in honor of the Great Spirit," the high priest said. Everyone in the court bowed their heads, the king included, and mumbled, "Blessed be the Great Spirit."

The high priest raised his head. "To celebrate the new moon tonight, the maize god requires a sacrifice."

"Yes. We have been expecting you," the king said, his voice reverent. "Bring the sacred choice."

Everyone in the court turned toward the doors. Ammon wondered who the king was issuing an order to, but he didn't have to wait long. A moment later, two guards entered, leading a young man, whose hands were bound in front. He looked to be about fourteen or fifteen. His body was bruised, marked by dried blood, his longish hair matted about his face. But instead of the wild eyes Ammon would expect of a prisoner, his face was docile, childlike even.

The guards stopped in the center of the room, and the high priest approached, looking the man over from head to toe. "An excellent sacred choice. The Great Spirit will be pleased, and the maize god will bless the bringing in of the harvest as we return his heart to the earth."

Ammon felt the blood drain from his face. This young man was going to be sacrificed. He knew about these diabolical practices, of course, but knowledge was different than seeing the actual victim.

"The royal court will attend the sacrifice at sunset," the king said, his face glowing with pleasure. The priests left with the bound man, and suddenly, the attention was back on Ammon. Pahrun escorted Ammon to the stand before the king again.

The king motioned for his wife to join him once again. The court visibly relaxed after the priests left, and Ammon felt the tension in the room dissipate.

The queen left the dais and walked to her husband's side, linking her arm through his. She gazed up at Ammon. Although he towered over her, he felt like a young boy in her presence. Here was a woman whose husband held his life in his very hands.

She looked at him for a moment, and he saw compassion in her eyes—*a mother's eyes*, he instinctively assumed. A mother who was raising children of her own. He wondered how she could bear to see the young prisoner on his way to the sacrifice.

"You're very far from home," she said.

"Yes." Ammon bowed his head in respect, though his mind was still reeling from the priests' visit.

"And you've come alone?" the queen asked.

Ammon took a steadying breath, trying to answer in a natural voice. "My brethren have traveled to other parts of the land."

"Your *brothers* have come into Lamanite territory as well?" the king asked.

Ammon raised his head. "They, too, wish to serve the Lamanites." *And the sooner we can teach them, the more lives will be saved from the demands of human sacrifice.*

The king stared at Ammon in amazement.

The queen smiled up at her husband. "Whatever will we do with a Nephite prince?"

Hope flooded through Ammon as the king smiled at his queen with true tenderness. This was a king who listened to his queen. Perhaps they now believed him and would accept his offer. The king squeezed his wife's hand, causing a pang in Ammon's heart. It was like watching his own parents together—the connection between husband and wife plain in a mere glance or gesture.

The king looked back at Ammon, a frown back on his face. "I wonder if the Great Spirit would accept a Nephite as a sacrifice?" His face twisted into a cruel smile, the exact opposite of how he had looked at his wife.

"Lamoni," the queen said in a voice so quiet Ammon was sure no one else in the court heard except him and the king.

The king's gaze stayed on Ammon, as if it were looking right into his soul. Ammon returned the gaze, holding his breath in anticipation. After a few seconds of absolute silence, the king said, "Do you truly desire to dwell among the Lamanites in my land?"

"Yes," Ammon said, letting himself breathe again. "I wish to live here among your people. Perhaps until the day I die."

The king's brow quirked again. "And you pledge you're no spy?"

"I am not, Your Highness." His pulse increased.

"I will find out if you're lying to me, and if you are, you'll be delivered to the altar of the Maize Temple . . ."

"I am no liar," Ammon said. "I make this pledge on my life."

Despite the murmuring whispers among the court, disturbing the silence, the king's steady gaze remained on Ammon. Hope flooded him as Ammon saw something change in the king's eyes—the hard, questioning gaze had softened.

Ammon held his breath, hardly daring to accept the new hope, yet, at the same time, praying fervently in his mind that he could.

A small movement from the queen caught his attention. She leaned toward her husband, her eyes moist, as she surreptitiously nudged him.

There was an almost imperceptible nod from the king toward his wife, then he said, "Guards, release him! Untie his bands."

Ammon's heart soared as the guards hastened to do the king's bidding. When the pressure around his wrists finally loosened, he exhaled with relief.

"Pahrun, return this man's ring," the king said.

Pahrun grinned and stepped forward, as if enjoying the ceremony. He twisted the ring back onto Ammon's finger.

"Son of Mosiah," the king said, holding out his hand. "I am King Lamoni. Welcome to the land of Ishmael."

"Your Highness," Pahrun said, arching a thick brow, "what will the high king say?"

Again ignoring him, Lamoni stretched his hand out farther. Stunned, Ammon grasped the king's hand, though his was dirty and his wrist raw from the bindings. At least his was not dirty from ordering the death of others.

"Your arms," the queen said with a slight gasp. She turned to a group of women behind her. "Bring water and ointment to treat the man's injuries."

The king nodded with approval. "Come," he said to Ammon. "Tell us about your family."

He followed the king toward the throne where he commanded his guards to arrange some cushions for Ammon to sit on. Lowering himself to the soft cushions, he swallowed against a lump in his throat. He moved as far away from the statue of the jaguar god as he could. All of the fasting, all of the praying, the painful journey through the jungles of Ishmael . . . He silently offered thanks to the Lord for this king's acceptance. Then he silently prayed for the soul of the young man who was about to be sacrificed.

Two women approached him, obviously servants by their plain clothing. The women avoided eye contact as they washed his wrists and applied a *curaio* salve to his chaffed skin then to the arrow wound in his shoulder. He took the opportunity to wet his hair. It had grown too long for his taste over the past weeks. He'd enjoy having it shorn off again.

"Bring our guest food and drink," the king said as the women departed. Pahrun ordered a slave to bring Ammon a cup of water and a bowl of various fruits. Ammon picked a guava and took one bite. Although he was starving, he couldn't seem to eat.

Pahrun withdrew the dagger he'd confiscated. "Tell us about your daggers." He looked at the king. "This prince makes his own weapons."

The king reached for the weapon and, turning it over in his hands, admired the craftsmanship. "Impressive. I haven't seen a blade with this contour before."

"The curved end makes it easier to skin an animal," Ammon said.

The king held the blade up. "Only an animal? Or do we have a warrior in our midst?"

Ammon lowered his eyes, suddenly uncomfortable, and the king laughed. "Your stature gives away at least part of your story."

The queen settled next to her husband's throne, and the king set the dagger aside and extended his arms. "Share with us the news from your homeland."

Ammon hesitated. The borders of the land of Zarahemla had been fairly quiet for about a year, with no skirmishes between the Lamanites and Nephites. But there was always a palpable tension between the two societies. Emissaries and merchants from each tribe always traveled with guards.

Ammon told him the most general things he could but spoke most about his journey into the wilderness. The king was mystified that Ammon would leave his inheritance to become a servant in a foreign land, but Ammon felt blessed that the Lord had softened the Lamanite king's heart to some extent—although there was still a long way to go in order to soften the heart of a man who allowed the bloodshed of his own people.

As the light began to change, the king smiled and held up his hands. "Let us go to the Maize Temple."

Ammon looked around at the people, yet no one's expression reflected the horror he felt in his heart. He had no choice but to follow the king's procession. Ammon soon found himself walking along a wide road in the heart of the land of Ishmael.

The city was beautiful. Ammon had never seen so many temples; it appeared there was one for every Lamanite god that Ammon was aware of. The temples weren't large, most no bigger than a home. At the top of the steps that led to each temple was a platter of burning incense. Priests came out of the temple entrances to watch the king's procession. Ammon wondered if they all used human sacrifice.

They reached a market square that appeared to be the center of the city. An elegant ceiba tree rose from the center, and it, too, was surrounded by incense and small offerings of food.

"Not too much farther," King Lamoni boomed as he caught Ammon staring at the surroundings. Ammon didn't know who was staring more, him or the Lamanites as he traveled in the king's company.

On the other side of the market plaza, a hill rose, and at the top was a magnificent temple, larger than any Ammon had ever seen. The number of stone steps reached into the dozens. The pristine white of the steps was marred by a dark brown stain running from the top to the bottom, right down the center. Ammon wanted to ask what the discoloring was from—perhaps flooding—but then realized he already knew the answer. The steps were stained with the blood of other human sacrifices. His stomach clenched as he raised his eyes upward to see the two massive altars at the top of the steps on either side of the main temple building. One altar was clean, but the other one smoked from a burning animal carcass—at least he hoped.

Someone must have given a signal of some sort the moment king arrived because almost immediately, several priests exited the temple. To Ammon's dismay, the prisoner was with them. They led him to the clean altar and tied him down. The young man didn't move, didn't protest. The surrounding priests started chanting to the Great Spirit. The words were foreign to Ammon, but his stomach knotted in anticipation. He stole a glance at the king, who was bowing his head and mouthing the same words as the priests.

Perspiration prickled Ammon's skin as the surrealness encircled him. The chanting grew louder, more forceful, and that's when Ammon saw the high priest raise a long dagger over his head. Ammon closed his eyes, but that didn't block out the screaming.

* * *

Ammon stared at the food in front of him, thinking of the young man who'd been brutally sacrificed. It was nearly dark by the time the king's procession had returned to the palace. Ammon wondered if he would have been better off in prison, but then he might have come to know the young man whose final words on earth were screams of agony as the priests cut out his heart.

Ammon sat with Pahrun and the king, along with several other members of the court. The evening meal had been placed upon the table, platters of steaming maize cakes, sectioned fruit, avocados, chili peppers, fish, and various other meats, including broiled tapir. It had been weeks since Ammon had seen so much food in one place.

"Was that your first witness to a sacrifice?" the king asked.

"Yes," Ammon said.

The king chuckled. "You'll grow used to it. Here in the land of Ishmael, our gods are quite demanding."

Ammon ate very little as he listened to the king regaling stories of previous prisoners who were selected for sacrifice. They used to put up a fight until the high priest came up with an excellent suggestion of administering a hallucinogenic beforehand. Setting down the slice of meat he'd been trying to work through, Ammon gave up on eating. "I shouldn't be eating at your table, O King," Ammon said. "After this, I'll eat with the servants, where I belong."

The king clapped his hands together, his smile directed at Ammon. "You must meet my children. They'd love to see a real Nephite prince—imagine, our enemy has come to *serve* us." Lamoni grinned with delight. "A prince who insists to be treated like a servant . . . Tell me, Nephite. What are your skills?"

Ammon hesitated then told them about being chased by a wounded tapir.

"We'll not send you out with the king's hunters, then," Pahrun said as those around the table laughed.

"We won't send a prince hunting for anything," Lamoni said. "He is much more valuable to us at court with all of his knowledge and training. Pahrun, we must convince him to stay at court."

Ammon knew the king meant to use him to strategize against the Nephites. "Your Highness. I am sincere when I say that I only want to be a servant, whether it be scrubbing your steps or caring for the horses."

"We'll change your mind yet," the king declared. "First, we must find you some new clothing. You can't wear those rags in my court."

Those surrounding the table laughed again.

"As you've noticed," Pahrun joined in, "we have much warmer weather here in Ishmael than in your northern country."

"You certainly don't want to wear a full tunic like a woman or a priest," the king added.

More laughter.

Ammon smiled but inwardly cringed. He felt more comfortable in his Nephite clothing—dingy as it now was. In the presence of the abundant wine, the glittering eyes of those watching as if to soak in every word the king said, and the calculating look in Pahrun's eyes, memories of his past life resurfaced, the ones he'd tried to forget.

The king leaned toward his wife and whispered. The queen's eyes widened, but she nodded.

Just then, everyone's attention went to the doorway of the throne room. The king's children entered the room, two girls and one boy. The eldest girl looked to be about his sister's age; Cassia was nearly nineteen. Lamoni's eldest daughter was dressed similarly to the queen, the bright colors of her tunic offsetting her rich brown skin. The younger girl looked at him quickly then busied herself cooing to a small bird that sat on her shoulder.

The older girl stared at Ammon with the same curiosity the people of the court had. When her father started talking, she glanced down.

Lamoni introduced his children, one by one: the boy, Pacal, who looked to be about ten years old, then the girls, Romie and Meztli.

When Meztli, the eldest, stepped forward, her expression turned nervous. Ammon didn't blame her—after all, he was a stranger and an enemy in her eyes.

Lamoni stood and walked to his daughter then put an arm around her shoulders. "Ammon, my friend, this is my eldest daughter. I'd like to offer her as your wife."

Ammon nearly fell over in surprise. The look on Meztli's face was one of terror.

He didn't know what to say—the king had been friendly to him, but this was the last thing Ammon had expected. It was clear the king was determined to create a political alliance—to force Ammon's services in the court. It seemed his hesitation was too long because the king said, "If you don't care to marry my eldest daughter then consider Romie. She'll be ready to marry in another year or so."

Ammon looked from Meztli to the younger sister. Romie couldn't be more than sixteen. He'd heard of Lamanite tribes intermarrying the children of royalty to ensure political fealty. But to marry a Nephite to a Lamanite? Was the king trying to guarantee a relationship between his people and the Nephites?

The younger girl didn't look as terrified as her older sister, but then again, she was quite preoccupied with the small bird that sat on her shoulder, feeding the bird and stroking it.

"I thank you from the depths of my heart and soul," Ammon said, finally finding his voice, though his mind was still reeling. "Both of your daughters are beautiful, but . . . I did not come here seeking a royal alliance or to spend my days as a member of the court." Pausing, Ammon sank to one knee. "I have come to be your servant. Please forgive me for not accepting your generosity."

The king's eyes rounded with astonishment.

Out of the corner of his eye, Ammon saw Meztli wipe a tear from her cheek. Her lip trembled as her father removed his arm from her shoulders.

The king strode to Ammon. "Tomorrow you'll start your service, then," Lamoni announced. "Pahrun will find a place for you to sleep and show you your duties in the morning."

Ammon rose to his feet. Pahrun motioned for Ammon to follow him, and as they left the throne room, Ammon cast a glance at Meztli. A shy, relieved smile touched her mouth as their eyes met.

He followed Pahrun along the hallway, feeling overwhelmed with gratitude. The king had listened to him and seemed to trust him. He said a silent prayer of gratitude then turned to asking the Lord to protect his brethren and help them be well received in the other lands.

"The king's daughter looked surprised you turned her down." Pahrun interrupted Ammon's silent prayer.

"Perhaps surprised but very relieved."

Pahrun chuckled and looked over at him. "That too."

They left the main hallway and went down some stairs, reaching the courtyard where Ammon had originally met Pahrun. "This way."

The pair walked along a lane that soon opened into it a circle of simple huts. Pahrun stopped and eyed Ammon in the moonlight. "You're unlike any Nephite I've ever met."

"Have you met many Nephites?" Ammon asked, thinking of the fair-skinned woman who'd nearly shot him in the jungle.

"Some. Mostly through trade, although there are some living among our people," Pahrun said. "The guards said that you were stopped by Moriah's daughter."

Ammon thought of the woman who spared his life. He wanted to ask about her but didn't dare. "Who's Moriah?"

"He's the clothier for the king. Moriah came to the land of Nephi about ten years ago from Zarahemla. Perhaps you knew him?"

"The name isn't familiar," Ammon said. "I was just a boy then."

Pahrun nodded, as if in deep thought. "Guards patrol the area, so any misstep you take will be reported." He waved suddenly toward one of the huts. "You'll sleep in there. Two brothers share it. They rise before dawn, so they're likely asleep." He started walking toward the hut. "I'd better make introductions so you don't wake up with a dagger at your throat."

Unease spread through Ammon as he followed Pahrun. Ammon wished he'd been given his dagger back. Pahrun opened the door without knocking. The interior of the hut was dim, and he had to stoop to enter.

Two heads immediately lifted from the cots in each corner.

"Men," Pahrun said. "A new servant is here to work with you—by order of the king."

The men's eyes widened, visible in the moonlight spilling through the doorway, as they took in Ammon's fair skin.

He stepped forward. "I'm Ammon."

"Corien is a herder of the king's flocks," Pahrun said. "Kumen works for the head blacksmith."

The two men looked at Ammon then nodded. Neither spoke but lay back down to sleep.

"About the best welcome you'll get, I suppose," Pahrun said. He slapped Ammon on the back. "I'll send over a cot tomorrow. Sleep well, prince of Zarahemla."

He turned and left Ammon, muttering as he walked out and made his way back to the lane.

Ammon scanned the sleeping figures—they seemed intent on ignoring him. Even though the light was dim, he could see there was no extra bedroll or rug. He briefly wondered if it would be more comfortable in the jungle grass outside but decided if he went out he might be mistaken for an intruder again and recaptured. Though he was beyond exhaustion,

Ammon knelt and poured out his heart to the Lord, thanking Him again for his safe arrival and pleading that his brethren would find such acceptance. Since his pack hadn't been returned to him yet, he lay down on the earthen floor, relaxing his head against his inner arm. Regardless of the hard floor, it didn't take him long to fall asleep.

CHAPTER 4

There is no peace, saith my God, to the wicked.
—Isaiah 57:21

A hand tightened about Ammon's neck, choking off his breathing. He struggled against the weight of the unseen assailant. With a sudden burst of energy, he flung the man off and sat up. Something furry brushed past him and yelped. Opening his eyes, he blinked in the gray light coming through the open doorway. A small dog sat a few paces away, staring at him.

Ammon rubbed his neck, disoriented, then realized he'd been dreaming. And the strangling hold must have been the dog curling up next to him.

"Hello, boy," Ammon said. The dog wagged its short tail and pounced.

He laughed and scratched the wriggly thing behind the ears, trying to avoid its wet tongue. Ammon looked around the small hut—the two bedrolls were empty, and a smoky scent hung in the air. Hoping it was the morning meal well underway, he stood and stretched. He left the hut, the dog jumping at his heels.

Dawn had long since cracked the night sky's blackness, bringing a softness to the dark clouds hovering overhead. The air smelled damp; rain felt imminent.

Ammon looked around for signs of life, but the huts were deserted. The smell of smoke grew stronger, so Ammon set off toward it, along the path he and Pahrun had walked the night before.

He arrived at a pavilion of sorts—a tall roofed structure with open sides. Several cooking fires were going, and dozens of men had gathered to eat.

Ammon walked two more steps toward the pavilion, and a hand encircled his neck. He was suddenly pitched to the ground.

His head smacked the hard earth. His mind went black for an instant. When his eyes blinked open, he saw a thick man crouching over him.

"Who are you?" the man demanded, whipping out a dagger and holding it dangerously close to Ammon's neck.

Ammon's hand shot out and twisted the man's arm. He was on his feet in an instant, ready to wrestle the dagger away. The man was quite a bit older, maybe by twenty years, but he was built like a large tapir, making the colorful cape he wore seem skimpy in comparison. Before Ammon could make another move, a second man appeared. "Gad, leave the Nephite alone. He's with us."

Ammon recognized the man who spoke as the man he shared his hut with—Kumen. He was short, his hair long, nearly to his shoulders. But his forearms rippled with strength, probably from pounding a lot of metal.

Gad's eyes narrowed on his broad face. "I wasn't told about any Nephite working for the king."

"Pahrun brought him in last night," Kumen said. "And he'll be working for *you*. And by the way, you just attacked a prince from Zarahemla." He laughed at Gad's stunned expression, then he turned to Ammon. "This is your new employer." He waved a hand at Gad, who nodded, his eyes still narrowed with displeasure.

Gad stared at Ammon. "You're a prince?"

"*Was* a prince," Ammon said, brushing his hands off.

Gad's thick eyebrow lifted, but before he could speak, Kumen said, "You're early today, Gad."

"Wanted to round everyone up and get an early start," the blacksmith said, his gaze trailing back to Ammon in curiosity. "I have other things to tend to this afternoon."

"I'm ready." Kumen handed over a maize cake wrapped in a leaf to Ammon. "This is for you. Thought you could use some sleep this morning, but tomorrow you're on your own." He offered a lopsided smile, revealing crooked teeth.

"Thank you," Ammon said and took a bite from the cake. He followed the two men along a twisting jungle path. Several other men fell into step with them, though no one replied when he greeted them. Give it some time, he told himself. He'd keep his head down and work hard. Eventually, he'd earn their trust.

By the time they reached the blacksmith shop, Ammon was drenched in sweat from the humidity. He wished he'd had his water skin with him to drink along the route, but even if the guards had returned it, there hadn't been an opportunity to fill it anyway. The other men were obviously used to the humidity and didn't seem affected by it.

The men all set to work, and Ammon followed Kumen around. He spent the better part of the morning pumping the bellows for the furnace. The task was tiring, but it was fascinating to watch Gad at work. He ran his shop like a grand production, orchestrating each task and each worker so that everything fell together in tandem. Pounding rang through the shop, and the men had to shout over it to be heard. The heat from the fire was intense, nearly suffocating Ammon for the first couple of hours.

When Gad finally called out a break, Ammon stepped outside, reveling in the cool moist air of the impending rainstorm. The men sat together, eating tortillas and drinking water the blacksmith had provided.

Ammon drank his fill of water, knowing he'd sweat it out within the hour.

During the break, Ammon felt Gad's gaze on him. When the rain started, the other men stood to go back to work. Gad said, "Nephite, I need to speak to you."

Ammon stiffened, wondering if he'd be berated for his slower work. The other men worked like lightening, but it would only be a matter of time before he'd catch up to the others' pace. Gad waited for the men to leave before he spoke.

"You're quick on your feet," Gad said, studying Ammon. There was respect in his eyes. "It seems you've been trained to fight by an expert. You were quick to react when I threw you on the ground."

Ammon was speechless; he hadn't expected that train of thought.

"I might be able to use you," Gad continued. He paused as a clap of thunder rippled from the sky. "You'd be an unexpected opponent and probably have tactics that wouldn't be anticipated since you come from another land."

Opponent? Tactics? "What do you mean?" Drops of rain spotted his face, and he wiped the drops away.

"There's a match tonight," Gad said, his eyes gleaming. "I'll sponsor you."

Anxiety rose in Ammon. "What kind of match?"

Gad smiled, showing his gapped front teeth. "A fighting match. The best fighter earns plenty of silver."

"I don't want to fight anyone," Ammon said, although he was flattered that Gad thought he was a good fighter. The rain strengthened, spotting Ammon's tunic, cooling him off. "I'm here to work and serve the king."

Gad threw back his head and laughed. When he sobered, he wiped the rain from his face. It was falling steadily now. "You're a strange Nephite. But I like you. And you'll make me proud tonight."

"I—"

"Let's get out of the rain and back to work. I'll come fetch you after supper tonight. I think you'll find the rewards to your liking."

Ammon was shooed into the blacksmith building, and the noise became immediately deafening. Each time Ammon looked over at Gad, the large man smiled. The blacksmith left before the end of the workday, so Ammon didn't have a chance to protest further.

The rain had stopped by the time they started the walk back to the servant huts. No one spoke—exhaustion written across everyone's faces. But the mention of fighting gnawed at Ammon.

Once he and Kumen reached their hut, they found Kumen's brother, Corien, waiting for him. The two brothers looked almost identical; the only difference was that Corien's hair had been shorn off except for one long braid that trailed down his back.

"Welcome," Corien said to Ammon with a quick glance from where he sat cross-legged on the floor.

"Thank you," Ammon said. Corien looked down and continued working on carving a piece of leather.

Kumen settled onto his cot, looking exhausted, and promptly closed his eyes.

In the corner of the hut was a familiar-looking pack. Ammon's things had been returned. He searched through the satchel to see what they had left. His sling and dagger were there; everything but his bow and quiver of arrows was inside. And they had taken his sword. But he breathed a sigh of relief when he saw the vellum scrolls. It was like a cloak of reassurance to have his scriptures intact.

Settling on the floor, he unrolled the one that was the most tattered— the most well read. As he read through the prophecies concerning the coming of Christ and how through His Atonement mankind could be redeemed, Ammon's heart warmed. He didn't know exactly when and how he'd begin teaching about the Lord to these Lamanites, but he would be ready when the Lord revealed the proper time.

After reading for several moments, he turned to Corien, who was still bent over his handiwork.

"What are you making?" Ammon asked.

Without looking up, Corien said, "A sling."

Kumen sat up, instantly alert. "What for?" he asked, anger in his voice.

Corien kept his dark head down and remained silent.

"Tell me you didn't volunteer." Kumen rose and crossed to his brother then stood in front of him with his arms folded over his chest.

"I did." Corien finally looked up, his black eyes meeting his brother's foreboding gaze.

The two brothers stared at each other.

"What did you volunteer for?" Ammon asked.

Kumen turned to Ammon, fear in his eyes.

"Corien thinks he can guard the king's flocks better than the last lead herder," Kumen said. "But what my brother has forgotten"—he threw a pointed look at Corien— "is that the last one was executed."

"Why? What happened?"

Corien put the sling aside and rose to his feet. He set his mouth in a firm line and looked directly at Ammon. "What my brother is trying to say is that he doesn't think I'm skilled enough to protect the king's flocks."

Kumen shoved Corien's arm. "I didn't say that." He turned to Ammon, talking quickly, "The king's flocks have been scattered several times over the past month. King Lamoni threatened the lead herdsman with execution if it happened again. Four days ago, the man was executed. Thrown into a den of wild animals."

The image made Ammon's stomach turn, although perhaps it shouldn't have been too much of a surprise. He well remembered the look on the king's face right before the human sacrifice. "Why is the punishment so severe?" He looked from one brother to the next.

"The flocks have been scattered so many times that the king's wealth in animals has been cut in half," Corien said.

Ammon's mind raced as he thought of Corien going into danger. "Who's scattering the flocks? Wild beasts?"

"No," Kumen broke in before Corien could answer. "A band of rebels. We don't know where they come from. They paint their faces, and no one has been able to recognize them."

"How many herders does the king send at a time?"

"Five or six," Corien said. "The king asked for a volunteer to replace the last leader, and I decided to do it." His mouth formed a straight line of determination.

"You can't," Kumen said.

"It's too late," Corien hissed. "The pay is higher, and I'll be able to marry Beyla sooner with a better income." He held up the sling. "With this, I'll scare off the rebels. The flocks will be safe, and the king will reward me with silver." He tossed the sling at Kumen, who flinched. Then Corien left the hut, muttering under his breath.

Kumen's face fell as he watched his brother leave.

"If I offer to go with Corien, and if the king would allow it, would they let me switch from the blacksmith shop to guard the flocks?" Ammon said.

Kumen swung around and looked at him, eyes narrowed. "You? To guard the flocks? What does a prince know about being a herdsman?"

"Not much," Ammon admitted. He stooped and retrieved the sling from the floor. Holding it up, he said, "But I do know how to use this."

***

Elena scurried to the reed door and pushed it open. She wanted to run to welcome Abish, but she waited like a proper hostess for the woman to make her way up the path.

When Abish lifted her gaze, Elena smiled and was rewarded with Abish's contagious grin. Although the Lamanite woman was only a couple years older than Elena, Abish seemed much more knowledgeable and wiser. She'd been serving in the palace since Elena could remember. Abish's wide face and dark eyes were captivating, but it was her personality that attracted others to her.

She was known as an excellent storyteller and spent hours entertaining the queen and her children. Elena had only heard a few of Abish's stories but loved each one. She told tales of faraway lands and long-ago royalty.

Elena knew little about Abish's childhood, only that she'd lost her mother as a child then, more recently, her father. But Elena didn't feel comfortable prying more information from the woman. Besides, she so cherished Abish's pleasing disposition. It was no marvel that Zaman wanted to have her for a wife.

"Come in," Elena said when Abish reached the house. "My father and brother are out back. I'll go fetch them."

"Wait. I brought you something," Abish said, lifting up the basket she carried.

Elena peered inside and gasped when she saw a wriggling rabbit—possibly the smallest she'd ever seen. "Oh!"

"It's for you—as a pet, if you want," Abish said. "It's a small breed from the land of Middoni. They don't grow very big and are very popular with the king's children right now. Of course, there are always too many, and the king tells his cook to prepare them for supper." She leaned close to Elena and whispered, "That sends the children into tears, and the king changes his mind—until the next day!"

Elena laughed. "I can imagine the children telling the king not to cook the rabbits." She reached for the furry bundle and lifted the trembling body. "What's wrong with her?"

"It's a *he*," Abish said. "And he's just nervous."

Elena held the trembling rabbit to her chest, lowering her chin against its fur. "All the way from the land of Middoni—no wonder he's scared."

"Well, he was born *here*," Abish said in an amused voice.

"Elena!" a deep voice called from the yard.

"My father," Elena said. "Let me tell him you've arrived." She hesitated then placed the rabbit into the basket.

"Of course," Abish said. "I'll just wait in here."

"Oh, yes," Elena said, her cheeks flushing. "I am not always such a terrible hostess." She led Abish into the front room. "Have a seat on any cushion, and I'll return very soon."

Elena hurried through the house just as her father reached the back door. "Abish is here," she said.

He straightened, his demeanor changing from her father to an expert clothier. He strode by her and welcomed Abish with a deep bow. Even though her father was technically considered a higher status than a servant, he was always very respectful to anyone who worked for the king or queen. "Come to the hut in the back courtyard," he said. "The samples are ready."

Elena followed Abish and her father to where her brother stood proudly by the hut they used to house all of the cloth, feathers, and beading. Zaman locked gazes with Abish, and she flushed. A smile touched his mouth, although he remained as formal as possible.

Abish went inside the hut with Moriah, and Elena waited outside with her brother, hoping that Abish would be pleased with their new designs. Her father had allowed Elena to personally design one of the capes that she hoped the queen or the princesses would like.

Elena whispered, "Has Abish received permission of marriage from the queen yet?"

"Not yet," Zaman said, walking away to check on the quetzal cages.

Disappointment swelled in her, knowing the queen valued Abish quite a bit. *If she were to marry, would she still work at the palace after her marriage?*

When Elena's brother was out of sight, she leaned close to the reed door, hoping to overhear the conversation inside the workroom.

She was well rewarded when she heard her father speak.

"My daughter has made a few of her own creations," her father said. "She has developed a fine skill, which will only grow better. Perhaps the queen and her daughters are looking for something to wear to the Maize Festival?"

Elena held her breath, waiting for Abish's response, but the woman's murmur was too quiet to decipher.

Elena walked around the small building, hoping to find a better place to hear. She stopped just short of the window and crouched below it. But it was too late. Her father was discussing the designs for the upcoming feast for the high king.

"This headdress will please the queen," Abish said.

"Thank you. Zaman has also been working on this for King Lamoni," her father said.

Abish said, "I think King Lamoni will garner a lot of attention wearing it."

Elena heard the excitement in the woman's voice. She smiled, happy for her father. Abish was a very good judge of the king's and queen's preferences.

Before Elena could leave, Abish and her father came out of the building. In Abish's arms, she carried a large wrapped bundle. They immediately noticed Elena.

"I was—" she began.

Abish laughed. "Your designs are very nice, Elena. I'll be taking these to show the queen." She lifted the bundle.

Elena's face flushed. "You mean—"

"Yes," her father said. "Abish will be taking them now."

Elena clasped her hands together. "When will I know what the queen thinks?"

Abish looked at Elena's father, amusement on her face, then back to Elena. "Have your father bring you by the servants' quarters tomorrow night. I'll deliver word from the queen."

Zaman stepped next to Abish, and as if by unspoken agreement, he walked her to the front courtyard. As their heads bent together in conversation, Elena felt a bit envious. Zaman had someone who would love and take care of him. Her father had had the same thing with her mother. *One day*, she thought, *I'll want someone too.*

But not a man old enough to be my father.

* * *

Ammon had never eaten so fast in his life. But he had to. At least two dozen servants surrounded the low table, and at first glance, there wasn't enough food to go around. The meal was disappearing quicker than he could grab it. Food had always been plentiful at his table in Zarahemla.

Night had fallen, and burning torches surrounded the pavilion, casting garish shadows on the men's faces. In this light, the Lamanite servants looked fierce, and they weren't even of the warrior class. Their bodies were hardened after days spent in tough labor in the service of a king they all seemed to respect and admire.

Corien and Kumen sat at opposite ends of the table, still not speaking to each other. A few congratulated Corien for being assigned the position of lead herdsman. They didn't seem to have the concern that Kumen had. Maybe it was just a part of their life. It seemed if you succeeded in the service of the king, you lived. If you failed, you died. Although the Lamoni he'd come to know in his short time in this land seemed to be a fair and just man, perhaps there was something more he didn't understand.

"Finished?" a gruff voice said behind Ammon.

He turned to see Gad standing over him. Ammon wiped his mouth on the sleeve of his tunic and stood. "I've thought about the fight and your invitation, and I think I should pass. I appreciate—"

Gad slapped a hand on Ammon's shoulder and laughed. "You're so polite. I suppose you learned that in your father's court—diplomacy." He moved his hand and waved it toward the eating men. "As you see, we're like scavengers. When someone throws you a bone, you take it."

His hand was back on Ammon's shoulder, this time gripping it hard. "You *will* come with me. I've already placed the wagers, and they're expecting you."

"They?" Ammon said.

"He's fighting?" Kumen was next to him, a half-eaten turkey leg in one hand. His former despondency had suddenly fled. "Everyone! Ammon will be fighting in the circle tonight!"

A few men laughed; some of them cheered; the rest just stared at Ammon in surprise.

"Let's go," Gad said.

"I'm coming too." Kumen grabbed another piece of meat from the table. Several others rose and joined them, Corien included.

They rushed Ammon along a path, propelling him in the opposite direction of the palace and the market square. The trail wound through the jungle, gnarled but well used. Ammon tried to protest further, but the men had broken out into a boisterous song.

Gad kept a firm grip on Ammon's shoulder as they walked, the path growing darker by the moment. The foreboding of the invitation to fight grew stronger. He didn't want to be here. He wanted to be sitting around a fire sharing the message of the Lord—not headed for a fight. But he knew he was outnumbered. The moonlight was sporadic overhead, peeking through as the clouds raced across the sky, although the lack of light didn't seem to bother any of the men. They moved with a surety, as if it were the middle of the day.

Up ahead, the trees took on a yellow glow. *Torchlights. There must be a crowd.* His heart sank at the thought of being used for entertainment. They stepped into a wide clearing devoid of anything but flat earth. Surrounding the clearing, rocks had been arranged with torches propped between them. A large circle had been mapped out with animal bones, and at least a dozen men milled about, all turning when Ammon's group arrived.

Now two dozen men had assembled, ready for a spectacle.

"Well, well," one man said, stepping forward. It was Pahrun. He wore a feathered cape topped with a headdress that looked like the head of a deer. He strode to Ammon and looked him up and down. "How did your first day go with the blacksmith?"

"Quite well," Ammon said.

Pahrun smiled at him then Gad. "A Nephite for a Nephite."

"Zaman is fighting tonight?" Gad said.

"I thought it would be fitting," Pahrun said, eyeing Ammon again as if to assess his size and strength.

"How much?" Gad removed a leather bag of coins tied to his waistband.

"Twenty silver onti."

Gad gave a short nod. "Bare hands?"

"Of course," Pahrun said with a chuckle. "I don't want the king's new servant bleeding to death."

"Agreed," Gad said, and both men clasped hands.

A young man stepped forward. *Must be Zaman. Tall, well built, but not intimidating.*

As the man moved toward Ammon, the torchlight fell on his face. The lighter skin, the close-set eyes . . . Ammon recognized him as one of the men from the jungle when he had been captured. The man who'd called out to the woman who'd almost shot him.

"Zaman," Pahrun said. "Tonight you'll fight Ammon, the new Nephite who claims to want to live in our land until he dies."

Someone shouted, "Which may be tonight!" The men laughed.

Pahrun lifted his heavy arms. "Silence! We're not animals here but seasoned fighters skilled in the art of combat." He looked at Ammon. "No weapons, *prince*. Stay inside the circle or forfeit."

"How is the fight won?" Ammon said.

"Either when the conch shell signals the end of the fight or when one of you is dead."

Sharp dread twisted Ammon's stomach. This was more serious than he thought. He didn't want to fight anyone—he'd come in peace, to serve and to teach the gospel. He had never backed down from a challenge, but this felt wrong. This was not why he had come to the land of Ishmael. He ignored the laughter floating through the crowd and assessed his competitor. He appeared almost bored, whereas Ammon's heart pounded furiously.

Pahrun whispered to Zaman while the men retreated and perched on the rocks surrounding the clearing.

Ammon looked for Gad or Kumen, but they'd moved back as well. He wiped the perspiration from his face. Pahrun left Zaman's side and walked to the outer part of the circle. Then he lifted his hands. "Begin!"

"Come on, *prince*," Zaman growled, his eyes fierce.

Ammon barely had time to consider how he was going to best this Nephite-turned-Lamanite before the man leaped toward him.

Ammon spun out of the way and brought his elbow down on Zaman's back. Zaman slammed into the ground with a grunt but rolled and was on his feet in an instant. Then he crossed the space and smashed a fist into Ammon's stomach.

Oof. Ammon bent over, gasping for air.

Zaman's hands encircled Ammon's head and flipped him onto the ground. Landing on his shoulder, he felt it pop, sending searing pain through his arm. He thought he heard Kumen shouting his name, but it sounded far away. Ammon groaned and rolled over.

Zaman's foot pressed against his chest, and when Ammon blinked his eyes open, he saw the glint of a dagger descending. Fear jolted through him—there weren't supposed to be knives. Maybe the conch shell would sound, but instead, the men shouted encouragement—for or against him, he didn't know. As the haze left his vision, he gripped Zaman's wrist, twisting it until he cried out. This was no game, and missionary or not, he wasn't going to let someone stab him. Fury built in Zaman's eyes, and with his free arm, he lashed out. Before Ammon could dodge, Zaman's fist plunged into his nose.

The cartilage in his nose dislocated, and his head jerked backwards. "Ahhh!" he cried out as an inferno of agony seared from his nose to the back of his head. Ammon released his hold on Zaman and covered his face with his hands. His eyes burned with tears, and when he lowered his hands, they were covered with blood.

With a belly full of rage, he wrenched the dagger from Zaman's hand, and it dropped to the ground.

"I thought there were no weapons," Ammon grunted as he scrambled for the fallen dagger. No longer holding back, he elbowed Zaman in the side of the head, knocking him to edge of the circle.

As Ammon reached for the dagger, Zaman clawed at his legs, pulling him backward. Ammon tried to shake him off, but the man was now up to his waist.

His nose still throbbed, but he forced himself to react. Hand clenched around the dagger, he flipped over, throwing Zaman off balance. Ammon leapt up and yanked Zaman to his feet, one arm locked around his neck, the other hand holding the dagger precariously close to his face.

The man gasped for air, but Ammon tightened his hold until he felt Zaman's body start to tremble. Ammon briefly caught the stares of the crowd, which was now silent, watching in anticipation.

"Give up, Zaman?" Ammon hissed in his ear.

The man struggled but couldn't escape the iron hold. At last, he said in a guttural voice, "Yes."

Ammon released him slowly, remaining tense and ready should Zaman change his mind.

Zaman turned, rubbing his neck. His face was a mixture of red and purple, but he grinned and held out his hand. "Good fight."

Ammon hesitated. This man had cheated and tried to kill him—and now he wanted to congratulate him? Finally, Ammon extended his blood-stained hand and gripped Zaman's.

"Get the man a rag!" someone shouted.

Several in the crowd chuckled. Kumen rushed forward and handed Ammon a piece of cloth.

Gad called out, "I knew I put my faith in the right fighter." A round of laughter filtered through the men.

"I'm not really a fighter." Ammon spat blood on the ground, sick at having to defend himself in a commissioned fight. "I'm—"

"I know, I know," Gad interrupted. "You're only here to *serve the king*." More laughter.

Pahrun approached, shaking his head and chuckling. "You're going to have to keep a close eye on this one." He handed over a leather bag of coins to Gad then appraised Ammon again. "Work starts early. You'd better get back and wash up."

Ammon nodded, feeling dizzy as he did so. His face throbbed with pain, and his stomach felt no better. Kumen and Corien walked with him as he passed through the gathering. Several men were exchanging coins owed on their wagers. A few clapped him on the back, and one man called out, "Next time, we need to allow the daggers from the beginning."

"Then one of them will sneak in a sword!" another shouted.

Guffaws followed Ammon out of the circle. He stumbled back along the jungle route, trying to focus on steady breathing as he kept the pace of the two brothers. He felt faint and sick to his stomach, but he didn't want to complain or slow anyone down. Frustration escalated. He was grateful the king had accepted him so well, but he felt like he was walking backward instead of forward. He didn't want to be labeled as a fighter. He wanted the people to respect his service to the king so that when the opportunity came to teach about the Lord, they would view him as a man dedicated to their king and the people, not as one who joined the fighting circles to earn money. His message was one of peace and salvation—he had to find a way to help them see that. Tonight, he'd done just the opposite.

CHAPTER 5

And the fruit of righteousness is sown in peace of them that make peace.
—James 3:18

As soon as Ammon awakened, he knew something was wrong. Light spilling through the single window in the hut told him it was midmorning. He turned his head toward the door and winced at the shooting pain in his face. Kumen and Corien had let him sleep in—probably due to his injuries—but he wasn't going to make much of an impression if he appeared to be the laziest servant in the land of Ishmael.

Gritting his teeth, Ammon sat up, and gingerly touched his nose. It was definitely out of place and extremely swollen. He grabbed a water skin and took a long drink of the stale water. Then he was on his feet, taking several deep breaths to steady his spinning head.

The flocks, he suddenly remembered. He was supposed to go out with Corien today. He scanned the hut for the sling Corien had been working on the day before. It wasn't in sight. Ammon went to his own pack and took out his sling and dagger. He needed to be ready to help Corien. He hoped the men hadn't left yet for the fields. He also selected one of the scripture scrolls to carry with him, just in case there was an opportunity to teach any of the herdsmen in the fields.

Ammon stepped out of the hut and found only sunshine and a deserted collection of buildings. He hurried to the pavilion that housed the meals, but no one was there either.

He decided to travel to the blacksmith building—hoping Kumen could direct him to the fields. He set off at a half run, stretching his aching muscles.

The day had already grown hot by the time Ammon reached the blacksmith's. His stomach was empty, and his face throbbed, but he was determined to make good on his promise to help Corien with the flocks.

When Ammon stepped inside the sweltering building, the men looked up from their work. Kumen met his gaze. He wore only a loincloth, his torso covered in perspiration. "What are you doing here?" he called out, crossing to Ammon.

"I was supposed to go with Corien to the fields," Ammon said. "Has he left?"

"Yes," Kumen said, using a rag to wipe the moisture from his face. "But you can't go to the fields yet. The king has to approve all herdsmen."

Gad joined them. "You look terrible."

"I look that good?" Ammon said with a half smile—it was all he could manage.

Gad assessed him, pride in his eyes. "You might have surprised the other men last night, but you didn't surprise me." He held up a hand to stave off any protest. "I know you don't want to fight anymore, but you might change your mind." He opened his large sweaty palm, displaying a dozen silver onties. "These are yours."

"I don't need them." He wanted only to serve, not become a paid fighter.

"You will, my friend," Gad said. "You might want to live here the rest of your life but certainly not in a hut with Kumen and Corien."

Kumen cracked a smile.

Gad pressed the silver into Ammon's hand. He took it, feeling the weight of the coins. It had been a long time since he'd held any sort of wealth in his hands.

Gad continued, "I was about to send Kumen on an errand to fetch a purchase from Zaman and his father. Why don't you go with him and stay out of the worst of the heat."

"Isn't Zaman the man who almost sliced my neck with a dagger?"

"The very same," Gad said, chuckling.

"That might not be such a good idea."

"No harm was done, right?"

Ammon let out a breath of air, casting a sideways glance at Kumen. "All right."

As the two men left the blacksmith shop, Ammon said, "How does one ask the king about joining the herders?"

"You'll have to wait until they return—to find out if their journey was successful or not," Kumen said in a rigid voice.

"Why is the penalty so stiff?" Ammon asked. "Why does the king threaten to execute the lead herdsman?"

Kumen looked past Ammon, as if searching for any who might be listening. "The king thinks there's dissension among his servants. This threat is to force them to come forward. Unfortunately, he also has to carry out his order of punishment. Besides, the flocks are being preserved for the high king's feast. To scatter those flocks is to insult Lamoni's father, the high king over the entire land."

"Your brother seemed prepared . . . and determined," Ammon said.

"That's what I worry about," Kumen said. "He'll take risks, trying to prove his loyalty to the king. To volunteer for this assignment is the way to prove absolute allegiance."

Ammon had seen it in Corien's eyes. The man was determined to protect the king's flocks at all costs to prove his loyalty. "How long has he been betrothed?"

"A few months," Kumen said. "He's been saving for a long time in order to build a hut of his own."

"He can have my silver," Ammon said as they reached the main road.

Kumen studied him. "I really don't understand you." He looked away, shaking his head.

They passed several merchants along the road who ignored the two servants. When they reached a bisecting road, Kumen said, "Here we are." He turned onto a lane that led to a home surrounded by a courtyard.

"What exactly are we picking up?"

"Zaman and his father are clothiers for the king. Gad likes to mingle with the aristocracy, and he ordered a new cape. He'll be wearing it to the high king's big feast next month."

Ammon's palms felt sweaty as they approached the house. He wasn't afraid of Zaman but certainly didn't want any sort of a rematch. There must be another way to befriend the Lamanites and get them to trust him.

Kumen rapped on the reed door. The thatch roof extended over the doorway, making a nice pocket of shade. The door squeaked open, and Ammon found himself staring into a pair of hazel eyes framed by thick eyelashes. Definitely *not* Zaman.

"Hello, Elena." Kumen bowed slightly. "Is your brother home?"

Her eyes stayed on Ammon. "Come inside," she said in a quiet voice.

Ammon walked into the cool interior, feeling the woman's gaze on him. He knew she remembered him, despite his mashed face. Her eyes had flickered with recognition. He studied her, wondering about her—she had spared his life when she could have easily released the arrow and killed or seriously injured him. He expected her to disappear to fetch her brother, but instead she stood openly staring at him. "What happened to your face?"

"I was in—"

"He's new in the blacksmith's," Kumen broke in. "A small accident."

The woman's eyes narrowed as if she didn't quite believe the explanation. She hesitated for a moment as if she were going to ask something else. Instead, she turned and went into another room, which Ammon assumed was the cooking room, and a minute later, Zaman appeared, chewing something.

"The Nephite is back!" Zaman boomed. Then he winced. "Oh—you don't look so great. Sorry for that."

"Sorry for *what*?" The woman's voice piped up behind Zaman. She stepped from behind him, her eyes scowling at her brother. "Did you have something to do with this?"

Zaman's pale skin flushed, and he smiled down at his sister. "Nothing for a woman to be concerned about."

Her fist shot out, and she punched her brother in the arm.

"Elena," he said in a warning voice.

She narrowed her eyes then left the room.

Zaman turned back to the men. "She's been living in a household of men too long—sometimes she acts more like a little brother." He rubbed his arm self-consciously. "Have a seat. What brings you to my home?" Before they could reply, he turned his head and called out, "Elena, bring in refreshments!"

Something clattered in the cooking room, drowning out a muttered response.

Kumen sat on a nearby cushion. Ammon followed but felt hesitant to do so. Weren't they on a business errand? Regardless, the cool house was much nicer than slaving away in the blacksmith building.

"She'll be back in a moment. She might take her time, but she'll be back," Zaman said as if he still had to justify his sister's behavior.

Ammon hid a smile.

"So what brings you to my home?" Zaman asked.

"We're on an errand for Gad," Kumen said. "He said you had a special cape ready for him."

"Ah, yes. We finished it just this morning. I'll fetch my father in a moment." Zaman focused in on Ammon. "Does it hurt much?"

"Only when I move," Ammon said in dry voice. It was obvious that Kumen was comfortable with this man, but Ammon was still annoyed that Zaman had cheated in the fight.

Zaman chuckled, flexing his hand. It looked swollen as well. "You know I wasn't really going to use that dagger—it was just for intimidation."

Ammon met the man's dark eyes. He might be trying to blend in with the Lamanites, but he still bore the appearance of a Nephite, no matter how he dressed. Ammon thought he'd uncovered a deeper understanding of the man. "Was I the last to find out?"

Zaman ducked his head, his expression a bit sheepish. "Fights rarely end in a death," he said.

That wasn't much more comforting.

"I knew it was a fight!" a woman's voice interrupted. Elena came bursting into the room. Her brother's face darkened at her sudden appearance.

She carried a bowl and cloth. "The refreshments will have to wait," she said, throwing her brother a sharp look.

Elena walked toward Ammon. She dipped the cloth into the bowl she carried.

He froze, not knowing what he should do—bow? Stand? What was the Lamanite custom when a woman approached?

"Hold still." She raised the cloth, smeared with some sort of paste or ointment, and touched it to his face.

Ammon flinched.

"Don't worry, I'm not going to injure you like my brother did," she said. "But you should probably close your eyes."

Ammon obeyed, though it felt strange that this woman would be so compassionate to him again. Apparently, she didn't feel the need to use an arrow to keep him at arm's length.

"He's fine," Zaman said, grumbling. "Leave the poor man alone."

"He's not fine," Elena shot back. "And it's apparent that no one has given his injuries a second thought. There's still dried blood on his face."

Ammon opened his eyes a slit, but when Elena turned her attention back to him, he snapped them shut.

"I can't believe him," Elena muttered. "He's always trying to prove something."

"I heard that," Zaman said.

Elena's touch was light, causing almost no additional pain as she applied the salve along his nose and below his eyes. The skin on the back of Ammon's neck prickled as he grew increasingly self-conscious under Elena's touch—especially in front of the men. "Thank you for not killing me in the jungle," he whispered.

She didn't respond for several seconds, but then she said, "You're most welcome."

Although his eyes were closed, he heard the smile in her voice. Her hand touched his, turning it over. "What's this?"

Ammon opened his eyes and pulled his hand away. "An old scar."

Their gazes locked for a moment. "We defected from Zarahemla too," Elena whispered.

"I can hear you, Elena," Zaman said.

Ammon was about to reply, to explain that he hadn't defected, when Zaman piped in again, obviously directing his comment at Elena. "You might not agree with everything I'm doing, but at least *I* get out of the house."

"I get out of the house sometimes," Elena retorted, applying more salve on Ammon's face. "Although, I manage not to break noses in the process. Does Abish know how you spend your nights?"

A rustling sound told Ammon that Zaman was on his feet. "That's too much salve, Elena. He has enough on him to heal every injury for the rest of his life."

The anger in Zaman's voice was real. He wondered who Abish was. Whoever she was, Elena knew how to take a jab at her brother. Ammon pulled away from Elena and chuckled.

Her hand went to her hip as she looked at him. "What's funny?"

"You and your brother remind me of me and my brothers," Ammon said. "We could argue about anything, no matter how small, day or night."

Elena's mouth twitched, but Ammon saw she wasn't about to give up a good fight with her brother. She turned on her heel and strode out of the room, the cloth in her hand. "A fine way to welcome someone from our homeland," she muttered.

Zaman's face flushed. "The homeland is dead to us, Elena. Just like Father says. *Dead!*"

She paused at the cooking room door. "Of course," she said in a neutral tone. "Just as Father says." Her tone was no longer argumentative but accepting. She glanced at Ammon, and he thought he saw more color in her cheeks. She lowered her eyes and turned into the cooking room. The men sat in silence, and a moment later, Elena reappeared with a tray. This time she was stone quiet. She set the tray of sliced maize cakes and fruit down and left without another word.

"Well, this looks delicious." Kumen reached for a piece of cake.

Ammon reached for one too. He wondered why Zaman and his family had left Zarahemla. What could have happened that made them despise it so much? And how did they end up here?

Zaman sat down and shook his head. "I must apologize for my sister," he said in a quiet voice. "She wouldn't like me saying this, but she truly doesn't leave this house very much. She struggles socially, and no matter how much my father and I talk to her, she hasn't been able to get over her temper." He looked at them, alarm dawning in his eyes. "She, of course, has many other skills, all of which will make her a very *marriageable* woman."

Kumen burst out laughing then reached over and slapped Zaman on his shoulder. "Your secret is safe with us. Right, Ammon?"

He nodded, his mouth too full to answer, but his thoughts were on the woman with the fiery temper.

"I thought you'd come with your brother instead. Where is he?" Zaman said, looking much more relaxed with his sister out of the room.

"Corien is with the herdsmen today," Kumen said, his tone deepening.

"Already? Is it true he volunteered to be the lead?" Zaman asked.

"Yes," Kumen said.

Zaman said, "Brave man. I hope he went armed."

"He made a new sling yesterday," Kumen said.

"Oh? He should have taken the one I bought at the market the other day. It was made in the land of Shilom. The sling is much finer and thinner than the ones I've seen. I wondered how it compares."

Ammon leaned forward. "Can I see it?"

Zaman lifted a brow. "Interested, are you?" He left the room for moment and returned with a sling dangling from his hand.

Ammon examined the workmanship. The leather was thin and narrow. A fine piece of workmanship. "Maybe it's for smaller rocks?"

"The merchant told me that it fits different sizes of rocks, and it's more accurate."

"Can I try it?" Ammon said.

Zaman grinned. "Why not? Follow me."

They exited the front of the house, and Zaman picked up a small stone from the ground. He handed it to Ammon. "Try this size first."

Ammon took several steps away from the men then pointed to a pistachio tree about thirty paces away. "Let's see if it'll reach the lowest branch." He let the sling extend to its fullest length then placed the rock inside the pouch. With a single smooth motion he had it twirling in the air, then he gave it a sharp release.

The stone sailed through the air, falling just short of the mark, but the aim was true.

"Let me try," Zaman said, using about the same size stone and aiming at the same mark. His sailed way off course. He picked up another rock and held it toward Ammon. "Try it again."

Ammon took the rock, and this time he kept the momentum of the sling a bit faster and released earlier.

The rock embedded itself into the lowest branch.

All three men stared at the target for a moment. Then Zaman turned to Ammon, his eyes wide. "Remind me never to get into a sling competition with you."

Ammon loaded up another rock, this one a bit larger, and tried again. Same aim, same speed, and the rock snapped into the branch, cracking the wood.

"All right," Zaman said. "That's enough damage to my tree."

Kumen laughed.

Handing over the sling, Ammon withdrew his own from his tunic. "This will go nearly twice that distance."

Zaman narrowed his gaze and eyed the sling.

Ammon loaded it with a rock and pointed. "Over to that second tree. At the base." Seconds later, the rock was embedded in the dirt.

"Let me see that." Zaman concentrated as he aimed for the same spot, but his shot landed several paces short and to the right.

"Did they teach you that in your father's palace?" Zaman asked.

"No," Ammon said. "It's something I learned when I got hungry in your wilderness."

"Impressive," Zaman said. "Would you like to see our workshop in the back courtyard? Then I'll get Gad's new cape wrapped up."

Ammon glanced at Kumen, wondering if they'd already used up too much time for this errand.

Kumen didn't hesitate. "Of course."

They entered the house again and walked through the cool interior to the back door. "By the way," Zaman said in a half whisper, "Gad would be one of those to not mention my sister's temper to. He's widowed, as you know, and has paid her some high compliments."

"I heard that," a female voice called out from their left.

Zaman shook his head and hurried through the hall. "She's impossible." He motioned them out the door. "The workshop is just over there. Go ahead and see it; my father's inside."

As Ammon and Kumen left the house, they heard Zaman speaking to his sister. Kumen put a hand on Ammon's arm and stopped to listen.

"You need to be more gracious when we have visitors," Zaman was saying.

"I was gracious to them," Elena responded. "You're the one who broke that poor man's nose."

"He's not a poor man if you must know. In fact, the king seems besotted by him. He's a former prince of Zarahemla but gave up his right to the throne. He's a deserter to his birthright and people. Regardless of what the king thinks, he's just a lousy runaway Nephite—hardly trustworthy at this point."

"Why does that make him not trustworthy? Maybe he had a good reason to give up his throne. We left Zarahemla as well."

A pause then Zaman's voice. "Don't ask so many questions. I saw how you looked at him. How nice you were to him."

"I wasn't—"

"He's no good, Elena," Zaman cut her off. "Besides, Gad asked about you last night. Father's invited him for supper tomorrow night."

Ammon didn't hear her reply because he tugged Kumen away. Kumen elbowed him. "She might have a bad temper, but she *is* quite pretty."

Ammon raised a brow.

"Don't get the wrong idea," Kumen said. "She's pretty in her own way but not my type of woman. Let's say I enjoy the sweeter ones."

Ammon chuckled as Zaman exited the house. He caught up with them, and they walked together to the workshop. Just before they reached it, a man stepped outside.

"Father, we have visitors," Zaman said.

"Moriah," Kumen greeted with a bow.

"Stand up, my man," Moriah said, his eyes flitting in Ammon's direction. He was obviously Nephite by birth but dressed more like his son. The light color of his skin contrasted with the vibrant aqua of his kilt. He wore a heavy gold necklace about his neck and several rings on his fingers. If Ammon had seen him at court, he'd have assumed he was just another member of the elite, although with fair Nephite skin.

"Who's your friend?" Moriah asked, appraising Ammon.

"The Nephite who was captured a few days ago along the borders of the land," Kumen answered.

"Ah, is this the Nephite you fought last night, Zaman?"

Zaman looked surprised that his father knew about it.

"Looks like it hurts," Moriah said.

"Only when I'm awake," Ammon said.

Moriah chuckled then grew serious, looking at Ammon. "I've heard about you. A deserter. It appears we have something in common." His thin brows drew together. "Though I wasn't born into the royal family nor did I give up a kingdom."

Ammon offered a half smile. "I've come to live among the Lamanites, just as you and your family, sir."

"Yes, so you have," Moriah said. He waved a hand toward the small hut. "Come into my workshop. And you'll see how much a Nephite can accomplish in this Lamanite land."

Kumen let out a low whistle.

Ammon stared at his surroundings. He'd never seen anything like it. Wooden posts stuck straight up out of the ground, displaying a rainbow of various capes. They were in different stages of being finished, all unique designs. A curtain hung down in the middle of the room, separating a smaller group of capes. Several low shelves contained headdresses, some made of feathers and beads, others of animal heads. Ammon remembered the deer headdress that Pahrun had worn the night before.

One headdress was especially impressive—a jaguar head with jade carvings in place of its teeth.

Moriah pointed out a few of the capes, naming the citizens who had ordered them. Kumen nodded, as if he knew each one.

"And this is Gad's new cloak," Moriah said, removing a cape with green and yellow feathers covering most of it. Light brown fur served as the edging.

"Remarkable," Kumen said, fingering the fur lining.

Moriah looked pleased. "Do you want to try it on?"

"Oh no," Kumen said. "I'll get it dirty."

Moriah held the cape out to Ammon. "Surely you've worn finery like this before—or maybe not. You wouldn't see much of this type of thing in Zarahemla, eh?"

"Not in these styles," Ammon said. As a prince, he'd had fine clothing but nothing this elaborate or garish.

"Take it to Gad," Moriah said, "and tell him I want payment at tomorrow night's supper." He turned and pulled a length of woven linen from a shelf then carefully wrapped the feather cape in the linen. He secured the bundle with a thin piece of rope.

Kumen took the bundle, and they turned to leave.

"Wait," Moriah said. "What's your name, Nephite?"

"Ammon," he said, turning to face the merchant again.

With a nod, Moriah said, "I remember seeing you as a boy. It was at the harvest festival. You were sitting between your parents, looking proud—like you were soaking in all that would be yours someday."

Heat rose in Ammon's neck as he thought of the privileges he used to take for granted. "That was a long time ago. Much has changed since then. Other things have become more important."

Moriah brought a hand to his chin, regarding Ammon thoughtfully. "I wonder," he said in a low voice, "what would make the prince regent flee his homeland—with all of his brothers?" He narrowed his eyes, his gaze part glare, part curiosity.

Letting out a breath, Ammon wished he could explain the true purpose of his mission. But the pit in his stomach confirmed to him that the time wasn't right, nor was Moriah the right person.

Moriah huffed through his nose in response to Ammon's silence. "Someday I'd be interested in hearing the real story." His gaze bore into Ammon's. "I certainly hope you're telling the truth—for everyone who's involved."

"Yes, sir," Ammon said.

Zaman interrupted, pointing to a headdress. "What do you think of the jeweled headdress?"

"It's the most amazing work I've seen," Kumen said. "The king will love it."

"It's a gift for his father. We'll present it at the high king's feast next month."

"*You're* going to the feast?" Kumen asked, his voice incredulous.

"Father is," Zaman said. "And I plan to accompany him one way or another." He shot a challenging but hopeful look in his father's direction, which Moriah seemed to purposely ignore.

The men left the hut, and Zaman walked with them around the house to the front courtyard. Although Elena was nowhere in sight, Ammon found himself straining to see some sign of her.

He thought about Gad coming to the family's home for supper the next night—with all of his wealth. It would be a prestigious match for her, it seemed. He wondered what she thought of Gad. Perhaps she was thrilled at the possibility. Regardless, it was none of his business. He made every effort to not look back at the house as they left the courtyard, but he failed miserably.

CHAPTER 6

For this shall the earth mourn, and the heavens above be black.
—Jeremiah 4:28

Elena watched the Nephite leave with Kumen through the side window of the cooking room. She was amused when the Nephite looked back at the house not once but twice. He probably thought she was raving mad to be acting like she had. But seeing Ammon's face bruised and swollen had sent her into a frenzy. *Yet, why should I be concerned about a man I don't even know?* Zaman fought at the jungle circle a couple times a week, something that would make their father furious if he knew, not to mention Abish. But her brother claimed to need the extra silver and said it wasn't as dangerous as it seemed.

Seeing Ammon had changed her mind. Her brother could have been hurt or killed. The Nephite was no man of small stature.

She turned away from the window and moved to the cooking fire to check on the soaking beans. She added some mushrooms to simmer in the pot. As she stirred, she worried that if something happened to her brother, she'd be forced to marry so her future would be secured. Her father wouldn't be around forever. She wasn't concerned about Abish coming into the home and taking over—in fact, Elena would enjoy having another woman around and someone to share the work with.

Maybe I could fill Abish's position with the queen and live and serve in the palace. But Elena knew she wouldn't like the confined lifestyle, with its regimen and constant company. She enjoyed her privacy and independence. She loved the walls of this home. They were thick and secure, keeping her away from the prying eyes of the Lamanite women. She'd never truly be like them, so it was pointless for her to even try.

If she married, she'd have to interact with more women, shop at the marketplace regularly, discuss children's ailments, and socialize with husbands and wives. All she wanted to do was stay home—where she was needed and where she was comfortable. She would be happy taking care of her father for the rest of her life. She didn't want a husband—didn't want to share a home with some stranger. Especially a man like Gad, who already had children.

Elena put down the stirring stick and walked back to the window. The men had just reached the gate of the front courtyard. She suppressed a smile when the Nephite's eyes strayed a third time. Her brother had referred to him as a prince who had failed his country, but she didn't believe that. No prince would leave his land to become a servant to his enemy. There must be a valid reason that he left. Yet, she could imagine Ammon as a great leader—he had a commanding presence and an authoritative quality about him. *And if it weren't for his battered face*, Elena admitted to herself, *he might be quite handsome.* Her heart quickened as she realized she already knew what he looked like without the bruising. Though the meeting in the jungle had been short, she'd had enough time to get a good look at him. She wondered about the scar on his hand. Was he a fighter like her brother? Did he also need extra silver, perhaps to create a home for a betrothed?

Now her face was warm. Why was she dwelling so much on the Nephite? Probably because he was different from Gad. Ammon looked at her differently and spoke to her differently, and she wasn't afraid or nervous around him. She turned away from the window, deliberately trying to think of something else as she returned to the pot of beans. But the image of Ammon shooting that tree with a sling came to her mind. She'd never seen anything like it. She remembered that Zaman had promised to take her target shooting this afternoon. Since the encounter with Ammon in the jungle, he'd seen the wisdom of his sister being more prepared.

"Elena," her father called from the courtyard, interrupting her thoughts.

"Coming." She walked out of the house, stepping outside into the bright courtyard where her father waited. "Will we be going to speak with Abish about my designs tonight?"

"If there's time," her father said. "More importantly, you need to come with me to market and select a fine meal for tomorrow."

Elena's mouth went dry as she instantly realized the only reason her father would need her to present a fine meal. Gad.

"Gad, the blacksmith, is coming for supper."

Her heart sank. Why did they have to meet him on the main road? And why did Zaman have to discuss her skills? "Zaman told me." She paused, thinking that she might dissuade her father about the marriage *before* Gad's visit. "He's old enough to be my father."

Her father let out a patient sigh. "He's a good man, Elena. He also has plenty of wealth." He looked at her tenderly. "I want you to be well taken care of. I wouldn't hand you over to anyone I thought wouldn't make a good husband."

She looked down at her twisting hands, tears collecting at the back of her eyes—tears she refused to let anyone see. "I know, Father." She lifted her face and kissed his cheek. "Must I go to the marketplace, though?"

"You must meet the meat vendor and get used to purchasing the meat—it will be your duty as a wife."

Elena pushed back her fear of being around so many people who might stare at her. "I'll get my scarf."

Once she was in the privacy of her bedchamber, she brushed angrily at the hot tears that had defiantly escaped. She'd known this day would come, but so soon? She'd trusted that her father would choose a good man. But why did he have to be so much older and one with so many children? There were five of them—one daughter married, a year younger than Elena, another daughter just fifteen, and three boys. How could she be a mother to children that were more like siblings? She didn't think Gad would let her spend much time in her bedchamber.

The bedchamber. That was another worry. She didn't understand all the intricacies of love, but she knew enough to know she didn't ever want to picture her and Gad . . . together . . . like that.

Stop thinking about it. Or the tears would never stop. She took a deep, shuddering breath then tied the scarf securely about her head. *There was no official betrothal, and maybe Gad wasn't even interested,* she tried to console herself. Yet, that broad smile showing his gapped teeth came to her mind, and she knew that he was *very* interested. He'd been a widow for more than two years, longer than most men waited to remarry.

Her other option was the temple. Women, most whom had no marriage prospect because of poverty or some deformity, entered the temple and served as priestesses. It was an honorable life and brought prestige to the family. The family was well compensated for the daughter's life of service, and the family was blessed by the gods with posterity for their immense sacrifice.

I could be a priestess, Elena thought, *and live my life in quiet peace among the walls of the temple. Perhaps the Maize Temple, where my mother's soul has been prayed over.* It wasn't the first time she'd considered becoming a priestess. The only thing that prevented her from telling her father was that she couldn't bear to leave him. She would miss him too much, and she knew he depended on her with her mother gone. Who would take care of him? Perhaps Abish, but it wouldn't be the same.

When she was ready to leave, Elena followed her father obediently to the grand plaza that had been built around the sacred ceiba tree. Its height was majestic as its sturdy trunk rose to the heavens. Small statues and platters of incense were stationed about the tree—where plenty of the villagers placed tokens of their deepest prayers, hoping that the ceiba would grant them. Elena and her father stopped before the tree and bowed their heads, saying a short prayer before passing by.

When they crossed through the plaza and into the first portion of the market, Elena hoped her scarf would conceal her from curious gazes. She didn't like being in such large crowds, and when she did visit the market, it was usually first thing in the morning when fewer people were about. They used to stare at her hair and skin when she was younger, before she thought to cover up with a scarf. Elena kept her eyes averted as her father stopped to talk to various people. As they entered the busier section, she clutched her father's arm to keep from being jostled and separated.

They passed by the vendor displays of fine lengths of cloth, jade jewelry, and shells made into almost anything from decorations for leather sandals to necklaces and hair pieces.

"What about a new robe?" her father asked.

"I don't want to purchase a robe when I can make it myself," she said.

"There's no time to make yourself anything new before tomorrow night. If you see something you like, let me know."

But Elena didn't want to purchase anything to look special for Gad. He was certain to notice the new cloth and would think she was interested in attracting him. The crowds were daunting, and Elena kept a hold of her father's arm as he made his way to the meat quarter.

Her father stopped at a merchant's stall. "This vendor always gives me a fair cut for the price," he said, nudging her forward.

"Ah, Moriah," the vendor said. "Who have you brought with you?"

"My daughter, Elena. She will choose the meat today."

The vendor pointed out several sections of tapir meat, explaining the tenderness of each. When Elena made her choice, the meat merchant wrapped the raw hunk with leaves.

"Thank you," Elena said, taking the meat. Her father placed it in his satchel.

"I will always have a good price for you," the vendor said with a bow.

Moriah grinned then turned to Elena. "Would you like to browse the clothing stalls now?"

"No," she said. "I'll just wear what I have at home. I don't need new clothing."

Moriah embraced her and kissed the top of her head.

"Father." Her face warmed. "Everyone will stare. Let's go."

"They can all know I'm proud of my beautiful daughter," he said.

Her face heated again, and she tugged at her father's arm. "Come on!"

A young boy tore past them, shouting, "An execution! In the plaza!"

"By the king's orders," another shouted.

"He'll be hanged," someone said.

"No," the meat merchant said. "He'll be thrown into the animal den like the last lead herdsman."

Elena's hand tightened on her father's arm. He looked down at her, his face suddenly pale. "We should go home," he said in a low voice. "The crowds can get into a frenzy when there's an execution."

Too horrified to speak, she followed silently. Elena had never seen an execution but had heard all about them from her brother. They always seemed needlessly cruel, but her brother had explained that the king himself had to follow the rules he had set forth to the people.

She and her father pushed their way through the jostling crowd. They'd have to pass the main plaza on the way back.

As they neared the ceiba tree, Elena's stomach clenched. A platform had been carried in, and on top of it stood a man she recognized. Kumen's brother, Corien.

Elena averted her eyes, but it was too late. She turned her face against her father's shoulder, her breath coming in gasps. She squeezed her eyes shut against the terrifying image. The naked body. His anguished cries. The ropes around his wrists. The blood.

She followed her father, blindly, her eyes blurred with tears. The crowd thickened, and the noise grew—some were shouting, some cursing, others wailing. Her father's arm was pulled from hers, and Elena searched for him frantically, but the pressing crowd had swallowed him whole.

Elena was alone in a maze of people. She shoved through the mob, away from the sickening spectacle. When she'd cleared the thick of the crowd, she ran toward home, desperate to get as far from the horror as possible.

* * *

Kumen chattered on the way back to the blacksmith building. "Corien will want you to show him how to hit those long distances too. He won't be back for a couple of days, but maybe you can teach me a little. He'll be impressed."

Gad was outside when they arrived at the shop. His eyes lit up when he saw the bundle Kumen carried. He handed it over then went inside the shop, leaving Ammon and Gad facing one another.

"Thank you." Gad stopped Ammon before he could enter. "What's on your face?"

"Besides two swollen eyes and a broken nose?" Ammon said. "Zaman's sister fixed me up with salve."

"Elena?" A smile appeared on Gad's face, and he leaned in to examine Ammon a bit closer. "She did a nice job. Another fine skill the young lady possesses."

Is he keeping a tally of Elena's skills? Ammon felt bothered that a man this age was paying so much attention to a woman like Elena—who couldn't be more than nineteen or twenty. He was about to ask Gad the ages of his children when a young boy ran up to them. "It's an execution!"

Gad turned to the boy, putting a hand on his shoulder. "Tell me, son."

Ammon saw the likeness between the two.

The boy's eyes flitted to Ammon for a second then back to his father. "The king's herdsmen lost the flocks to a band of rebels. The king has ordered the execution of the lead herder. He'll be slain within the hour."

Gad's jaw flexed. *"Corien?"*

The boy nodded, his eyes wide with fear. Ammon felt as if he'd been punched in the stomach.

Gad cursed. "Go home and tell your brother to come and close up the shop."

"Can I come to the execution?"

"No," Gad said, his voice stern.

When the boy had scurried off, Gad glanced at Ammon. "Wait here," he said.

Ammon's mind churned as he waited. This wasn't happening—he'd just been with Corien the night before. Maybe it wasn't too late, and they could plead for mercy. The workers filed outside, chatting as if they were taking a regular break. Gad's worried gaze met Ammon's.

Gad cleared his throat. The massive man shifted his weight from one foot to the other. "I have news from the palace. The king's flocks were scattered again. The king has made his orders clear, and now there will be an execution."

"No!" Kumen cried out. "Not my brother." Kumen sank onto a nearby rock and buried his face in his hands.

"We're finished working for the day," Gad said in a quiet voice. "Everyone can leave." The workers murmured condolences to Kumen then left.

Ammon turned to Gad. "Can nothing be done?"

Gad shook his head, his expression sorrowful. "It's the king's edict. Made just days ago after the flocks were scattered by rebels. Corien volunteered to lead the new group of herdsmen . . . He's worked in my shop . . . Said he wasn't scared by a band of ruffians. Wanted to prove his loyalty to the king. But now . . ."

As Gad's voice trailed off, Ammon's stomach felt hollow.

He crossed to Kumen, praying that he'd be able to say the right thing. He crouched down to Kumen's level. "I'll come with you."

Kumen raised his head, his face tearstreaked. "My brother didn't have to go, but he thought he'd earn more respect in the king's eyes."

Ammon's throat was too thick to speak.

"Don't you understand?" Kumen continued. "He shouldn't have volunteered. It was a death sentence from the beginning. This didn't have to happen."

Settling next to Kumen, Ammon listened as Kumen talked about his brother. How foolish his brother was. How he'd always seemed to get into one scrape or another. And now this.

Ammon's heart clenched as he thought of his own brothers—alone, each in foreign territory. What challenges had they met? Had they been welcomed as he had?

Gad crossed to them. "Here, drink this." He held out a flask of agave wine.

After a long swallow, Kumen wiped his mouth then stood up, his reddened eyes filled with resolve. "I must go plead with the king for my brother's life."

"No," Gad said, putting a hand on his arm. "It will only anger him further. We don't want two executions."

"Then I'll go in my brother's place," Kumen announced. "It's better me than him. He is betrothed to marry. I have nothing . . . and if my brother is killed, I'll have no one." His voice wavered on the last sentence, and Ammon felt a sting in his own eyes.

"The king won't change his mind—not for this," Gad said. "It's too serious. He made the announcement in front of the whole court. If he goes back on his edict, then he'll lose the respect of the people."

"He'll show he's a merciful king by sparing my brother's life." Kumen spoke rapidly, his eyes wide. "I'll *make* him understand." He wrenched free of Gad's grip and started to run toward the main road.

"Kumen!" Gad shouted and ran after him.

Following, Ammon easily overtook Gad as they chased Kumen. Ammon wasn't sure where the man was running to at first, but it became clear as they reached a crowd gathered at a central market square. A giant ceiba tree towered over the throng. A platform rose above the heads of the people, giving everyone a clear view of the man who stood on the top of the scaffold.

Ammon caught up with Kumen, who had stopped, staring in disbelief at his brother. Corien had been stripped naked. His limbs looked bloodied and bruised, and a thick rope laced around his wrists and ankles.

Gad joined them and grabbed Kumen's arm. "Take his other arm so he doesn't try to stop the guards," he said to Ammon.

Ammon gripped Kumen's arm, but he sensed Kumen was done running. Grief and horror twisted his face as he stared at Corien.

"The sentence has already been given," Gad said. "The king's entourage is gone, and only the guards remain."

Ammon's stomach twisted furiously as the crowd's shouts grew louder. A ripple of conversation passed through the people, some speculating on who the rebels were, others talking about the execution.

The guards steered Corien off the platform. "What are they doing?" Ammon asked Gad.

"They're taking him to the wild animal pit," Gad said.

A boy ran past them, shouting, "To the animal den!"

They both looked at Kumen, but he seemed oblivious to the shouting. "We need to get him away from here," Gad said. "If he causes a commotion, he might be arrested."

But the thickness of the crowd intensified, pushing them along. Kumen became alert again and started to call out, "Corien!" He yanked his arm from Gad, but Ammon kept his hold.

"Gad!" Ammon shouted, but he was lost in the hundreds of people. Kumen continued to cry out for his brother in the commotion. Ammon felt helpless as they were shoved along, and the only thing he could do was keep a hold of Kumen's arm.

The crowd pushed through the plaza, past the platform and the large ceiba tree. The crowd propelled them along a narrow path that led into the jungle. Ammon tried to steer Kumen off the path, but he kept his determined pace.

The path opened into a clearing that reminded Ammon of the fighting circle from the night before. But instead of a large area outlined by animal bones, this one contained a large pit—one similar to an animal trap. The feeling of horror in Ammon's stomach told him this pit was much larger and much deeper than what it took to simply trap a single animal.

What was even more awful was the sight of Corien, held fast by several guards, perched on the bank of the pit.

The guttural cry from Kumen was a sound Ammon hoped to never hear again. It wrenched at his heart and soul, piercing him straight through.

"Corien!" Kumen screamed.

Ammon stumbled along with Kumen, keeping a firm hold on the man. The crowd parted, letting the two of them through, as if they knew who Kumen was.

Ammon was able to stop Kumen before he reached the edge of the pit, opposite Corien. The brothers' eyes locked, and Corien gave a simple nod. His jaw was set, his lips in a firm line, eyes blazing. Across his cheek was a long cut that still bled, either from protecting the flocks or from the guards' abuse.

"Stop!" Kumen screamed, jerking away. He lunged for the pit, and Ammon pulled him back, earning a shoulder in the face. He bit back his own pain and focused on using all of his strength to restrain Kumen. He'd already caught the guards' attention.

Corien stared at his brother's desperation. He looked up at the sky as if it had the answers. Then, without provocation, he threw himself forward into the pit. His body turned and dropped as if it were happening very slowly. The crowd went dead silent. Then Corien disappeared from view.

A series of unmistakable growls and shrieks followed, and several in the crowd screamed and backed away.

Kumen dropped to his knees, sobbing and clawing at the dirt. Ammon sank to the ground next to Kumen, holding him down, preventing him from following his brother into the pit. Ammon ignored the burning tears on his face and the new throbbing in his cheek as he held onto Kumen.

"Let me go!" Kumen clawed desperately at the ground.

"Never." Ammon intensified his grip, feeling that Kumen was quickly losing strength. *Please, Lord,* Ammon prayed silently. *Help me keep this man safe. Help me comfort him.*

CHAPTER 7

Train up a child in the way he should go: and when
he is old, he will not depart from it.
—Proverb 22:6

When Elena reached the courtyard of her home, she wiped tears from her cheeks, but they fell faster than she could make them disappear. She hadn't even known Corien, but every part of her body imagined the fear, the terror of the moment of falling into a pit of wild animals. The glaring yellow eyes, the low growls, the menacing teeth, the first tear of flesh . . .

The pain would be hot and searing. And that's as far as she could let herself imagine. It was horrible to think about, to even hear about. Everyone had been talking about it as she'd fled the plaza. She'd run, covering her ears, not caring if people thought she was strange or childish for being so scared.

She opened the gate to the yard, her racing heart starting to slow, though her body continued to tremble. And the tears wouldn't stop.

Her thoughts turned to Corien again. How did he endure knowing he was about to die? What did he think in his last moments of life as he was led to the animal den? Did he wonder what it would feel like? Did he wonder what would happen when he died—where his spirit would go—now that he'd broken the king's edict? Would his spirit go to heaven?

She barely remembered attending the Church in Zarahemla. When she'd begged her mother, she'd tell Elena small things about the Nephite religion. But since her mother's death, her father had refused to discuss any of it. Her mother had been attacked by a jaguar when she was on a bird-collecting trip with her father. Her father had warded off the wild beast, and they originally thought her mother would live. But then infection set in, and nothing the healer did, nor the praying priests, could reverse the fevers. Regardless, the priests of the Maize Temple had offered many sacrifices in her mother's behalf. And now her father and brother gave generous donations to the Maize Temple at every moon.

The most devout Lamanites made the largest donations, and her father made sure his donations were noted.

She wished she could ask someone about what would happen to Corien's spirit. What would the Nephite, Ammon, say? She wondered again where the scar on his hand had come from. The priests in the Lamanite temples drew their own blood and let it fall upon the altars to honor the Great Spirit, proving that they were devout above all other citizens. Had Ammon's scar on his hand come from a similar ritual in Zarahemla?

Elena looked through bleary eyes at the goddess statue of Chak Chel that sat next to the front door. She slowly walked toward it. Her father had bought the statue a few months after her mother's death. It was supposed to bring them strength and wellness, this goddess of war and medicine. Today the goddess seemed to have her eyes closed.

"Elena?" a female voice called out behind her.

Startled, Elena turned, sure that her face was blotchy, her eyes red. "Abish?"

"I saw you leave the marketplace. I could tell you were upset." The open, sweet expression on Abish's face was too much for Elena. She started crying again and threw her arms around her friend.

"I don't understand how the king can be so cruel," Elena whispered. She drew back and covered her mouth. "Why did this have to happen—?"

"It's horrible," Abish said, touching Elena's arm. "Corien was such a hard worker, a sweet man, who only wanted to prove his loyalty."

"Why couldn't the king make an exception?" Elena asked.

Abish hesitated then said, "Many outside of the court don't understand how important it is for the king to follow his own rules." She looked past Elena, her eyes troubled. "But I must confess, I don't exactly agree with the king's edict, even if he is convinced there are dissenters among his own servants." She looked behind her. "Let's go inside."

Abish led her into the gathering room where they sat together on a set of cushions.

"Where will Corien's spirit go?" Elena blurted as soon as they were seated.

Abish looked decidedly uncomfortable as she twisted her hands together.

"I wish my mother were here to explain it," Elena said.

"You mean about what the Nephites believe?" Abish whispered.

"Yes," Elena said. "Haven't you wondered as well?"

"I have," Abish said, her face flushing slightly. "I've asked Zaman about it, but he doesn't like to talk about Zarahemla, so I think I'll try to ask Ammon some questions."

Hope sprung inside Elena. Perhaps she could ask Ammon as well. "He'd be happy to answer them, I'm sure."

"I hope so," Abish said in a quiet voice.

Elena wrapped her arms about herself as a sudden chill went through her. The events of the day came flooding back. Corien would have no chance against the wild animals, just as her own mother hadn't. "Do you remember your mother?" she asked.

Abish looked surprised at the question, and her answer was slow to come. "I don't remember her very much anymore. I was only three years old when she died. But my father . . ."

Elena watched her carefully. "What was he like?"

"He was a humble man," Abish said. "Quiet but intelligent. He used to study old documents and records from the temple that the priest would sometimes let him bring home. He'd study them in the evenings after he was finished cleaning."

"Did you visit the temple with him often?"

"Until I was about fourteen. Then the priests forbade me to accompany my father." She looked away from Elena's gaze. "At least that's what he said at first. Later, when he secured a position for me with the queen, he told me the real reason."

"What?" Elena said in almost a whisper.

Abish hesitated for a moment. "I'd been noticed by one of the priests, and he wanted me to join the order of the priestess and serve in the temple."

"That must have been an honor to be noticed," Elena said. Perhaps if Abish hadn't wanted to marry Zaman, they could have served together in the temple.

Abish's gaze flickered with confusion. "Not an honor, necessarily."

"One of the girls in our neighborhood was called to be a priestess," Elena said. "Her family became wealthy for the rest of their lives. I've thought about it as well, but my first loyalty is to my father. If anything were to happen to him, though, I think I'd choose the temple over marriage."

Abish's face drained of color. "The price of becoming a priestess is very, very high."

"I know," Elena said. *Because you can't ever marry or have children but are eternally bound to the gods.* She let out a sigh. "It sounds like a quiet yet very spiritual life."

"My father forbade me to ever take the oath," Abish said, vehemence in her voice.

Elena looked at her with surprise. "Why? He couldn't have known you'd fall in love with Zaman."

Abish grabbed her hands. "Elena, you're old enough to know these things. Without a mother, you have been kept in innocence."

"What do you mean?" Elena said, feeling wary.

"The temple priestesses serve many functions, many of them noble. They're keepers of the sacred relics, in charge of preserving them. They sew beautiful robes for the priests, and they spend a lot of time in prayer. The priestesses take many oaths—one of which is the virgin oath."

Elena knew this. So why did Abish's voice sound so foreboding?

"Although for the girls who take an oath to be virgins, lifelong virgins," Abish said, "it's not as it seems."

Elena stared at Abish.

"It's true they don't marry, and they don't ever have husbands," Abish said. "But their bodies are used in rituals."

"What do you mean?" Elena whispered.

"My father called it temple prostitution."

Elena's heart slowed. "You mean—you mean . . . men come into the temples?"

"The *priests* perform fertility rites in order to fully worship the gods and goddesses. They use the priestesses during these rites."

Elena's hands started to tremble, and she clasped them tighter. The words sounded in her ears, but she couldn't quite grasp their full meaning. One part of her told her fertility rites in the temple were too unbelievable, too horrible to comprehend. The other part of her realized that it was a valid reason for Abish's father to forbid her from taking the priestess oath.

"*All* of them do this?" she asked. "The priests and the priestesses . . . together?"

"Yes," Abish said, her eyes brimming with tears.

"How can that be? The priests are celibate men—that's part of their oath."

"Celibate in the public sense," Abish said. "But the rituals that take place between the priests and priestesses are reenactments of the joining of a man and woman."

No, Elena thought. *How could they?* Rising, she crossed the room, taking several deep breaths. Everything she'd assumed about the priestesses was false. They weren't lifelong virgins but women who were used in a terrible manner.

"Elena," Abish said in a soft voice, coming to stand next to her. She placed her arm across Elena's shoulders. "I'm sorry to have to tell you this."

"Does everyone know about this? The royal family?"

"Yes," Abish said. "The king supports these practices and believes his family is blessed because of them." She took a deep breath, panic in her eyes. "I just wanted you to know the truth—although I am still loyal to the king's family, not everything is easy to live with." Her face changed, going from worry to determination. "I've . . . had some good news this morning. It was why I was in the marketplace searching for Zaman when I saw you. The queen gave her permission for our marriage."

Despite her recent shock, Elena smiled and threw her arms around Abish's neck. "We'll truly be sisters!"

Abish patted her. "Yes, truly."

"Have you told Zaman?" Elena asked, drawing back.

Abish's face reddened. "Not yet. Don't tell him you knew before him."

Elena couldn't stop smiling. "Thank you." She impulsively hugged Abish again. "Tell me exactly what the queen said."

"She apologized for taking so long but gave me her blessing. She said I could work for her as long as I wanted to."

"I'll watch over your children for you—I'll be like a second mother to them."

"Elena," Abish said, her tone serious. "I don't expect you to work in our home. You might not think so now, but you'll have your own family someday."

"Perhaps." Elena looked away. "I certainly don't want to serve in the temple anymore." She wondered if she should tell her about Gad and her misgivings. Instead, she moved away from Abish and stood. "I should begin supper preparations."

"Do you need help?" Abish said.

"No," Elena said. "I mean, you probably have to return to the queen after being absent for so long."

"Yes, you're right." Abish stood and touched Elena's arm. "I hope you'll feel better."

"I will." She held her tears back until Abish left. She thought of the tenderness between her brother and Abish. Would she ever have that with a man? Fresh tears came to her eyes as she thought about Corien—he'd been betrothed, saving money to provide a home for his bride. Now he'd never see that happy day. *Maybe I'm not so bad off*, she thought. *I have my life and my family.* She went through the motions of preparing supper without focusing on what she was doing.

More than an hour passed before her father and brother returned. "Elena!" her father called out.

Elena hurried out of the cooking room. She met her father as he came inside the house. In his hand, he held the wrapped piece of tapir. "For supper tomorrow night."

Her father put it in the cooking room then returned to her side. He looked at her and frowned. "Still upset about Corien?"

"I—" Her voice quivered, so she settled for a deep breath then said, "Yes."

"Would you like to come to the burial services with Zaman and me?"

A shudder passed through Elena.

"Following the services"—her father continued—"we can visit Abish and see if she has any news about the reception of your designs yet."

She nodded, suddenly feeling numb inside. She hadn't even thought to ask Abish about the festival clothing. Elena felt different now, different from the person who'd been so excited to create festival clothing for the queen, but now it didn't seem to matter much at all. Not when a man had been brutally executed that day. And not after learning the truth about temple priestesses.

"Very well," her father said, his voice gentle. He put a hand on her shoulder. "I'm sorry you had to see the man just moments before his death."

Elena blinked against the burning that had started in her eyes again. "Where will his spirit go?"

"He was a good man from what I've heard. I hope he'll go to one of the higher levels of heaven. Just like your mother." He pressed his lips together then put his other hand on her other shoulder. "You must get the meat salted and soaked for the big supper tomorrow. Remember, Gad will be coming. He knew Corien and can tell us more about him. He might even be at the funeral tonight."

"Perhaps we should change the supper with Gad."

"No," her father said. "I know this is a big step for our family—but you're no longer a girl, and we must face the future. Postponing the supper won't make it any easier. Besides, you know the queen gave permission for Abish to marry your brother?"

When she nodded, he continued, "That will change our home. Abish will want her own household to run and raise their children in."

"Father." Elena put her arms around him. "I don't have to marry. Who will take care of *you?*"

Her father stroked her hair and chuckled. "You'll be welcome to come over any time to care for me. When Zaman marries, I consent to be fussed over twice as much." He drew away and looked her in the eyes. "But you need a place to call your own, with your own children."

Elena wrinkled her nose. "Gad has enough children already."

"If you're married, children will come, Elena," her father said in a quiet voice. "Do you know the explanation?"

Elena flushed and stepped away from her father's embrace. "I know enough. I don't need you to tell me."

Her father's face grew red as well. "I'm pleased to hear that."

Elena moved past her father, toward the cooking room. "I'll begin those supper preparations."

Her father looked all too relieved to be done with the conversation.

Once in the cooking room, Elena found the largest bowl and placed the tapir meat inside. She poured water over the meat then added plenty of sea salt. The cool water felt good on her hands and wrists. Her thoughts turned again to the looming supper guest tomorrow night. She couldn't imagine what it would be like to be married to Gad. She'd always hoped that she'd marry a man closer in age—and someone she at least found attractive. Her mind skimmed through the available men she knew in their area.

But as each name popped into her thoughts, she immediately dismissed them. Too short, too loud, too boring, too old. Of course, the options opened further if she didn't just consider successful merchants or blacksmiths and considered men who were of a lower class—like servants to the king. Yet, she knew her father would never let her marry anyone who was considered a lower class than her family. He'd spent too many years earning the status for their family. Her brother could marry Abish because he'd provide a good living. But Elena had to marry someone of equal or better status.

That includes Ammon. Although he might be a former prince, he's now a servant. Her face started to burn again, and she pushed thoughts of him to the back of her mind.

She focused on the tapir in front of her. She'd let the meat soak overnight so that by the morning it would be tender and flavorful. It would take most of the next day to cook. She had only one more day to prepare for her meeting with Gad. The decision was out of her hands, and she would no longer consider the possibility of becoming a temple priestess. Her chest constricted as the inevitability of marriage began crushing in around her.

CHAPTER 8

For by grace are ye saved through faith; and that not
of yourselves: it is the gift of God.
—Ephesians 2:8

Evening descended like a gentle cloak, reminding Elena that the end-of-harvest month was her favorite time of year. At nightfall, the temperature cooled just enough to make walking outside pleasant—not too cold or too hot.

She walked alongside her brother and father as they headed to the north side of the palace to the main servants' quarters. *A funeral ceremony was being held; although*, she thought with a shudder, *there was no body to pray over or to bury.*

They arrived in a clearing surrounded by a half dozen huts. A long line of people led to one of the huts, so Elena assumed it was where Kumen lived. They took their place at the back of the line. It moved forward slowly. Pockets of conversation around the clearing were subdued. Torches had been lit in front of the hut, flickering against Kumen's grief-stricken face as he received condolences. Elena glanced behind her; the line of people extended across the clearing. It was amazing how many people knew the brothers.

"Kumen," her father said as they reached the front of the line.

"Thank you for coming, Moriah," Kumen said, clasping his hand. Then Kumen turned to Zaman. The two men embraced, both with tears in their eyes. Elena swallowed against the lump in her throat as the men talked about Corien.

When Kumen turned to greet her, she said, "I'm sorry about your brother." She was surprised at how relatively steady her words came out.

Kumen nodded, his eyes still watery. They moved on and left the line, walking toward a group of men. Her breath caught when she saw Ammon among them. He wore a dark tunic and stood nearly a head taller than most. As if he'd sensed her presence, he turned, his eyes catching hers.

Elena looked away quickly before her face flushed at being caught watching him, but Ammon was already crossing toward them. He greeted her father and brother. Next he gazed at Elena. "Are you staying for the ceremony?"

She was surprised that he'd asked her the question directly with her brother and father standing there. "Yes," she said.

Her father looked back and forth between the two, his expression questioning.

Zaman barely concealed a scowl. "We're all staying for it." The words were polite, but underlying them was hostility that Ammon was paying attention to her.

Elena shot her brother a warning glance. He'd already caused Ammon enough trouble. The swelling on his face had grown worse since that morning, and the bruising was even darker, plainly visible in the torchlight.

Her father extended his hand toward Ammon. "I must thank you."

"Thank him for what?" Zaman cut in.

"For sparing your life," her father said, looking at Zaman then gripping Ammon's hand. "When I saw him at our home, I just assumed that my son had won the fight. But from what I've heard since, it was quite the opposite. It seems that you were very merciful."

Zaman grunted. "That's not true. Look at his injuries."

Elena stared at her brother. Like her father, she'd assumed that Zaman had won the fight and thought Ammon's broken nose was evidence of that.

Her father chuckled softly. "Gad told me the story, son. You fought unfair, and when Ammon turned the fight in his favor with little effort, you realized your error fairly quickly."

Zaman folded his arms across his chest, his face flooding with anger. "I was only following Pahrun's orders."

Ammon stepped forward, interrupting the two-sided conversation. "I know Zaman's intent wasn't malicious, but I didn't appreciate the surprise."

Narrowing his eyes, Zaman studied Ammon. "I should have listened to the rumors. When I saw you, I didn't think you'd be much of a challenge."

"What do you mean?" Moriah said. "Look at those arms—like steel. There's not a bone of laziness on his body. His height alone gives him the advantage."

Zaman's face remained expressionless, refusing to acknowledge Ammon's strong physique.

"He'd been beaten by the palace guards the day before, so I thought he wouldn't fight as hard," Zaman muttered.

Elena's stomach clenched as she thought about what Ammon must have been through when the guards dragged him to the palace. "What were the rumors?"

Everyone turned to look at her, including Ammon. Her cheeks flushed, but she held Ammon's gaze.

"Yes, what rumors?" her father added.

Zaman answered for Ammon. "That he carries a satchel full of knives wherever he goes—that he's some sort of an expert in creating the perfect dagger," he said in a mocking voice. "I wanted to see what he'd do unarmed, with a knife at his chest."

"Ah," Moriah said. "This is all making sense." The expression on his face said that he was teasing his son. He looked at Ammon. "Are these rumors true?"

Ammon lifted a shoulder. "Determine that for yourself." He removed a satchel tied to his waistband and opened the drawstring. From the leather bag, he withdrew four daggers.

Elena suppressed a smile by clamping her mouth shut as she watched Zaman's incredulous expression.

Moriah gave a short nod then looked at his son. "I think you've met your match."

"I've seen you with a sling," Zaman said in a reluctant tone, "but how are you with these?"

"Fair," Ammon said. "I'm more interested in the craftsmanship than in the use."

"Can I see one?" Zaman asked.

Ammon handed one over.

"Magnificent, aren't they?" a voice boomed.

The group turned to see Pahrun, dressed in his utmost finery for the funeral. He wore a deep scarlet cape that flowed over his shoulders and reached to his knees. His waistband was decorated with intermingling shells and jewels. From his own satchel, he withdrew a dagger that looked remarkably like the ones in Ammon's possession. "Ammon said I could keep this one, said he had plenty of others." Pahrun placed a hand affectionately on Ammon's shoulder.

"And I'll extend the same offer to my new friend," Ammon said.

Zaman's eyes widened. "That's very generous of you. Are you sure?"

"Of course."

"Thank you," Zaman said, real appreciation in his tone.

What is it about this man? Elena wondered. *He's only been here for a couple of days—in enemy territory—and already has a circle of friends.*

"Maybe your sister would like one as well?" Ammon said.

Her attention snapped back into focus. "Me?"

"You seem to have command with a bow and arrow, but what about a knife?" Ammon's eyes glinted with humor.

Elena was sure she was bright red, and she was sure her brother and father noticed it. "I don't think I could use one as a weapon. It's not like a bow and arrow—with a dagger you have to be very close to your target to use it."

"With an arrow, she's merciless on a poor tapir," Zaman said.

Thankfully, Pahrun interrupted and took the attention away from her. Zaman's claim wasn't entirely accurate. She'd shot a tapir only once, and her brother had to finish it off. "The others are gathering for the ceremony."

Elena followed the men as they joined the group of mourners. Kumen stood in front of his hut, waiting for everyone to assemble. She held back from the family and friends, not feeling entirely comfortable since she hadn't known Corien well.

Gad arrived, and Kumen quickly greeted him. Elena moved to the back of the crowd, avoiding Gad as much as possible. Her brother and father were somewhere in the middle, standing with Pahrun and Gad. She was grateful he hadn't seen her yet because he would have surely come to stand at her side.

The ceremony started with a speech from Kumen about his brother's fine attributes. As he spoke, tears sprang to Elena's eyes, memories of her mother resurfacing in the somber atmosphere.

One of Corien's friends stood and began to speak. Someone tapped Elena's shoulder, and she turned to see it had been Ammon. He didn't say anything but held out a piece of cloth.

She shook her head, not sure what it was meant for. One side of Ammon's mouth lifted as he leaned toward her and wiped her cheeks with it. Elena drew in her breath and took the cloth from his hand. "Thank you," she whispered.

She expected him to move away, but he stayed near, so near that she could hear him breathing. Her arms prickled at his proximity, and she tried to ignore him and pay attention to the ceremony. Perhaps Ammon was waiting for her to return the cloth. She hoped Zaman wouldn't see them standing together; his sour mood would return.

A priest from one of the temples stood, wearing pale brown robes embroidered with dark thread. "Tonight I offer a blessing upon the soul of Corien. Tonight he will meet his judgment, and his obedience to the temple customs will be determined. He'll then be assigned to one of the seven heavens." He looked up at the sky before continuing. "This man was a poor servant, but he made his donations to the temple regularly; therefore, I pray that the god of death, Ah Puch, will be merciful to him and recognize his humble contributions to the maize god."

Elena wrapped her arms about her. Tonight she saw the priest differently than she ever had before. After Abish's revelation about the temple rites, she had begun to doubt for the first time. Besides, the priest's words made her feel uncomfortable. How could a person's life be summed up by their donations to the temple? It all sounded so cold, so methodical. She thought of her mother, remembering her face, her voice, her touch. A person should be judged on everything they did—how they lived their lives, not just by their donations.

Ammon shifted his position so he was standing next to her. His eyes were closed, and he was mouthing words. What was he doing?

Suddenly his eyes opened, and Elena quickly looked away but not before Ammon saw her. "Sorry," he whispered. "I was saying a prayer for Corien's soul."

She couldn't help but stare at him in surprise. His eyes looked moist as if he were genuinely sad about Corien's death—a man he'd only just met. Now his attention was on the priest, as if he were listening to every word.

Why would a Nephite pray for a Lamanite? And who was he praying to? Questions continued to burn through her, and she wondered what Ammon believed. Her mother had only told her about a few Nephite beliefs.

She turned to him and whispered, "Do the Nephites believe in the seven heavens?"

Ammon didn't move or react, so she decided he hadn't heard her. She faced forward again, trying to concentrate on listening to the priest's words. "A person's obedience is shown by his abundant donations. Poor or wealthy, all must worship the maize god with generous contributions."

She felt a pressure on her hand, and she realized Ammon was tugging her backward. She took a few steps back with him, so now they were separated from the main crowd.

"The Nephites who are members of my church believe in one heaven," Ammon whispered, sending a fluttering through her. His hand was warm, making her very aware that he still held her hand.

She concentrated on his words: "It has three kingdoms," he said. "People are assigned to a kingdom depending on their faith and level of obedience to the commandments."

Elena had heard of "commandments" before from her mother. She nodded, warmth now spreading to her face at Ammon's nearness. "And the underworld? Do the Nephites believe in that?"

Ammon released her hand—taking with it his warmth. "Yes. It's a place where murderers, liars, adulterers and thieves go—those who break the commandments."

Elena's hand felt empty and cold with the absence of his, but she pressed on, knowing she had limited time to question him. "What about Corien? He broke the king's edict."

"I think," Ammon whispered, "God will be merciful to him. Although it was an earthly king's commandment, the actions of the other Lamanites were out of Corien's control."

It was what she hoped. The poor man deserved a good afterlife. "What about his temple offerings? The priest says they were very small."

Ammon's mouth set in a tense line then he said, "We believe that God will judge us on our obedience and righteousness, not on our earthly wealth. We all make sacrifices according to our stations."

"My mother told me a few things about the Nephite God," she said in a whisper as the priest finished talking.

The crowd began to move and converse among themselves.

Her father was walking toward her, Gad with him.

Ammon straightened. He was looking forward again, his expression concentrated as if they'd never had a conversation.

* * *

Elena's hands shook as she poured the final layer of honey on the amaranth mixture. The treats would set in time for refreshment after the regular supper. Except this was no regular supper. Gad would be at the house at any moment.

She stored the honey pot and rinsed her hands with water. She dried and then clasped her hands together. It would not do to appear nervous. Her father and brother would notice, and Zaman might use it as an opportunity to tease or embarrass her.

"There you are," her father said, coming into the cooking room. "I thought you said the meal was ready to serve."

"It is," she said. "I just wanted to add more honey."

Her father touched her loose hair. "Go prepare yourself. Your appearance and manner are more important than the food tonight."

"Father—"

"Not another word. I want you to consider Gad. Open your heart to him, my dear. Don't close it before even considering what it might be to become his wife." He touched her chin. "He's an important man, wealthy, and will provide you a good and comfortable life. And . . . he's enamored with you. If I thought there were someone better for my daughter, I wouldn't ask you to entertain his proposal."

Elena looked away from her father's imploring eyes. She took a deep breath, resolving to follow her father's wishes—to at least *think* of Gad favorably, even if it were for this one evening. She nodded and excused herself.

Once inside her bedchamber, she let the doubt creep back in. Gad was a well-respected man. Yes, he was much older than she was, but it wasn't uncommon for a widower to marry a young woman—one who could finish raising his children and care for him as old age set in.

Elena perched on a stool before a small table containing vials of dye and miniature bowls of powder. She plaited her hair while looking at her reflection in the metal square. It wasn't Gad's age or his several children that made Elena hesitate. He was so . . . different from Ammon. She felt like an object in Gad's presence; whereas Ammon treated her like a friend, someone who was worth getting to know and caring about. Someone who looked beyond homemaking skills that she might or might not possess.

Leaning forward, she dipped a thin brush into the vial of black dye. With a steady hand, she darkened her brow as Abish had explained to her. Then she used a different brush to dip into the red dye to stain her lips. Elena wondered what type of painting the Nephite women did in Zarahemla. Her thoughts turned to Ammon and his family—what was his mother like? Was she a beautiful queen with all the finest in everything?

Elena dabbed powder on her cheeks then reached for the bottle of essence. She'd made it herself from oils and plumeria. She dotted the scent onto her neck and chest, wishing it were Ammon coming to supper. He and Zaman seemed to like each other now. She smiled at the possibility of suggesting it.

She shook the thoughts about Ammon away—he was a servant, not wealthy and important like Gad. *Do I want wealthy and important? Although*, she reminded herself, *Ammon had been wealthy and privileged in his former life.* She was impressed that he'd given it up but also curious as to why. She couldn't imagine Gad leaving everything as Ammon had.

I'm thinking of Ammon again when I'm supposed to be considering Gad. She rubbed at the excess powder on her cheeks as she thought of Ammon taking her hand at the burial service the night before. Her face flushed at the memory. He hadn't meant anything by it, she was sure. But the comfort he offered was exactly what she'd needed at that moment. It was as if he somehow knew her.

A shuffling sound outside her door caught her attention.

"Elena? Our guest has arrived."

She'd been so caught up in her thoughts that she hadn't even heard Gad arrive.

"I'm ready," she said, placing the brush back on the table. She took one final glance at her reflection. She looked several years older when painted—an effect her father would certainly be pleased about.

As Elena entered the gathering room, Gad's presence filled the entire space. His voice boomed, echoing off the plain walls and captivating her brother and father.

"Ah, there she is," Gad said, his eyes not missing one aspect of Elena's appearance.

She dipped her head in acknowledgment, though her stomach twisted. She'd caught her father's and brother's triumphant grins. *I've done well, maybe too well.*

In a couple of strides, Gad was standing in front of her, his hand extended. Elena's heart thumped with nervousness as she let him take her hand and kiss her cheek. Her pulse increased as he lingered, his lips staying close as he spoke, "I hope your cooking is as delicious as your appearance."

Her stomach hardened at the words, and she drew away as soon as she dared, casting a glance at her father. Gad's words had been too bold. Her father must have overheard, but he simply smiled and invited Gad to sit.

Elena disappeared into the cooking room, her face flaming with heat. How dare he say that—and in front of her family?

She put her hands on her cheeks, but her hands were just as hot as her face. Taking several deep breaths, she grabbed the first tray. As she delivered the first course, Gad's eyes went to her figure as he smoothly continued his conversation. He was telling some story about his brother, Loki, whom she heard was homeless most of the time, spending his days and nights drinking.

She surmised that Gad expected her to be impressed as he boasted of the many scrapes he'd bailed his brother out of. Gad was the good son, the caretaker in his family—at least that's what he emphasized several times.

Elena left and hovered in the cooking room, waiting for them to finish the first course. Once they finished, she brought out the tapir covered in a guava sauce.

As she was clearing the first course, Gad said, "You must sit with us, then you'll see my enjoyment of your meal firsthand."

With trepidation, Elena sat between her brother and father. She ate with her brother and father when they were in private but not when they had guests in the house. Gad gave her a self-satisfied smile then reached for the tapir. He took an exaggerated bite.

"Delicious!" Gad declared. "My children will be envious when I tell them what Elena prepared for supper tonight. They'll wish they were here as well." He threw her a meaningful look.

Elena looked down quickly, not wanting to encourage him and furtively hoping her father wouldn't suggest the entire family come to visit. Would her mothering skills be scrutinized too? Thankfully, Gad returned to the topic of his brother.

"Of course, Loki often spends the night in my home—my children love their uncle. My only rule is that he can't bring certain, questionable women with him." He laughed. He talked as he ate, making it difficult to look at him politely. "I don't think he's heeded my advice much, though." His gaze was on Elena again. "If my situation were to change, then, of course, I'd have to be even more strict about who spends the night in my home."

Elena forced herself to keep her mouth shut. This man just admitted that he allowed harlots in his home. Her face flushed as she tried to keep her gaze on the food. Who was to say that those seedy women were just for Gad's brother? Many men entertained harlots, married or not. She didn't know if she could trust Gad.

"How's your business, Gad?" her father asked, mercifully changing the conversation.

Gad talked about blacksmithing details that Elena might normally find interesting if they came from a man who didn't harbor drunks and harlots in his home. Her stomach churned, refusing to enjoy even a bit of the food she'd spent so much time preparing.

When her father's wine cup was empty, Elena jumped at the chance to leave the table and disappear into the cooking room for a few moments. Once alone, she caught her breath and gripped her hands together so she wouldn't start banging things around or throw a jug at something or *someone.*

She put her frustrations into scrubbing the dish she'd cooked the tapir in. She blinked against her stinging eyes—just because Gad owned a home and ran a business didn't make him a moral man. She wondered about his first wife and what she'd been like. More importantly, what had she endured? Had her brother-in-law frequented the house in the days that she was alive, bringing strange women? What about the children?

"Thank you for the meal," a voice said behind her.

Dread touched her. Without turning, she knew who stood in the doorway. Knowing she couldn't be rude, she looked over at the visitor. "You're welcome."

Gad straightened from his slouched posture against the entryway and walked toward her. "Your father said you wouldn't mind if I came and thanked you personally."

Elena resumed scrubbing.

Gad stopped right behind her, placing his hands on her shoulders. They felt thick and heavy, stifling through her clothing.

Elena stopped scrubbing, wishing she dared to push his hands away. "We're pleased you could join us," she finally said. She turned slightly, moving away from his hold, but his hands remained.

His smile was broad as he slowly leaned toward her.

Her heart pounded in fear, and she took the risk of stepping forcefully away. "I think my father called your name." She kept her gaze steady, hoping to sound convincing.

Gad's hands fell from her shoulders but remained very close. "Ah." He gave a knowing nod. "Your brother said you were quite timid. Not used to people." His fingers came up to touch her chin before she could react. "Another desirable quality. A man wants a woman all to himself. One who will be happy in the home."

Elena didn't know whether crying on the spot would make him leave, but she was willing to try. Or maybe she could laugh like she was mad.

"Sir?" It was Zaman in the doorway.

Elena had never wanted to embrace her brother so fiercely.

He looked from Gad to Elena, and Gad dropped his hand.

"My father asked that I walk you home and carry the leftovers for your family to enjoy."

Gad turned with a smile to Zaman. "Thank you. They'll be most grateful."

Elena busied herself arranging the leftover food into a basket then turned away without a word and began scrubbing again as the two men left. When she heard the gate to the courtyard snap shut, she ran to find her father. A light came from the shed in the backyard, and she burst into the workroom.

Her father turned as she fell to her knees and grabbed his hands.

"Please," she cried. "Please don't promise me to Gad. I couldn't bear living in his house and being his wife."

"Elena," her father said in a firm voice. "You must think through this more. You do not know what you are asking."

Elena hung her head, knowing very well what she was asking. If Gad should ask her hand in marriage, her father wouldn't be able to turn him down unless he wanted to jeopardize his livelihood. So there had to be a very valid reason—one that Gad wouldn't already know about. If she were already promised to someone else . . . but that wouldn't work because Gad knew she wasn't. Or if she had decided to take an oath as a temple priestess . . . She shuddered at that thought and what Abish had revealed to her about priestesses' duties.

She rose to her feet and faced her father, seeing the love and concern on his face. She knew he really did have her best interest at heart. That made it all the harder. She kissed him on the cheek and turned to make the short walk back to the house.

Why? She wanted to cry to the gods and goddesses, or whoever was out there taking petitions. Inside her bedchamber, she sank to her knees and prayed, not sure of who was listening but hoping her pleas would make a difference. *Why do I have to face this decision? Can I not just live as an unmarried woman? The temple is no longer an option, so please help me.*

CHAPTER 9

*The God of my rock; in him will I trust: he is my shield . . . and
my refuge, my saviour; thou savest me from violence.*
—2 Samuel 22:3

Two Weeks Later

Drums pulsed through the late afternoon air as the Maize Festival com-
menced. Elena waited in anticipation for the arrival of the royal family.
Abish had told her that the queen and her two daughters would, in fact, be
wearing Elena's creations. She'd been working nonstop over the past two
weeks on the clothing to get it ready in time. It had been an excellent excuse not to see Gad again, although he didn't know the costumes were her
personal creations. He'd come several times to the house, and each time
her father had offered his apologies. But Elena knew that Gad expected to
see her today.

   She kept close to her father near the front of the crowds since her
brother had already been swallowed up by a group of friends. The throng
of people was already heavy and jostling for position as everyone watched
the priests on the platform in the center market square.

   Then the conch shell sounded, sending a pulse of excitement through
the gathering. Elena turned as the royal banner came into view. Its deep
scarlet color contrasted against the pale violet sky. It wasn't until the family
ascended the platform that Elena could see their clothing. Hot pride
burned through her at the spectacle. The queen and her daughters wore
heavy jade jewelry on their necks and arms. Their tunics were fitted and
pale yellow. Around the waistline and hem, Elena had stitched an intricate
flower pattern with colored beads. Their capes were short, falling mid-
back and were of the most brilliant blue feathers. They looked spectacular.

When the royal family was settled, a group of performers walked onto the stage and reenacted the labors of the harvest season. When they concluded, the priests took over, blessing the royal family, the people of the land of Ishmael, and all future crops. The high priest held up a basket with several birds inside and took them to an elaborately decorated altar set on the edge of the platform. He slit the birds' throats, each in turn, then lit them on fire.

As the dark smoke rose in the air, the sun made its final descent and disappeared as the priest concluded with a final blessing. The king triumphantly rose to his feet and raised his hands. "Let the Maize Festival begin!"

The people cheered, and the royal family stayed on the platform as servants carried a table and food right to them. Even from her position, the food looked delicious—steaming platters of maize and squash with delicacies, such as quail eggs, honeyed treats, and cacao drink.

Elena shadowed her father as he moved through the crowd and spoke with friends. She spotted Gad, wearing a fine cape her father had made. He wore no shirt but had painted red and black designs across his torso and arms. Gad looked fierce in his costume and was speaking to a group of men in animated tones. He was not hesitant to show off his wealth. That day, word had reached them that the king had bestowed upon Gad the honor of representing the feathered serpent god. He would be part of the ceremony that blessed the maize crops the following day. The honor would last an entire year until the next Maize Festival.

Her father halted in his steps, obviously spotting Gad as well. "We must congratulate him," he said, turning to Elena.

"You go," she said. "I'm tired from all the work, and I think I'll return home."

"It will impress him if you come with me."

"It will also encourage him too much," Elena said in a quiet voice.

"He was more than gracious this morning when he came to visit."

Elena remembered the conversation she'd overheard between her father and Gad. He'd come to their home to ask if she'd accompany him to the Maize Festival. When her father had said it wasn't appropriate for a young, unmarried woman to accompany a man who wasn't her relative, Gad had made his intentions clear about asking Elena to marry him. Her father had stalled, said that Elena had been so busy with sewing that they hadn't had time to discuss a betrothal. He'd asked for more time, and Gad had conceded. Meanwhile, Elena hoped his attention would be drawn elsewhere.

Her father was silent for a moment. "Wait for a few minutes over by the pottery stand, and I'll come with you."

"No," Elena said, pressing her hand on her father's arm. "This is an important time for you to associate with potential customers. Everyone must know that you completely outfitted the royal family tonight—you'll gain many new customers. Besides, Gad is wearing one of your capes."

"With your help," her father said.

"Of course, but that can't be known yet. I don't want *him* to know. Maybe after this festival is deemed a success or perhaps after the high king's feast next moon."

"My dear Elena," her father said, leaning to kiss her cheek.

She smiled, feeling her eyes burn. Her father had taken a great risk in stalling Gad's marriage proposal. She hoped her father could maintain his good name and relationships in the community and that Gad's new honor would steer his attention away from her reluctance.

Elena melted into the crowd, keeping an eye on her father. She didn't want Gad to see her, so she put some distance between them. From afar, she watched her father approach Gad. Gad seemed to greet her father in a friendly manner, but it was difficult to tell. She pretended to examine a painted ceramic jar as she frequently glanced in her father's direction.

Gad was still talking, as if he'd just continued what he'd been saying before her father had arrived. Relief coursed through Elena. Yet, the little sleep from the last couple of weeks crowded into her body, and exhaustion pervaded her thoughts. The festival would last most of the night and into the next day. Her father wouldn't stay out too late, but her brother would likely stay out all night.

She moved through the crowd toward the main road that led from the plaza. Several vendors had set up along the road, taking advantage of the crowds that attended the festival celebrations. The torchlights only extended so far, and soon Elena walked in the moonlight. People scurried past her, always in groups of friends, leaving the plaza to another destination. Elena felt a pang in her heart, and the consequence of her delaying to accept Gad's marriage proposal settled a bit deeper. If she were to accept his offer, she knew she would be drawn into his circle of friends immediately. Even though she'd be a much younger wife, she'd gain respect. But what would the cost be to her own happiness? Yes, for now, she was alone. Again. Yet, she would be happy living at home and caring for her father's comforts, which might cause her brother more angst, but ultimately, she'd settle for a life of being unmarried.

I'll be fine, she decided. *I'll manage. I always have.* Elena was grateful for the cape she'd brought and pulled it over her shoulders, keeping most of the night's cool wind away. A lump in her throat formed, but she ignored it, resolving she'd rather be alone than with a man she didn't love.

My parents chose each other, and I want the same thing, she thought.

She turned along the path that led to her home when she realized someone was walking behind her, quite close. She glanced over her shoulder. A large man slowed in his steps, and in the glint of the moonlight, Elena felt her heart slow.

"Elena," Gad said in a voice just above a whisper.

She hesitated, wanting to flee to the safety of her home. But would that stop Gad from following? Maybe he had a message from her father.

"Hello," she said, taking a few more steps until she reached the gate to the courtyard. She put her hand on it, as if she were giving him just a moment before heading in.

He strode up to her and swung his cape off of his shoulders.

Elena winced at the odor that emanated from him. She guessed he'd been drinking plenty of wine. But his gaze seemed steady enough as he put his hand on the gate—over hers.

She exhaled but didn't move her hand.

"Your father is a good man," Gad said. "This is a fine cape." He laid it across the gate.

She was unsure what to expect now and suddenly wished she'd waited for her father.

"And I was told you were a good woman, a pure woman," he continued, moving slightly closer to her, his hand pressing on hers until she felt the grooves of the wood. "Yet, I'm not so sure anymore."

Elena drew back, her hand still trapped. "If you're talking about how busy I've been this month, I can explain."

Gad's mouth quirked into a smile. "That's not necessary. I think I already understand. No father would continually put off a suitor, no matter how busy the woman was."

"Perhaps there has been a miscommunication," Elena said, her pulse increasing.

"Miscommunication?"

She nodded, hoping he'd let go of her hand. Instead, he gripped her arm with his other hand. "I think the miscommunication was between *us*, my dear."

A chill spread through Elena, and she tried not to lash out. This man was much bigger and stronger than she—what chance did she have against him?

"I just cornered your father outside the market square. I asked him if there was anything—anything at all—that might prevent you from marrying right away."

Elena stilled, her stomach nauseated.

"Do you know what he said?"

She was afraid to ask.

"That you still pine for your mother and not having another woman in the house has ill prepared you for the rigors of raising a ready-made family."

Anxiety filled Elena—on one hand, she wanted to run to her father and thank him; on the other, she wondered what the consequence of Gad's displeasure would be.

"Do you know what I think?" Gad said, his voice low and harsh. "You're plenty of age to be married, and your mother has been dead many years. Certainly enough time to recover. And from what I can see, you are fully able to work. You'll figure out anything new fast enough. I think you're a temptress; you lead men to think you care for them."

"No," she said. Her face burned at the suggestion. "I don't even know any other men." *Not any other Lamanite men.* "My father is very protective of me."

Gad moved closer, one palm touched her cheek, the other hand went to her waist. "What do *you* want, Elena? Without your father here, I want to hear the answer directly from your lips."

"I wish for more time before I marry," Elena said, her heart pounding in panic, "to whomever it may be. A man like you shouldn't have to wait. If you want to retract your intentions, no one has to know."

He glared at her, his palm pressing against her skin. His hand slowly moved behind her neck, forcing her to look at him. "Everyone already knows about my interest in you—I haven't been quiet in my intentions."

"I hope that you'll respect my wishes, Gad," she said, trying to keep her voice from trembling.

"Your father might claim that you aren't ready to marry and that you aren't ready to leave his home, but I know a woman's fancy—you are playing me. You encouraged him to invite me for supper. You dressed in your finery and served a meal." His grip increased, his eyes boring into hers. "You don't know what you're giving up. You think you live in comfort now—what you could have had with me is security for the rest of your life and your children's."

"I might never marry," Elena said, her eyes burning. "I've always been content to work for my father."

Gad's jaw flexed, his eyes flashing. "With one word from me, your father's business will no longer exist. The king has made me the next feathered serpent, and the very gods will listen to me now."

Her throat constricted.

"Your father and I could combine our business and be two of the most successful men in the land of Ishmael—after the king . . ." His voice was deep, and he lowered his head toward hers until Elena could smell the sweat of his skin and feel the heat of his breath.

She pulled away from him, but he strengthened his hold before she could twist out of his grasp.

"Elena," he whispered in a harsh tone. "You *will* be mine. And I'll wait no longer." He shoved her beside the gate, pushing her back against the wood.

She tried to turn away, but his arms were massive, restraining her as if she were a child. "Please don't," she cried out, but his mouth pressed against hers, choking off her protest. *Stop!* her mind screamed, but no sound came out as Gad forced his kisses upon her.

I will be ruined. I'll be forced to marry this man. Tears stung her eyes as she clawed at his shoulders to no avail. She broke away for a violent instant and screamed. Then Gad's mouth was on hers again.

"What's going on?" someone shouted, pulling Elena from her haze of desperation.

Gad lifted his head but didn't release her. "Leave us," he growled through gritted teeth.

"Let her go!" the man commanded.

Gad turned, and Elena took the opportunity to squirm away and scrambled over the gate, ruining her tunic in the process. But she didn't care. She didn't know who had interrupted them, but she wasn't going to face any more embarrassment. Gad shouted something at the intruder, and a fierce argument ensued. She didn't pause to catch the words as she fled toward the house, slipping once and scraping her leg. Ignoring the pain, she stumbled on until she was safely inside. In the dark, she fumbled her way into the cooking room and grabbed a large knife.

Her breath came in gasps, and she shook all over, but she forced herself to the window to watch the courtyard. Her heartbeat thudded against her ears, and she held back the sobs that threatened, wanting to hear what was happening. She'd escaped—with only a few forced kisses from Gad. But what if Gad followed her inside? And what would her father do when he found out? Would she be ruined?

Fear consumed her as she thought of Gad's threats to force her to marry. If someone hadn't come along, what else might have happened? Her stomach dropped as a man came through the gate and into the courtyard. The man was thinner than Gad, and unlike Gad's bare torso, he wore a tunic. It wasn't him.

Relief filled her, but she kept the knife in front of her. She blinked against the stinging in her eyes to better focus as the stranger came into view.

Ammon.

And he was alone.

Elena didn't know whether to laugh or sob. Crying seemed easier. Leaving the cooking room, she made her way to the front door and cracked it open. Ammon stood in the courtyard, waiting.

She watched him for a moment, unsure of what to say, how to explain. Maybe he just thought Gad's advances were a common occurrence in their Lamanite city. Maybe he thought they were betrothed, but then why did he make Gad let her go?

Elena stepped outside, the knife still clutched in her hand. Their gazes met. In full view of Ammon, she saw the blood on his hands and a long cut on his neck.

"You're hurt," she whispered.

He tore his gaze from her and looked down at his hands as if he hadn't been aware.

"Did Gad . . .?" she started.

"I'm all right," Ammon said. "He's a bit worse off."

Elena crossed to him, hardly daring to breathe. Her eyes darted past Ammon. What if Gad came into the courtyard with a weapon?

She looked at Ammon's neck. "You need to bind that." Then she looked down. "And your hands are covered with blood."

Ammon turned them over, seeming in a daze. "I don't think it's my blood. I'm afraid Gad's nose might be broken."

"Where is he?" Elena said in a quiet voice, worried he'd show up at any moment.

"He won't be coming back," Ammon said.

"How do you know? He could be even more furious than ever. He might gather some men . . ." Her voice trembled as the enormity set in. "I—I evaded his marriage proposal, and he's determined to make me marry him. No matter the cost. That's why he—" Her voice choked off, and she brought a hand to her mouth trying to control the emotions burning within her.

"I'm sorry I wasn't here sooner," Ammon said. "But you'll be safe now. Your father and brother will take action once they hear."

The anxiety only increased, but she didn't want Ammon to know it. What would her family say?

"Elena." Ammon's voice sounded strained. "Do you have water I can clean up with?"

She swallowed back her emotion. "Certainly. Come inside."

"I'll just wait out here."

"No," she said. "We need to get the bleeding on your neck stopped."

He followed her, somewhat reluctantly, but she had him sitting on a stool in the cooking room and the fire stoked in a matter of minutes. She pressed a cloth against his neck. "Hold this in place while I fetch the water. There's a full jug at the back door." She left, and when she returned, Ammon was placing more wood on the fire.

"You're supposed to be sitting down," Elena said. She poured the water from the jug into a bowl, her hands trembling slightly.

He turned. The light was considerably brighter now, and several more scratches on his face and neck were obvious. The bleeding had slowed, but she made him sit down again so she could work. "Hold still," she said in a quiet voice as she touched the wet cloth to his neck. Being so close to him was completely different from being around Gad—maybe it was because she instinctively trusted Ammon. She knew he'd never harm her. He flinched a couple of times as she cleaned the blood from his neck, but he remained still for the most part.

"All finished," she said, stepping back. Her breathing calmed as she moved from him. Just his presence filled her with ease.

Ammon dipped his hands into the bowl of water and washed the blood off. His knuckles were scraped and bruised but looked fine otherwise. She couldn't help but notice that all of the swelling and bruising had left his face since the last time she'd seen him. His jaw and nose had strong lines, and his eyes were as warm and welcoming as ever.

When she realized she was staring, she spoke before he could notice. "How did you best Gad? He's such a large man."

Ammon raised his gaze to meet hers. His formerly tense expression relaxed. "He's old."

Elena fought back a smile. "He's not *that* old, and he's very tall."

Ammon dried his hands and stood, towering over her, amusement in his eyes. "I'm nearly as tall, and I'm much faster."

She let her smile through. "Yes, you are. Thank you."

But he didn't return the smile; instead, his expression sobered. "I might have made it worse."

"I can't imagine anything worse," she said.

"I can."

His words were quiet, full of meaning. Elena looked away, clasping her hands together to stop the trembling. She hoped he wouldn't notice. "Thank you for stopping him."

He was staring at her; surely he noticed her fear.

"What will your father and brother do?" he asked.

She lifted a shoulder, trying to act less worried than she felt. "My brother is already angry at me for waiting to make a final decision about Gad's proposal. My father will be angry at Gad's actions, but what can he do?"

"Report him to the king." His voice was confident.

She held back a scoff. "That won't happen. Even women who *are* defiled are beneath the king's attention. Women who've been wronged are usually forced to marry, or they become a priestess in the temple and forsake all chance of ever marrying and raising a family."

Ammon watched her closely as she spoke, his expression one of disbelief.

"Gad can't force you to marry him."

Tears flooded her eyes, and she turned away so Ammon wouldn't see. She walked to the cooking fire and gazed at the flames. "I'm afraid he has more power than I thought." She took a shaky breath. "He threatened to bring down my father's business, and he has the power to do it. He could bring our family into disgrace with a few rumors. He's found great favor with the king, and he's desperate to keep that favor because of his brother, Loki, who is a former legion commander. Loki is said to be a drunk and wholly depends on Gad's income. Gad won't let anything get in the way of his influence with the king."

"I've heard his brother has spent time in prison," Ammon said.

"Yes, but Loki is let out time and time again because of his history in the king's militia." Elena discreetly dried her cheeks with a clean cloth.

"So Gad is the dependable brother of the family?"

"In comparison—although I don't feel like he's trustworthy."

"I agree," Ammon said. "Especially after what he did tonight."

His soft words, full of concern, filled her eyes with tears again. She remained facing the fire, not able to look at him.

His response hung in the air, and she tried to think past it. When she finally felt in control, she said, "Would you like something to eat?" She turned from the hearth and reached for the bowl that contained the leftover beans from supper, keeping her gaze lowered. "I can fix you something."

"No thank you." Ammon crossed to her, and the warmth of his hand alighted on her shoulder. "You should rest, Elena," he said. "I'll wait outside until your father or brother comes home. You won't have to worry about Gad. I'll talk to them and explain what happened."

Elena set the bowl of beans down. "Don't." She finally looked at him. "I need to explain—take responsibility. Tell them I'll do what they ask. I can't risk my father's livelihood and all he's worked so hard for."

Ammon stared down at her then slowly lifted his hand and touched her chin. She met his eyes, her heart pounding fiercely.

"You shouldn't offer yourself as a sacrifice in this way." His gaze held hers, and in his eyes, she saw the truth of his words. But did she have the courage to act on it? Tears burned against her eyes, but she blinked them back furiously, refusing to cry in front of Ammon.

"Elena," he said, touching her arm.

The concern in his voice released the tears she'd been fighting against. She could no longer hide them. His arms came around her, and she stiffened, wondering if he saw her as a weak child who needed to be comforted. Then she rested her head against his chest and wrapped her arms around Ammon's waist. For the moment, she felt safe, secure. He didn't say anything, just held her as she cried. She cried for her father, for her family, but also for fear that Gad might come after Ammon now.

When she was able to speak again, she said, "What if Gad retaliates? He's a powerful man with plenty of influence, and you are—"

"Only a servant," Ammon said, his chest radiating warmth as she held onto him. "But he'll have to wait until I return."

Elena released him, and he dropped his arms. "Where are you going?"

"I volunteered to take the king's flocks out tomorrow."

Elena stared at him. "You?" Her stomach hardened as a hundred concerns flowed through her. "But Corien—"

"I know," he said. "When I came to the land of Ishmael, I told the king I wanted to serve him all of my days—whether they are short in number or long."

"You can't—it's a death sentence, Ammon." She stepped away from him, new fear thudding through every limb. "What if those rebels come again and scatter the flocks? The king will have you executed."

A faint smile touched Ammon's mouth, as if he found her worry unnecessary. "God will preserve my life, if that is His will."

"*God?* The Nephite God is strange indeed. Why would you tempt your God?"

"I'm not tempting Him. I'm following His will."

Anger burned through Elena now. "You just told *me* not to sacrifice—but that's what you're doing. Why would your God want you to come all this way just to die? What's the purpose of that?"

"Only God knows the full purpose of my coming to this land," Ammon said, his tone patient. "My sacrifice would further the Lord's work. I can only follow His will. When the time is right, I'll share God's message with this people."

"And what's that message?" Elena shot back.

His expression remained composed, not rising to her angry response. "I hope I'll be able to share it with you someday. When I return, I'll offer Gad a formal apology for striking him but make it clear that he was in the wrong for treating you this way. From what he said about you at the blacksmith shop, I had a completely different impression of your relationship with him. But now I know that you have no desire to marry him. He needs to know that."

The anger deflated in Elena, but the fear remained. "I think I made myself clear." She gazed at Ammon in the firelight, her heart twisting. "Don't worry about me, Ammon. You need to take your own advice and leave the king's flocks be. Don't be so foolish."

A subtle smile crossed his face, and his voice was distant when he said, "I've been foolish enough in my past. I know the difference now. Serving the king is far from foolish."

She took a step toward him. "I don't understand you. Why did you give up your kingdom? What could have possibly driven you away from a throne and palace?" She scanned his fresh injuries. "Look at you—bruised and bloody from fighting a blacksmith for the honor of some woman—a woman below any prince's notice."

One of Ammon's eyebrows lifted. "You think I shouldn't be noticing you?"

"That's not what I meant," she said quickly, her face heating up.

His gaze didn't leave her face. "What did you mean?"

Elena looked down; her cheeks were surely on fire. "You may have risked too much in stopping Gad. Perhaps you shouldn't have interfered in Lamanite ways."

He let out a heavy breath, but still she didn't dare look at him.

"I don't regret interfering with Gad," he said. "I do regret that I lost my temper—I might have been able to reason with him. But seeing what he was doing to you . . . It seems I lost my sense of self-preservation."

"You don't seem to have any sense of self-preservation," she said. "In fact, it's as if you *want* to risk your life."

"Elena," Ammon said, his voice suddenly urgent. He stepped closer, and in one swift motion, his hands cradled her face gently. If her face had been warm before, it was burning now.

"No matter what happens out in the fields, no matter if I live or die, I'll never regret coming here and meeting you. I just hope you can forgive me if I've let you down. Know that I will be praying for your safety and your happiness while I'm out in the fields."

She gazed at this Nephite from her homeland as the firelight flickered around him. He had battle scars and the strength to fight off a man twice his size, but his touch was softer than a feather. She lifted her hands to his shoulders, careful to avoid his wounds, knowing that she was perhaps fulfilling Gad's statement that she was not a woman with pure thoughts.

She hesitated, waiting for Ammon's reaction, but he didn't move, didn't shirk away. His gaze seared through her, his expression intense. Serious. But his eyes were warm and ardent.

She lifted up on her toes the same moment he bent down, and when his face was just a mere breath from hers, someone called her name from outside.

Elena paused, her eyes locking with Ammon's. "It's my brother."

CHAPTER 10

The hand of the Lord shall be known toward his servants,
and his indignation toward his enemies.
—Isaiah 66:14

"You're not coming," Ammon told Kumen as he slipped a sling into his pack, next to the vellum of scripture. They'd be with the flocks for two or three days, and Ammon wanted to be prepared in case the Lord called upon him to teach.

"I won't let you fail like my brother." Kumen's eyes blazed in the early morning light. They'd fallen asleep after an argument the night before, and Kumen still wouldn't give up.

"I'll be fine," Ammon said, remembering he'd just said that to Elena a few hours ago. He turned away from Kumen, refusing to listen to anymore arguments. Elena's face had haunted him all night, and he'd had little sleep. He could still feel the intensity of her gaze, the touch of her skin—but he needed to focus on the task at hand, his real purpose for serving the king.

He hadn't been able to get her off his mind after their meeting at the funeral. At first, he thought there might be some promise between them, but that was before Gad started talking about her in the blacksmith shop. He'd spoken as if they were already betrothed and would marry soon.

It wasn't until last night when Ammon was able to see Elena's true feelings about Gad that hope set back in. Hope for what, he wasn't sure—and now wasn't the time to focus on it.

After reading some of the scriptures the night before on the suffering Christ would go through in His mortal life, Ammon felt strengthened. He was being asked by the Lord to do only a small part. Christ would be the one to suffer for all mankind; Ammon's challenges were but minor.

He'd spent the night half praying, half sleeping. He worried about Elena; he worried about leading the king's flocks. But he knew it was the right thing to do. If the Lord's will was that he'd fail at this mission, so be it, but he'd be prepared to protect the king's flocks at all costs. Another dagger went into the pack. Kumen was still talking, but Ammon ignored him and strapped a third knife to his waist. He couldn't be too prepared.

He wondered if he'd even make it to the fields without retribution from Gad. The man was powerful, as Elena said, and had many friends. He might be waiting outside the hut door right now.

Zaman had been furious when he'd arrived home the night before since he'd already heard Gad's version of events. Fury turned to astonishment when he saw Ammon there. Zaman had taken several minutes to calm down enough to hear Elena's side of the story.

Elena had tearfully recounted the events to her brother, including bandaging Ammon's wounds.

Zaman had said to Elena, "Gad came to me and told me that you had betrayed him." He had hesitated then continued. "I told him I'd make you apologize . . . but now, it seems I might have been mistaken."

That statement from Zaman had given Ammon hope, but even after Ammon had clarified what Gad had forced upon Elena and after it seemed Elena's brother was on her side, Ammon still worried. Hope and determination had drained from her eyes as her brother had talked about forgiving Gad of his small mistake. *He was only eager, like any man in love,* Zaman had claimed. He'd then reiterated Gad's success and influence in the community.

Elena had glanced at Ammon a few times during the conversation, but the light had gone from her eyes. She seemed defeated, and that's what worried Ammon the most. He might return from the fields and find her a betrothed woman—and he didn't think it would be for the better. She was afraid of Gad, didn't trust him, but would she bury all of that to provide a life of ease for her father and brother?

That's not all that's bothering me, Ammon thought. His anger at Gad was more than just protecting the virtue of a woman—but of that *particular* woman. He'd come to care for her in a way that was more than he thought possible, although it was not in his plans. Serving the king for the rest of his life wouldn't provide a viable home for any woman, let alone children. He didn't know how long he'd be in the land of Ishmael, but the missionary life was no place for a family.

Shame poured through him. He'd seen the look of trust in Elena's eyes, and he knew he was letting her down—or would be when or if she expected anything more of him. Under any other circumstance, he would be able to admit that he was more than interested in her—but not now.

Kumen was talking again, and Ammon turned to look at him.

The man held out a sword that had belonged to Corien. "Take it," Kumen said. "I wish my brother would have carried it with him."

Ammon took the weapon. Its weight was familiar, and he missed the sword that the king's men had confiscated when he'd been captured. He turned the sword over, the muscles in his wrists remembering past moments of instructing his brothers to sword fight. They'd always been afraid to get into serious contact, but the weight felt steady and sure in Ammon's hand, lifting his confidence.

With a sling, he could inflict some damage. With a sword, he could truly defend. The thought of combatting with a sword against a fierce Lamanite should have brought fear, but instead, a calm washed over Ammon. Warmth spread through him as he felt the assurance of the Lord touch his soul. Ammon realized he would be strengthened as he set out to defend the king's flocks. The Lord would not abandon him.

He looked into Kumen's anxious gaze.

"Thank you, my friend," Ammon said. "I'd be honored to take it with me."

Kumen gave a brief nod, his eyes shining with pride.

"But," Ammon continued, "you'll need to stay here. You're all your mother has. Who will provide for her if something happens to you? The king has threatened that *all* the herdsmen will die if something happens to the flocks."

"Then the death of my friends will be on my conscience if I don't help you. I can't let you go without you knowing the dangers. I grew up here, and maybe it didn't help Corien, but I'm not as impulsive as he."

Ammon let out a sigh. "What will Gad say if you don't show up for work today?"

He'd told Kumen about Gad's actions last night, so there were few secrets between them.

"Please let me come. Gad can add me to his list of complaints," Kumen said. "If the flocks are scattered, I promise to tell the king it was all your fault."

Ammon laughed. He lifted the sword, its weight comfortable in his hands. "How good are you with a sword?"

"Better than Corien," Kumen said, his tone hushed.

Ammon lowered the sword and looked directly at Kumen. The man's eyes were wide with eagerness and near desperation. "All right," Ammon said.

Kumen whooped and gripped Ammon's shoulder. "You won't be sorry."

"Let's get out of here before Gad shows up," Ammon said.

He wanted to apologize to Gad, but it would be well for a few days to pass in order for Gad's temper to cool down. Even though Gad had been drunk and unreasonable, Ammon regretted injuring the man—perhaps he should have tried to reason with him more.

Ammon followed Kumen out of the hut. The morning was still fresh with heavy dew on the surrounding trees. They walked along the path toward the first courtyard of the palace, where they were to meet the other herdsmen and Pahrun. When they arrived, Pahrun waited with several guards.

The herdsmen sat on the steps, looking wary. When Ammon entered the courtyard, they stood as a group, assessing their new leader.

"You're late," Pahrun said, a grimace on his face. Despite the early hour, he was dressed to the hilt—glittering jewels at his neck and fingers, feathered cape, and a jade-decorated leather band around his head.

Ammon extended his hand. "I've brought a new recruit."

Pahrun looked at Kumen, surprise evident on his face. "Are you sure, Kumen?"

The man nodded.

"I'll let Gad know where you are then," Pahrun said.

"Thank you," Kumen said.

Pahrun cleared his throat and turned to Ammon. "The king would like to speak with you before you depart. Leave your weapons here."

Ammon placed his pack and sword on the steps that led to the palace entrance, wondering if this was an ordinary request as he and the other herdsmen followed Pahrun inside. They wound their way through the corridors. It was quite a different trip than the one in which he'd been freshly dragged in from the jungle. The hallways were quiet in the early morning, the men's footsteps echoing against the cool air.

Inside the throne room, the sweet aromas of a hearty morning meal met Ammon's senses. His stomach complained—it was too early for the servants' morning meal, so he and Kumen had gone without.

King Lamoni looked up from a platter of sliced meat as the men were escorted in.

"Ah, there you are," Lamoni said.

Ammon bowed, along with the others, then straightened to meet the king's gaze.

"Looks like you got into a bit of a scrape."

Pahrun chuckled at the king's comment. But Ammon kept his expression straight. "Did you have parting advice for us, Your Highness?" he asked.

Lamoni's eyes narrowed slightly as he brought a cloth to his grease-covered lips. His gaze landed on Kumen. "I'm surprised to see you here. Do you trust Ammon to lead the flocks?"

"I do," Kumen said.

"All right," the king said, looking a bit uncomfortable as he shifted on his throne. "Each of you knows the seriousness of watching over the flocks. They must all be returned or the penalty of death will fall upon *all of you*." His eyes moved to Ammon's and then to the shocked faces of the other herdsmen. Ammon could tell by the look on the king's face that his increased threat had produced the reaction he had hoped for. It was obvious the king was serious about the importance of his flocks. He then turned back to Ammon. "After the flocks are watered, you and the men will return and prepare my horses and chariots. That same day we will ride to the land of Nephi for my father's great feast, and there, we will deliver the flocks."

Ammon dipped his head. "As you wish, O King."

Lamoni stared at him, as if he were expecting some sort of question. He finally said, "Do you know how to prepare a horse and chariot?"

"Yes," Ammon said. He turned to the men flanking him. "Come. Let's move out before the dew dries." He bowed another time to the king then turned and strode out of the throne room. Pahrun and the other guards scurried to keep up, and Ammon felt the king watching his back until they disappeared.

* * *

The sun turned the grass gold as it spilled over the horizon. The heavy dew started to evaporate as Ammon and the other servants made their way toward the waters of Sebus, driving the flocks ahead of them.

By the time they reached the water, the sun had crested the eastern hills and Ammon was already warm with exertion. The humidity in the air seemed to cling to every thread of his clothing, keeping the moisture against his skin. As he watched the animals drink their fill, he had the sudden desire to plunge into the water himself. Instead, he found a rock to perch on and took a swig from his water skin. Five other servants, including

Kumen, had come to Sebus. The men separated and surrounded the flocks, anxiously watching from various locations as the sheep meandered along the shoreline, drinking at their leisure.

On the other side of Sebus was a line of trees that thickened on its way up the hillside into an impenetrable-looking jungle. From Ammon's vantage point, he could detect any movement or the arrival of another party.

But there was no movement, no perceived threat, and the peaceful morning continued. Ammon eyed the ground. He spotted a few rounded rocks and picked them up. They would spend two or three days here, so perhaps the rebels were taking their time in showing up. Still, he wanted to be prepared. He mulled over the rocks in his hand then tossed the less-than-perfect ones to the ground. The rest, a dozen or so rounded stones, he placed next to him.

Eventually, Kumen walked over to Ammon and joined him on the rock. His earlier anxious expression had lightened considerably.

"Maybe we should find a new place to sleep when we return in a few days," Kumen said. "Gad might be waiting for you."

Ammon picked up a couple of the round stones and turned them over. "I look forward to speaking with Gad. I have a lot to apologize for."

"Apologize? You have nothing to be sorry for."

"I do," Ammon said. "I used force when I could have used reason."

Kumen's voice rose. "I've seen Gad drunk before—and if he was anything like I can imagine, I think force was the only answer."

"Perhaps," Ammon said, his stomach twisting as he recalled the event. "Perhaps not."

The rest of the day dragged on with no appearance of any rebels. The second day passed much the same. Ammon spent some of the time shooting stones with the sling, but mostly he watched the flocks and the treeline. During the more quiet moments, he pulled out the vellum of scriptures and studied them. He read about the Creation and about their first parents, Adam and Eve. He had the words practically memorized, but reading over them brought him comfort and assurance. It was like the Lord was speaking to him, making promises, and offering hope. Looking over the fields, he tried to imagine what it would be like to be the first man to witness so much.

A few times, Ammon was tempted to share something about Christ with Kumen or one of the other king's servants, but the Spirit continued to stall him.

On the third day, with still no appearance of questionable men, they began to make preparations to return the well-fed flocks to the king. Kumen watched Ammon add a few rounded stones to his pack. "How about you show me some of your tricks with a sling before we leave?"

"There are no tricks," Ammon said. "Only a lot of practice."

"I don't know about that," Kumen said. "I've had plenty of practice, but I can't get the distance on it."

"Maybe you need to throw harder," Ammon said.

"Then it's less accurate."

Ammon removed his sling from his pack and placed a round stone into the cup. "See that tree over there?"

Kumen followed Ammon's gaze to a tree about thirty paces away. Just then, one of the other servants called out, "Another flock is coming."

Kumen gripped Ammon's arm and whispered in a fierce voice, "Look over there! It's the rebels!"

Several Lamanites appeared at the top of the hill that rose above the other side of Sebus. They drove a flock before them.

Adrenaline shot through Ammon as he watched the slow approach. He didn't remember hearing that the rebel band drove their own flocks. "How do we know it's the same men who scattered the flocks from before?"

"I'm not sure," Kumen said. "But it appears they want to cause trouble. Why else would they water their flocks in the exact place as the king's? See the man wearing the armbands?"

Ammon picked the man out of the approaching group. They were still too far away to identify faces, but a large man in the middle wore leather armbands around his dark arms.

"I'm guessing he's the leader," Kumen said in a quiet voice. "Oh no, look at how many are coming." He started counting. "Twelve, thirteen, fourteen, fifteen . . . There are three times more than the last report."

A chill rushed through Ammon. Had they heard that he was leading the flocks? Was this supposed to be some sort of revenge on the "Nephite"? The Lamanites reached the other side of Sebus, ushering their flocks to the water. So far they were ignoring the king's servants, but that did nothing to ease Ammon's worry.

Ammon counted seventeen men. Not only were the king's servants far outnumbered, but it wouldn't be too hard to scatter their flocks because they had spread out along most of the shoreline.

"We should gather the flocks to one side," Ammon said. "Maybe the men are friendly. Maybe they aren't the same rebels. Surely they know whose flocks we're watching over."

Kumen looked down at his light brown kilt with the royal insignia, just as all of the other servants. "They know."

The king's servants made their way toward Ammon's perch, looking over their shoulders frequently to assess the movement of the other Lamanites.

One of the men spoke in a rapid voice. "It's them. I'm sure of it. I recognize the large man—the leader. It's the same one who was there when Corien was out here. His face has paint on it—so do the others. It looks like they've gathered some recruits."

Kumen jumped off the rock, his hands curled into fists.

Ammon joined Kumen just as he spotted some movement among the Lamanites. Everyone turned to watch as the Lamanites began their destruction. The leader was shouting and running toward the animals closest to his own flocks.

The king's flocks reacted instantly, bolting and fleeing from the shores. They scattered in different directions until it became a massive chaotic movement. A few ran into each other in the confusion. Most tore through the grass and brush and ran in different directions, some disappearing into the jungle.

"The king will slay us all!" one of the servants cried out, staring in horror at the fleeing flocks.

Ammon kept his attention on the leader as the large man walked back to the other Lamanites, his hands in the air. Over the lamenting of the servants, Ammon imagined he heard the man laughing and gloating over his success. Ammon straightened, and he suddenly knew he had to act. Peace settled over him, bringing calmness. The Spirit flooded his soul, and he knew the Lord would deliver him somehow. This is what he'd come for, what he had prepared to do.

Kumen tugged at his arm, his voice rising in panic, "We'll be executed like my brother."

"No," Ammon said above the lamentations of the servants. Before he could explain, the other servants sank to the ground on their knees, a couple of them weeping loudly.

"My friends," Ammon said, looking from Kumen to the other men. "Do not fear."

"These wicked men have sealed our fate," one cried out, sinking to his knees and covering his face with his hands.

"Stand up," Ammon said, the calming presence of the Spirit still with him. "Stand up and do not fear, my brethren."

"The king will never forgive us. It's too late."

Ammon walked to each man and touched his shoulder. "Be of good cheer. Let's go find the flocks. If we hurry, we can catch them all. We'll bring them back and return them to the king." He looked around at the men, who were starting to listen to him. The Lord would help them. These men looked at him with wide, trusting eyes. Ammon knew that if he could bring back the flocks to the king, these men would be his friends for life; they'd listen to anything he said. "We'll bring them back to Sebus, and the king will not slay us."

The men rose to their feet and squared their shoulders, understanding that Ammon's suggestion might work.

"There are six of us—it won't take long. Our lives are at stake. We must do this." Ammon tried to keep the excitement out of his voice, but it coursed through his heart. It was as if the Lord were showing him the way, and all he had to do was follow through. "The animals will follow our lead—we are simply sending them in the opposite direction they've run. We'll guide them back to the waters of Sebus."

"Let's go," Kumen echoed, determination replacing the fear in his eyes.

Ammon divided the group into three parts. "We'll each go a different direction. We must hurry before they get too far."

They started running in their assigned directions, and Ammon watched them for several seconds, making sure they had a chance of getting ahead of the scattering animals. Then he took off in his own route, staying clear of the rebel band. The rebel Lamanites watched the king's servants with amusement, occasionally hollering encouragement and mocking them.

Ammon ran toward the line of trees and plunged into the brush that preceded the heavier trees. He came upon three sheep and shooed them back toward Sebus. "Go on," Ammon urged, prodding them until they bolted toward the lake. He moved through the dense foliage, shooing them out one by one. He was grateful they followed each other out of the jungle. Then, after several minutes of hiking, he didn't come across any more. The flock would slow down to graze after the initial fear had left them, so he'd likely found them all.

He pushed back through the jungle, and the noise of his approach drove the lagging animals ahead until Ammon exited the thickest portion of trees. On the other side of Sebus, several servants were driving animals toward the water. Relieved they'd made good progress, Ammon offered a silent prayer of thanks.

He again skirted the group of rebels, careful not to antagonize them. They sat, crouched together, talking among themselves. They stared at him as he passed, and Ammon inadvertently caught the gaze of one of the Lamanites. He was clearly the leader. Something about him was familiar; maybe he'd seen him in the marketplace or on his way to the blacksmith's shop. Ammon tried to memorize the man's features so he could report them to the king.

When Ammon reached the other servants, he was out of breath but triumphant. They stood among the flocks, keeping one eye on the flocks, the other on the Lamanites across the waters.

"Well done, my friends," Ammon called out. The others met him with several relieved grins.

Kumen jogged over to Ammon, his expression worried again. "We gathered the flocks, but how will we get rid of those Lamanites?"

"Hopefully they'll get bored," Ammon said. He didn't have any qualms, so the Lord must still be guiding and protecting him.

"Oh no!" one of the servants cried out. "They're coming around the lake. They'll scatter the flocks again."

Ammon turned to see the leader walking slowly, deliberately, around the lake toward their flocks. Several of his men followed.

"Stay here and keep the animals surrounded," Ammon said. "I'll go speak with them."

Kumen and the other servants burst into action and hurried to the outer perimeter of the gathered flocks. Ammon located the sword he'd left by his earlier perch and strode back to the shoreline, reaching it just as the leader rounded the final curve. A half smile crossed the man's square face. His build reminded Ammon of a warrior, but the man looked sloppy in appearance, as if those days were long past and he now spent too much time in leisure.

The leader stopped, and Ammon halted, locking gazes with the man. Scars ornamented the Lamanite's body, intimating fierce battles in the man's past. The man's gaze was steady, his body unflinching, as if he weren't at all worried that one of the king's servants had come to confront him carrying a sword. The leader nodded his head once, and behind him, another Lamanite ran up. The man nocked an arrow and aimed it toward the king's flocks.

"As a servant of the king and the protector of his flocks," Ammon said in a loud, clear voice, "I order you to leave the king's property alone."

The man cast a sideways glance at the leader then released the arrow. It flew into the center of the newly gathered flock. Several sheep bolted, creating a ripple effect of confusion.

"Bring them back together," Ammon yelled to the servants. They rushed into action and coerced the flock back into a tight group.

The archer glanced over at the leader, who folded his arms across his chest and nodded again. He again nocked an arrow and aimed toward the flocks.

"I'm asking you for the last time to leave the flocks alone," Ammon said. "I have been commissioned to protect the king's flocks with my very life. If you attempt to scatter the flocks again, your lives will be in danger."

The leader's face twisted into an ugly smile. "You're sorely outnumbered."

The archer took aim, once again ignoring Ammon. But before the man could release the next arrow, Ammon dropped his sword and took out his sling. An instant later, he had it loaded, and with two rotations and a flick of his wrist, the stone flew straight at the Lamanite, hitting him in the center of his forehead. The man fell backward and hit the ground, his limbs twitching.

Ammon removed another pebble from his pouch as the leader stooped over the fallen Lamanite.

"He's dead!" the leader cried out. He looked at Ammon, his grisly face filled with disbelief.

Holding the leader's gaze, Ammon loaded another rock into his sling.

"You killed my man!" the leader shouted again, his voice escalating in amazement. He grunted as he stood up and stared at Ammon. Clenching his hands into fists, he cursed. Then he called to the other men who'd held back.

Ammon's heart pounded as he wrapped the sling once around his hand to shorten the length as the other Lamanites rushed to join their leader. He didn't know if he could defend himself against so many with merely a sling. But a calm feeling coursed through him, clarifying in his mind what he needed to do.

"Kill that Nephite!" the leader screamed, his face darkened in fury.

Ammon barely heard him as he lifted the sling and started to rotate it. Several men rushed forward. Ammon released the next rock. It struck one of the Lamanites in the forehead, stopping him midstep. He collapsed.

The rebels stopped, their expressions stunned as they watched their comrade lie on the ground, unmoving.

The leader was at the fallen man's side in seconds, lifting his head. The body was still. The Lamanite leader turned to stare at Ammon. He raised a trembling hand and screamed, *"Get . . . him!"*

The men fumbled with the satchels at their waistlines, taking out their own slings and aiming them toward Ammon.

He let out a breath of air, relaxing his shoulders and staying rooted in one place as the stones fell short.

"Get your clubs and slay him, you fools!" the leader growled. The men scurried into action, grabbing clubs. Now they acted as a group and ran toward Ammon.

He loaded the next rock, swung, released. Three. They kept coming, quickly closing the distance but not too quickly for Ammon. One by one, he methodically struck down three more men with his sling until there were six slain on the ground. The remaining men hesitated as their comrades lay still on the shore.

"Kill him! Or I will kill you!" shouted the leader. The men leapt forward, charging at Ammon, clubs raised over their heads, yelling.

Heart pounding, Ammon reached for the sword. Six slain, and these men still wouldn't give up. They'd be upon him if he relied only on the sling. His body felt as if it were on fire, and his heart felt as if it were pounding out of his chest as he stood his ground, waiting for the first man to close the distance. The Lamanite's eyes were dark with rage, and he was screaming as loudly as he could.

Ammon bent his knees and swung upward as the man's club came down toward Ammon's head. Instead of clashing with the club, his sword connected with the man's arm midmotion. The Lamanite screamed in agony and dropped to the ground, his arm severed. Ammon stepped away from the bleeding man, hardly having time to think beyond the next attacker. He kept his sword aloft and his stance ready as the second man charged, his shouts filling the air. This man was more burly, more sure of himself, and had his club raised over his head. Again, Ammon met the man's arm with enough force to sever the arm.

The two men's anguished screams mixed with the next man's yells as he sprinted toward Ammon.

He switched the sword to his left hand and raised it just as the Lamanite brought down his club. The man shrieked, but Ammon only heard his own heart thudding in his ears. Perspiration dripped into his eyes, and he blinked against the stinging to see his next assailant. Another man came, then another. Ammon lost track of how many men charged him but instead focused on blocking the blows, severing the arms of many.

Their screams of pain were in the background now, a ringing sound that only meant he'd defeated another man and was moving on to the next foe. Then there were two of them coming, running toward him at the same time.

The size of one told him it was the scarred leader. Ammon's heart rate doubled as he braced himself to fight off two. He swung his sword as the leader descended upon him, making contact with the man's fast-moving club but missing the man's arm. The other Lamanite wrapped his arms around Ammon's legs and pulled him off balance.

On the ground, Ammon rolled out of the way of the next attack, keeping the sword in his hand. He raised his sword with both hands just as the second Lamanite came crashing toward him with a club. Again, he avoided collision with the club but met the man's arm. The man's arm was detached, and he fell backwards with a cry.

The Lamanite's blood covered Ammon, but he didn't have time to get out of the way. Thick fingers reached around Ammon's neck and dragged him backwards. Ammon twisted, trying to break the hold. He knew it was the leader. He gasped for air, writhing against the pressure. Using all of his strength, he swung the sword over his head and brought it against the man's flesh, striking between his shoulder and neck.

The grip around his neck loosened, and Ammon fell back, his chest heaving. He rolled over and staggered to his feet, still gripping his sword in one hand. Arms littered the ground, and Ammon's stomach started to revolt. The sound of screams and yells rushed into Ammon's ears and filled the air as the rebels ran toward the hill, gripping their injured arms. He looked down at the leader—the man's head was nearly severed, his eyes open but unmoving.

The leader was dead.

How many have I killed? What have I done? Hot bile formed in his throat, and he sank to his knees. He hardly noticed the remaining couple of rebels who stared at him in horror. But they soon regained enough composure to turn and flee after the others. They ran toward the trees, leaving their flocks behind. Ammon crawled toward the water, dragging his sword with him. He didn't make it far before he retched in the dirt. His stomach seized again. Shouting filtered through his mind, but he heard only the thudding of his heart and his gasping breaths until someone touched his shoulder. Ammon spun, weapon in hand.

"It's me," Kumen said, stepping away, his eyes wide. "Are you all right?"

Ammon wiped the back of his mouth with his hand. It came away bloody. He looked down at his bloodstained clothing. The throbbing in his head turned into a throbbing that consumed his body.

"How did you conquer so many men?" Kumen said.

Ammon opened his mouth to speak, but his voice was silent. He looked over at the dead leader, the gruesome death, and he turned and retched again.

He collapsed in the dirt, his body spent, his mind hazy.

Kumen stood over him for a few minutes then walked over to the dead leader. "That man is Gad's brother, Loki," he said in a quiet voice.

Ammon closed his eyes and groaned. That's where he'd seen that face before. He rose slowly to his feet, forcing himself to look at the dead leader. The man's final act in life had been yet another violent battle. The stories that surrounded the crisscrossing scars on Loki's arms and bare torso would forever be silent now. Even in death, Ammon sensed the man's power and former might.

The other servants ran up to him on the shoreline. They gazed at the scattered carnage, stunned into silence, and then one of the servants knelt before Ammon. "You are the greatest warrior I've ever seen."

The king's servants sank to their knees, bowing their heads. One of the servants offered praises as if Ammon were some sort of idol to be worshipped.

"Who are you?" Kumen cried out.

"Stand up," Ammon said, taking a step backward and shaking his head. "You know who I am."

Kumen threw himself forward, prostrating himself onto the ground. "Have mercy upon us, Great Spirit." The other men fell to the ground as well.

"Rise, my friends," Ammon urged them. "I am *not* the Great Spirit." The prostrated men didn't move. "We have to finish our work and return the flocks to the king."

No one stirred, and several of them were muttering some sort of a prayer.

Ammon barely heard them. He turned away and staggered the rest of the way to the water's edge. There, he plunged into the water, feeling numb. *Gad's brother is dead. And I've killed him.* Ammon soaked his body in the water, scrubbed his face and neck, and felt the tenderness where Loki's fingers had choked him. Ammon realized he was bleeding; the wound on his neck from the other night had been reopened.

Ammon sank into the water, going completely under the dark coolness. He stayed beneath the surface until his chest felt as if it would explode. Then he came up, gasping for air.

Exhaustion consumed his body, and he wished he could stay beneath the water and not see death everywhere. *What will Gad think when he discovers that Loki is dead?* He groaned at the thought. *Will Elena and her family be punished further?*

Someone was calling his name, sounding far away. Ammon tried to focus on cleaning as he scrubbed at the blood on his hands and forearms. He touched his face; one side of his mouth was swollen. His tunic shirt clung to him, though it was torn, stained, and useless. He took it off and futilely tried to rub out the stains.

Wearing only his kilt, he strode out of the water. Kumen and the other men had gathered the arms into a pile, their faces grim. They had also dragged the slain men from the sling together in a heap. Ammon averted his eyes.

"Seven are dead," Kumen said when Ammon approached. "You defeated six men, plus their leader—a leader who has commanded some of the fiercest battles our people have seen."

Ammon gave a short nod. Of all the men to scatter the flocks, he couldn't believe it was Loki, Gad's brother. The man had left him no choice, but still, Ammon's heart twisted as he thought of the grief and anger Gad was soon to experience. Why did the Lord direct him to replace Corien? To defend the king's flocks? To kill the rebels? *I must have faith*, Ammon thought. *The Lord must have a plan.*

The other servants, finished with collecting arms and dragging bodies, gathered around Ammon.

The servants fell to their knees again. "Please have mercy on us, O Great Spirit."

"I told you who I am," Ammon said. "Don't worship me."

They lowered their heads to the ground, calling out praises.

"Come," Ammon said more firmly. "We must not delay our duties to the king. He is expecting our return with the flocks. Gather the rebel's flocks as well."

Finally, Kumen raised his dirt-streaked face. Ammon held out a hand, and Kumen rose to his feet.

Ammon strode toward the flocks and herded them in the opposite direction of the waters, back toward the king's fields. Several minutes later, Kumen caught up with him to help.

At the top of the first hill, Ammon paused to make sure the other servants were coming as well. They walked in a group, carrying the severed arms like war trophies.

Ammon turned away, his stomach taut again. The day was far from over, and he could only pray that the Lord would continue to direct him and that this wouldn't become more complicated.

CHAPTER 11

But the Lord is the true God, he is the living God, and an
everlasting king: at his wrath the earth shall tremble.
—Jeremiah 10:10

Elena stared in horror at her brother.

"He cut off several arms and killed who knows how many men," Zaman said, his face a mixture of awe and fear. "They say he used a sling to slay many men then cut off the arms of the rest—with one swing of the sword."

"One swing of the sword?" Moriah asked. "Who *is* this Nephite?"

Moriah stood in the courtyard with them as Zaman delivered the incredible news about Ammon.

"Is Ammon all right?" Elena asked.

Zaman snapped his head around to look at her. "*Ammon?* He's like a beast—a warrior ten times over! No one's said how *he's* doing, but there are dead men—possibly dozens—and you ask how *the Nephite* is?"

Elena closed her mouth and gripped her hands together. *Is he alive? Is he injured? How does one man kill so many with no help?* She shuddered to think of him in a bloody battle. Her stomach twisted at the description of the gruesome scene, but she still worried about Ammon's well-being. *What led him to so much violence?*

"The king and all the court have gathered to hear the servants' story," Zaman said. "They had to send several of the king's guards to gather all the dead. Father, let's go!"

Moriah hesitated.

"I won't be able to get past the palace guards without you," Zaman said.

He reluctantly agreed, and the men hurried out of the courtyard as Elena stared after them, stunned. *What happened at the waters of Sebus?*

To Ammon? She took a step toward the gate and then another. Before she knew it, she was running out of the courtyard and into the jungle, taking the shortcut to the palace rather than following her brother and father.

By the time Elena reached the outer courtyard of the palace, a large crowd had gathered, though they were being kept out by the palace guards. Panic rose in her chest as she assessed the number of people. She had to reach her father and brother. Swallowing hard, she pushed through the onlookers until she saw them. They'd just arrived, and she joined them on the way to the gate. She took her father's hand, knowing she might be turned away as a lone woman. He glanced at her in surprise, but just then the palace guard allowed them entrance, and Elena passed through the gates, her hand still clenched in her father's.

They hurried along the massive halls, joining other small groups of dignitaries, everyone speaking in hushed voices.

Elena's father and brother hesitated just inside the throne room. A good-sized crowd had gathered, and they wound their way through the tightly packed people to afford a better view.

The king was questioning a group of men whose kilts were bloodstained.

As Elena drew closer, she saw the gruesome pile of arms in front of the row of servants. *The arms Ammon severed.* She stared at them, finding it difficult to tear her gaze away, horrible as the sight was. Then she scanned the servants for Ammon—although their backs were to her, she'd recognize the lighter skin. He wasn't there. She swallowed at the sudden thickness in her throat and focused on King Lamoni. His face was shaded deep red as he threw out question after question.

"Surely Ammon is more than a man." The king looked at the pile of arms spread on a rug at his feet. He lifted his gaze again to look over the hushed crowd. "Is he the Great Spirit?" His tone was quiet, but it pierced every listening soul.

The people remained silent.

"Has the Great Spirit come to punish my people because of our executions?" King Lamoni said, more to himself than to the servants.

The queen stepped forward, taking her husband's arm, her face absolutely pale.

Kumen spoke up, "We don't know if he's the Great Spirit." The other servants nodded their agreement. "But I do know Ammon can't be slain by your enemies. They tried to scatter the flocks a second time, yet he was able to slay all of those men by himself. I've never seen a man with such power."

The king placed a hand over his wife's as he inhaled deeply. "He must be the Great Spirit and was sent to save your lives so I wouldn't order your executions."

Kumen fell to one knee. "If the Great Spirit has preserved our lives, we are at his mercy."

The king turned and looked at the various stone idols flanking his throne, one representing the Great Spirit. With his wife, he knelt and bowed his head. Several people in the court sank to their knees as well. "We thank thee for thy mercy, O Spirit," the king cried out.

Elena sank to her knees, along with her father and brother, although many questions milled through her mind about the Great Spirit appearing in a man's form. She thought about the other men he'd bested rather easily—her brother . . . and Gad. The crowd echoed the king's praise to the statue. After a few minutes of fervent worshipping, the king rose to his feet and turned to face the servants again.

"Where is this man? This man who has such great power?"

Elena held her breath as everyone looked at the servants for the answer.

Kumen spoke for the group of servants again. "He's feeding your horses, preparing them for the chariots you ordered for the high king's great feast. We are not with him because we came here to report first." The other servants nodded vigorously.

The king looked at each of the servants, his expression incredulous. "He did all of this," he waved his hand, "then went to the stables to prepare the *horses*?" Lamoni stroked his chin, looking down at the pile of arms. "Surely, there has never been a servant as faithful as this man. He's following *all* of my commands—to *perfection*."

He left his wife's side and walked to the large throne. Putting his hands on the armrests, he was silent for a moment, keeping his back to the people. When he turned around, his face was pale. "Now I know with a surety he *is* the Great Spirit." He looked to his wife, who had covered her mouth in awe. "I want to speak to him, ask him questions, but I don't dare."

The king sank into his throne and put his face into his hands. He didn't move for a long space of time. Some of the crowd left, thinning the amount of people in the room, but the place was stifling, the stench from the severed arms growing stronger.

As each minute passed, Elena worried more and more about Ammon. *Where is he? Is he injured? Ill?* The pile of severed arms and the crowd made her feel dizzy. She leaned toward her father. "I need to go out for a moment."

He nodded absently, and she slipped out of the room. The openness of the hallway was a relief, and Elena inhaled deeply. Her steadiness slowly returned and with it her desire to find Ammon to see if he was all right. *He must be*, she decided, *if he is feeding the horses.* But her heart pounded to think of what condition he might be in. He was stubborn, and injured or not, he'd still perform his tasks.

She hurried along the hallway, wondering if he were indeed the Great Spirit. Her heart clenched. If he was, he wasn't a mortal man. She couldn't expect any sort of relationship from him. But what about his claim to be a Nephite prince? A group of people exited the throne room, and Elena stepped aside then moved to the wall, changing her mind about searching for Ammon. She couldn't face him. He'd probably see right into her heart and know her desire for him. He would laugh—this powerful being. A man greater than the king himself!

She leaned against the cool wall, closing her eyes. She thought of all the things she'd said to him—what had he thought of her?

"Elena?"

She opened her eyes, blinking against the sudden brightness. Ammon stood in the hallway. His torso was bare, making him look like a native, save for his fair skin. He had several scrapes on his arms, and the wound on his neck looked like it had been reopened.

"Ammon," she whispered, her voice cracking. "Are you—How—" Her eyes filled with tears.

He crossed to her, grabbing both of her arms. "What's wrong? Is it Gad again?"

Elena's voice caught. She couldn't answer. She shook her head, her eyes flooding with tears. Ammon was alive and well. But who *was* he, this man she'd been afraid for? This man she'd been worried about since he left with the king's flocks? Until this moment of seeing him close-up, alive, and breathing, she hadn't realized how important he'd become to her. Her mind reeled. How could she be in love with someone she'd known for such a short time? It wasn't possible. Ammon was the Great Spirit. "I—I thought something had happened to you."

Ammon wiped the tears from her face with his scarred hand. "I need to report to the king. Wait for me here. I want to speak with you."

Elena grabbed his hand and squeezed it. It was warm and calloused—just like a man's would be. Ammon drew his eyebrows together as he enclosed her hand with his. He squeezed back gently then pulled away. "Wait here."

Elena released him, feeling as if all warmth had just left her body as he strode toward the throne room.

After several tempering breaths, she followed and reached the throne room in time to hear Kumen's voice speak above the hushed crowd. "Rabbanah, the king desires you to stay."

Ammon was facing Elena's direction as if he were about to leave the room. Their eyes locked briefly, and Elena saw something like relief as he gazed at her. But all too soon, he turned back toward the king.

Ammon spread out his hands and said, "What is it you wish of me, O King?"

Elena held her breath, anticipating the king's response, but he said nothing. She had to see what was happening, despite Ammon's request. She slipped into the room, searching for her father. When she found him, she stood next to him, looping her arm through his, hoping to steady her trembling body.

***

"What do you desire of me, O King?" Ammon asked the king again. He'd been waiting for the king's response—but the man made no move to answer. The king's eyes flitted from Ammon to the pile of severed arms then out to the crowd. At one point, the king gripped his throne and made a move to stand, but instead he sank back as if all of his energy had left him.

Ammon looked into the eyes of the gathered Lamanites around the throne room. Many bowed, though most just stared at him in awe. Elena was in the crowd; he was glad to see she'd stopped crying. Her father and brother appeared to be fine, so Ammon could only attribute the tears to the possibility that she'd heard about Gad's brother's death. Ammon hoped Gad wouldn't retaliate against her family. When Ammon faced the king again, he waited for the king to give him instructions. Another moment passed, and still the king said nothing. Everyone in the court looked from the king to Ammon, anxious because of the silence.

Ammon continued to wait for the king to speak, wondering why Lamoni hadn't answered yet. Was he angry? Was he trying to come up with a punishment? Ammon had followed the Lord's promptings at the waters of Sebus, but still he worried about the king's reaction. He started to pray silently. *Please, Lord, direct me. Help me know the right words to say . . .*

When Ammon concluded his silent prayer, warmth spread through him as the Spirit whispered, telling him that he needed to open his mouth. The right words would be given to him. Resolute, Ammon took a step forward, not entirely sure of what the outcome might be. But just as he obeyed the Lord's promptings at the waters of Sebus, he did so now. He met the king's gaze and said, "Did you send for me because you've been told how I defended your servants and flocks?"

The king gave a brief nod.

Ammon exhaled in relief, feeling the assurance of the Spirit as he continued in a quiet voice. "And is it because I slew seven of the Lamanites with a sling and a sword to defend your flocks?"

Another nod from the king.

"And because I smote off the arms of the others who raised their clubs against me?"

The king's eyes widened.

Ammon bowed low. "Why are you speechless, Your Highness?" he asked. "I am but your servant, following your commands."

The king slid from his throne to the floor and knelt. He clasped his trembling hands together and said, "Who *are* you? Are you the Great Spirit who knows all things?"

Ammon raised his brows, wondering why the king would think he was the Great Spirit. Did others in the room think that as well? By the awed silence, Ammon guessed they did. A smiled touched the corner of Ammon's mouth as he shook his head. "No. I am not."

The king stared at him for a moment, but his expression was still confused. "How do you know the thoughts of my heart?" the king said. "And by what power did you smite off all of those arms?"

Warmth flowed through Ammon's body. The moment had come. A voice again whispered to his mind, a voice that could only be the Spirit: *Lamoni is ready to receive my teachings.* It was as if the Spirit was shouting at him. All the prayer, all the scripture study, all the preparation—and now the time had arrived. He was grateful the Lord had answered his prayers, although not in the method anticipated.

Ammon crossed to the king and in a bold move took the man's hand. "Rise and stand. I am no Great Spirit. Do not pay homage to me."

The king rose to his feet, his body quivering as he gripped Ammon's hand. "Will you tell me how you did this? I will give you whatever you desire." His voice grew in strength and conviction. "I will guard you with my own armies, although you are more powerful than they."

Ammon released the king's hand. "It is not necessary, O King. I only want to tell you of the power I've used to conquer your enemies. The one thing I desire is that you will listen to my words."

The king's eyes stayed on Ammon's face. "Yes, oh yes," he whispered. "I will believe all of your words."

The king had been humbled and astonished. He was like a little child, ready to soak in the truth. Ammon's heart leapt, and he took a steadying breath, feeling the strength of the Spirit like fire in his limbs. "Do you believe there is a God?"

"What do you mean?" the king asked.

"Do you believe there is a Great Spirit?"

"Yes."

"The Great Spirit is God," Ammon said. "Do you believe that this Great Spirit, who is God, created all things which are in heaven and in the earth?"

The king drew his eyebrows together. He glanced at his wife then back to Ammon. "Yes, I believe that he created the things on the earth. But which heaven do you speak of?"

"I speak of the one and only heaven, the place where God dwells with His holy angels."

"Is heaven above the earth?" the king asked.

"Yes," Ammon said. "God looks down on all the children of men, and He knows the thoughts and intents of our heart. He is the one who created us."

"I believe your words," the king said in a slow, measured tone.

Ammon wanted to shout for joy. His body felt lighter than the air.

"Were you sent by God to us?" the king asked.

"I am only a man, created in God's image, as all people are," Ammon said, his chest expanding with elation, "but I was called by His Holy Spirit to teach your people so they will be brought to a knowledge of the truth. A portion of the Spirit dwells within me so that I have knowledge and also power according to my faith and desires."

It was as if Ammon were floating because so much light had filled his soul. He could not deny the presence of the Spirit in the room and knew the others could not either. Ammon had the scripture scroll tucked in his waistband, but he knew the words by heart now—and it was as if the Lord were enlightening his mind as he taught. Ammon continued to speak of Christ and the salvation of mankind as the king listened, staring at him in wonder, and as the surrounding group of people remained hushed. Kumen and the servants who had been in the fields with him sat on the stone floor, listening intently as Ammon told them about the creation of the world and of Adam and Eve.

Ammon rotated as he spoke, including all those in the room who were listening. He told them the story of their father, Lehi, to which the Lamanites nodded with familiarity. But with the tangible presence of the Spirit in the room, the story had full meaning and more clarity.

After relating the travails of Lehi's family, he taught the king about the plan of redemption. "Christ will come and fulfill the plan that has been in place since the beginning of the world."

The king raised his hands over his head and cried out, "O Lord, have mercy! According to Thy abundant mercy which Thou hast had upon the people of Nephi, have mercy upon me and my people."

And then he collapsed to the ground. The crowd gasped, and the guards scurried to the king's side. He didn't move, didn't speak.

"Call a healer!" the queen shouted. She knelt by her husband and cradled his head. "Lamoni, wake up."

Ammon made his way forward, but the guards had already lifted the king and were crossing the throne room, passing through the gathering.

"Take him to our bedchamber. Send the healer there," the queen called out, hurrying after those who were carrying her husband.

As soon as the guards had lifted the king into their arms, Ammon felt the reassurance that the king would be all right. He wanted to reach out to the queen, comfort her, and tell her that her husband was under the power of God. He knew all too well that the dark veil of unbelief was being cast away from King Lamoni's mind, just as it had for Alma the Younger back in Zarahemla. Ammon had carried Alma back to his father, who knew immediately that Alma wasn't dead but was being taught by the Spirit. Joy surged through Ammon as he thought about the king undertaking this conversion process. Ammon's prayers had been answered beyond anything he could have comprehended when he set out on this mission.

He turned to find someone to explain it to—Pahrun, even Kumen, but they were nowhere to be seen. Many were leaving to spread the news about the king.

Several people had remained, watching Ammon, but their expressions were filled with confusion. Finally, he spotted Elena, and their eyes met briefly. He started toward her, but she and her family were swept up in the tide of the crowd. Zaman trailed Elena, and Ammon decided he could reach him first.

"Zaman!"

He didn't turn but continued through the doors.

"Ammon," someone said, touching his arm. He turned to see Kumen.

"Let's go back to the hut," Kumen said, "Until there is news about the king."

* * *

Elena reluctantly followed her father and brother home. Her father kept his lips pursed as Zaman ranted.

"This could get very dangerous," Zaman said. "Nothing but trouble has occurred since that Nephite came to our land."

Elena wanted to protest, but she was still trying to grasp all that she had seen and heard. Although she burned to speak with Ammon, she would be grateful to sort out all of the information in the privacy of her own bedchamber.

"If something has happened to the king—" Zaman cut himself off.

"When the healer arrives, we'll know what's wrong," Moriah said.

Zaman shook his head, groaning. "I should have used my dagger on the Nephite when I had a chance."

"You wouldn't have won the fight," Elena murmured.

"What?" Zaman said, stopping to glare at her. "How can you say that?"

"Didn't you see the pile of arms?"

"Humph," Zaman said. "So he's good with a sword, but he is only a man, after all." He turned and continued walking.

Once they reached their homestead, Elena went through the motions of preparing the meal. She didn't know who'd be eating it—she couldn't imagine taking one bite for herself. After setting the maize kernels on the fire to simmer, she made the escape to her room. Her brother had stormed out of the house earlier, and her father sat quietly in the front room.

She sat on her bed and closed her eyes, remembering what Ammon had said to the king: *I am not the Great Spirit.* Elena let out a slow breath, allowing relief to flood her body. *He's just a man—an incredible and powerful man, but a man.*

She lay on her back, keeping her eyes closed. It had been so warm in the throne room, not a warmth that made her perspire but a warmth that seemed to fill her on the inside. *Peaceful.* That was a better word. When Ammon spoke about the heavens, she'd remembered what he'd said when they had stood together at Corien's funeral. Was this the same place that God and His angels dwelled?

She moved onto her side, gazing at the small goddess statue her father had given her. She reached for it and turned it over in her hands. The piece of stone seemed cold and dead in her hands, completely unlike the warmth she had felt when Ammon had taught the king about the plan of redemption.

For several moments, Elena stared at the figurine, willing it to communicate with her through a thought or a feeling. There was nothing. She wondered about the consolation she'd felt before but then decided maybe it was her own consolation and she'd given the goddess the credit.

She set the idol back in its place and rubbed her head, wishing she could talk to her father or brother about it. It was plain how her brother felt about Ammon's actions, but what about her father?

"Elena?" her father's voice called outside her door. "Abish is at the house."

Elena sat up and wiped her cheeks. "I'm coming out." She rose and straightened her clothing, glancing again at the idol. She decided to ask Abish what she thought—she would know what was going on at the palace. Heart pounding, Elena left her room to greet her.

Abish stood in the doorway. She was usually a small woman, but at this moment, she looked as if she'd grown in stature. And her face absolutely radiated.

"What's happened?" Elena said, rushing toward her and clasping her hands.

"I've come to speak to your brother," Abish said. "But he isn't home."

"What about?" Elena asked. "Is the king doing better?"

"No," Abish said, her expression temporarily falling. "The king is the same."

"Then what—"

Abish allowed a small smile to emerge that broadened into a grin as her eyes glowed even more intensely. "Perhaps we could take a walk together."

Elena glanced over at her father, who had waited in the cooking room and had overheard everything. He nodded, and Elena linked arms with Abish and led her to the front courtyard. They avoided the main road, keeping to a narrow side path.

"Tell me your news. It must be fantastic," Elena said after she couldn't stand the wait any longer.

"Did you hear what Ammon taught?" Abish asked.

"Yes, I was there with my father and brother—I don't know what to think about his message," she said all in one breath. "What did you think of his words?"

Abish stopped on the path and turned to face Elena. "Oh, my dear. I can't believe I can finally speak the things of my heart."

"What do you mean?" Elena said.

"Everything Ammon said is true. The God the Nephites believe in is the *true* God." Abish's voice caught with emotion. "I've known it for many years, yet I dared not confess it to anyone."

Elena stared at her. This woman who was as close as a sister had *Nephite* beliefs? "How did you know? You've never been to Zarahemla to hear the Nephites preach."

"My father had a vision." Abish clasped Elena's arms. "Before his death, he shared it with me. That's when he made me promise never to become a priestess."

"What did he see?" Elena whispered.

Abish looked past Elena as if she were in some sort of trance. "My father spent most of his life cleaning the temples. In return, he was allowed to take home records to read. Sometimes he shared the histories with me about the Lamanite people."

Elena nodded; she already knew this much.

"Some parts of the stories of our ancestors always bothered him."

"What?" Elena asked, although she wondered if she wanted to know. Abish was speaking of things that were never discussed in her household.

"Have you heard of the Liahona?"

Elena narrowed her eyes. It sounded familiar.

"God sent the instrument to our father Lehi. It only worked when he and his family were righteous. It took many years for them to travel from Jerusalem to our land," Abish said. "Why did it take so long, my father wanted to know?"

"Laman and Lemuel didn't want to leave their homeland," Elena said. "Didn't they try to return and claim their inheritance?"

"Not exactly," Abish said. "My father learned that Laman and Lemuel tried to kill Nephi and Lehi several times. Their unrighteous behavior made the Liahona stop working. Only when they repented did the Lord help them again."

"Is this what your father had a vision about?"

Abish took a deep breath. "In my father's vision, he was taught by the Lord. He learned that Nephi was given the patriarchal role by the Lord— and not because he was the favorite son, as his brothers claimed. It was the *Lord's* decision."

Elena stared at Abish, whose eyes were moist.

"The Lord is *real*, Elena. He's not a wooden or stone idol on the steps of the temple. He's the Lord who brought us out of Jerusalem and the one who the Nephites continue to teach about." Abish brushed at the tears on her face. "I know Ammon is speaking the truth. The things he taught are true."

The warmth that Elena had felt in the throne room crept back in. "What about the king? Will he recover?"

"The Lord has the power to destroy a person," Abish said, surety in her voice. "I don't know what happened to the king or what will happen to him. But none of it is Ammon's doing."

Elena still had so many questions, but she couldn't deny the way she felt inside at Abish's words.

"I just wanted you to know how I felt," Abish said. "I'll tell Zaman as well when I see him."

"Maybe you should wait. He's very upset about the king."

Abish opened her mouth then shut it. "Very well, at least until the king recovers."

The two women walked slowly along the path until they reached the turnoff for Elena's house.

"I must go now," Abish said. "The queen is in need of great comfort, and she may call on my services." She embraced Elena fiercely. "I hope you will come to know the true God as I do."

Elena watched Abish leave. Abish's expression was as if the sun had appeared after a long storm.

Elena wrapped her arms about herself as she walked slowly home. Did she believe in the vision Abish's father had? She'd seen with her own eyes the evidence of the power Ammon possessed—and he claimed it was through the power of God. At the gate to her courtyard, she paused. *What do I really feel inside? What did I feel in that throne room when Ammon spoke?*

Warm. She thought. *Peaceful.*

She looked up at her home. Had her father felt the same thing? Her brother had made his feelings clear. Confusion settled over her again— and what about the king?

She crossed the courtyard and opened the front door. There, in the front room, stood her father and Gad.

CHAPTER 12

Be ye not unequally yoked together with unbelievers: for what
fellowship hath righteousness with unrighteousness?
—2 Corinthians 6:14

Gad put his thick hands on Elena's shoulders, his eyes black, his gaze intense. She tried to pull away, memories of his forced kisses causing her to shudder, but his grip was too tight.

Elena glanced at her father, hoping he'd intervene, but he avoided her eyes. Had he finally given his consent for marriage? Was there no way out now?

The words that came out of Gad's mouth were not what she had expected. "He killed my brother!"

Elena opened her mouth to question, to understand, but Gad rushed on, his fingers digging into her flesh. "That Nephite! The one who nearly killed me the other night . . . *He* killed my brother!" Gad's eyes grew wild as he shook her. "Don't you understand? My brother was at Sebus."

Suddenly Elena understood. "Loki?" She could barely get the word out.

"Who is this Nephite?" Gad pressed. "How do you know him? How did he happen to come by your house the other night?"

"I—" Elena pulled away, grateful when Gad's hands dropped. She took a step backward, glancing between her father and Gad. "I can't believe it—your *brother*? He was trying to scatter the king's flocks?"

Gad threw his hands in the air and groaned. "I tried to keep him out of trouble, but he was weak. Easily influenced. He served honorably in the militia, defending our borders against the filthy Nephites. Just because he became caught up in the wrong group of men doesn't mean he had to be killed for it." He sank into a pile of cushions, covering his face with his hands. "Ammon had no right! He acted in the name of the king as if he were the king. My brother deserved to defend his actions in court."

Elena looked at her father's ashen face then at Gad's. A lump formed in her throat. The man was suffering. Loki had deserved punishment for scattering the flocks—but was Gad right that Loki had a right to defend his case before the king?

Suddenly, Gad leapt to his feet, his face flaming. "I'm going to kill Ammon!" he shouted. "I don't care what he told the king—he's a *murderer*. And now the king . . ."

Zaman burst into the room. One look at his expression, and Elena knew he'd just found out about Loki as well.

Gad rushed to Zaman, his eyes bloodshot with anger. "Will you stand by me?"

"I will," Zaman said.

The two men embraced. "On my life," Gad said as he pulled away, his voice quaking, "I will seek revenge upon the man who killed my brother."

"I will come with you," Zaman said. In a flurry and before Elena could react, they were out the door and running, her father following behind them.

"No!" Elena screamed. But her plea was silent to them. She grabbed the door to steady herself, her body throbbing with fear. "What's happening?" she cried out. "What is happening to us all?"

* * *

The sun had nearly set when Elena pulled herself out of her stupor. She didn't know how long she'd sat on the ground in the entryway of her home and sobbed.

It was probably too late now. Gad and her brother could have already taken revenge upon Ammon. But if so, no one had come to spread the news. She dried the tears from her face. Surely bad news would have reached her by now. That fact alone gave her the smallest of hope.

She took a deep, steadying breath, determination building within her heart as she thought of Ammon still alive. He'd killed or maimed more than a dozen men. Three more wouldn't be too much more. Fear for her brother and father escalated, combining with the fear for Ammon's life. She didn't know if her heart could stretch any farther without breaking. If what Abish said was true, Ammon had been sent by the Lord to teach them the truth. And now he'd be killed for it.

Elena pulled herself to her feet with resolution. She walked to her bedchamber and selected a dark scarf then covered her hair and tied the scarf beneath her chin with trembling hands. She crossed the courtyard just as dusk settled, casting its purple-gray tones over the stone wall.

It didn't take long for her to reach the circle of huts that housed several of the king's servants. If Ammon was gone, she might be able to find out some information from Kumen.

She slowed in surprise when she saw four men standing in front of the hut—the king's guards. What did it mean? Had there been an incident? Was she too late?

She approached the guards, trying to read their stoic faces. "I'm here to see Ammon."

One guard stepped forward and asked her to take off her cape then checked to make sure she carried no weapons.

Relief built in Elena. If something had happened to Ammon, wouldn't the guard say something?

"What's your name?" the guard asked.

When she told him, he walked to the door and knocked.

Ammon opened it. She almost didn't believe he was real. He must have noticed the wild disbelief in her eyes because he motioned for her to come inside.

A figure rose in the corner of the room, and Elena barely registered that it was Kumen. When he saw who she was, he stepped out of the hut.

"You're here—*alive*," she said. "The guards . . ."

"Yes, the queen has been merciful," Ammon said, narrowing his eyes.

"I—it's my brother. And Gad. They—" Her voice choked off, and she looked away, forcing herself to take a deep breath.

"If this is about Loki, then I already know," Ammon said.

She looked at him. "You knew it was Loki?"

"Not at first." Ammon's gaze faltered. "Let me tell you what happened."

"Wait," Elena said, her voice wavering. "Tell me first what's wrong with the king. Is he dead too?"

"I don't believe the king is dead. A friend of mine had a similar experience where he was overcome by the Spirit of the Lord." He touched Elena's hand, but she drew it sharply away. "Please sit down. I have much to tell you."

Elena sat across from him, watching the changing shadows on Ammon's face as he spoke in the dimness of the hut, broken up only by the flickering oil lamp in the room. The story he told her was even more fantastic than Abish's claim about her father's vision.

"In Zarahemla, I was visited by an angel—a heavenly being sent by the Lord." He spoke with such reverence and emotion that the hairs on Elena's arms stood straight up until she shivered.

"My brothers and I . . . we were not always faithful to our church . . . and the Lord saw fit to chastise us. He sent an angel to intervene. We fell to the ground when the angel spoke. Alma was also with us—but he became unconscious." Ammon gripped his hands together in front of him, and Elena detected the pain in his eyes. She marveled that the Lord would send a message through an angel and wondered what the angel had said to the men, but she didn't want to interrupt Ammon. "We were so afraid," he continued. "We had no one to turn to; we'd been estranged from my family and his. We finally saw no choice but to take Alma's body to his father."

He looked up, his eyes shining. "The high priest knew immediately why his son was unconscious. In fact, he rejoiced because he knew Alma was being taught by the Lord."

"And you think that's what's happening to the king?" Elena whispered.

"It's what I'm praying for," he said, his voice matching her whisper. "Until I see the king, I won't know for certain."

Elena nodded; his answer seemed honest enough. But what about the angel? Was an angel visiting the king right now? She inhaled, trying to comprehend if such a thing were true.

"Elena," Ammon said, his voice so quiet that she wondered if he'd really spoken.

When she looked up, his eyes were on her.

"I've done things in my past that are unspeakable. I want you to know that I did not come to your land thinking I'm superior to anyone. I'm truly a humble servant—first of the Lord, second of the king. Whether I die of old age or at the hands of someone like Gad, I'll go to the grave a repentant man. Unless it's the Lord's will, I'll no longer fight back if someone comes to seek revenge on me."

Elena blinked against the burning in her eyes. How could he be so passive? She stood and crossed the room then turned and looked back at him. How could he not fight back? He'd just bested seven men to defend the king's flocks. Why couldn't he defend himself against Gad or her brother? Even as she thought it, her heart ached. She could never choose between her brother and Ammon.

He rose and walked toward her, holding out his hand, palm up so that the deep scar was clearly visible. "This scar reminds me every day of an oath I took for the wrong reason."

She studied the horizontal scar—a shiver ran through her. "You made a blood oath?"

"It was an evil promise, a secret combination," he said. "I spilled my blood to prove my loyalty to the deceiver. But now I will gladly spill my blood to fight *against* the deceiver. That's why I've come into the heart of Lamanite territory, where the goodness of God has been blocked by the dark clouds of the adversary for too long. Each morning I make a new oath as the sun comes up, an oath that I will serve only one God the rest of my life."

"This is why you gave up your throne?" Elena asked.

"Yes," he whispered.

Amazement swept through her. "Why would you give up a wonderful life for your *enemies*?"

"I don't consider the Lamanites my enemy. I love them like my own family. I pray day and night that I'll be able to share the Lord's message among this people, no matter the toll on myself." He held her gaze, and she almost forgot to breathe.

"The toll has been great indeed." Elena took his scarred hand in hers and brought it to her lips. She kissed the rough skin. He watched her but made no move. She closed her eyes for a moment, his warm hand still in hers, as she searched her heart. She knew he had been born a prince and was meant for something greater than defending the king's flocks, yet in her eyes, his greatest service had been making her feel valued.

"I believe you," she whispered. She heard him exhale, and when she looked up at him, his eyes were wet. She leaned forward and wrapped her arms around his neck, soaking in his warmth, his strength.

"Elena—" he said, his arms encircling her.

"You don't have to say anything more," she said. "Just know that I believe you. No matter what happens to you, or to me, I believe in you."

A heavy breath escaped him, and he tightened his hold. "You must go now," he said into her hair. "I don't want you here if someone comes."

"I want to be here."

"No," Ammon said, pulling away and gazing at her, his hands still at her waist. "Kumen will protect me. I don't want this to involve you. If it's my time—"

"Don't say that."

He leaned down, his forehead almost touching hers. "If it's my time, I don't want any retaliation to come your way."

His breath was sweet on her face, and she wondered if his heart was pounding as hard as hers. What if this were the last time she saw him alive? Could she stop Gad? Or Zaman? What would the cost be? She couldn't lose Ammon—wouldn't lose him. She lifted her face and pressed her lips against his. He went absolutely still. But then he was kissing her, pulling her into his arms, and lifting her from the ground. Elena melted against him, lost in his embrace as she prayed in her heart—to a new God—to preserve this man's life.

CHAPTER 13

Discern between the righteous and the wicked, between him
that serveth God and him that serveth him not.
—Malachi 3:18

Two Days Later

Ammon paced inside the hut as Kumen kept watch out the door. Death threats had been made against Ammon. At all hours of the day Lamanites, some intoxicated with wine, others intoxicated with confusion and anger, shouted threats outside his hut. Four guards were currently stationed outside the hut by the order of the queen. Still more guards patrolled the surrounding jungle, turning away groups of protesters or the occasional lone crazed man. The longer the king remained unconscious, the higher the tensions rose in the city. And everything seemed to point to Ammon. He had been blessed that the queen hadn't thrown him in prison, or something worse, but had decided to preserve him.

Two days had passed since the king had fallen to the ground unconscious—two days of mourning by the majority of the people. Two days since Elena had kissed Ammon.

A flash of warmth swept through him as he thought about her—her trusting eyes, her declaration that she believed his teachings. *One woman in the land of Ishmael believes me,* he thought, his heart aching anew. And it was someone he cared more for than his own life. He'd pled with her to take no risks, to speak to no one about her visit, to keep her beliefs silent.

He didn't know if the land of Ishmael was on the brink of civil war as the people became more and more vocal in taking sides—for or against Ammon. But he didn't want Elena in the middle of it.

It wasn't supposed to be this way, Ammon thought, stopping to stare at the sword propped in the corner of the hut—the sword that had taken many lives in a matter of moments. He hadn't wanted to harm anyone; he had merely wanted to defend the king's flocks. He hadn't meant to drive a deeper wedge between himself and Gad or cause Elena's family more pain.

And he hadn't meant to return Elena's kiss. She obviously knew his true feelings about her now, which would make it more painful if the events in the land of Ishmael didn't end well.

"Someone's coming," Kumen said, walking into the room. "Someone from the palace."

Ammon stopped. "A servant? Another guard?"

"A woman servant."

"At least I'm not being arrested," Ammon said. He stepped out of the hut into the morning sun as a woman approached the guards. They questioned her, and one of the guards searched for weapons.

The woman's eyes met Ammon's, and he recognized her as a servant he'd seen about the palace in the company of the queen. Her dark hair was pulled severely back from her face, making her look older than she probably was. She wore a dark cloak over a plain brown tunic bearing the royal insignia. Her hands fidgeted nervously.

In his heart, Ammon prayed it was good news—that the king had awakened.

"Sir." The woman bowed her head. "The queen requests your presence in her chamber."

"The queen?" His heart leapt. "Has something happened to the king?"

"He's still the same."

The same. At least he'd have a chance to speak with the queen. He'd wanted to explain everything to her, to console her, but he hadn't had the opportunity. She had not summoned him, and he couldn't have approached her without her consent. "Thank you," Ammon said.

He grabbed his own cloak and followed the servant along the path. The guards followed as well, carrying out their orders to protect him. "What's your name?" Ammon asked the servant.

The woman hesitated for a moment then said, "Abish." As they continued to walk, the servant cast a backward glance at him but said nothing more.

Inside the palace, the halls were hushed. Dark rugs hung over the windows, allowing very little light to enter and signifying that the court was in mourning. Servants moved to the side as Ammon passed by. As his eyes adjusted to the near darkness, he noticed the hollow-eyed stares following him—fear of him and fear for their king.

Abish led him along a corridor then stopped at a set of large doors. She tapped on one of the doors and waited. A moment later, the door creaked open. A young woman stood there, dressed much the same as Abish. She looked over at Ammon, and relief covered her face.

"Come in," she whispered, averting her eyes. "The queen is expecting you."

The guards waited outside the chamber as Ammon entered.

The room was overheated—a fire blazed in the hearth in the corner of the sitting room. Beyond a collection of cushions was another pair of doors.

The queen rose from the cushions as soon as she saw Ammon. Even though she was a petite woman, she commanded a presence that Ammon immediately felt.

He bowed as the queen looked him over. "O Queen, how may I be of service?" When he lifted his head, she was still regarding him. Her eyes didn't hold the fear of the servants in the halls but were dark with distress.

"The servants of my husband believe you're a prophet of a holy God," the queen said in a halting voice. "They believe the words you spoke to my husband and that you have the power to do many mighty works."

Ammon nodded, his heart swelling. So the king's servants truly believed.

"If this is the case, I ask you to go in and see my husband," she said. "He has lain upon his bed for two days and two nights. Some say that he is not dead." Her voice faltered. "Others say that he is dead and that his body stinks. They want to place him in the sepulchre." Her eyes grew moist. "I don't think his body stinks like they say. I believe he's alive."

Ammon prayed the queen was right and that King Lamoni wasn't dead. He crossed the room, and the queen stepped aside, lifting her hand toward the connecting doors. Ammon pushed open the door.

A wide platform bed stood in the middle of an elegant chamber. Another fire roared in the corner hearth, making the heat almost unbearable. The king lay on the bed; his torso was bare, but a rug covered him from the waist down.

The windows were draped, but the room was brighter than the sitting room. Even when Ammon first entered the chamber, he sensed the king was resting peacefully. Ammon crossed to the side of the bed and gazed down at the man who was under the power of God.

When he awoke, he'd have remarkable messages to share with his people. Ammon's mind flashed back to Alma the Younger's similar experience. Alma had remained unconscious for three days. Ammon reached for the king's hand, hearing a gasp from one of the servants who occupied the room.

Warmth permeated from the king's hand, and tears stung Ammon's eyes. He could almost imagine the unbelief that had fallen away from the king's mind like a veil and the light that now filled the king's heart and mind. The Spirit comforted and assured him as he held the king's hand.

Ammon turned to the queen, who stood with her hands clasped in front of her, her eyes wide. "Your husband is not dead," he said. "He is asleep, being taught of God. Tomorrow he will rise again."

The queen's hand came to her mouth as tears filled her eyes. She sank to her knees and reached for Ammon's hand. He took her trembling hand. "Do you believe my words?"

She whispered, "I have no witness except for your promise and what the servants have told me. But I will believe that my husband will rise tomorrow, and I will not bury him."

Ammon held her gaze, feeling the power of her faith pulse through him. He marveled that this woman had never seen an angel nor heard the voice of the Lord. She hadn't been taught the principles of the gospel or the Lord's commandments. Yet, she believed. "You are blessed because of your great faith," he said. "I have not seen such great faith among all the people of the Nephites."

The queen rose to her feet, tears streaking her cheeks as she clasped Ammon's hand. "Thank you for coming. Please," she said in a tremulous voice, "please return tomorrow morning." She released Ammon and turned toward her husband. Sitting next to him, she grasped his hands and watched him.

Her face looked smooth; the weariness and worry had fled. Abish crossed the room and knelt by the queen's side. After several moments of silence, Ammon murmured his farewell. Abish lifted her head to watch him leave, a faint smile on her lips.

* * *

"He says the king will rise this morning," Zaman's voice boomed through the house.

Elena flinched at the sound. Gad had been at their place over the past three days, ranting and railing against Ammon, making Zaman's hatred against Ammon even stronger. Together, they laid their plots against Ammon, trying to find a way around the queen's guards. "The guards are patrolling the surrounding territory, questioning and searching everyone. It looks as if we aren't the only ones who want the man dead. We'll just have to be more patient, wait until the queen sees the truth of her husband's demise," she'd heard Gad say more than once.

Zaman had readily agreed.

At least Gad had mostly ignored her over the past couple of days. With his mind occupied with the death of his brother, he'd seemed to have forgotten her presence.

Elena had spent as little time as possible in the house, except when it was pouring rain. She'd worked on clothing orders, sitting silently with her father. The worry was plainly etched in his face, but it was as if he were too afraid to voice his concerns.

Thunder sounded, causing the roof to shudder above. *Why did the storms have to come* this *week?* If there were any time to be housebound, this was not it. The two men in her home who were cursing, ranting, and plotting murder made her sick to her stomach. And the sleepless nights worrying over Ammon and the king made it no better.

Elena stepped into the front room and switched the empty wine jug for a new one as the rain started up again. Gad was sprawled on the cushions, staring at the wall, and Zaman paced the room. Neither acknowledged her presence.

She crept out and made a detour to her bedchamber. For the hundredth time, she knelt next to her bed and squeezed her eyes shut. She didn't know how the Nephites prayed, but she did know they prayed a lot—or at least Ammon did.

"Please, God . . . or the Great Spirit who is called God, preserve the king's life. Soften the hearts of Gad and my brother. Preserve Ammon's life that he might fulfill his mission." The back of her throat ached. She couldn't imagine what she'd do if something happened to Ammon—at the hands of her brother, no less.

"O God . . . preserve those I love." She let her head fall into her hands. "Even—even if it means I must give up Ammon." Hot tears burned. She was willing to do it. But did the Nephite God strike bargains? If she made a promise, would He make a promise back? "I'll give up Ammon if it's Thy will . . . even if it means I must marry Gad." Her chest constricted as she held back a choking sob. If God did make bargains, she was ready.

"Elena, are you coming?" her brother's voice sounded through the walls above the rain.

With shaking hands, she wiped her face. She smoothed her hair unconsciously, although she doubted the men would notice her disarray. "Coming where?" she called as she stepped into the hallway.

"To see Ammon fail," Zaman said. "Our plans have been changed. All we need to do is show up at the palace and let Ammon condemn himself. We'll be ready to heed the people's command and get rid of Ammon."

Gad's bitter laugh filled the air as she entered the gathering room.

"I . . ." She looked at the men as they stood in the entryway dressed in their finery. Her brother wore his best cloak, and Gad had thrown on a feathered rendition designed by her father. Both men had swords strapped at their waists. Fear pulsed through Elena at the sight of the weapons. "Yes, I'm coming."

As the men walked out into the drizzle, she took her cloak from the peg by the door and draped it over her head and shoulders as protection from the rain. Her only comfort was that their weapons would be confiscated upon entering the palace. "What about Father?"

Just as she spoke, her father appeared from around the side of the house, already wearing a cloak. He joined them as they hurried across the courtyard. She linked her arm through her father's. He merely nodded at her presence.

On the main road, they joined a throng of people, all heading the same direction—toward the palace. Once they reached the royal courtyard, Elena was amazed to see the numbers gathered there. The mass of people reminded her of the mobs from a few days before when Ammon had defended the king's flocks.

A group of priests had perched on the stairs leading to the palace, calling out condemnation upon Ammon's soul. Pahrun stood near the main entrance, surrounded by guards. At the base of the steps, a row of guards had been stationed to keep the crowd at a distance.

Gad and Zaman pushed their way through, Elena and her father following. As they reached the bottom of the steps, Gad called out to Pahrun. When he saw their group, he motioned for them to come up.

The guards parted then quickly moved together to block some men who tried to follow the small party.

Elena's heart pounded as she ascended the steps. Would the king truly rise? She had to believe. Ammon's very life was at stake. She clung to the words he had spoken to her—that the king was not dead. *He must not be dead.*

To Elena, it proved something that the queen had sent guards to protect Ammon instead of throwing him into prison or otherwise condemning him.

Pahrun greeted their group with a grim smile and opened the doors just enough that they could slip inside the palace. He followed them in after shouting orders to the guards to let not one more soul inside.

"The time is drawing near," Pahrun said. "The Nephite said the king would rise this morning."

"All will be proven soon, then," Gad said, his voice harsh but wary.

"Yes," Pahrun said, casting a triumphant glance behind him. His eyes strayed to Gad's sword, but he said nothing, made no order for him to leave his weapon behind.

Elena's eyes trailed to Gad's side where he kept a hand on the hilt of his sword. Her stomach knotted at the sight, and knowing her brother was armed as well made her wonder if she had enough courage to face what might happen next.

Pahrun moved ahead of their group and led the way. Several corridors later, Elena realized they were not going to the throne room. They walked through a part of the palace she'd never been in. Pahrun slowed when they arrived at a wide hallway. Half of the hallway was filled with people, quietly whispering to each other. By their dress, Elena recognized them as members of the aristocracy. She felt very out of place. She hadn't dressed as her brother and Gad. Even her father wore a fine cloak. Hers was plain, dark, and coarse.

Pahrun bullied his way through the crowd, and the people moved for him as Elena followed with the other men. They entered a spacious room containing several couches and embroidered wall hangings. The area was crowded, but no one was sitting. Through the open doors to the adjoining room, Elena saw the queen and her children kneeling next to a large bed. Upon the bed lay the king.

Elena's eyes widened as Pahrun led her and the men into the king's private chamber. They stopped at an open area just inside the doorway, next to a tapestry-covered wall. Gad and Zaman both kept their hands on their hilts, their eyes fixed on a man standing at the foot of the bed.

She looked to see who'd captured their attention. *Ammon.*

The swelling in his face was gone, and the bruising was barely noticeable. He wore a clean tunic and looked as if he'd bathed recently. He was a different man from what Elena had seen when the pile of arms had been displayed in the throne room. He wasn't smiling, but his whole expression seemed to glow, exuding confidence, his presence filling the room. For the first time in three days, her worry fled, leaving in its place a tangible feeling of assurance.

She wished she could talk to him. Hear his words of comfort. When she realized he still watched her, she flushed, remembering their shared kiss. Then she remembered her bargain with God, and it was as if a cold jug of water had been poured over her head.

Ammon looked at Gad's burly form then back to her, his expression questioning. She swallowed, trying to fight the dryness in her throat. Ammon wouldn't approve of her bargain, but looking again at him and knowing how much she cared for him, she resolved to do what she must.

Ammon's attention shifted. The queen rose and turned to face the assembled people. Quiet rippled through the gathering as she clasped her hands together. "My husband is not dead." She held out her hands, and her children moved to her side. All of their eyes focused on the sleeping king, waiting.

Time seemed to move slowly as everyone waited in silence, watching for any sign of movement. Elena noticed others she recognized in the room—Kumen with the other servants who had been in the fields guarding the flocks, as well as Abish and a few female servants she had seen many times. Her gaze went back to the king but strayed yet again to Ammon. The intensity with which he watched the king brought a lump to her throat. His lips were moving slightly, and she knew he was praying.

The king's hand twitched, and the crowd gasped.

When his eyes opened, one of the servants fainted. Elena groped for her father's arm and held on. Her legs suddenly felt unsteady.

King Lamoni slowly pushed himself up on the bed and swung his legs over the side. He stood and held out his hand to his queen. "Blessed be the name of God, and blessed are you."

The queen cried out with joy. Seeing her expression made Elena's heart nearly burst. The king was alive. Truly alive.

He took a step toward the queen, his hand still outstretched. "For, as sure as you live, behold, I have seen my Redeemer. He will come forth and be born of a woman. And He will redeem all mankind who believe on His name."

Along with the others in the room, Elena was speechless. Warmth traveled the length of her body, from her head to her very toes. The king had seen the

Redeemer in a vision. Tears fell onto her cheeks as the king took another step and grasped his wife's hand. Together they knelt, their expressions filled with joy and wonder.

The room was absolutely still as the people stared at the king and queen. Then Ammon was on his knees, his hands clasped together as he looked at the ceiling. The words coming from his mouth were now audible as he prayed aloud, thanking and praising God.

The king and queen sank to the floor, unconscious, eyes closed, bodies unmoving. Ammon followed, collapsing into unconsciousness.

CHAPTER 14

The Lord preserveth all them that love him: but all the
wicked will he destroy.
—Psalm 145:20

All around Elena in the king's chamber it was as if the servants and people of the court came out of a stupor. The king, the queen, and Ammon were lying on the floor. She knew they weren't dead. They were being taught by the Lord. Murmurings rose as the people questioned what had happened. Elena wanted to tell them what was happening, but she was in a daze, trying to comprehend the sight before her. Kumen cried out to God, raising his hands toward the heavens and asking for the Lord's forgiveness. The other servants who had been with him and Ammon at the fields joined in.

Elena felt a hand pulling her.

"Hurry, before we are struck down too!" Zaman said. "If the evil can overcome the others, we'll be next. We must get help." He had her arm and tugged her out of the room, their father and Gad pushing their way out too.

Elena wanted to resist, to stay in the king's chamber, but she felt weak, as if all her energy had been depleted. Others were leaving, but many of them stayed. As they exited into the hallway, Elena turned to look behind her. Those in the king's chambers had all fallen to the ground. She tugged against Zaman's grip. "They aren't dead," she said.

His expression was a mixture of fury and fear. "You're coming with us."

Her father's hand went to her back, and he helped push her along.

Gad hurried ahead, calling out for the king's guards. Several of them appeared at the end of the hall. "There's a great evil upon the king and his family. All the servants who were in the king's chamber have fallen to the ground."

"No, wait," a woman's voice shouted behind them. Elena turned to see Abish running toward them.

Abish came to a halt in front of them, catching her breath. "I saw you leave with the others," she said, looking from Elena to Zaman. "It *is* the power of God, *not* evil, that caused the king and queen to fall to the earth. They are being taught by the Lord."

Zaman gripped Abish's shoulders. "You have been deceived, Abish," he said in a gentle yet tense voice. "The queen has been tricked by Ammon, and now she has forced her beliefs on you."

"No, Zaman," Abish said, her eyes filling with tears. "You must believe me." She looked at Elena. "They're not dead. There is no evil. The power of God is at hand in that room." She took a deep breath, her pleading expression focused on Zaman. "My father had a vision many years ago, and he taught me the truth."

"You're mad," Zaman spat out, his expression hardened with anger. He dropped his hands from her shoulders.

"Abish is right," Elena said. "Ammon is the Lord's missionary."

Zaman turned his gaze on his sister. "Not you too—" He broke off, his eyes wild. "I forbid both of you from going back in there. You've been tricked by an enemy to our king."

Abish backed away, shaking her head. "You're wrong."

"We must warn the people," Zaman said. "You women, stay here. Father, guard them."

"Zaman, don't do this," Abish said, her voice cracking. "Listen to your heart."

But his expression was dark, cold.

"I'll keep them here," Moriah said, turning his stern gaze on Elena. Although his expression was serious, she saw the hesitation there. Zaman and Gad took off running.

Abish clung to Elena's arm. "They'll spread lies and the people will panic. I must tell them what's really happening." She lowered her voice. "Stay here. Tell those who come the truth."

Elena nodded, her eyes burning. Before her father could react, Abish left at a run in the opposite direction of Zaman.

In the cool hallway, Elena waited with her father. She turned to him. "You must believe, Father. You were in the king's court when Ammon taught us about the true God. You heard with your own ears. You saw the king rise from his bed—just as Ammon said."

"Zaman is right," he said. "There is no other explanation. Ammon has brought evil to our land."

She grabbed his hands. "Why won't you believe?"

"There are reasons we left Zarahemla—I refuse to let our land be taken over by Nephites."

"Ammon doesn't want to rule us," Elena said, her voice turning desperate. If only she could convince her father, he could stop Zaman and Gad's plans. "He's here to teach us about the true gospel."

"That's what he *wants* us to believe," her father said as a guard ran past them, shouting something. Her father watched the guard then turned back and whispered, "Do you know anything about the government in Zarahemla? The Church and the government are one and the same. King Mosiah listens to the prophet Alma more than he does his own advisors. Ammon wants to rule here."

"Then why did Ammon turn down the offer of marriage to the king's daughter?" Elena asked.

Her father went silent.

"You don't have an answer," she said. "It would have been an important part of his plan, *if* he had a plan. Which he doesn't."

"Perhaps it was all part of his manipulation of the king," her father countered.

Elena didn't have time to respond. Around the corner at the end of the hall, several palace guards arrived, escorting a group of priests from the temple. They barely glanced at Elena and her father as they walked by. But she heard their biting words.

One priest, who shuffled in his old age, was the most vocal. "We are paying the price for allowing a Nephite to dwell in our court!"

A guard shot back, "The king brought this evil upon himself for slaying his own servants who let the flocks scatter."

More priests arrived—women among them, the priestesses of the temple. They almost never left their sanctuary, so Elena marveled to see them now. Their spotlessly white tunics were covered by delicate linen robes. Their arms were painted with intricate designs—with paint that never came off. Elena used to think they were beautiful, but now it made her shudder.

Then a voice that Elena knew well came from the end of the hallway. Gad was back with her brother. Several other men were with them—their appearances were rough, beards overgrown, bodies unwashed, kilts stained. They looked as if they'd been in a brawl—black eyes, lacerations, bruises.

"Who are those men?" Elena asked her father.

"They—" He paused, his eyes widening. "They're Loki's friends."

Understanding swept through Elena. These were the men who'd scattered the king's flocks, the men whom Ammon had fought against in the name of the king. At least these were the survivors.

Her father grabbed her arm and pulled Elena out of the way as they passed. Then he tugged her along with him, following Gad's group. They hurried along the corridor until they reached the king's chambers again. The guards and priests were in the king's sitting room, arguing still.

Elena pressed herself against the wall that faced the chambers. The king and queen were still lying on the floor, unconscious, with many servants who had also fallen. Ammon was still on the floor as well.

Gad walked right into the middle of the arguing priests. "Look at all of them. That Nephite caused this."

Everyone's attention went to the king's chamber. "He's a sorcerer, bringing evil to our land!"

One of the injured rebels shouted, "He killed our brethren. He's a Nephite, and the king allowed him to kill our friends with no punishment!"

The arguments broke out fresh again as some argued that Ammon was evil and others blamed the king for the evil in executing his own servants and allowing Ammon to slay the Lamanites. Elena's mind churned. She craned to see Ammon again—hoping he'd wake up and calm these people.

Suddenly, Gad withdrew his sword and held it high in the air. Dread flooded through Elena. He turned in her direction, and their gazes briefly met. Elena's throat constricted at the murderous expression on his face— one of pure rage.

"In the name of the land of Ishmael and in defense of our king," Gad shouted for all to hear. "I will have my revenge on my brother's life."

"No!" Elena shrieked as Gad plunged through the priests and into the king's chamber. But her cry went unheard as Gad rushed toward the prostrate Ammon.

"Ammon!" Elena tried to scream, but the only sound that came out was a strangled cry. She watched in horror as Gad closed the distance between him and Ammon and lifted his sword.

Elena pushed through the priests as panic tore through her body. She had to stop Gad, but it was as if her body had slowed and she was wading through a pond thickened with mud.

Ammon didn't wake, didn't move. With a burst of speed, Gad swung downward, but instead of completing the forward motion, Gad's legs buckled beneath him. He sank to the ground, the sword dropping from his grip. His body landed with an echoing thud in the suddenly silent room.

His head snapped against the floor, and his body went still.

Someone gasped. Elena didn't move as she stared at Gad's body.

Zaman rushed forward and broke the silence. He touched the man's neck then pressed his head against his chest.

Elena held her breath, her pulse pounding throughout her body.

"He's dead!" Zaman's voice strangled out. He turned to look at the mute crowd. "He's dead!" he repeated in a pained voice.

Shock rippled through Elena—how could he be dead? Ammon hadn't touched him. No one had touched him. All around her, the priests and guards backed out of the room, casting furtive glances in Ammon's direction.

Zaman twisted and looked at Ammon's body, his expression mixed with wonder and fear. He scooted away from the sword as if it were a poisonous snake. Slowly, Zaman rose to his feet and backed away. He pointed at Ammon and opened his mouth, but no words came out.

The rebel Lamanites gathered around Zaman, and the murmuring started again. Elena's eyes burned with tears as she tried to comprehend what had happened. Ammon had told her he would be protected by the Lord, that he could only be slain if it was the Lord's will.

Gad couldn't kill Ammon; that was clear. But how had Gad died? Then it struck her—the Lord had protected Ammon; the Lord had struck down Gad.

"He *is* the Great Spirit," someone said, and other voices joined in with agreement. More people were arriving by the moment. Apparently, there were no longer guards blocking the palace entrance.

"No, he was sent by the Great Spirit," someone in the crowd called out.

"He's a monster!" one of the rebels shouted. "How many more will die in his presence?"

"He's been sent from the Nephites to torture us," another called out.

"It's because of our iniquities," a guard said. "Ammon was sent by the Great Spirit to afflict us. This is the Great Spirit who has always attended the Nephites but destroyed the Lamanites."

Elena wanted to cover her ears to shut out all the arguing. It seemed disrespectful to have the helpless, unconscious king and queen lying so close as their people argued over their fate. The crowd had shifted and pushed Elena near the corridor where she could no longer see Ammon's still form.

A warm hand touched hers, and Elena turned. "Abish?"

The woman was out of breath, her face flushed with heat. "What's happening?" Abish asked.

As Elena quickly explained, Abish's expression went from amazement to dismay. "I sent Ammon's accusers here to see for themselves," she said. "But it has not helped." She gripped Elena's hand and pulled her close. "Have the servants awakened?"

"No, not even Ammon."

Eyes brimming with tears, Abish said, "I must go into the chamber. I must tell the people the truth."

"Abish," Elena warned. "These men are looking for someone to blame. If you go in there—"

Abish's hand slipped from Elena's, and before she could finish, Abish had disappeared into the king's chamber.

Elena wended her way through, trying to keep up with her friend. When she squeezed into the bedchamber, Abish was already kneeling next to the queen. The people were hushed, watching what the servant would do next.

As soon as Abish grasped the queen's hand, the queen opened her eyes. The people gasped as the queen smiled and rose to her feet. Abish reached to help her, but the queen's legs were steady, and her eyes shone as she gazed at the people. "O blessed Jesus, who has saved me from an awful hell. O blessed God, have mercy on this people!"

A ripple of warmth shot through Elena. It was as if her very soul were on fire. The queen looked over the heads of the people as she continued to speak, but the next words made no sense to Elena. It seemed that the queen spoke in another tongue, although her face was radiant, making the subject matter clear. The queen was praising God.

She stooped down and took her husband's hand. He opened his eyes, a similar expression of joy on his face. Gasps echoed through the people. He rose to his feet with little effort and gazed over the murmuring crowd. His eyes swept past Elena and then dropped to Gad's body on the floor. The king was quiet for a moment then looked up, comprehension in his eyes.

"Please listen," the king said, his voice soft yet firm. The crowd quieted. "Ammon has brought us the truth, and I have been taught of the Lord. Everything Ammon taught has been confirmed in a vision as I lay upon my bed. God created the world, just as Ammon said, and also created Adam, our first father."

Elena listened as the king recounted the words of Ammon that he'd taught in the throne room. Her skin prickled as the king testified of God and the plan of salvation. Around her, people shifted, and she sensed their restlessness. Looking over at her father, she saw him absorbed in the king's words. But her brother's expression remained closed, dark.

"While you were unconscious, Ammon killed Gad!" Zaman called out.

Ammon woke at that moment. He rose to his feet and stood next to the king. He looked over at Gad's body on the floor. Surprise registered on his face, then he turned his gaze to Zaman.

Several of the rebel Lamanites stepped forward. But Zaman raised his hand and spoke for them. "This Nephite has brought evil upon us. He has slain *your* people. Is there no justice?"

A priest stepped forward. "Ammon has tricked you—tricked the court." He pointed to the servants on the ground for emphasis.

One of them stirred—Kumen. He slowly opened his eyes.

"I have not been tricked," the king said. "My heart has been changed."

Kumen was on his feet. "My heart has changed too. An angel has declared the truth of Ammon's words." His eyes were moist as he gazed at the people. The other servants who had fallen awakened and rose to their feet, making similar declarations.

Elena listened to them all while feeling and hearing the murmurings around her. How could these people not believe what they could see with their own eyes?

Zaman ordered the Lamanite rebels to lift Gad's body, and they carried it out of the room, with Zaman following. Many others left as well—priests, priestesses, guards.

Elena's father turned to her. "We must leave."

"I want to hear what the king and queen have to say."

He hesitated, looking about the room. Those who had been arguing had already left, and those who remained were calmly listening to the king. "Have Abish walk you home, then."

"Thank you, Father," Elena whispered.

"Don't be too long," Moriah said. "There will probably be a ceremony for Gad tonight."

The thought immediately sobered her. She felt a little guilty as she realized she'd been more intent on hearing the revelations of the king and queen than on dwelling on the fact that Gad was gone.

Elena searched the crowd for Abish. She moved to the woman's side, and Abish linked her arm through hers then leaned over and said, "Are you coming to the baptisms tonight?"

"What do you mean?" Elena asked.

"Ammon has invited all the believers to a baptism at the river tonight." She let out a sigh. "I'm going to be baptized—at last!"

Elena tuned back into what Ammon was saying. While she'd been speaking with her father, the king had stopped talking and Ammon had taken over. "Through baptism you enter into a righteous covenant with the Lord," Ammon was saying. "This is the first step in following the Lord's commandments and becoming a righteous people."

Several people clapped for joy.

Abish joined in the clapping. She turned to Elena, searching her eyes. "You must come tonight—we can be baptized together."

"What about Zaman?" Elena whispered.

Abish's expression faltered. "I don't need his permission. He doesn't understand, but I'll help him to—someday."

"I don't think my father would give me permission, especially after what happened to Gad."

"Perhaps it will take a little time for them to accept the truth," Abish said. "But you can still come and watch me be baptized."

Elena thought of Gad's upcoming burial services—she'd be expected to attend. "I don't know. This is all still so new."

"Just look inside your heart," Abish said in a low voice then turned her attention back to Ammon.

I am, Elena wanted to say. Ammon's voice filled her heart. She had seen for herself true miracles. There was no way she could deny who Ammon was or who had sent him to her people.

But the price had been high for her family. As she watched Abish's rapturous expression, Elena wondered how much higher it would go.

CHAPTER 15

*Discern between the righteous and the wicked, between him
that serveth God and him that serveth him not.*
—Malachi 3:18

Elena walked home, Abish at her side. They were both quiet, lost in thought about the amazing things that had just taken place.

"I can't wait to tell Zaman that I'm getting baptized tonight," Abish said.

"Maybe you should wait," Elena said.

"Wait to get baptized?" Abish asked in a surprised tone.

"Either that or wait to tell Zaman. He's very upset about Gad and blames Ammon for his death, as well as Loki's."

Abish blew out a breath. "Gad shouldn't have tried to kill the Lord's servant."

"I know," Elena said, her stomach churning with confusion. "But Gad has become close to my brother and father."

Abish linked her arm through Elena's and slowed their walking. "Zaman will come to know the truth."

Elena refrained from arguing. Maybe Abish knew her brother better than she, but she doubted it. She'd never seen him so angry. He'd spent the last three days plotting Ammon's demise with Gad, and now Gad was dead.

The courtyard looked deserted when the women arrived at the house. Elena wondered where her brother and father had gone, but just as she was saying good-bye to Abish, Zaman came through the gate.

His face was drawn and pale. He focused on Elena, not seeming to notice Abish. "Where've you been?"

His voice was tight, controlled, and Elena's heart plummeted as she sensed the anger there. "I stayed at the king's chamber and listened to what they had to say."

Zaman stepped in front of her, his gaze searing into hers. Suddenly, it was too hot—the afternoon sun seemed to intensify, causing perspiration to form along Elena's neck.

"I thought you were coming with me," he said. "Then I turned and you and father were both gone."

"Father left a little after you. He gave me permission to stay—"

"Father said you begged him to stay," Zaman practically growled. Finally, his eyes went to Abish, but his expression only hardened. "I heard what you said to the people. You were claiming the opposite of what I had told them."

Abish took a step forward, placing her hand on his arm. "Please let me explain. Let's go inside where we can sit down."

"No," Zaman said, shaking her hand off his arm in one swift motion. "Explain to me here. Now."

Abish took a trembling breath but kept her head held high. "What Ammon says is true. All of it. My father had a vision and shared it with me many years ago. When Ammon testified of God in the king's throne room, it was just as my father had taught me." Her eyes shone as she spoke, and her voice was filled with emotion.

Zaman folded his arms across his chest, keeping his eyes narrowed. "You support a lying Nephite who claims that a murderous God is who we should be worshipping? Is this another fable you tell the queen's children?"

"No. This is no story. God has always had His vengeance on the wicked," Abish said in a quiet voice.

Zaman's lips twisted into a sneer. "So Gad and Loki were wicked? In whose eyes?"

"The king's." Abish's voice rose in defense. "Loki was no good—everyone knows it. Why would he be foolish enough to lead a rebel band and try to destroy the king's property? Loki's the traitor. Ammon was just doing his job—defending his life and the king's flocks. And it's obvious that the Lord was on Ammon's side, not Gad's, when Gad tried to kill a defenseless man."

"It was one of Ammon's tricks," Zaman spat out. "Some sort of evil-doing. Maybe he poisoned Gad."

"While he was under the queen's guard or lying unconscious in the king's chamber?" Abish's eyes burned with anger and disbelief.

"He might have bribed someone else to do it," Zaman said. "He has plenty of dogs following him."

Elena flinched at the words. Her heart thudded as Zaman continued his rant.

"I just came from Gad's house. I carried his dead body to his children, who are now *orphans*," he said, all of his anger directed at Abish. "*You* didn't see their expressions of misery. Who will care for them now? A good man has died, and he did nothing but try to avenge his brother's senseless death."

Abish took a step back, shaking her head.

"You've been bewitched, Abish, and now you're influencing my sister with your stories of your father." He took a ragged breath, his eyes wild. "I won't let it happen. Leave my property now. I won't allow my sister to associate with traitors. I left Zarahemla once, and I won't allow it back into my home."

Abish backed away, her eyes glistening with tears. "Zaman—"

"Go!"

She turned and half ran, half stumbled out of the courtyard, banging the gate as she left.

Elena's chest constricted, and she took a gulp of air, but it wasn't enough. She felt faint—the sun, the argument, the emotional turmoil she'd experienced that day.

She turned from her brother and walked numbly toward the house. *Father will make some sense of this.* Tears tugged at her eyes as she thought about Abish. Abish had been so sure Zaman would be supportive. She hadn't even told him about the baptisms.

As she entered the house, she thought of Gad's children and her throat tightened. Gad had made some serious mistakes, and now his children were orphaned. She looked up to see her father standing in the front room, looking out the window. By the look on his face, she knew he'd seen the whole interchange between Zaman and Abish.

He turned toward her, his face pale, his eyes layered with dark circles of sleeplessness.

"Father—" Elena started but was interrupted when her brother burst into the house behind her.

"Gad's funeral is tonight." Zaman's voice was despondent, dull, but his eyes flickered with pain. "I've arranged the service, and he'll be buried next to his brother."

"What do his children need?" Moriah asked in a quiet voice.

"His oldest daughter and her husband are moving back to Gad's for now," Zaman said. He crossed the room, his hands twisting together in agitation. Then he turned to look at Elena.

She wished she could disappear at that instant.

"I don't want you to go anyplace where you might run into Abish," Zaman said, his voice cold.

Elena froze, wondering if she had the courage to battle him. Would this pass? She knew his anger was at its peak—the strain of all that had happened, along with Gad's death, had sent him to the edge of reason. If she was quiet and complacent now, tomorrow, or the next day, she might be able talk to him more sensibly.

But Zaman wanted direct answers now. "Promise me you'll stay away from her and her poisonous words."

"I—" She glanced at her father for help, but his usually warm eyes were steely. "We're all upset, Zaman. Let's discuss this tomorrow." Her pleading voice only seemed to antagonize him further.

"Tomorrow? Tomorrow the king and his cohort—that conniving Nephite—will have all the people bowing at their feet!"

"Ammon isn't conniving."

Zaman's eyes narrowed. "Do not speak that name in our home. He's the worst conspirator of his kind. Coming here and pretending he wants to be a servant. Ha! Did you see how the king was ready to offer his daughter in marriage? It's only a matter of time before he's signaling for the Nephite armies to invade."

Elena had tried to remain calm, but her brother was being absolutely ridiculous. "You're speaking fool's words, Zaman. Ammon is who he says he is. He's not a conspirator—if Loki and the rebels had never come against the king's flocks, he'd still be working in Gad's blacksmith shop."

At the mention of Gad, Zaman's face darkened. "How dare you put the blame on Loki? Next you'll be blaming Gad, just as Abish did."

"Is that why she left?" her father asked.

"She's on that Nephite's side," Zaman answered, but his attention was still on Elena. "Promise me you'll not consort with her or any of the believers."

She shook her head, looking to her father for agreement.

Her father's jaw was set firm. "The city is in upheaval, Elena, and we must keep our bearings. We must cling to what we know, what we've always known. Just because a Nephite comes into the city and persuades the king to believe in a new God doesn't mean we have to follow him. Our people have died."

Elena squeezed her eyes shut to block out the grim gaze of her father. "Who are we, really? Are we Lamanites or Nephites? Ammon says that we are all children of the same God. Why do we always have to be against each other—taking each other's lives, lands, and homes? Why can't we coexist in peace?"

"That's *exactly* what he wants us to believe so we let down our defenses," her father said.

Zaman turned away sharply, as if restraining himself from another outburst. It was just as well for Elena. She'd rather reason with her father anyway.

"Ammon doesn't have a hidden plan, Father. He's speaking the truth. I believe him," her voice trembled, but she didn't care. Zaman had been right. This couldn't wait until tomorrow. "I was there—so were you—I saw the king rise at the appointed time. I heard the queen testify of the Lord. Her words were like a warm rug that covered me from head to toe."

"The king rose from his bed as part of the production," Zaman cut in, whirling around to look at her. "It's part of the trick to convince us to fall under Ammon's spell. He has the king and queen under his control, and they're acting their parts."

"No." Elena brought her hand to her heart. "I can feel the truth in here."

"I won't lose you," her father said in a quiet voice. "Your mother is gone, and all I have left are my children." He took her hand and pressed his lips against it. When he raised his eyes, Elena was torn at the tears she saw in them.

"I love you, and I don't want to see you harmed," her father said, Zaman nodding in the background.

Elena's throat clenched. She loved her father and brother with everything she was. She understood their concern and their protection, but in this case, it was unwarranted.

"Gad is gone," her father continued. "He was to be your husband."

Tears filled her eyes. Not because she wouldn't marry Gad—it seemed his faults were all exonerated upon his death—but because of the loss to his children.

Her father released her hand. "As much as I would miss you, I'd rather send you to serve in the temple than to see you dissuaded by the evil that grows daily in the king's court."

"No—"

"I want you *safe*, Elena," he said. "Happiness will come when you reconcile yourself to your fate."

"Don't send me there," Elena nearly shouted, pulling away from her father.

Zaman's glittering eyes were on her. "Promise us, then. Promise you'll stay away from *him* and all his teachings."

Her father nodded in agreement, and Elena's mind spun. She felt sick. "I can't," she whispered. "I—I want to be baptized into his church."

Zaman barked out a laugh. "And become like sheep. Running in the streets and praising a God we've never heard of until three days ago? There's even talk that the king is forming a new church with Ammon—a church that Ammon will be the head of. Is that what you want? To throw away all of our beliefs and worship Ammon?"

"They aren't worshiping Ammon. They're worshiping—"

"I don't want to hear it, Elena." Zaman's eyes darkened as he studied her. "I've noticed the way you've looked at him. In fact, Gad noticed as well. It was no small coincidence that Ammon threatened Gad's life, then somehow Gad miraculously fell to his death." His voice was full of venom. "You're infatuated with Ammon, aren't you?"

"I'm not infatuated with him," Elena said, her heart pounding in her ears. "I'm in love with him."

Her father and brother stared at her in shock.

"What did you say?" Zaman growled.

"You don't know what you're talking about," her father said nearly at the same time.

"What? That I don't know what love is, or that I couldn't possibly love a Nephite?" Elena's voice trembled.

Zaman raised his hand with fury in his eyes, ready to strike her. Elena backed away.

"I do love him," she choked out, tears spilling onto her cheeks. "I'm sorry it doesn't fit into anyone's plans."

"It will never fit into anyone's plans," Zaman said. "You're under his spell and will do anything to get his attention—even get baptized."

"That's not why I want to get baptized."

Zaman laughed again, sharp and bitter. "If you so much as see that Nephite, speak to him, or even listen to one of his filthy sermons, you'll be locked in the temple faster than you can strap on your sandals." He took a stuttered breath. "And if he steps foot near our property or I hear that he's spoken your name, you will spend the rest of your life in the temple."

"Father," Elena said, turning from her brother's wrath, hoping to find a shred of forgiveness in her father's eyes.

But his gaze was decisive. "Zaman is right. We must keep ourselves completely separated from the fool. When the king comes to his senses, we'll be considered his allies. We've worked too hard to become a part of the society to take any chances now. If we sympathize with Ammon in any way, people will remember *our* Nephite roots. If you take any risks, Elena, you'll pay dearly. And you'll have no one to blame but yourself and your own disobedience."

Zaman's words struck Elena to the core. She had to warn Ammon, tell him that he was forbidden to see her or come near her home. But how?

* * *

The river swirled about Ammon's ankles as he took the first steps into the dark ripples. He turned to see if King Lamoni needed any help walking into the flowing water, but he'd already handed over his cape to a servant and was grinning broadly as he stepped in beside Ammon. The moon provided just enough light to see the larger rocks in the river, but the king had brought along dozens of torches that now lined the riverbank, making it look as if a large festival were taking place.

Ammon's breath caught in his throat as he looked at the gathered crowd on the bank. So many had already committed to baptism. All of the servants who had been in the fields with him that fateful day, including Kumen, were there and many of the queen's servants, including Abish.

On the walk to the river, she'd caught up with Ammon and told him about her father's vision. Ammon had been amazed that this woman had kept the truth to herself for so many years, afraid of being considered a traitor to the Lamanites, although in her heart she knew about the true God.

Nearly bursting with gratitude, Ammon continued walking through the cool water until he reached the center of the river where it rose to his waist. He thought of how he and the king had been in discussion about how best to establish the Church in the land of Ishmael. They'd talked about organizing congregations and building synagogues. Ammon could hardly believe all that was happening and how well the teachings of the Lord were being received by so many. King Lamoni joined him, and

Ammon gazed at those standing along the bank and felt his heart swell. All of those people were waiting to be baptized. It took his breath away. He thought of his brothers and wondered if they had been able to convert any Lamanites, if they'd tasted this sweet reward.

He turned to Lamoni, whose eyes were moist with emotion. They clasped arms. Ammon looked to the heavens, toward the moon and the countless stars. He thought of his forefathers and the stories he'd heard of baptizing multitudes of people. Alma the Elder had baptized hundreds into the Church at the Waters of Mormon. Here, tonight, was Ammon's own Waters of Mormon. Peace flooded through him. The words that had been passed down from priest to priest, generation to generation, came to him.

"O Lord," he cried out, "I pray that Thou wilt pour out thy Spirit upon Thy servant, that he may do this work with holiness of heart."

He took a steadying breath as emotion rocked through him. The crowd on the riverbank was completely silent; even the river seemed to grow quieter, more reverent.

"Lamoni, king of Ishmael, I baptize thee, having authority from the Almighty God, as a testimony that you have entered into a covenant to serve Him until you are dead as to the mortal body."

Lamoni exhaled, his grasp firm on Ammon's arm.

"May the Spirit of the Lord be poured out upon you," Ammon said, his voice trembling. "And may He grant unto you eternal life, through the redemption of Christ, whom He has prepared from the foundation of the world."

Ammon strengthened his grip on the king as he plunged Lamoni into the cool water. When Ammon pulled the king back up, they both smiled at each other.

Lamoni embraced Ammon, soaking his torso.

"Thank you, my friend," Lamoni said, his voice thick. He turned to the crowd and lifted his hands. "Praise be to the Lord!"

The people cheered. The king strode to the bank, extending his hand to his wife. She stepped into the river and let her husband lead her to Ammon.

"The queen desires to enter the waters of baptism," Lamoni said as he handed her off to Ammon.

Ammon took the queen's delicate hand and began again.

Following the queen, Ammon baptized each of their children, Pacal, Romie, and Meztli. Then, one after another, Ammon baptized the people.

Many embraced him, and others hurried back to the waiting arms of friends and family. Throughout the evening, Ammon couldn't help but look for Elena. She'd been in the king's chamber when he'd talked about baptism and the establishment of the Church. He knew she believed. But he also knew she was obedient to her family.

A woman stepped into the water, making her way toward him with a broad smile. It was Abish. By the time she reached him, tears were on her cheeks, but her smile was unwavering.

Ammon took her hand, meeting her smile with his own. Abish's face glowed with excitement. A lump formed in Ammon's throat as he thought of how long she'd waited for this moment.

Following Abish's baptism, the king took his family back to the palace. There were only a few remaining now, since most of the people had gone home.

Ammon baptized the last of those waiting on the riverbank. Only as he finished the final baptism of the night did he realize how exhausted he was. The strength of the Spirit had maintained him over the past few days, and even during the sleepless nights, he'd had stamina. But as he walked out of the river for the final time, his legs barely held him up.

Kumen waited on the bank with a large rug that Ammon gratefully accepted. "Thank you."

"No, my friend, thank *you*," Kumen said. A couple of torches remained, casting a faint orange glow on their faces. "What you've done will change the land of Ishmael forever. I only wish my brother could have been baptized as well."

"The Lord will take care of him," Ammon said. "He was a good man."

Kumen nodded, falling silent for a moment. "Let's get you back to the hut before you get any colder."

Ammon shivered beneath the rug. He was tired, yes, but he knew his mind wouldn't rest for a while. "Go on without me. I'll be there soon. I'd like to stay out here for a while longer."

Worry crossed Kumen's face. "There are many who voiced their distrust against you—I don't think you should be alone."

"Don't you think that if it were the Lord's will that I die, it would have happened sometime in the last three or four days?" Ammon said.

"You're right." Kumen chuckled. He bade farewell to Ammon then moved up the bank and onto the path that led back to the community of servant huts.

Ammon watched his retreating figure, mixed emotions pulsing through him. Tonight had been incredible, and he was overwhelmed with the number he'd baptized. Just performing the baptismal ordinance had confirmed again to Ammon the decision to come to the Lamanite people and teach the gospel.

He found a grassy spot on the sloping bank and sat down, pulling the rug about him. He wasn't that cold anymore, but a breeze had picked up. He wished he could have shared his triumphs with his brothers. His throat tightened as he thought about Aaron, Omner, and Himni. The idea of them working and teaching among the Lamanite people, just as he was, had brought him comfort many times. Yet, even with the incredible success that Ammon had met, there was still some serious resistance. He knew that each of his brethren had certainly met with their own triumphs and losses.

His reflections turned to prayer until he was praying in his heart for the welfare and safekeeping of those he loved, both the missionaries and the family he'd left behind in Zarahemla. He prayed for those who didn't come tonight to be baptized, that their hearts would be softened. He prayed that he and King Lamoni would be directed in how best to establish the Church throughout the land. Then he prayed for the one woman he'd particularly hoped to see tonight on the riverbank.

Several moments later, he opened his eyes and watched the moving river. Something sounded behind him, and he turned to see a figure walking through the trees above. Ammon scrambled to his feet, wondering if someone else wanted to be baptized but had come too late. The alternative might be someone who wanted to harm him, but he'd take the risk.

"Wait!" he called out. The figure paused then continued walking. "Elena?"

It looked like her, but he couldn't be positive. Sand-colored hair gleamed in the moonlight, and the woman seemed about the right height.

"Elena?" he called out again as he sprinted up the bank. The woman stopped again. This time she turned.

"Did you just get here?" he asked as he strode up to her. He noticed the tears in her eyes. "What's wrong?"

She looked down, avoiding his gaze.

She might be late, but at least she came. "There will be more baptisms later this week." Ammon hesitated. "Did you come to be baptized?"

She lifted her eyes to his. "I can't."

His body went cold. He knew she believed; he could *feel* it even now. He could barely get the question out. "Why not?"

She looked past him as if trying to muster the courage to speak. "My family is against it, you're preaching, as you've probably guessed. They've been deeply wounded by Gad's and Loki's deaths." Her desperate gaze finally met his. "I shouldn't even be here. If my father and brother knew I was out here talking to you—"

"Elena," he broke in. "I'm very sorry lives were lost when I was defending the king's flocks."

"I know," she said. "It's not just Loki and the other rebels."

"I had nothing to do with Gad's death," Ammon said. "You must recognize that it was the Lord's doing."

Her voice was a whisper when she answered, "I know that too."

He put his hands on her shoulders. "Then listen to me, Elena." She glanced up at him but looked quickly down again. "You can make your *own* choice about the Church. I won't force you to be baptized, just as your father and brother shouldn't force you to *not* be baptized. It's your choice, not *theirs*."

She shook her head. "You don't understand. They provide my home, my food, everything. I love them, and they're my family. I can't betray them—even if it means going against what I most desire."

"Is baptism what you desire?" Ammon asked.

"Yes," she said, finally lifting her gaze to meet his. Her eyes were wet again. "I want to be baptized, to covenant with God, and to have the blessings the king and his family will have."

Relief filled Ammon. She did want to be baptized. He lifted a hand from her shoulder and smoothed the hair that cascaded along her back. "I'll speak to your family," he said in a soothing voice. "When the pain of Gad's death is lessened, they'll listen to the truth."

"No," Elena said in a rush, her eyes widening. "They can't know I've spoken to you tonight . . . after . . . after they've forbidden me to."

"I won't tell them I spoke with you."

"They'll know," she said. "If you come, they'll know, and I'll be punished."

His stared in disbelief. "What do you mean, *punished?*"

"My brother said he'll send me to the temples where I'll be made a priestess."

Anger surged through Ammon. "A priestess? But—"

"I know. I don't want that. It's considered an honor and brings wealth to the family, but how could I? Especially since I know about the true Church."

Ammon clenched his jaw, angry at Zaman all over again. "Why would they threaten to make you a priestess? Just to keep you from getting baptized?"

"Not just that," she said, her tone reluctant.

"Then what?" Ammon tried to read her expression, but she kept her eyes averted. He waited for her to answer, wondering what else her family was afraid of.

Finally she spoke, her voice barely above a whisper. "I told them that I was in love with you."

Her words thundered into his heart. He stared at her, at a loss.

"I should have never said something like that to my father and brother, but they dragged it out of me. They say it's the real reason I want to be baptized. They can't believe that the Great Spirit is God or that I've felt His presence. They said if they see you at our home or they hear that you've spoken my name or even that you've looked at me from across the crowd, they'll send me to the temples." She paused to take a breath. "They only think I'm infatuated with you."

She let out a frustrated sigh and closed her eyes for an instant. Ammon's pulse was throbbing wildly, but he still didn't speak, trying to absorb everything she'd said—that she loved him, that she'd told her family.

"But I'm not . . . *infatuated* with you. I know . . . I love you." Her eyes were moist, and her voice trembled as she continued. "I also know that I can't ever marry you. You're a prophet—you're going to be the leader of the Church in all the land—you're royalty whether you claim the throne or not. And . . . my family despises you." She was crying now. "And I'm sorry I kissed you. It was wrong of me. You probably see me as a temptress, as one more trial to overcome as you fulfill the Lord's mission." She turned away, hands covering her face. "Good-bye, Ammon."

He reached out to stop her, but she fled from him, her cloak billowing behind her.

He shed the heavy rug about his shoulders, knowing he'd have to catch her before she got to the main road, before anyone could see them together and report back to her family.

She was quicker than he expected and had a good lead already. His exhausted body slowed him down even more. But he pushed his limbs to the limit, increasing the pace of his strides, until he caught up with her.

She shrieked when he grabbed her waist. When he spun her around, she was still crying.

"Elena," he said in a winded voice as he wrapped his arms around her and pulled her against him. She stiffened, but after a few seconds, her arms went around his waist. They stood together for several moments, hearts pounding from running, each of them trying to catch their breath.

She started to pull away, but Ammon kept his hold. "Don't run away from me again," he murmured into her hair. "I'm going to be a missionary the rest of my life. I don't expect the Lord means for me to never marry. But I have no home, no way to provide for a family except by the labor of my own hands at the mercy of others. I'm at the direction of the Lord as to where I'll live and whom I'll serve."

"I know."

He drew away and lifted her chin until she was looking at him. "I don't have all the answers right now. But I do know I feel the same way about you."

Her eyes widened.

"Don't look so surprised." A smile tugged at his mouth. "I love you too." Her lips softened into a shy smile.

"Whatever happens," he said, his tone serious, "know that I didn't come here with any thoughts of marriage until I met you. My heart was bent toward service and not taking any rewards for myself."

"Is that why you turned down the king's invitation to marry his daughter?"

"One of the reasons," Ammon said. "I didn't want the king to think I was here for a political alliance, which the marriage would have become." He hesitated. "Also, I didn't want to marry someone I didn't love." He ran his fingers along her cheek. She leaned into his palm and closed her eyes.

"But it won't work between us either, will it?" she said in a quiet voice.

"Don't give up yet, Elena. I need to consult with the Lord."

Her eyes blinked open, and he saw worry in them.

"I think I know His answer already," she said, her voice dull.

"You'd be surprised at how merciful the Lord is." He smiled gently. "He wants His children to be happy, even a Nephite missionary like me." He raised his other hand and touched her other cheek so that he was cradling her face. "The Lord knows I love you."

Her eyes widened again, and Ammon grinned. He could hardly believe he could tell her now, but then again, he could hardly believe he'd waited until she said it first.

"Can you wait for me . . . to ask the Lord?" he asked, his gaze intent on hers.

She let out a slow breath, her eyes questioning. "I'll wait. But how will I know when you get the answer?"

"I'll find a way to contact you," he said.

A small smile touched her lips. He slowly released her and twisted the ring from his finger. His heart pounded as he thought of the meaning of the ring. It represented his lineage and his claim to the Nephite throne. But his heart pounded even harder when he thought of the woman he wanted to wear it.

Elena watched him, curiosity in her expression. With his right hand, he untied one of his armbands and removed the thin strip of leather that wound around his upper arm several times. He slipped the ring onto the strip then tied the ends of the leather together, creating a simple necklace.

He raised the necklace and placed it over Elena's head. She lifted her hair out of the way, and the ring settled onto her chest. She blinked up at him, fresh tears in her eyes.

"So you don't forget whom you're waiting for," he said.

A smile blossomed on her face.

"And . . . I also want you to be clear that I'm *not* sorry you kissed me," he said.

He cradled her face with his hands again and leaned down, gauging her reaction. When her eyelids fluttered shut and she lifted her face, he closed the distance. He touched his lips against hers, lightly at first, then deeply as she responded by wrapping her arms around his neck and pulling him closer.

CHAPTER 16

It is better to trust in the Lord than to put confidence in man.
—Psalm 118:8

He said he loves me, Elena thought, trailing her hand along the tree branches. A branch snapped back into place behind her.

"Shhh!" Zaman hissed, walking several paces from her as they searched for a quetzal nest.

But Elena hardly paid attention to her brother. *Ammon said* the Lord *knows he loves me*, she clarified in her mind. Coming from Ammon, that was probably the highest compliment he could pay. *And I'm wearing his promise.* She lifted a hand to her chest and touched the concealed ring that hung from a thin leather strap beneath her tunic.

Her cheeks burned, and her heart raced as she thought about Ammon and his words to her the night before.

"There," Zaman pronounced.

He'd interrupted her thoughts, and Elena looked up. In a high tree towering overhead, they could see a nest peeking through the leaves.

Zaman brought a finger to his lips as Elena studied the position of the nest. A long green-feathered tail extended over the side.

Zaman motioned for her to go around to the other side of the tree as he climbed the lower branches.

She crept quietly to her position and laid the net on a fern at her feet. Then she carefully pulled out an arrow and waited for her brother's signal. When he was nearly halfway up the tree, he lifted his hand and motioned over his head. He wanted her to aim above the nest, to hopefully cause the quetzal to fly downward into one of their waiting nets. Zaman braced himself against the trunk, his feet perched on the branches and a net stretched between his hands.

Elena let the arrow fly, and it crashed through the leafy branches above the nest.

The male bird squawked and tore out of the tree, its feathers a blur of color. This time, Elena was ready with her net raised in the air, her focus solely on the flying bird. She nearly stumbled and let go of the net as the quetzal flew into it and struggled furiously.

In a matter of seconds, her brother had dropped out of the tree and thrown a second net over the writhing bird. His jaw set in a determined line, and he wrestled the bird until he held it firmly and had tied its beak.

From his kneeling position on the ground, he looked up at Elena, a triumphant grin on his face. "Well done."

Elena smiled back, the praise warming her temporarily.

"These will be the final feathers needed for the king's cloak. We need to have it ready by tomorrow to present to Abish. The Moon Festival is only a week away. Although the king has made some foolish decisions, we need to stay in his good graces. The aristocracy will continue buying from us if the king does."

Elena wondered if she'd be able to go to court with her brother and father to deliver the festival clothing. Ammon was sure to be there. She envisioned Ammon's warm eyes in her mind, and she smiled.

"What?" Zaman asked.

"Nothing," Elena said, forcing herself to appear sober. "Can I help with the cloak?"

"We'll ask Father. You know he's been very particular about the king's wardrobe."

Elena followed her brother out of the thick of the jungle. She absently kept her hand at her chest, touching the necklace that lay beneath her tunic. Her brother looked back at her a time or two with a puzzled look on his face. She dropped her hand and tried to look more somber so he wouldn't become suspicious.

As they reached the main road, she pulled a scarf over her head. It was the color of charcoal to signify that she was in morning. Zaman also wore a belt of the same dark color. They would dress this way for seven days to honor Gad.

Elena pushed away the guilt she felt rising within her. In the jungle, among the trees and birds, her confidence had increased. The likelihood of Ammon marrying her seemed possible. But here, along the main road, heading back to her home, she felt as if she were entering prison.

She'd always been happy to stay home for the most part, but now that she was being forced to and Zaman or her father constantly had her under their watch, home was a prison, one that blocked out two people she loved—Abish and Ammon.

She lagged behind Zaman until he hurried her along, impatience in his voice. She increased her pace after that and even reached the courtyard gate before him. As soon as she reached the gate, her father came hurrying out of the house, his expression troubled.

"I have news," her father said, looking from one to the other. "Come inside after the bird is taken care of."

Elena followed her father inside, while Zaman secured the quetzal in the cage in the back courtyard. He joined them in the gathering room, his expression wary.

Her father was pacing, clenching his hands together. As soon as Zaman entered, their father spun and said, "The king isn't attending the Moon Festival, and neither is the rest of his family."

It took a few seconds for the news and its impact to settle in. Elena opened her mouth to ask questions, but Zaman jumped ahead of her.

"No one in the family is going?" Zaman asked. "But what about the ceremonial clothing we made?"

Her father's face paled as he sank onto a cushion. He brought his fists in front of him. "There will be no ceremonial clothing." He raised his gaze, his eyes rimmed in red. "We've lost our commission."

"For everything?" Zaman asked, his voice belligerent.

"Not for everything. At least . . . I don't know yet. The family still has all the unworn clothing they were supposed to wear to the High Feast." Moriah let out a frustrated sigh. "There will certainly be more occasions, but if he ignores this one, what about the next festival after that?"

Elena rubbed her forehead. The news couldn't be as grave as it seemed. "Perhaps the king will purchase the clothing since it is ready, and we won't lose the cost invested."

"Perhaps," her father muttered, but his fists remained clenched together, his expression wan.

"It's Ammon," Zaman growled. "If it weren't for his stories and distractions, the king and his family would be preparing for the festival. We'd have our compensation this week."

"The Jaguar Feast is in one moon's time," Elena said, thinking of when the king would want to wear new ceremonial clothing.

"For the *Jaguar Temple*," Zaman shot out. "The Jaguar priests are not members of the king's new church. If Ammon has his way, that's another god cut out of our traditions. The king will probably remain in his customary kilt on that day and not attend the festival. No need for the jaguar headdress, feathered cape, or luxuries for the queen. No need for your designs, sister."

Elena's face stung as if she'd been slapped. Her brother was right on one level, but certainly all was not lost. The king might still desire the costumes her family created—there were many other uses.

"I know what you're thinking," Zaman said, turning on her. "But you are wrong. The king won't want the costumes at all now. Ammon is to blame. It's just one more thing that he has tricked the king into. Now do you think accepting Ammon's word is worth the price?"

He crossed to his father and put a hand squarely on his shoulder, his fiery gaze still on Elena. "With one event, Ammon has endangered the Lamanites and has stolen our family's occupation—our legacy that we were to pass down to our children, one that Father has spent years building up." He wrinkled his nose in disgust. "What else is Ammon planning on taking from us?"

"We'll consult with the king and ask what type of clothing he'll now require," Elena said. "We haven't been replaced by any other clothiers. We're still in his good graces; surely he won't cast us off for any reason."

"Unless that reason is a conniving Nephite who wears nothing but plain tunics."

Before Elena could reply, someone rapped at the door. Zaman's eyes narrowed, but he didn't move, so Elena rose and crossed to the door to open it.

A short man waited there, his arms and torso thick and muscled. It was Dedan, Zaman's friend who was a border guard. He was armed, as usual, with a sword strapped to his side as if he'd just left his position. She wondered why he was at her doorstep instead of at his guard post.

"I'll fetch my brother," Elena said by way of a greeting. "Would you like to come inside?"

"No thank you," Dedan said in a noncommittal voice. "I'll wait for Zaman out here." He averted his eyes as if he were trying to avoid her gaze. She shrugged and turned to call Zaman. He came into the hallway and pushed past her without a word.

He and Dedan walked into the courtyard together.

Elena went back into the gathering room. Her father had stood as well and was going out the back door. She took off her scarf, grateful for the movement of air again.

Curious, she looked out the window as Zaman and Dedan crossed the courtyard and went around the side of the house.

She walked through the hallway and peeked out the back entrance just as her father met them in the back courtyard. There was some discussion, and her father went into the workshop.

Zaman disappeared into the workshop for a moment and returned with a sword. Dedan withdrew his own sword, and the two entered what seemed to be a serious discussion. Then the two friends started to spar.

Elena knew it was friendly, but it still made her nervous to watch. Every once in a while, they'd stop and Dedan would instruct Zaman on a better movement. Dedan had been well trained, and he was teaching Zaman.

The pit in Elena's stomach grew by the moment. Why would Zaman choose now to brush up on his sword fighting? Did this have something to do with the costumes the king no longer required? But Dedan couldn't have known about the costumes. Then a sickening feeling hit her. Was her brother planning another attack on Ammon? She shook her head, muttering to herself. He wouldn't dare. No one would dare after what happened to Gad and Loki—would they?

With her pulse drumming, she stepped into the courtyard. Zaman and Dedan didn't pay her any attention. She stood, watching them with her arms folded. Finally, they broke, and Zaman barely glanced at her. "Go help Father, Elena."

She didn't move. "What are you doing?"

Zaman lifted his sword, still not looking at her. He lunged toward Dedan, who easily avoided the weapon. "Leave us."

"Why?"

"Elena, go help Father."

Her cheeks burned, but she wanted to hear it from him. "What are you planning, Zaman?"

Dedan's sword came crashing against Zaman's. Her brother blocked the blow, but it was a lucky block. His arm gave out long before Dedan's did.

"Let's try that again," Zaman said, keeping his determined gaze on Dedan.

"You'll never be his match," Elena said in a quiet voice.

Zaman didn't respond, but she knew he heard her. Dedan glanced over, his eyes full of guilt.

So Dedan did know Zaman's plan. And it had been planned *before* Zaman knew about the lost commission.

She swept past the men and stepped into her father's workshop. Her father had already started to reorganize the costumes. If he was surprised to see her instead of Zaman, he didn't say anything. It appeared he knew about and supported Zaman's foolish plans.

Why am I the last to know? Then again, why am I even surprised?

Her father handed over a cape that would belong to one of the king's sons. Long green feathers made up most of the cape, but at the top, he'd started to sew in a row of soft white feathers.

"We need to remove the top row of feathers. An aristocrat's son might like less decoration."

Elena's hands trembled as she took the cape. She examined the type of stitches her father had made. They were very small and neat. It would take hours to undo them. "Father?"

"Hmm?"

"What is Zaman planning?"

He refused to meet her eyes. "Just finish the cape."

She let out a breath of frustration, but her father kept his head bent over the headdress he'd turned his attention to.

In her heart, she had wished—no, prayed—that Zaman's temper would cool, that he'd see reason. During Gad's funeral, she'd shed plenty of tears, but on the others' faces she'd only seen anger. Zaman's included.

She'd hoped that a new day might soften his resolve a little. If anything, it had just strengthened it. In the jungle, he'd almost seemed his old self, but now, she understood that he'd been calculating, expecting Dedan to be at their home when they were finished. The lost commission had only added to Zaman's vendetta.

When is he planning to attack? Elena wanted to know. Who else was involved? Obviously, Dedan and her father knew. How many would Ammon have to fight against?

He was protected under the king now. Not only did the Lord seem to protect him at every turn, but the king and queen were also devoted to him.

I shouldn't worry, Elena thought. But she did. More now than ever. Would her brother be struck down just as Gad? Or maybe there would be a terrible sword fight. She knew her brother would be at the losing end. Why did he keep trying to fight against the truth?

Elena had difficulty concentrating on unpicking the tiny feathers on the upper collar of the cape. Her fingers felt clumsy and thick, and they slipped twice, giving her needle wounds that throbbed.

"Father," she finally said, ready to scream if she didn't break the silence. "Zaman will be killed."

She'd caught his attention, and he lifted his head, blinking.

"You know he's no match for Ammon," she pressed.

"It's not a question of whether he'll win or lose," her father said. "It's a question of honor."

"For whom? Gad is dead—Gad went to avenge his brother, and now they're both dead," Elena said. "Will Zaman do the same? When does it end? How many fools will die before they understand?"

Her father's face reddened.

Elena's mouth felt parched. Perhaps she'd gone too far. But it was the truth, and she had to speak it.

"Your brother will not rest until he's done what he thinks is right."

"What he *thinks*?" she asked. "Father, I *know* this is wrong, no matter how many ways Zaman looks at it. If Ammon were in the wrong, the king would have him punished. Zaman isn't the law. He's being disloyal by going against the king."

"The king will thank him later, when the trance Ammon holds over him is broken. And that can only be accomplished through Ammon's death." Her father's tone grew urgent. "You must forget him, Elena. You're perhaps too young and innocent to understand the consequences of your actions if you stand in the way of your brother."

Elena gritted her teeth. Her father was on Zaman's side, through and through.

She bent over her work, blinking rapidly so her vision wouldn't cloud with her stinging tears. Her brother and now her father were making it more and more difficult to choose. How could she choose between her own family and the man she loved? She hoped it wouldn't come to that. But with each passing hour, the possibility seemed more and more likely.

CHAPTER 17

Blessed is the man that trusteth in the Lord, and whose hope the Lord is.
—Jeremiah 17:7

One Week Later

Ammon greeted the congregation as he stepped beneath the large canopy. Nearly one hundred people had gathered to hear his message. It was astonishing to see all of the eager faces lifted toward him and smiling at him.

It had been a week since the night of the first set of baptisms—a week since he'd met with Elena and told her to wait for him to get his answer from the Lord. Each morning and night he'd petitioned the Lord, and he had yet to receive a confirmation.

But Ammon tried to stay confident that the Lord would answer in due time. Ammon only wished he could speak with Elena and console her so she didn't worry. And he still hoped to see her at one of the meetings— signifying that her family had softened their hearts.

Meanwhile, he was careful to stay away from Elena's homestead. He didn't want to give fuel to any rumors. He suspected Zaman had contacts in many places.

As he stepped on the platform at the front of the assembly, the crowd quieted. Although there were many children in the audience, they, too, seemed to be paying attention. His gaze landed on Abish in the front row. Her familiar face created a pang in his heart.

She offered a wan smile, as if she understood the thoughts running through his mind.

Ammon scanned the crowd, seeing mostly people he didn't know. At the base of the platform, Kumen waited for any summons. He'd been assigned to travel with Ammon throughout the land and share his witness of Ammon's words.

As he did at the beginning of every teaching opportunity, Ammon spoke about the Creation of the earth and taught about the heavens where God and His holy angels dwelled.

The congregation nodded as he taught them how each person was created in the image of God. After speaking about the creation of Adam and teaching the significance of the fall of man, he invited Kumen to join him on the platform.

Kumen had been nervous the first few times, but now he spoke with seasoned confidence. "Many of you have heard about the three days King Lamoni was overcome by the Spirit of the Lord. I was there when it happened. I saw him fall to the ground, and I saw him rise up and testify of Jesus.

"What many of you don't know is that the second time the king and the queen were overcome by the Spirit, I was as well. I sank to the ground and had a wonderful vision. An angel appeared to me and taught me about the plan of redemption—the very plan that Ammon will now teach you."

Kumen stepped aside, and Ammon moved forward again.

As he spoke to the people about the plan of redemption and how it was prepared from the very foundation of the world, he could see the Spirit working upon the congregation. The peace and warmth was palpable. Tears streamed down many people's cheeks, and most sat with their hands clasped together, intently listening.

As Ammon concluded, he had tears in his own eyes when he asked, "Who would like to join the Lord's Church and be baptized in His name?"

Nearly every hand shot up. A flood of emotion coursed through Ammon.

Someone at the back of the congregation stood and began to clap loudly. At first, Ammon thought it was a joyous new member, but the man broke away from the crowd and walked along the perimeter of the group, still clapping.

"Well done, Nephite!"

It was Pahrun. His cape was a brilliant yellow, almost blinding in color. He strode toward Ammon. "You've managed to recruit dozens more people, leading them into your lair."

Ammon's mouth dropped open. He hadn't seen or heard from Pahrun since the king's revival. Pahrun hadn't been baptized, but Ammon hadn't realized he was one of the rebels working against the Church and the king.

His wardrobe didn't seem to suffer any.

More astonishing was who followed Pahrun as he walked—Zaman and several other Lamanites.

"Wait, my people!" Pahrun said, his voice booming over the murmuring in the crowd. "Wait and consider carefully. Do not be dissuaded by this stranger—this man who came into our land under false pretenses. I was there when he first crossed the palace threshold. I was there to examine his goods—and do you know what he carried with him? All manner of weapons. More daggers than any man could use in a lifetime."

He had the attention of the crowd now. "He didn't come in peace. He came to fight. He came to steal your hearts away, weaken you, then attack." Pahrun's cold gaze pierced Ammon. "In fact, I had to force his own name out of him—it was a like a dirty confession. You should have seen it. If I hadn't recognized the royal emblem of Zarahemla on his ring, we might have never known his true identity."

Ammon felt as if he were facing a raging fire as he watched Pahrun's advancement. But it was the man behind Pahrun that drove the most pain through his heart. Zaman. Had he fallen so far already? He'd been vocal enough when Gad had died, and he'd forbidden his sister from getting baptized. Yet, as far as Ammon knew, Elena had been obedient to her family.

He looked from Pahrun to Zaman. Three other men stood with them, and they looked familiar, but Ammon didn't know their names. As the crowd cleared to let them through, he saw their brandished swords.

Kumen immediately drew his dagger and moved in front of Ammon.

"No," Ammon said in a quiet, commanding voice, moving to the side of his friend. "I will face them and answer their accusations."

"This could be a bloodbath," Kumen said, his voice strained. "Women and children are here—"

"Pahrun is right," Ammon said in a loud voice that sailed beneath the palm canopy, his gaze locked on Pahrun. "I had wished to serve the king without being treated any differently than any other servant. I was afraid my identity would affect the way some people viewed me. It's proved to be quite true, apparently."

Before Pahrun could respond, Ammon continued. "Pahrun is also right that I carried many weapons with me. An overindulgence on my part, I'm afraid. I had no idea what to expect while traveling in the wilderness, and although I'm quite handy with a sword, I knew that smaller weapons would be more effective in securing a meal of a rabbit or squirrel."

The people nodded their agreement while Pahrun's face went red.

Ammon stole a glance at Zaman, whose expression was almost blank. It was as if no emotion flowed through the man's body. He was simply following Pahrun.

Gazing back at Pahrun, Ammon added, "I did not mean to hide my identity exactly but perhaps delay it a bit until the time was right to share more information with the king."

"You came here to weaken our defenses against our enemies," Pahrun said through gritted teeth.

"Pahrun," Ammon said, "I don't want to fight. I came in peace, and that hasn't changed."

"You don't want to fight, or you aren't able?" Pahrun said. "Where is your mighty sword or your crafty sling? When your weapons are scarce, you suddenly claim peace."

"I will not fight you, Pahrun. Say what you will."

Kumen stepped in front of Ammon, his dagger raised. "But *I* will fight."

Several men in the front row formed a line below Ammon, daggers drawn. "We'll fight too."

Pahrun's gaze went from Ammon and the men assembling to defend him. "I refuse to battle against my own people. They may be tricked—but they'll come to know the truth soon enough." Pahrun took a step back. "This I can promise, Ammon, prince of Zarahemla: you will not live to see another full moon."

* * *

Elena pulled the scarf over her head, securing the dark cloth beneath her chin. Her heart hammered as she crept out of her room. She couldn't risk bringing a lamp or a light of any kind. Tonight she must rely solely on the moon.

The visit by Abish earlier that evening had been a great risk to them both. Abish knew about Elena's confinement, but she didn't think this could wait. Abish was right. Even though Pahrun's threat to Ammon was that he wouldn't live to see the next full moon, she agreed with Abish that the men would act quickly so that no one would be ready.

So Elena made herself ready and refused to fall asleep. The reward came when, well after the moon had reached its zenith, she'd heard whispered voices in the courtyard. She peered out her window to see the silhouettes of several men, and her heart nearly stopped at the sight.

They were hard to distinguish in the dim light, but she was certain that one was her brother and another was Dedan.

Tonight, she exhaled. *They're doing it tonight.*

With a shaking hand, she removed the dagger she kept beneath her bed and strapped it to her waist. With her scarf secure, she slipped out of the house, hoping her father wouldn't awake and look in on her. He hadn't for many years, but if he should choose to do so tonight . . .

The men had already disappeared into the night, but Elena could guess where they were going. And if not, then this would be a wonderful time to be mistaken.

Oh, Abish. Thank you for your warning. The woman's dark, pain-filled eyes seemed to float before her. Zaman had refused to speak about Abish, and neither woman knew if there was marriage in the future. He hadn't officially cancelled the betrothal, but it was almost as if he had.

Elena hurried as fast as she dared, trying not to stumble or trip along the jungle path. The moonlight was spotty at best, seeming to weave in and out of the shadows at will. *Please, Lord, protect Ammon.* She took a deep breath, trying to put her confidence in Ammon's God.

But that promise didn't necessarily transfer to Ammon's friends—Kumen or even the king or queen. A new thought of terror entered Elena's mind. What if her brother were planning on assassinating someone other than Ammon? She wouldn't be able to stop it. She couldn't even get close to the palace without the proper escort.

She resolved to go to Ammon's hut first—to give him the warning.

Once she reached the circle of huts, she waited for several moments in the protection of the trees. The place was so quiet. No movement or light came from anyone. She looked again at the moon as it cast its silent witness downward.

She crept around the buildings until she reached Ammon's hut. She was afraid to step out into the moonlight and knock on the reed door. But she had to warn him somehow. She scooped up a handful of pebbles and tossed them onto the thatch roof. It would sound like rain from the inside, but perhaps Ammon or Kumen would realize it wasn't raining.

Three men exited the hut almost immediately, carrying swords. For an instant, she worried that it was her brother's band—already finished with their foul deed. But when Elena recognized Ammon's fair skin and two of the king's guards, she wavered between running into Ammon's arms and hiding completely. She settled for standing where she was and waiting for him to spot her. It took him only seconds. He motioned for the guards to remain where they were, and then he was at her side.

"What are you doing here?" His expression was a mixture of worry and joy. He resheathed the sword at his waist.

"Zaman's plotting something against you. He might be coming tonight."

He took her hand and led her around the side of the hut, out of the direct gazes of the guards. Ammon stopped and scanned her from head to toe, as if checking for injuries. "I'm not worried about Zaman. Are *you* all right?"

She bit her lip. "I'm all right, except for having to stay at home all the time. And not seeing you," she finished in a whisper. She peered up at him, her heart tumbling as she realized how much she'd missed him. Now that he stood in front of her, it was as if she missed him even more. She never wanted him to release her hand. But maybe what had happened between them had all been in her head. After all, it had been more than a week since their last meeting. Maybe things had changed.

Ammon lifted his other hand and smoothed a piece of hair that had escaped her scarf. Her skin felt as if it would burst into flames. His hand strayed to her cheek then slid behind her neck. He leaned in, whispering, "I thought we'd agreed you wouldn't take this risk. I don't want to have to come to the temples and fight off a horde of priests."

Elena smiled, and he grinned back. So maybe he did still care for her, or else why would he be practically holding her?

She gazed at him as he stared down at her, soaking in his features. She had memorized his face, seen it every night before she fell asleep and then dreamed about him all night. She wanted to wrap her arms around him, feel safe in his embrace, feel his kisses again, but she hesitated. Zaman could be here any moment, or he could be carrying out his plot against the king right now. "Ammon, the risk I'm taking is nothing compared to what my brother has been plotting."

"I know all about it, Elena," Ammon said, his fingers tugging back her scarf and tangling into her hair. "I don't even live at this hut anymore. The king has given me secure chambers to sleep in. He also assigned guards to follow me around."

Elena nodded, but she still didn't understand. "Why are you here now?"

"I've come to fetch my belongings. I don't know if I'll ever be safe here again." He paused, his expression grave. "Elena, I haven't received an answer yet."

The breath went out of her, and she felt cold all over.

"I wanted to tell you; I wanted to come, but I didn't want to take the risk." His lips twisted with amusement. "The risk *you* are now taking. I can see I have a lot to learn."

Despite his teasing, Elena felt sick. Empty. Hollow.

Ammon's hand slid around her waist as he moved in closer. "It doesn't change the way I feel about you. We just have to be patient." His arms encircled her.

She wrapped her arms around his waist. "I missed you so much."

A quiet exhale vibrated his chest. "You can't even guess how much I've missed you."

The warmth returned with full force.

He lowered his head and kissed her neck. A shiver trailed all the way to her toes. "Elena," he whispered, his breath warm against her neck. "You shouldn't have come."

"I had to—Abish came to warn me and told me to be on my guard."

He lifted his head to gaze at her. "Tell her she won't have to worry for a while." His eyes went from hazy to serious. "I am leaving for Middoni in the morning."

Elena could only stare at him. Was this another mission? How could he leave now? "How long will you be gone?" she said, her voice sounding thick and unnatural in her ears.

"The Lord has told me that my brother Aaron and two other missionaries, Muloki and Ammah, are in prison there."

"In prison? But what if they capture you too?"

"The king is coming with me."

Elena let the information settle in, but she couldn't dispel the worry.

It was as if Ammon could sense it. "King Lamoni wants me to meet his father, King Laman. We didn't make it to the great feast, but he wants me to travel with him to explain and also to teach him about the plan of redemption."

The information made her feel numb. How long would Ammon be gone? Could the new converts in the Church remain strong in his absence? Abish had told her about the interruption Pahrun had caused at the assembly earlier that day.

"The Lord warned me that Lamoni's father would seek my life," Ammon said, "and that I should go to Middoni instead."

Elena stiffened. "The high king can find you in Middoni."

"I will put my trust—"

"I know, I know. You'll put your trust in the Lord." Elena smiled softly at him, although her heart ached. How could she deserve a man like this—a man who was so good, so loving, and who, no matter what he claimed about his past, was the purest man she knew?

She pushed against his chest playfully. "Go, then, my missionary. Go and save your brothers. I'll just stay here and wait some more."

He smiled, and Elena rose up on her feet and pressed her mouth firmly against his.

It was as if Ammon were waiting for her to make the first move, but he was clearly ready to make the second. His strong arms lifted her from the ground, nearly taking her breath away as he held her against him, kissing her.

"I knew I should stick around." A voice pierced the night air.

Ammon's arms stiffened, and he released Elena.

She turned to face the person who was watching them, with no doubt in her mind who it was. Zaman stepped into full view from a set of trees. The moonlight glinted eerily off the sword he carried.

Elena reached out to grasp Ammon's arm, but he'd already stepped in front of her, his sword drawn.

"No, Zaman," Elena choked out as her brother stepped forward with his face pulled into a sneer. "I'll call the guards!"

Zaman barked out a laugh. "My men have already taken care of them."

Her stomach recoiled. "What did you do?" she said in a horrified whisper.

Zaman lunged forward, his sword lifted and ready to strike.

"Stop!" she cried out.

In one swift motion, Ammon raised his sword to meet Zaman's. The impact of the swords caused Ammon to step backward, knocking him into Elena. She lost her balance and fell to the ground. Her hands slid along the dirt and rocks, and she came up with small pebbles embedded in her palms. She brushed them off, ignoring the pain as she focused on her brother and Ammon.

The swords collided again. Ammon's brow was furrowed in concentration, perspiration standing out on his skin. But he looked calm compared to Zaman's raging expression.

Her brother attacked like an animal, lunging with fury, swinging his sword with all his strength.

Out the corner of her eye, Elena saw more movement. She turned to see Dedan and a couple of other men walking out of the trees from their hiding places.

Her heart rate doubled at the sight of Pahrun. Even if Ammon bested Zaman, these men could attack. All the men carried swords in their hands. Her pulse drummed as she thought of her brother possibly fighting to his death. Or to Ammon's.

Tears stung her face, and she covered her mouth with her hand, feeling as if she were going to be sick.

The men were circling each other now. She wondered if Ammon saw the others who'd arrived. How would he fend off so many? "He's done nothing to you, Zaman," she cried out.

She shrank back to the ground, looking for a stick or a rock, anything to divert the fight, although she knew she'd be a weak comrade to Ammon. She had to convince Zaman to back off.

"I'll do whatever you want, Zaman," Elena called out. "I know I broke my promise, and I'll accept my punishment. Just leave Ammon alone."

"It's too late for that now," Zaman said. "Shut her up, Dedan."

Elena turned to glare at Dedan. But there was no mercy in his eyes, and before she could scramble away, he grabbed her. A handful of dirt and rocks fell from her hands.

Dedan didn't look too happy to be holding her captive, but he kept her arms pinned behind her so she couldn't escape.

With a satisfied grunt at her capture, Zaman sidestepped and lunged for Ammon again. Ammon sidestepped as well, avoiding the wild swing.

"You have no right to force your sister into the temples," Ammon said. "Let her go." His breathing was heavy as he continued to play Zaman's game.

"You have no right to even *look* at my sister," Zaman growled. His chest shuddered as he panted for breath, and he wiped perspiration from his face with his other hand.

It was plain to Elena that her brother was starting to tire, causing her to tremble now for an entirely different reason. How would she explain to her father if her brother were killed? Could she look at Ammon the same again? She struggled against Dedan, wishing she'd warded him off with her dagger. But he'd been too fast. His grip turned to bruising, and she stopped moving.

She seethed as she looked back at the fighting men. Ammon had been watching her struggle.

"Watch out!" she called as Zaman made another move.

He'd lost concentration for barely a second, and the edge of Zaman's sword caught him on the shoulder. Elena cried out. Ammon sucked in his breath but didn't lose a beat as Zaman swung his sword upward. Ammon leapt out of the way and brought his sword down on Zaman's with such force that he screamed.

He cursed and switched hands. The hand previously holding the sword hung limp at his side. Elena wondered if Zaman's wrist was broken or sprained. Ammon slowed and stood still, watching Zaman struggle to take up his position again. With a slight shake of his hand, he deflected the next blow from Zaman.

Then the next part happened so fast that Elena didn't have time to register it until Ammon had tripped Zaman and pinned him to the ground. Zaman's sword had flown several paces away, and Ammon was now bending over him, poised to bring the sword down on his neck.

"Let your sister go free," Ammon said in a harsh voice. Zaman's eyes bugged out as he stared at Ammon face to face.

"Let her go now. You're not the first man I've killed."

Zaman spit in Ammon's face.

Ammon grabbed Zaman's head and brought the sword against Zaman's chest. Sobs tore through Elena. Was she about to see her brother's death?

Ammon brought his sword closer until its obsidian shards pressed against Zaman's throat. "Free her."

A gurgling sound came from Zaman's throat as he spoke. "Let her go, Dedan."

Elena's legs buckled as Dedan's tight grip suddenly loosened, sending shards of pain through her as the circulation returned to her arms. She nearly stumbled but was able to keep herself upright.

She moved to the other side of the fighting men until she stood next to the hut. She pressed her back to the hut, taking strength from it to steady her legs.

"Now promise me you'll let her make her own decisions and not force her to serve as a priestess in the temple," Ammon said.

A smile twisted onto Zaman's face. "That's a difficult bargain."

Ammon grabbed a fistful of Zaman's hair again and lifted his head up.

"All right," Zaman gasped, his eyes widening.

"On your *life*," Ammon demanded. "So that I know you mean it."

"On my life."

Ammon released Zaman's hair, although he kept the sword pressed against his neck. The two locked eyes for a long moment, then Ammon released him.

Zaman exhaled.

Ammon stood, looking down on him. "Remember your oath that you made in the presence of God and witnesses whom you'll be accountable to if you break it." He looked over at Elena. "Are you all right?"

She nodded, numb all over. At some point the tears might come, but for now, she could only stare.

Her brother sat up, rubbing his neck and looking a bit stunned.

"Anyone else want to clash swords?" Ammon asked, looking at Dedan then the other men. No one moved or spoke.

Ammon turned, his gaze finding Elena again. He strode toward her with his jaw set firm. Blood stained his tunic from the cut on his shoulder, and she could see the fire and determination in his eyes. If she hadn't been leaning against the hut, she might have sunk to the ground.

He was alive, and he'd spared her brother.

A shape loomed behind Ammon.

"No!" Elena cried out just as the person collided with Ammon. Ammon spun as he fell to the ground, landing nearly at her feet.

Elena looked up to see her brother's eyes wild with fury. Ammon rolled and dodged the first blow then met the second with his sword.

Ammon was at a disadvantage because he was still on the ground and Zaman was standing over him. In his position, leverage with a large sword was almost impossible. He rolled again with his sword still in his hand, but Zaman's next blow wrenched the sword from Ammon's hand.

Elena gasped as Ammon leapt to his feet and rushed Zaman.

Horror flowed through her body as she expected Zaman to run Ammon through, but instead, Zaman staggered back, screaming.

Elena froze as she saw the blood seeping through Zaman's fingers as he gripped his upper arm.

Her heart thundered as she wondered if Ammon had cut it off. But with what? His sword was on the ground. Instinct propelled her to run toward her brother.

She skidded to a stop and bent over Zaman, who was writhing on the ground. She didn't know if she wanted to see the extent of his injuries but knew she had to look so she could help him.

His arm extended from his shoulder, apparently still attached. But the blood had saturated his hands, making it difficult to see the extent of his injury.

"Let me see your scarf," a voice said above her.

With trembling fingers, Elena untied her scarf and handed it to Ammon.

He knelt by Zaman and removed his hand that covered the wound. Zaman cried out again at the movement.

Ammon slipped the scarf beneath the bleeding arm and tied it securely above the gash.

Elena could see it now. He was losing a lot of blood.

Ammon straightened and wiped his hands on his kilt. "He needs a healer. The gash will have to be sewn."

Dedan stepped forward from where he was hovering between indecision and fear of Ammon.

"Be quick about it," Ammon said in a sharp tone.

Dedan and the other men lifted Zaman, who cried out as they moved him. His eyes were closed in pain and defeat, but Elena exulted that the injury wasn't worse.

As they moved away, casting furtive glances in Ammon's direction, he turned to face Elena, his expression grim.

"I didn't want to injure him." His eyes searched Elena's. "I'm sorry for this—I didn't want to fight at all."

"I know," she said, looking up at him. His shoulder was still bleeding, and new scrapes had appeared on his face. A shudder went through her. Zaman had made an oath and had attacked Ammon again. He'd broken the most binding oath possible.

"Elena, are you sure you're all right?" Ammon asked. "Did Dedan hurt you?"

She shook her head, eyes burning, not trusting herself to speak. Immediately, his arms went around her, and she held onto him, leaning her head against his chest. She concentrated on his breathing, his heartbeat, the fact that he was alive and well. Zaman's plan had been soured, but had it died? "Your shoulder," she whispered after a moment.

"That can wait," he said. "I need to check on the guards."

Elena followed him, holding his hand, dreading what they might find.

In front of the hut, the two guards lay motionless. Ammon immediately crouched and checked to see if they were breathing. "Both still alive."

Elena exhaled in relief.

Ammon looked up at her, his expression strained. "I have to alert the palace."

Elena started to nod then paused. "It will save time to fetch the healer ourselves. One lives not too far from here."

He stood and took her hand. They hurried around the side of the hut, where he fetched his sword, restrapping it to his waist. "Let's go. Then I'm taking you home. Your father needs to hear about this."

Elena knew he was right. *But what will my father's reaction be? Will he be livid once he sees Ammon and hears what happened to Zaman?*

From the ground, he also retrieved a dagger. Suddenly, Elena realized that when Ammon had rushed Zaman, he'd used his dagger to slice his arm.

Ammon slipped his hand in hers, his other hand on the hilt of his sword.

Once they alerted the healer and Ammon was assured that the guards would be well taken care of, he walked Elena home.

They stayed to the jungle paths, avoiding the main road and not saying much. Elena's heart seemed to pound in her throat—making it too difficult to speak. The only thing that kept her from breaking down into sobs was Ammon's warm hand in hers, clasping it firmly.

Once they reached the gate, Elena was exhausted. A short time earlier, she'd left this courtyard believing she'd be saving Ammon from harm. And now he was injured, her brother was injured, and two guards had been attacked.

She turned to look at Ammon as he opened the gate. His eyes met hers automatically, and it was as if a silent understanding passed between them.

He brought her hand to his lips and kissed her knuckles, then he pulled her beneath the nearest trees, concealing them from the moonlight that bathed the courtyard. One of the windows of the house was illuminated. Her father was up, waiting. Surely he'd seen her empty room and noted Zaman's absence. He clearly knew something was going on.

"When you go inside," Ammon whispered, "tell your father I'm here to speak with him about Zaman."

"All right." Her throat tightened again.

"Don't come out. This needs to be between us." His hand touched her face, caressing it from her cheek to below her jaw. "In the morning, I leave for Middoni, but when I return, I hope to have received an answer from the Lord."

Her chest expanded as she silently prayed it would be true.

"Until then," Ammon said, "I expect your father to protect you against . . . whatever might come."

A tear slipped down her cheek.

His fingers absorbed the tear, and he leaned over and pressed his lips against her forehead.

She inhaled, fighting back the deluge.

He pulled away gently and took a step back, his gaze on her.

She turned and walked across the courtyard. Halfway to the door, she glanced back, finding Ammon still watching her. He nodded once, and she took courage and entered the house to face her father.

CHAPTER 18

Ye are my witness, saith the Lord, and my servant whom I have chosen.
—Isaiah 43:10

Heavy dew lined the grass as Ammon followed the last chariot out to the road where two other chariots were waiting. The king would be joining him at any moment. In the early warmth of the sunlight, he examined the wheels of each chariot and checked the horses' reins. The third chariot contained gifts for the king of Middoni in hopes that it would help them negotiate the release of Ammon's brethren.

Servants busied themselves around the chariots and horses that were loaded with provisions for the two-day journey, while others brushed down the horses that the guards would ride. The king's ten-year-old son, Pacal, sat in the first chariot. Pacal had his arms tightly folded across his chest, stubbornly waiting for the arrival of his father. He'd asked to come on the journey, but the king had said no.

By the expectant look on Pacal's face, Ammon guessed he hoped to change the king's mind. Ammon knew it would be near impossible.

Not far from where Ammon stood was a group of guards who'd be traveling with them. He was surprised at the number for such a small party—at least two dozen were to accompany them and protect the king. *And me.* The king had been insistent that Ammon's enemies would continue to grow. After the incidents with Pahrun and Zaman, the king didn't want to take any chances.

Ammon was grateful for the king's concerns, but it also broke his heart that there was so much strife already between the Church members and the unbelievers. Wasn't it possible to live in harmony and respect one another's beliefs? The temple priests had endured the largest chasm, losing precious revenue when people stopped coming to their temples and bringing offerings. The priests' livelihoods had been threatened, and they refused to listen to Ammon's message. But he maintained hope that through prayer and the Lord's guidance he'd eventually reach some of the priests and convert them to the truth, just as his friend's father, Alma the Elder, had recognized the truth in Abinadi's preaching so long ago in King Noah's court.

"The king," a murmur went through the servants. Ammon turned to see the king and his usual entourage of various guards and advisors approach. His wife also walked with him. Her gaze made a beeline to her son. When Pacal saw his mother, he shrank inside the chariot.

Ammon refrained from chuckling at the sight. The queen said nothing as she strode up to the chariot and held out her hand. A reluctant son stepped out and took her hand, then she promptly led him away.

The king spoke to the guards then dismissed the servants and the advisors, who would report directly to the queen in his absence. He turned to Ammon, his expression serious. "Are you ready, my friend?"

Ammon bowed his head. "Yes, Your Highness."

"Let's go and free your brethren, then," Lamoni said, a slight smile on his lips.

Everything moved into action as Ammon stepped into one chariot and the king into another. One guard settled in the third chariot to drive it, and the rest of the guards climbed onto their horses.

Ammon held back his horse until the guard's chariot had pulled out. The king followed next, then Ammon steered his horse into action.

The morning air felt invigorating as the chariots picked up speed. They moved onto the main road, where people had come out of their homes to wave and watch the procession. They were too far east to pass by Elena's house. Regardless, Ammon felt self-conscious, hoping the new members of the Church wouldn't see him as being pretentious for riding in a royal chariot. He'd volunteered to ride a horse like the guards, but the king had insisted he take a chariot.

The events of the night before came rushing back to Ammon. The murderous look in Zaman's eyes caused him to shudder. There'd been no doubt in Ammon's mind that Zaman was prepared to kill him. It wasn't a bluff or a test; it was a premeditated fight to end Ammon's life.

And by the nature of the fight, Ammon knew Zaman had been preparing. He was quicker and stronger than at their first fight, when Ammon had quite easily bested him. This time, Zaman had more moves and stamina—but perhaps it was due to the anger behind his actions as well. Ammon prayed that Zaman would keep his promise to Elena.

Her trusting gaze filled his thoughts. He hadn't told her he loved her last night before he sent her into her house. He should have—he knew that now. The journey he was embarking on with the king could take him away for a long period of time.

The way Elena had looked at him had touched him, and he knew she still felt the same—though they'd been separated for a week. That meant she hadn't reconsidered after spending time away from him, hadn't come to her senses that their relationship might not work.

A faint smile crossed Ammon's face as they exited the city. The meeting with her father had gone much better than expected. At first, Moriah had seemed horrified that Zaman had been injured. He didn't seem too surprised that Zaman had attacked Ammon, though.

"I've come to request that you hold Zaman to his promise," Ammon had told Moriah.

"There should be no trouble if Zaman has made such a promise," Moriah said, his tone stiff.

"I agree," Ammon said with a bit of hesitation. "I just wanted you to know about the incident and what happened from my and Elena's viewpoint. She shouldn't be punished for her beliefs."

Moriah's eyes narrowed at that. Ammon couldn't clearly read his expression in the moonlight, but since the man seemed to be listening, Ammon continued. "She's been an honorable daughter, taking care of your home and helping you with your business. Any family would be proud to claim her."

Moriah's gaze softened.

Feeling encouraged, Ammon said, "Elena isn't the only one in the land of Ishmael with strong feelings about the Church. There are many who are coming to know the truth. I hope that someday you'll listen to the teachings of the Lord."

His stance unforgiving, Moriah said, "You don't understand our family." His voice was low, but his tone was firm. "We left Zarahemla for a reason, and now you've brought it back to our doorstep."

"The truth can't be denied, nor can it be run from," Ammon replied.

"I don't want your preaching," Moriah said with a shake of his head. "There are others who may listen, but it's not welcome here."

"I respect your wishes," Ammon said. "Please watch over your daughter. That's all I ask."

"I have always watched over her," Moriah said, his tone defensive. "That will never change."

Ammon decided to back down. He couldn't argue that Moriah had been a good father. In his mind, he was protecting his daughter. Yet, she was old enough to make her own choices now. "Thank you, sir," he said. He turned and left, hoping that by the time he saw Elena again, he'd have the Lord's answer.

"Beautiful, isn't it?" the king's voice interrupted Ammon's thoughts as he called out over the rumble of the chariots and horses' hooves.

Ammon looked over at the king, who waved toward a meadow. One side contained a series of springs, creating a large outcropping of yellow flowers throughout the meadow. A family of deer had been standing near one of the springs but had bolted as the procession passed by.

"Should we take one?" the king called out, prodding Ammon again.

"No," Ammon called back. "Let them stay as a family for now."

The king chuckled and slowed his chariot as they passed the springs. "That's what I love about you, Ammon. Always thinking of others first."

He laughed. "I guess it applies to deer as well." A sudden memory flashed through his mind of a hunting trip he'd been on with his brother Aaron and his best friend, Alma. They were all pretty decent hunters, but Alma seemed to have the expert's touch—or at least many fortunate shots. Once, when Alma had targeted a jaguar and had the perfect shot, he'd given it up. In disbelief and anger, Ammon had grabbed his friend's bow and tried to salvage the loss.

But the jaguar fled.

When Ammon turned to his friend in anger, Alma simply replied that the jaguar was a nursing female. At the time, Ammon didn't understand, but as he watched the family of deer, from the mother to the fawn, he understood the beauty of the creation cycle. There was a time when hunting was necessary, but there was a time when life should be respected.

His thoughts strayed again to Elena, hoping that Zaman would afford his sister the same respect.

By the middle of the day, the heat was so unbearable, even for the native Lamanites, that the entourage stopped to seek refuge in the shade of trees near a river. Ammon drank deeply from the cool, clear water then plunged into the depths, clothes and all. He spent the better part of the next hour lying on the grassy bank as the water droplets slowly evaporated from his skin and clothing.

He kept his eyes shut, though he knew most of the guards kept an eye on him. He recognized two of them as baptized members of the Church, but those two seemed to keep themselves markedly separated from the other guards.

As the air cooled, the party moved on, taking the same formation as before. Ammon stayed alert, fascinated with this new land of thick jungle, blooming flowers, and the constant noise of animals.

The guards ahead of Ammon signaled to slow down. He was immediately on alert as he slowed his chariot, matching the gait of the horses around him. The guards closed their circle about the king, who stood up in his chariot so he could get a better look at what was up ahead.

Seconds later, three Lamanite soldiers appeared on the road ahead of them. They rode abreast horses, each soldier wearing bright red capes— most likely denoting that they were royal soldiers—in service to another king.

Ammon slowed his horse to a stop, barely missing the guard's chariot in front, which had come to a dead stop.

Lamoni's group was deathly silent as they waited. Three more soldiers came around the bend, slowing as they saw Lamoni's group.

The soldiers formed a line until six horses blocked the path. Ammon couldn't see who else was in the procession because the soldiers blocked most of his view. In the stillness, the sound of a chariot was plain. It grew louder until Ammon could make out the wheels past the horses' legs.

"Stand down," a shout came from the person in the chariot. The six soldiers on horses parted, revealing the man who'd spoken.

Ammon stared at the man's fine clothing and display of a green feathered cape. Upon his head was a large headdress, which must have been extremely hot during the middle of the day. He was standing in his chariot, taking a good look at everyone. He was an older man, wiry and strong, whose narrow face sagged somewhat with age, but his dark, alert eyes missed nothing. They glanced at Ammon then behind him to King Lamoni.

"Father!" Lamoni cried out.

Ammon turned to stare at Lamoni then looked back at the stranger. *Lamoni's father? King Laman?*

The high king climbed out of his chariot, the feathered cape swishing about his thighs. He made an exaggerated movement and placed his hand on the hilt of an exquisite sword. Ammon couldn't help but notice the impressive workmanship. Two of the high king's guards rushed to his side, but he didn't acknowledge them. Instead, he strode forward, passing his own horses, and stopped right in front of Ammon's chariot.

"Who is this Nephite who travels with you like Lamanite royalty?" His voice was sharp and quick, as if he'd been issuing orders most of his life.

"Father," Lamoni said again, climbing out of his chariot.

But the high king kept his steely gaze on Ammon.

Lamoni said, "This is Ammon. He's my former servant—a man who is trustworthy in every way."

Finally, the high king looked at his son. "Why did you not come to my high feast? All of my sons were there—except for you!" His voice was not loud, but controlled anger and disappointment underlay its tone. "Why are you here, without your family," the king waved a hand at Ammon, "traveling with the son of a liar?"

Lamoni arrived at the side of Ammon's chariot. Ammon stepped out of his chariot so he wasn't towering over the two men. The high king watched every move, suspicion in his eyes.

Ammon held the man's gaze as Lamoni rehearsed the arrival of Ammon in the land of Ishmael, how he'd become a servant and defeated the rebel Lamanites.

"So this man is good with a sword. What of it?" King Laman said in a huff, though he eyed the sword strapped to Ammon's waist.

"His power is beyond any man I know," Lamoni said. "Even beyond your skill, Father."

The high king's eyes narrowed—his gaze assessed Ammon once again. "Instead of returning to boast of his successes," Lamoni said, his voice filled with awe at the recollection, "Ammon went to prepare my horses and chariots as I had asked."

Ammon watched the high king's expression harden with disbelief as Lamoni explained the vision he'd had when he'd been unconscious for three days and the establishment of the Church and baptism of many people.

"My wife had a vision also," Lamoni said, his eyes glistening. "She converted to the truth." Emotion was plain in his voice.

The high king took a step back, shaking his head, his gaze flitting between his son and Ammon. "Lamoni," the high king began, his voice low and threatening, "you're telling me that you've spared this Nephite's life and allowed him to live in your lands. Have you not learned anything from the education I provided? The Nephites are sons of a liar who robbed our fathers. And now his children continue the legacy by deceiving us in order to rob us of our property all over again."

"No, Father. We were wrong."

"Wrong?" King Laman spat on the ground. "You've been sorely deceived. Have you not provided this Nephite with a home and clothing?" His gaze slid to Ammon with distaste. "A chariot, food, the ability to travel among your people without question?"

"Yes, but—"

"And how do your people treat him?"

"For the most part, they treat him well," Lamoni blundered.

"Ah ha!" he said, triumph on his face.

"You must hear what he has to say," Lamoni continued.

"And be ensnared in his web of lies?" The high king pointed a finger at his son, his hand shaking slightly as his face darkened. "You will slay this Nephite spy. Right here, right now!"

Lamoni mumbled his disagreement as his father continued, "You'll not travel to the land of Middoni but will return to your own land where you'll beg forgiveness of your people. Of *my* people. You'll do as I say or lose your very kingdom."

"Father, no . . ." Lamoni's face had paled, but he remained standing straight, his shoulders squared. "I will not slay my friend. And I will not return to the land of Ishmael, but I'll go to the land of Middoni as I planned so that I may release Ammon's brethren." His voice quieted as he said with authority, "I have not been deceived. I know Ammon is a just man and a holy prophet of the true God."

Lamoni took a step forward. "Father, please listen to me," he said in a quiet, measured voice. "I have been a good son, and I've followed your counsel my whole life. When Ammon walked into my court, I was suspicious at first. I knew what you would say, but something about him was different from the beginning. I chose to make him a servant in my kingdom. It was not a decision made lightly, and I did not do it to dishonor you in any way." He took a deep breath. "And now that I know Ammon is a man of God, I will never turn my back on him."

The high king's eyes bugged out, and his mouth twisted into a white line. He yanked his sword from its strap then raised it, glaring at his son.

Ammon recognized the murderous look in the man's eyes. He'd seen it directed at him all too recently. He also knew what a precarious position

Lamoni had put himself in with his father. To defy his father openly was to commit treason. Ammon didn't want to fight the high king, but at the same instant, Ammon felt the power of the Lord settle on him, and he knew what he had to do. He crossed in front of the chariot and stood between Lamoni and the high king. "Do not slay your own son."

King Laman turned his lethal gaze on Ammon.

"But, if you *were* to slay him, it would be better that he fall than you," Ammon continued in a steady voice, holding the man's gaze. "King Lamoni has repented of his sins, but if you should fall at this time, in your terrible anger, your soul would not be saved."

The high king's mouth fell open, and his hand gripped the hilt of his weapon.

"If you did slay your son," Ammon continued, aware of the advancing soldiers but paying them no attention, "his blood would cry from the ground to the Lord his God, for vengeance to come upon you. Your son, Lamoni, is an innocent man, and if you should kill him, you would lose your soul."

The sword lowered slightly, but King Laman kept his eyes locked on Ammon. "I know my son is innocent. If I killed him, I'd be shedding innocent blood. But you—*you* are not innocent. You've fooled him and have sought to destroy him."

"I have fooled no one," Ammon said, crossing his arms over his chest. "I have only spoken the truth."

"Let's see how you do against a warrior who's never lost a battle! Stand back, guards!" the high king yelled and lunged for Ammon.

Ammon spun away, unsheathing his own sword in the process so that by the next blow, he was ready. The two swords cracked against each other.

Lamoni shouted, but his father wouldn't relent, and his attack was swift and fierce. If Ammon weren't trying to avoid getting killed, he would have been impressed with the high king's skill.

King Laman was quick on his feet. One second he was in front, the next he was swinging from the side. Ammon met the blows again and again, mostly defending. It didn't take too long for him to learn the high king's strategy. It was as if the Lord were directing Ammon, and he was able to anticipate the placement of the king's sword seconds before he acted. A couple of minutes into the fight, Ammon spotted the king's weakness. The king only fought with his right hand. Most warriors had been trained in combating with both hands in case of an injury. Ammon noticed the high king's left hand looked as if it had been broken or injured and had never fully healed.

When the next blow came, Ammon had his strategy in place, and the second his sword deflected the strike, he switched hands and caught the high king on the upswing. But instead of clashing swords, Ammon made contact with the king's right arm—not heavy enough to sever it but heavy enough to injure it.

King Laman stared at his bleeding arm in shock. Then his gaze met Ammon's with disbelief. Laman's soldiers rushed Ammon. He backed away, gripping his sword with his left hand held high.

Lamoni's guards stepped forward, their weapons brandished.

"No," the high king gasped. "The Nephite beat me fairly. Everyone stand down."

Ammon kept his sword raised until the guards backed off.

The king looked from Ammon's left hand to his right, seeming to understand that Ammon could spar equally with both hands. The king was too injured to fight now. Ammon circled the king then stopped in front of him, ready in case the king leapt into action.

The king loosened his grip on his sword and let it fall to the ground.

An outcry shot through the surrounding soldiers.

With his lame hand gripping his bleeding arm, the heat fled the high king's eyes, replaced by fear. "Have mercy," he said in a voice barely above a whisper.

Ammon remained still, weapon still ready.

"Spare my life, Nephite," the high king said. "I don't know who you are, but I've never fought someone of such power. It was as if you knew where I was going to strike each time. How could you know?" His eyes turned wild, and he licked his lips. "Please, spare my life."

Ammon lifted his sword until it was poised at the high king's chest.

The king's face drained of color, perspiration standing out on his skin. In that moment, every single one of his years showed upon his face.

"I *will* smite you," Ammon said, his voice low and even, "unless you grant me that my brethren will be released from prison in Middoni."

"S-spare me, and I will give you whatever you ask," he said, stumbling on his words. "I will even give you half my kingdom."

Ammon lowered his sword slightly, and the color started to return to the high king's face. Ammon looked for any glimmer of deceit in the king's eyes. Seeing nothing but desperation, he gave a short nod. "Very well.

If you'll grant that my brethren will be released from prison, and—" he glanced over at King Lamoni—"also that your son will retain his kingdom and that you'll not take revenge on him but grant that he may rule his people according to his *own* desires . . . then I will spare you." He took a shallow breath, his grip still firm on the hilt. "If not, I *will* smite you."

The high king looked from Ammon to his son as if he didn't dare believe. His gaze moved to Ammon's sword, which lay inert at his side. He lifted his eyes to Ammon, more color returning, his expression changing from fear to relief then to joy.

"Because you ask me something so simple in exchange for my life," the high king began, "I will send my request to release your brethren to the king of Middoni. And my son will retain his kingdom from this time and forever." He looked straight at Lamoni. "I will govern him no more."

The high king's face softened considerably. "I invite you and your brethren to come and visit me in my kingdom, for I would welcome you as a friend and desire to hear your teachings."

Warmth pulsed through Ammon as he processed the high king's words. The man's face had changed in a few short minutes—brightened, softened, grown wiser somehow. *The Spirit is almost tangible*, Ammon thought.

Lamoni stepped forward and embraced his father, trembling and smiling. They released each other then embraced again. The emotion in the high king's face caused Ammon's heart to ache as father and son clung to each other. He had no idea when he'd see his own father again, in this life or the next, but the reunion would be sweet indeed.

CHAPTER 19

Deliver me, I pray thee, from the hand of my brother.
—Genesis 32:11

She ran faster and faster. Yet, as always, her brother was just out of reach. Laughing. She kept stumbling as the light from the moon changed, filtered by the trees, making the forest path hard to follow. Her heart pounded in her throat as she sensed time was running out. Once the sun rose, it would be too late. She had to stop her brother before he reached his destination. Suddenly, he turned and grabbed her. If they'd been children, they might have wrestled until they were laughing and until all of their strength was spent. They'd then lie side by side in the grass, gulping in great breaths of grass-scented air.

But they were no longer children, and Zaman had murder in his eyes. He held her down as someone else's hands tied a scarf around her mouth. She struggled against the strong hands and tilted her head upward to see who else was her captor. When she saw his face, she screamed, except no sound came.

Elena's eyes flew open in the pitch dark. Her first thought was relief that she'd been dreaming. Her second thought was terror as the same hands in her dream pinned her to her bed, and she realized a hand was covering her mouth. She struggled to catch a full breath of air, but the hand pressed down harder.

She strained to see in the dark, but the pit in her stomach told her that one of these men was her brother. She gasped for air, feeling as if she might suffocate. Elena jerked with all her strength against the men holding her down. She tried to bite the hand over her mouth, but it was impossible to open her mouth.

"Give it to her," Zaman said, his whispered voice unmistakable.

Someone forced a bitter liquid into her mouth, and before she could spit it out or scream, the hand was covering her mouth again. Most of the liquid had dribbled down her chin and neck, pooling in her hair. She gagged, the taste bitter and gritty in her mouth, the texture of ground seeds.

Then she noticed the hands gripping her arms didn't hurt so much, and the pressure of the hand on her mouth seemed to lessen. She was quite tired, she realized, and decided she should probably try to sleep again. Maybe the men would eventually go away. Somewhere in her mind, she realized the drink they'd given her had forced her to relax. She didn't really want to sleep. She wanted to fight, get away, scream for her father. First, though, she'd sleep. When she awoke, she'd worry about getting away.

If *I awake.*

It was the last cognitive thought Elena had before she woke again in a chilly room, lying on a thin rug—so thin she could feel the hard coldness of a stone floor beneath her body.

She had no way of knowing how much time had passed. Elena brought a hand to her mouth—a scarf had been tied around it—cutting into the sides of her cheeks. Just as in her dream. *Maybe I'm* still *dreaming.* But, no, she knew she'd never felt so cold, so stiff, so tired before.

She tugged at the knotted scarf until it came loose and slid away. Her groggy mind tried to reconstruct the events that had brought her here. Wherever *here* was. She blinked her eyes, trying to adjust to the darkness of the room and make out any shape or form. Placing her hands beside her, she pushed her way into a sitting position, almost retching in the process. The pain in her head spread through her body, rocking through her stomach.

She clutched her middle and moaned. As she let out a slow breath, the sharpness faded, leaving in its place a dull but definite throbbing ache throughout her body.

The minutes passed, and the pain dulled further. When she could move without gasping, she felt along the floor. The stone was smooth and polished—a quality not found in many homes, unless they were the palaces of kings or houses of aristocrats who were members of the upper echelon. The only other possibility made her skin crawl.

The temple.

Elena felt the panic return, and she placed her palms flat against the stone, trying to steady herself. The darkness seemed closer, darker, suffocating her all over again. Was there no light at all in this room—this cell—she'd been dumped in?

Where was Zaman, and what about her father? Did he know about her forced capture?

She crawled until she reached a wall. The room didn't seem big, but it was larger than she'd guessed at first. She didn't know how long it took her to explore the circumference of the space, but she moved as quietly as possible, in case someone was outside listening.

When she reached the door, she examined it with her fingers from the top to the bottom. It seemed to be made of solid, smooth wood. Everything would be the best quality in this building even if it were to be used as a prison.

Elena had gone from one form of a prison to another. Any hope she'd had about reconciliation between her family and Ammon was starting to dissipate. Ammon could have been gone several days already; she had no way of knowing since she didn't know how long she'd been unconscious. The continued pain in her stomach and the way that crawling about the room had utterly exhausted her told her it had been awhile since she'd had food or water.

She slid her fingers along the base of the door, feeling for a space between it and the floor. There was hardly a space, and no light came from the tiny opening. Did that mean it was nighttime?

Elena sat back, drawing her knees up to her chest. Her throat burned with emotion as she thought about how far Zaman had gone—how deep his cruelty. How he'd betrayed her. He was no longer the brother she knew.

Please, Lord, she whispered. *Deliver me from this place.*

Tears stung her eyes, and she swallowed painfully. Her energy spent, she collapsed onto the floor. The stone rose up to meet her, its unsympathetic coldness encompassing her.

Her eyes fluttered shut. There was nothing she could do but wait, and she was so tired. The coldness had almost become warmth when the sound of footsteps seemed to reverberate in her mind.

She slowly opened her eyes as she realized someone was coming toward her door—or at least she assumed it was her door, unless there were other chambers like hers clustered together.

Her first instinct was to scramble away and hide. But she had canvassed the room, and there was no place to hide. As it was, she barely had the energy to scoot enough so that if the door swung inward, it wouldn't hit her.

The door swung outward.

A rush of warm, incense-laden air reached her as a shaft of light fell into the chamber. It wasn't as bright as she'd expected but more of a dull yellow.

A figure crouched near her. A thin woman—or girl, who looked hardly older than a child. She bent over Elena and touched her forehead. Elena flinched at the touch—it was so unexpected but became reassuring as the woman stroked her brow and whispered.

Elena tried to focus on the whispered words but realized they were more of a chant—perhaps a prayer that she was unfamiliar with.

She turned her face, blinking to get a better picture of the woman. "Who are you?" she croaked, her throat feeling as if it would cut off her words at any moment.

"Shhh—" the woman soothed. "Drink this." The woman's hand went behind Elena's head and lifted it up while simultaneously pressing a cup against Elena's mouth.

The wine was unlike anything Elena had ever tried. She guessed it was in a purer form than she'd ever tasted—the wine merchants at the market were known for diluting their offerings in order to make a larger profit.

A fiery warmth filled Elena's bosom, spreading throughout her limbs until it reached her toes. She pulled away and gasped.

"There. Much better," the woman's voice came again, this time sounding farther away.

In fact, Elena wondered if she were dreaming again. But the stone floor beneath her felt too real. She sagged against the woman's hold, and she felt her head gently lowered. By the time the woman rose to her feet, Elena felt as if a cloud had descended upon her mind—a cloud of peace and comfort.

As the door swung shut, she heard another set of footsteps.

Despite the grogginess that threatened to consume her again, she raised herself up on one elbow to keep herself more alert.

A hushed male voice was speaking to the woman who'd just given her the drink. But his tone was too quiet for Elena to make out anything. She was quite sure it wasn't her brother, but as her mind began to go blank with exhaustion, she realized she wasn't sure of anything anymore.

* * *

Ammon pulled his chariot to a stop along with the others to look over the central valley of Middoni that sat snug among a collection of hills. Smoke rose from various buildings and huts, and patches of brown dotted the landscape, evidence of a completed harvest. Ammon used the brief respite to take a drink from the water skin stored in his chariot. They'd been traveling hard since leaving the high king the day before. The long drink of water did nothing to quell the ache in Ammon's stomach. He'd had it all night and thought it had been the fresh deer from supper. But in the morning, his appetite was normal, though the ache persisted.

It's just worry, he admitted. *Worry about my brethren. How have they fared in prison? And, of course, Elena.*

He tried to push away the worry that seemed to grow with each passing moment. He'd be in front of the king of Middoni very soon. He released the harness so the horse could graze on the lush grass.

Ammon scanned the layout of the city below. Several smaller temples sat clustered together, not as grand as those in the land of Ishmael but certainly plentiful, representing various deities. Above the course way of temples perched a sprawling building. *The royal palace*, he assumed.

King Lamoni pulled up next to him, his face dusty and sweaty from the day's travel. "Let's hurry so your brethren won't have to spend another day in a prison."

"Thank you," Ammon said with a nod, gratitude spreading through him, softening the ache in his stomach. They'd said little that day, the noise of the chariots making conversation nearly impossible. But the night before, Lamoni had spoken of his childhood and growing up under his father's shadow.

"In all my days, I've never known him to lose a battle or a one-on-one fight," Lamoni had said. "When you bested him, he knew you were no mere man."

Ammon had smiled at that. It seemed the best way to get attention and respect from the Lamanites was to defeat them in a physical match.

Tears had shone in Lamoni's eyes when he had added, "My father has never let me stray far from his command. Although he gave me the land of Ishmael, edicts came nearly every moon with direction on how to perform my duties. Pahrun has been with me since the beginning—appointed by my father, of course."

Now, looking across to Lamoni—his kind eyes and determined face—Ammon's heart swelled; both at the thought of his new friend, who happened to be a king with great influence and power, and at seeing his brethren soon. He and Aaron had been inseparable as brothers since birth.

After being apart so long, it was unbelievable that they were now separated only by a small space.

"Let's go," Ammon said with a nod, his throat too raw to say much else.

At the king's command, the party started along the road that snaked downward toward the valley nestled between the hills.

As the chariots rolled along the bumpy road, Ammon saw a guard post not too far down the hillside. Noticing this first one made the others more plain. There wasn't a wall or fence surrounding the city, but the guard posts were plentiful, making it easy for visitors or intruders to be spotted. Ammon wondered where his brethren had been captured and taken to the king.

A conch shell sounded, announcing their arrival. By the time they reached the guard post, two dozen soldiers were standing at attention.

Two guards remained perched on top of the wooden platform that had been built to watch over the land.

"I am King Lamoni, come from the land of Ishmael," Lamoni called out, pulling his chariot to a stop. "I request an audience with your king with the blessing of the high king. I have brought many gifts."

A soldier, who appeared to be the commander, rushed forward and held out his hand. Lamoni extended his own hand, and the soldier examined the king's ring.

He turned and nodded to the other soldiers. Then he studied Ammon, suspicion in his eyes. Ammon realized that all of the soldiers were studying him.

"This Nephite is trustworthy. He travels with me."

The commander held Ammon's gaze for a long moment, then finally he stepped back. "We'll escort you to the palace," he said to Lamoni.

The soldiers surrounded the party and slowly led the way into the city. The procession drew crowds, and the Lamanite people pressed in to see who was coming into their land. They stared openly at the king and his guards, and children hid behind their mothers as Ammon passed.

Ammon tried to smile at a few, but that only scared them more and sent their mothers scolding and shaking their fists at the intruders.

They passed right through the market square. The vendors moved to the side with the customers. Goats scattered before the horses, some of them narrowly missing the hooves.

The crowd hushed as they passed by. Many followed behind, only stopping when the soldiers reached the palace grounds.

The soldiers directed the chariots to be parked inside the walls, and Ammon stretched his legs as he stepped out. Three of the soldiers loaded the gifts in their arms. They continued, leading them through a flat-stoned courtyard and up a series of steps. Fountains of water and miniature pools dotted the courtyard. Several women sat in a huddled group, watching the newcomers with unveiled interest.

One of the women had pale skin, reminding him of Elena. He swallowed thickly and looked away from her. The ache had returned with full force. *One thing at a time.*

At the top of the steps the stone structure of the palace loomed overhead, casting a cool shadow on the approaching party. The commander conferred with the guards at the palace entrance. Then the soldier turned. "Only the king and the Nephite may enter. The guards must remain outside the palace."

As the king and Ammon moved into the interior, he blinked against the dimness, taking in his surroundings. The floors echoed their footsteps as they walked in unison along a great hall. They stopped at a set of doors that the posted guard threw open upon the lead soldier's command.

They entered a large room that seemed surprisingly empty compared to King Lamoni's court; whereas Lamoni's court always teemed with family members, advisors, and various other villagers there to make requests, this room contained a couple of men, who appeared to be scribes, and a handful of guards.

A large man sat on the throne; Ammon guessed the king was a couple of finger widths taller than he. The king watched the entering party with a lazy gaze, with no motion to stand. One woman sat below the throne's platform. She wore heavy paint on her face, perhaps in an attempt to look older, but Ammon knew she was quite young—perhaps thirteen or so. The placid expression on her face told Ammon that she had grown quite bored attending to the king. His heart twisted—here was a young girl who should be home with her family, not serving as a harlot.

The commander walked about halfway across the room toward the king's throne then sank to one knee. The young woman watched the soldier with a bit more interest.

"Lamoni, king of the land of Ishmael, requests an audience with you, Your Highness." The commander kept his head bowed and eyes lowered until the king spoke.

"Rise," the king said, his gaze moving past the soldier to Lamoni, finally settling on Ammon with mild curiosity.

The king gripped the sides of his throne and propelled himself upward with a grunt. On his feet, he seemed to sway slightly, then he took a step forward. He descended the few stairs that led from the platform to ground level.

"Lamoni, my cousin!" the king said, his hand outstretched as a smile broke on the man's round face.

"Antiomno!" Lamoni replied, obvious relief sounding in his voice. He crossed the remaining distance to the Middonian king, and the two men clasped hands.

"What is the reason for the honor of your visit?" King Antiomno asked. His expression didn't match the excitement of his voice.

"First," Lamoni said, as if he sensed the king needed some warming up. "I've brought several gifts from home. I hope you and your family will enjoy them."

The soldiers, who had unloaded the goods from the chariots earlier, stepped forward. In their arms, they carried baskets of silver jewelry, fine leather, and luxurious furs.

"Ah," King Antiomno said, walking forward, his eyes shining with delight at last. He touched the length of a fur cape.

He lifted his shining and appreciative gaze to Lamoni. "We'll enjoy these gifts very much." He flicked his hand in the direction of the young woman who remained on her cushion near his throne. She came scurrying forward, and the king handed her a silver necklace. Her cheeks pinked as she took it and practically danced back to her cushion.

Ammon thought of his own sister, how she would never have to live this life. He wished he could teach this girl that there was a better way.

The Middonian king's gaze fell on Ammon—curiosity no longer concealed—although he spoke to Lamoni. "Surely you've spent all this time in travel for a reason—not just to bring your cousin gifts."

"You're right," Lamoni said. He crossed to Ammon and put a hand on his shoulder. He introduced Ammon as a trusted companion, leaving out most of what he'd told the high king. "I've brought Ammon with me to ask a favor of you."

The king's eyebrows lifted, creasing his meaty forehead. "A favor for a Nephite?"

A flash of a smile crossed Lamoni's face. "Perhaps another gift will make you feel more at ease listening to the Nephite."

King Antiomno crossed his arms over his wide chest. "Continue."

"You've recently captured Nephite intruders, correct?" Lamoni asked.

The king smiled broadly. "Yes."

"These men are Ammon's brethren," Lamoni said. "We've come with a personal request, as well as a request from the high king, to release these men from your prison and let them go free."

"The high king is interested in these vagrant Nephites?"

Lamoni withdrew a scroll of vellum from his waistband and handed it over to Antiomno.

The monarch took it, curiosity still in his eyes, and studied the seal and written request. Then he shrugged. "If the high king sends his request, then I suppose I can't say no." He looked up with a fixed smile.

Lamoni returned the smile. "Perhaps you need something more for your effort."

Antiomno waved his hand. "No, no. That won't be necessary." He looked from Lamoni to Ammon, as if still considering. With the vellum in hand, he turned to one of his guards and gave him the instructions. "Bring the three Nephite prisoners as well as their belongings."

Ammon's heart pounded as the guard left the room by the same way they'd entered.

"Make yourselves comfortable. It might be awhile," Antiomno said.

Ammon followed Lamoni to a low table where they both settled onto cushions. The king ordered some food then sat next to Lamoni. They entered into a conversation about other relatives, kings, and what happened at the high feast—leaving Ammon out the conversation.

The food arrived, platters piled with cooked sweet potatoes, mushrooms, eggs, and charred slices of meat. Ammon was famished, but he only ate one slice of meat. The ache in his stomach had increased, along with his pounding heart. It didn't help matters when King Antiomno called for the young woman to sit by him. The way he put his thick hand on her leg and stroked her arm made Ammon uncomfortable. He wished he could tell her about a better life, one where she didn't have to be subservient to the king in this way.

Ammon picked at the meat on the platter in front of him, wondering why it was taking the guards so long to bring his brethren. Maybe the prison was on the other side of the city.

Suddenly, the king stood.

At the same moment, the doors to the throne room opened. The guards appeared, leading three strangers.

Ammon rose to his feet as well, thinking that the guards had brought the wrong prisoners. The three men who stood in the entrance were bound together with thick ropes. Their bodies were painfully thin, their skin nearly as dark as Lamanites, perhaps from the sun or perhaps because they were part Lamanite.

The man in the middle sank to his knees, gasping in shallow breaths. The man on the right looped his arm under the fallen man's armpit and helped him stand again.

Then Ammon realized that these men didn't have dark skin but were dirty, covered in mud and their own filth. His throat constricted as he noticed they were naked as well.

The man in the middle was standing again, but his legs trembled. He took a deep breath and lifted his head, squinting in the light.

The instant Ammon's eyes locked with the prisoner's, he knew it was his brother Aaron. But he had changed so much.

Ammon raised his hand to his mouth as bile worked its way to his throat. These men had been beaten, starved, and left naked. *While I . . . I've been living like royalty.* Tears stung Ammon's eyes. He made his way around Lamoni and Antiomno until he was in front of the table.

"Ammon?" Aaron's voice was a whisper, but it filled the entire throne room. He reached out a hand, a smile separating the muck on his face for an instant before he collapsed.

The other two men, whom Ammon now recognized as Muloki and Ammah, fell forward as well—their wrists tied to Aaron's.

Ammon rushed to the men, sinking to his knees and pressing his hand against Aaron's neck. It pulsed, signaling life. Relief poured through Ammon, followed instantaneously by anger. "Untie their bands," he called out.

The guards acted as if they were statues.

"Untie them!" King Antiomno echoed.

The guards moved too slowly, so Ammon took out a dagger from his waistband and sliced the ropes.

Aaron let out a grunt, and a surge of joy rose in Ammon. "Can you hear me, brother?" he said, carefully rolling him over.

Lamoni knelt beside Ammon on the polished floor and handed over a cup of wine. Carefully, the two of them raised Aaron's head and gave him a drink. Aaron's eyes fluttered open, and he reached out to touch Ammon.

"Ammon—am I in heaven?"

"No," Ammon said. "But you will be soon if you don't have another drink."

"Still the demanding older brother," Aaron said in a faint voice.

While Ammon sat with Aaron, coaxing him to down the liquid, Lamoni gave Muloki and Ammah some wine.

"It appears you came just in time," Antiomno mused, standing over them with a goblet of wine in his hand. "Another couple of days, and they would have perished. They refused to eat Lamanite food."

Ammon doubted that but didn't say anything. More likely they hadn't been given any food. And just a few paces from them now sat a table laden with food. The anger and pain in his heart was so great he couldn't even respond.

Thankfully, Lamoni stood and faced Antiomno. "Thank you for their release. We'll take them with us now."

"Just as well," the king conceded. "They're smelling up the throne room." He chuckled then added, "I don't mean to offend *your* Nephite, but these Nephites have been trouble from the beginning. I'm glad to have them off my hands."

Two guards entered the throne room. One carried a thick bundle of vellum scrolls tied with string.

"Is that all that's left of their things?" King Antiomno asked. He took the scrolls and handed them over to Lamoni.

Lamoni accepted the scrolls then gripped King Antiomno's hand in farewell.

Ammon tore off his upper tunic and tied it around Aaron's waist. Lamoni removed his cape and ripped it in two, providing wraps for both Muloki and Ammah.

Ammon crouched and lifted Aaron. For a full-grown man, he didn't weigh much more than a woman. Ammon huffed as he carried his brother from the throne room, Lamoni following with the shuffling Muloki and Ammah.

They left the palace walls and stepped into the open air, where a crowd of nobility had gathered in the courtyard, no doubt having heard of the unexpected release of the Nephite prisoners. Ammon clenched his jaw as they passed the spectators and their curious stares. He wanted to lash out somehow, berate these people for how they'd treated men of God, but he knew he couldn't. These people might someday be taught the truth, and they'd remember his behavior.

The chariots had never looked so welcoming. As Ammon and Lamoni helped the men into them, Ammon shuddered to think what might have happened if he'd been even one day later. His brethren were in terrible condition, and there was still a risk that they would not make it. But the wine had revived them somewhat, giving Ammon hope.

"Let's go," Lamoni said, setting his chariot into action the moment the palace gates swung open. The same soldiers escorted them outside the borders of the land. By the time they reached the top of the first hill, it was nearly dark.

Lamoni had a guard scout a place to camp for the night near a river, not too far from the main road.

Ammon helped his brethren to the river where they washed weeks of grime and dirt from their bodies. They emerged looking refreshed, like new men. Lamoni provided them with new clothing that he'd sent a guard to purchase in Middoni.

The small group huddled around the cooking fire as the meat from several rabbits roasted.

"Where are the scrolls?" Aaron asked.

Lamoni asked a guard to fetch them and handed them over. "What are they?"

"The word of God. I thought I'd lost my scriptures," Aaron said in a pained voice. He held the vellum reverently, then he lifted his eyes, meeting Ammon's gaze. "How did you know to come?"

"The Lord revealed it to me." Ammon looked over at Lamoni. "Fortunately, I've become friends with the king of the land of Ishmael, who helped in your release."

Aaron and the others were incredulous when Ammon told him about King Lamoni's conversion, the many baptisms in the land of Ishmael, and the run-in with the high king.

Aaron shook his head, his eyes bright in the firelight. "You always did have it easy."

Ammon chuckled, though inside he ached for his brethren. He wondered about his other brothers, Omner and Himni. "Maybe your prayers for me were more effective than mine for you."

"I wouldn't doubt it," Aaron said, starting to look and sound like his old self. He stretched out his arms and studied his bandaged wrists. "I had hoped to find at least a handful of Lamanites who were willing to listen in the land of Jerusalem."

"Is that where you went first?"

Aaron nodded, bringing his arms back to rest on his knees. "After we separated, I traveled along the borders of Mormon then into Jerusalem." His eyes lifted to Ammon's. "Did you know the city was built by Amulon?"

"Yes, I think I remember learning that," Ammon said.

Rubbing his arms as if suddenly cold, Aaron continued. "There are two main groups of people there—the Amulonites and the Amalekites. The Amalekites wanted to hear nothing I had to say. I visited their synagogues and taught them the plan of salvation—well, I started to teach the plan of salvation.

"In each synagogue, I was thrown out," Aaron said. "So I started preaching in the streets, drawing crowds in the process. I was either ignored or taunted or children threw rocks at me—but that was essentially the worst of it."

He stopped for a moment, staring into the fire. "Did you know the people in Jerusalem follow the order of the Nehors?" Aaron asked.

Ammon slowly nodded. It sounded familiar, but when he was learning history and politics, he wasn't nearly as aware of it as he was now.

Lamoni cleared his throat and said, "Their priests are paid much like the ones in the land of Ishmael—the people support them through donations. They also believe all mankind will be saved no matter what."

"Yes," Aaron said in a quiet voice. He lapsed into a momentary silence, then his gaze seemed to snap into focus. "One man, an Amalekite, contended with me as I taught in one of the synagogues. He wanted to know if I'd seen an angel." His mouth formed a smile.

"And the answer was yes, of course," Ammon said.

Their eyes met over the fire. A jolt passed through Ammon—he'd missed his brother so much. It was a blessing to sit here with him, even though he knew their mission was far from over and they'd have to separate again.

"The Amalekite asked how I could know their thoughts and the intents of their hearts. How could I know they needed to repent?"

Muloki shook his head, letting out a small chuckle. "They've all asked that."

Aaron continued with a nod. "How could I know they weren't a righteous people? That was always the next question. The Amalekite argued that they've built sanctuaries and assemble to worship God—and God will save all men." He rubbed his face and sighed. "I asked the man if he believed in the Son of God, who will come to redeem mankind from their sins."

Lamoni leaned forward, intent on Aaron's words.

"The Amalikite said he didn't think I could know such a thing and that the traditions of the Nephites are foolish," Aaron said in a quiet voice. "Our fathers could not know either." He spread his hands wide, his gaze traveling to Lamoni's. "I opened my scriptures and read about the coming of Christ, the resurrection of the dead, and that there could be no redemption for mankind except through the death and suffering of Christ." His voice fell. "And the Atonement of His blood."

He stopped, his words heavy in the air, and stared at the fire. The only sound was the intermittent sparks popping. Finally, he wiped his eyes and said in a trembling voice, "They became angry and mocked my words. I couldn't make them listen to any reasoning after that."

He sighed, gaining control of the trembling in his voice.

Tears stung Ammon's eyes as he felt the disappointment and frustration his brother must have felt. It was all too familiar.

"After leaving the Amalikites, I crossed into the predominantly Amulonite neighborhoods." Aaron paused. "They were worse—much worse. They drove me out after a very short time. That's when I ended up in a village called Ani-Anti."

"Where I was preaching," Muloki said. All heads turned toward him. He tilted his head in Ammah's direction. "I'd been in Ani-Anti for several days before Ammah found me there. Soon after, Aaron arrived. Even with the three of us, they would not soften their hearts."

"Just as Aaron said," Ammah added, "we taught from the scriptures about the Atonement. But they could not believe that 'their' god wouldn't save everyone—even in their sins."

"What sins? They have no sins," Muloki said in a grave voice.

Those around the fire chuckled.

"We left Ani-Anti and traveled toward Middoni," Aaron said. "We met Omner and Himni along the way."

Ammon straightened, dread pressing against his chest. "Where are they now? What happened?"

"I don't know," Aaron said. "They weren't captured with us. We had split up after the reunion just outside of Middoni."

"The Lord only told me about you three," Ammon said, trusting that that meant his other brothers were safe for the moment.

Aaron studied Ammon for a moment. "We have a good deal to live up to."

"What do you mean?"

Aaron stretched, stifling a yawn. "Your success in the land of Ishmael brings me increased hope. Tomorrow I must start anew."

"You can barely walk," Ammon said.

"Then I'll start the next day," Aaron said, his voice light.

"Not if I can stop you," Ammon said, looking at his too-thin brother. "You need food and rest to get your strength back."

"Are you questioning my strength, O mighty sword man?" Aaron said, his smile lopsided.

Ammon raised his brow. "I am."

"In the morning then. Right here. Swords."

"What's the contest?" Ammon asked. "Who can *lift* a sword?"

"Ha." Aaron brought both his arms up and flexed. "What I might lack in strength, I'll make up in wit."

Ammon laughed. It was good to laugh again with his brother.

CHAPTER 20

I will not justify the wicked.
—Exodus 23:7

Elena woke with a start, her body covered in perspiration. Memories rushed back of her brother abducting her, of lying on a stone floor, and of being given wine. She didn't know for how long—hours, days?

Regardless, she sensed she was in a different room now. It was still quite dark, but the floor didn't feel the same as the previous cell. Her eyes roamed the room—a single oil lamp burned, casting leaping shadows against a stone wall. Elena sat up on the pallet she was lying on. Then her blood froze. Not two paces from her was another pallet, and someone was sleeping on it. Long, dark hair spilled over the rug. Elena released a faint breath—at least it was a woman.

As her eyes adjusted further, she saw there were four other pallets in the room, all with women sleeping on them.

Where am I? She stood, her legs feeling as if they'd give way at any moment. Her stomach rolled with nausea, and she sat back down, breathing deeply as the headiness passed. She tried to stand again, more slowly this time. When she was finally upright, she was out of breath.

Have I been ill? She'd never felt so weak in her life, even after the loss of her mother when she didn't want to speak to or see anyone for weeks on end.

She took one step then another, her head feeling as if it were detached from her body. Once she made it to the first pallet, she gazed down at the sleeping woman. She was beautiful and young. Markings wrapped around her wrists and lower arms—Elena had noticed them before on priestesses who had been at the various festivals. Each temple had their own symbols; these looked like maize stalks intermingled with flowers and other symbols.

So I'm in the temple of the maize god, Elena thought, a shudder passing through her. Before Ammon had taught the truth, she hadn't thought too much about the priestesses and their markings. But now she knew the nature gods were false idols. As Elena continued to gaze at the woman, she saw the uneven ridges of a deep scar along the priestess's chin, extending along her neck.

Elena sank to the floor, her strength giving out as she stared at the sleeping woman. She knew many of the priestesses of the temple were sent there because they had no marriage prospects. A deep, disfiguring scar, such as the one this woman had, would be a deterrent to a prominent marriage.

Elena wanted to reach out and touch the woman—maybe offer her some words of comfort. She should have more choices. Just because she had an unfortunate scar . . . but then Elena recoiled in horror. If what Abish had said about the priestesses were true, no man would want one of them . . . *used.* The markings of the priesthood could never be concealed. They were permanent etchings in the skin, filled with colored dye.

She gazed at the other sleeping forms, seeing the markings on their wrists and arms.

"Good. You're awake." The quiet voice startled Elena.

She turned to the woman with the facial scars. Her large, luminous eyes watched her calmly.

"Who are you?" Elena asked.

"I have renounced my former name. You may call me Sunray."

Elena stared at her. How could someone renounce her name? And why? She glanced about the room at the other sleeping forms, wondering if they had changed their names as well. "Where am I?"

The woman's face edged into a sweet smile. "You're in the private chamber of the priestesses."

Elena nodded, having guessed that. "This is the temple of the maize god?"

Sunray replied in a neutral tone, "Yes."

"How did I come to be here?" Elena asked.

A flash of disbelief crossed Sunray's face. "I didn't see your arrival, but I was told your grief was too great over your lost love. You wanted to forget the outside world and dedicate your life to the maize god."

My lost love? Ammon? Nausea rolled through Elena.

"I'm sorry to remind you," the woman said, rising from her pallet. "You must have loved him very dearly."

"Who—who's in charge? Who can I speak to?" Elena asked, desperation clenching her heart.

"Oh, my dear." Sunray nearly floated to Elena, her white sleeping robes hanging in soft folds about her thin body. The woman wrapped Elena in her arms. "Just let it go. Let the grief out. We're here to fill up your soul again. When you forget your old life and give yourself to the god of the harvest, you'll become a renewed vessel."

The woman's touch was familiar, and Elena knew this was the same woman who'd given her wine when she'd been alone in the dark chamber.

Elena shrank from her. "I don't want to forget," she choked out.

"I know." Sunray released Elena and handed over a jug that was nearby on a low table. "A drink of this will calm you."

Elena instinctively reached for the jug then stopped midmotion. "No, I'm not thirsty."

The woman laughed—her laughter tinkled like a child's. "You don't need to be thirsty to drink. This special drink will help you feel better."

Elena shook her head, stubbornness growing within her. If it was the same wine she'd been given previously, it would make her drowsy again. She wanted to be alert; she wanted to get out of this place.

The other women stirred in the room, and a couple of them sat up, wiping sleep from their eyes. Each in turn smiled at Elena, but no one spoke. Evidentially, these women weren't much for conversation. The women, for the most part, looked quite normal. Elena wondered about their outward scars, as well as their inward ones.

In unison, the women rose and lit several more oil lamps, and Elena was able to make out other parts to the room she hadn't noticed before. Tables lined the walls, some of them stacked with scrolls. The women took turns washing in a great basin in one corner of the room, sharing the water. But the women didn't seem to mind. Once dried off, they took elegant robes from pegs on the wall, exchanging their white sleeping robes for various colored drapes.

They dressed in silence, with occasional smiles. When the woman with the scarred face looked over at Elena, Elena felt embarrassed to be caught staring. It had been years since she'd been around another woman preparing for the day or the evening. Elena couldn't be sure which time of day it was now.

The women took turns in front of a square of polished metal, painting their faces until they looked quite astonishing, especially in the light of the oil lamps. Their already beautiful features were accentuated by the shadows.

"Join us." Sunray stood in front of Elena. She grasped her hand and pulled Elena to her feet. "We start the mornings with prayer then go on to our other duties. But today is special."

Elena slowly focused on her. "Why is it special?"

"Today you're awake. We'll begin your initiation."

"What—"

Sunray pulled her into a circle with the other women. They all crowded together, holding hands, and Sunray's quiet voice filled the space. The chant was similar to what she'd been chanting when she'd visited Elena in the dark room.

But instead of the calm peace it had brought before, Elena's heart pounded with discomfort. The repetitiveness of the words grated on her at first then began to lull her—just as the wine had.

She tried to stay alert, to concentrate on the faces before her—to look for someone who might be able to help her. But all of the women carried the same expression of compliance and acceptance.

The chanting ended, and the women released hands. Elena felt a cool touch of air as her hands were released—the perspiration drying almost instantly.

"Come. We will begin the initiation," Sunray said in an almost whisper.

"I'm sorry," Elena said. "There's been a horrible mistake . . ."

Sunray stepped right up to her and placed a hand on her shoulder.

Before Elena could move back, she felt a sharp pinch on her neck. She touched the sore spot, finding a long thorn embedded into her skin.

"What's this?" Elena said, wincing as she pulled it out.

The women smiled, and suddenly, Elena felt like smiling back.

Sunray's hand rested on her back, gently guiding her to the basin. Other women clustered around her as they undressed her and helped her into the water. Elena didn't resist—enjoying the feeling of being taken care of.

The water felt wonderful and soothing. Why had she been fighting against this? Sunray poured the calming water over her hair, and Elena closed her eyes as it cascaded over her.

She had almost fallen asleep, she was so relaxed, when Sunray gently urged her out of the water. The robe the women produced was made of fine linen, softer than anything Elena had ever worn before. Somewhere in the back of her mind, she thought about how her father would be interested in a fine material such as this. But the thought faded almost as quickly as it appeared.

Sunray led Elena to a stool, where she obediently sat as the women dried her hair and painted her face.

"Beautiful," Sunray pronounced.

Elena looked at her reflection. The person gazing back at her looked just like a priestess—elegantly painted and wearing a flowing robe. Faint surprise registered but was quickly dispersed as the women around her smiled and complimented her.

"We've never had a priestess with such fair skin," Sunray said, smoothing Elena's hair behind her ears. The gesture was comforting, motherly. "There, you're feeling much better, no?"

"I am," Elena said.

"Drink this," Sunray said, producing a cup of the sweet-smelling wine.

Hesitation stirred in Elena, but she couldn't understand why exactly. It was as if she'd forgotten something and couldn't quite remember what. She looked from the wine to Sunray's open, beaming face, and she took the cup. The wine was sweet and even more delicious than she'd remembered. *Why did I resist earlier?*

This wine was different—it didn't bring with it the exhaustion that had come over her earlier, but as it spread throughout her body, she felt a pleasant hum of comfort.

"Come," Sunray said, leading her to a low table, one that Elena had noticed earlier. Sunray draped it with a cloth. "Lie down, my dear."

Elena obeyed, and the other women approached, carrying vials of oil in their hands. One by one they applied the various oils, and Elena was absorbed into a delightful collection of aromas.

She closed her eyes as the women massaged the oils into her skin. She could now understand that the temple was the best place for her to be. The women would take care of her—something she hadn't had in a very long time. There was no strife in this chamber, only love and acceptance. No shouting brother or disappointed father. No people arguing over Ammon's preaching.

Ammon.

Her mind focused on him, then the image flitted away. Elena concentrated, knowing Ammon was important to her . . . somehow. She scrunched her eyes together, trying to imagine Ammon. What she saw took her breath for an instant.

In her mind, he was looking directly at her with those intense eyes. His fair skin was all too familiar, along with his customary red-dyed leather band around his head. His broad shoulders and arms brought back the memories of being held by them. His mouth moved, as if he were speaking to her, though she heard nothing. His expression looked worried, concerned, maybe even a little angry at something. Her heart hammered. What was he trying to say?

Elena's eyes snapped opened. Sunray hovered over her, stroking her face. "Are you all right?"

Then Elena remembered. She raised her hand to her neck to feel for the necklace, but it was gone.

"Where is it?" she whispered, her chest going hollow as the memories came back with full force. Ammon. The king. Abish. Her father. Her brother.

Sunray's expression softened. "When a woman enters the sacred walls of the Maize Temple, she leaves all reminders of her former life behind," Sunray said. Her hand moved to stroke Elena's brow. "In a few days, you'll forget all about your necklace and the ones on the outside. They will go on with their lives, thinking of you with fondness, of course, but you will reconcile your heart to a higher purpose."

Elena shut her eyes against the caressing of Sunray. *No,* she wanted to cry out. *Stop touching me.* But if she jumped up and demanded to leave the temple, would Sunray poke her with that poisoned thorn again and force more wine down her throat?

Elena opened her eyes and tried to tell her body to remain calm. She'd make Sunray and the other women think she was still under their influence, and she'd go along with their "initiation," all the while looking for an opportunity to escape the temple.

Where'd she go after fleeing, she didn't know. Even if her father were compassionate enough to take her back into his home, her brother wouldn't be. She could find someplace to hide for a while until she had a plan. She was familiar enough with the jungle, thanks to her tracking with her brother—the jungle would hide her well.

"We're ready at last," Sunray's gentle voice cut through Elena's frantic thoughts.

She sat up on the table, swinging her legs slowly to the ground and trying to act as if she were still influenced by the wine. She offered a complacent smile to Sunray.

"This is beautiful," Elena said, touching the neckline of her robe. The neckline was lower than she felt comfortable with. There were no sleeves, just as the other women's robes. One thing marked a difference between her and the priestesses. She had no markings on her arms.

"You're an impressive vision," Sunray said, smiling and taking her hand. "Come. We will now present you to the Holy Order."

Sunray led Elena out of the chamber, still clasping her hand. The change in air hit Elena like a cold river. She tried not to let it show in her expression though—especially since the effect of the wine was wearing off quickly now. It must not have been a potent mixture. Perhaps she was given the wrong one.

The women moved quietly but swiftly. They all had bare feet, making the sounds of their movement almost silent.

They'd stepped into a long corridor with high ceilings. Faint sunlight filtered through from somewhere above, but the corridor remained quite dim. Elena scanned for doors or passages that might lead out of the temple.

They turned a couple of times, continuing from one corridor to the next. Elena had never imagined a temple would be such a maze. She lost track of the number of turns, and she had no idea which direction they were going.

The floor started to slope downward, then suddenly, the women stopped. A small door that looked as if it were plated in gold stood before them. If they hadn't stopped, Elena might not have noticed it.

"The others will stay here—only I can accompany you into the priests' circle," Sunray whispered, her hand firm on Elena's bare arm.

Elena suppressed a shudder and kept her expression neutral. The women surrounding them stepped back, forming a half circle in front of the door while she and Sunray faced the door.

Sunray rapped on the door.

Without moving her head, Elena cast her eyes to the right then to the left, assessing how she could break through the barrier of women and make a run for it. But which direction would lead her out of the temple?

The door swung open, making only the slightest of creaks, and a man wearing a dark kilt stepped out.

A woven priest hat covered his shorn head, making it obvious he was a priest. But he did not wear the usual priest robes she'd seen worn throughout the land during festivals. He was also much younger than she had expected. Not that she'd paid particularly close attention to the temple priests, but they'd always seemed to be much older men.

This man didn't even glance at Elena, but his gaze lingered on Sunray.

"We are here to initiate a new priestess," Sunray said.

Only then did the priest look at Elena. His expression remained somber, but in his heavy-lidded eyes, she detected curiosity and something deeper, something Elena wasn't quite able to read.

The priest turned, stooping down to reenter the door. Elena followed at the prodding from Sunray and stepped into a circular room. The ceiling was much higher than she had anticipated, nearly that of the outside corridor. She wondered why the door had been so small.

Her attention immediately snapped to the half dozen pairs of eyes staring at her—all men. Another surprise. In the marketplace, the priests never made eye contact with the women, as if it had something to do with their purity and separation from women.

Not all women, from what Abish had told her.

As the thought swept dread through Elena, she noticed an altar in the center of the room. It was unlike the altars on the outside of the temple, which were built of large stones and reached up to a man's chest. She'd seen plenty of burnt sacrifices made to the gods when she had sometimes accompanied her brother and father as they made donations.

But this altar was a large rectangular shape, low and flat, and covered with a thick rug.

What was this altar used for? There was no smell of burnt animals in the air. Fear prickled along Elena's skin as she saw the ropes dangling on the sides of the altar. What did the priests have to tie down?

She raised her eyes to scan the men who stood in a circle. They all regarded her with open curiosity and interest, their eyes taking in every portion of her. She suddenly wanted to cover herself with a thick robe and wash the paint from her face. Her stomach twisted as her gaze went to the altar again. Sunray's hand was in hers again, guiding her toward the altar.

"No," Elena rasped, but Sunray didn't seem to hear.

Elena pulled her hand away, and only then did Sunray turn, her eyes questioning and confused.

The young priest was next to her, his hand on her arm. "Don't be afraid," he said in a whisper. The words were anything but comforting. His eyes narrowed, and he leaned close to her as his hand trailed up her arm. "You can trust everyone in this room."

Elena shrank from him, her eyes moving to the door. She'd just have to get around the priests, and surely the door wasn't locked, was it? She couldn't remember.

The priest looked at Sunray next. "I thought she had the wine."

"She did," Sunray said, alarm in her eyes. "She drank a whole cup."

The priest focused again on Elena, distrust in his gaze. He smiled and put his other hand on Elena's arm. "You should've had two cups, I suppose."

Elena's heart sank as the priest spun her and forced her to walk the remaining steps to the altar. She shouldn't have let them bring her here. What if there was no way out now? She'd waited too long to try to escape. "Please," she said, her voice trembling. "This has all been a mistake—I can't be a priestess." She turned to the priest, thinking surely this had happened before and they wouldn't force her to do the initiation.

The priest's grip tightened on her arms. "The instructions were made very clear when you arrived. In fact, we were warned that you might claim this was a mistake."

The other priests in the room nodded, and Elena noticed that their gazes no longer seemed curious but determined, even resolute.

Elena calculated how strong these priests might be. They spent all day in the temple, chanting, lighting oil lamps, and making animal sacrifices. It wasn't as if they were warriors.

Just as her legs brushed against the altar, Elena spun, wrenching out of the priest's grasp. She pushed past Sunray's extended arms and ran toward the door. She easily dodged another surprised priest. Reaching for the latch, she hoped the priestesses on the other side would be too startled to react. She yanked on the latch and pulled the door toward her, but a large hand slammed into the door, keeping it shut.

She kicked at the priest who'd stopped her, but his arms encircled her as another priest gagged her. The two dragged her back to the altar where they forced her to lie on her back. Within seconds, they had bound her ankles and wrists.

Frantic, Elena arched her body, trying to scream through the cloth stuffed in her mouth. She looked wildly about to see if anyone had one shred of compassion. But all the gazes that met hers seemed to be vacant wells.

She flopped back down onto the altar, fury pouring through her. The younger priest was next to her again, his expression calm, as if nothing had happened and she'd willingly climbed upon the altar. He removed a thorn from somewhere inside his robe and stuck it in her upper shoulder.

A sharp pain pierced Elena, and again she tried to scream. The priest was patient as she writhed. When her energy was momentarily spent, he stuck her again, this time in her upper thigh.

Elena squeezed her eyes shut as the pain in her thigh escalated. Tears ran down her face as she fought back nausea. Vomiting while she was gagged would surely choke her to death.

When the nausea passed, she opened her eyes and stared up at the ceiling. The poisoned thorn was already taking effect. Her vision blurred, and her breathing relaxed. She blinked against the haze as the pain in her shoulder and thigh lessened. She tried to turn her head, but all strength and motivation had left her.

Someone else stood over her. Another priest. This one looked older than any man she'd ever seen. The lines in his face were deep—and his eyes, where she might expect to see some compassion or understanding—were cold.

His hands pressed against her arm, and it took every effort she had to tilt her head down to see what he was doing.

Her heart clenched with helpless horror as he held a thin dagger above her skin. A vial of what looked like dark dye sat next to him on the altar.

Elena tried to move, but her body would not obey. She tried to keep her eyes open, but they closed of their own will—the final image in her mind was that of a knife descending to carve her skin.

CHAPTER 21

*When your fear cometh as desolation, and your destruction cometh
as a whirlwind . . . call upon me.*
—Proverb 1:27–28

Two days. That's all Ammon was able to delay Aaron. His brother was
perhaps the most stubborn Nephite he knew.

The final night, Ammon was restless while the rest of the camp slept.
The worry about Elena had only grown stronger these last days, and it
didn't help that he'd be sending his brethren off into the unknown again.
He knew their lives would be spared, but it had been proven that the
promise didn't make them exempt from all manner of persecution and
torture. They'd already suffered and had done so with a willing heart.
Ammon wished he could take their place. But he knew he had to fulfill
his promise to King Lamoni and continue with building the Church up
in the land of Ishmael.

When the moon was high in the sky, Ammon finally gave up on
finding sleep and climbed out of his bedroll. The air was surprisingly
cool. He wasn't too far from the fire, and the embers glowed hot beneath
the black wood. He pulled the bedroll closer to the fading fire and sat
thinking about all the events that had occurred in the last few days. They
were truly miracles.

Then why couldn't he shake the sense of foreboding? He searched
his mind and heart—focusing on Aaron and his brethren. Would they
be heading into danger the next day? *No,* he decided. The Lord had been
so clear in His command to come and fetch his brethren that it didn't
seem possible they'd be heading into the same situation they'd found in
Middoni.

Elena. He analyzed the conversation he'd had with her father. Moriah had been forthright, and his word was sound. Yet, Moriah didn't have complete control over Zaman. A chill rushed through Ammon's chest.

There. That was it. Zaman was the flaw, the cause for the angst. Even if Moriah had promised to protect Elena, it might not be entirely possible if Zaman were determined enough to punish her for her disobedience. *How much will Zaman risk to ensure that his sister stay away from the Church? Did our sword fight increase his hatred enough to take revenge on Elena?*

Ammon stood, his thoughts too tumultuous to allow him to remain sitting. He walked around the fire pit, worrying about Elena. *She's probably fine*, Ammon tried to reason with himself. Moriah gave his word. But no matter how much he wanted to fully depend on her father's word, he couldn't find ease.

Ammon reached his bedroll again. This time he knelt and clasped his hands together. Bowing his head, he began to pray.

"O Lord, O God, I kneel before Thee as Thy humble servant. The blessings on this journey have been great, and I praise Thee, O Lord, for the deliverance of my brethren. Continue to protect them, to bless them, and to guide them to those who are ready for Thy message." He paused, thinking of Elena.

"O God, I plead for the protection of Elena in the land of Ishmael. Bless her and preserve her. Soften the hearts of her family so Elena will be able to follow her own heart. Thou knowest how much I love her. I have come to Thee with this desire of my heart before and know that all things are in Thine own time. If it be Thy will, please let me know tonight if I can make her my wife. O Lord, let me know if this is the right course." He paused again, eyes closed as he waited, listening, feeling, accepting. The sounds of the night continued—the popping of the embers, the night critters, the rustling of the leaves in the nearby trees, the constant gurgle of the river—but dimmed as Ammon listened for the Lord's answer.

The feeling started in his chest—a warmth—faint to begin with but growing stronger as it spread along his torso and throughout his body. Ammon didn't dare move as the warm assurance filled him like a refreshing drink. His heart hammered, and tears stung his eyes, but he wasn't sad. He smiled, hardly daring to believe yet accepting the sure joy that flooded his heart and mind.

"Thank You," Ammon whispered. As the warmth faded, a mellow peace remained. At the conclusion of the prayer, Ammon lay back down again, finally able to rest. The Lord had given Ammon His blessing, and Ammon knew that all would be well.

What seemed like a short time later, Ammon awakened to the sounds of morning. The fire had been stoked, and Ammon's throat felt scorched from sleeping so close to the smoke. He blinked in the early dawn light and then remembered: *the Lord's confirmation.* He smiled to himself as he searched for his water skin. After taking a long drink, he sat on his bedroll for a few minutes, just soaking in the new day. His heart was light. He couldn't wait to see Elena. He knew there would be challenges in speaking with her family about it, but he believed the Lord would provide a way.

Aaron and the others were just waking up when Ammon was rolling up his bedroll. He found some tortillas and brought them over.

"Where'd you learn to serve?" Aaron said, his eyes still thick with sleep.

"I know, I know. Mother would be proud," Ammon said, handing him the tortilla.

Aaron grinned then took a large bite. "Much better than what they fed us in prison."

While they ate, Ammon put together three bundles for them to carry, each filled with provisions of dried meat, extra clothing, and bedrolls. They'd be heading out separately, which made it more important for them to have supplies.

"I'll only make it to the next tree with so much to carry," Aaron protested.

"You can't take too many supplies," Ammon said.

"I can." Aaron removed a second water skin from his bundle and an extra dagger Ammon had supplied. "One water skin and a dagger is plenty. I can catch my own food." He took out the wrapped pieces of dried meat.

"Aaron!" Ammon said.

"You sound like Mother."

"Someone has to if you're not going to take enough supplies," Ammon muttered.

Aaron straightened to his full height, towering over Ammon. He was still thin—too thin—but the two days' rest had produced nearly a miracle. He looked almost like his former self, and the healthy color was back in his face. "I may not be able to best you in a sword match, but the Lord will preserve me."

Ammon's throat constricted as he looked at his brother. "I know," he said in a soft voice, humbled by his brother's faith, despite what he had gone through so far in his missionary experience.

Aaron continued to unload his pack, and Ammon kept his mouth firmly shut. When Aaron had taken out almost everything that had been put in, he lifted the bundle onto his shoulder, his expression triumphant.

"My brother," he said, clapping a hand on Ammon's shoulder. The two embraced for a fierce moment. "Until we meet again."

Ammon's eyes burned as he pulled away. "God speed your way."

Muloki and Ammah approached to bid farewell. They'd left their packs a bit more bulky than Aaron's, for which Ammon was grateful—they'd need to do all they could to regain their strength.

Lamoni hovered, embracing each man in turn. Ammon knew the king's testimony had been strengthened as he'd heard the stories from Aaron and the others.

Ammon and the king stood together as they watched the three men depart.

"It was an honor to meet your brethren," Lamoni said in a quiet voice. "They're fine men."

"Thank you for coming with me and staying with them as they recovered," Ammon said. "I'm indebted for your help."

"No, I'm indebted to you and your brethren for abandoning your comforts and home in order to bring us the true gospel," Lamoni said.

"I have a lot of missionary work ahead of me," Ammon said.

"That you do, my friend," Lamoni said with a smile. "As soon as we return, we'll start the plans for building synagogues throughout the land."

"Then there's no time to lose," Ammon said. The peace from the night before had been replaced again with a worry in his heart that told him it was time to hurry back to the land of Ishmael—to Elena.

* * *

Ammon slowed his chariot, signaling the king to do the same. The feeling of foreboding had increased the closer they grew to the land of Ishmael. Lamoni pulled up beside him as the guards brought their horses to a halt.

"Something's not right," Ammon said in a low voice.

Lamoni looked ahead of them, scanning the road. "What is it?"

"I'm not sure." Ammon kept his gaze on the tree line. They'd traveled hard all day, stopping only for a couple of short breaks to water the horses.

They were still an hour from the border.

"Don't send the herald to announce our arrival," Ammon said.

Lamoni furrowed his brow. "Are you sure?"

"We need to be cautious. Once we cross the border, we should detour from the main road." Ammon glanced about him, feeling more nervous by the moment.

The party traveled slower now, the guards staying on high alert. They kept their weapons brandished as their gazes swept from the trees to the road. When the guard post came into view, Ammon withdrew his sword and kept it gripped in one hand while he controlled the horse with the other.

Ammon didn't recognize any of the guards, and Dedan wasn't among them either. The king passed by with just a short acknowledgement, and then they were on their way.

"Is there another road that will fit the chariots?"

Lamoni shook his head. "We can send a couple of the guards ahead with them."

"That's—" Ammon began then stopped as a whoosh of air passed by his cheek. An arrow landed a few paces ahead in the dirt. "Get down!" he yelled, crouching inside the chariot as another arrow sailed past, this one hitting his horse.

The horse bolted, throwing him against the rim of the chariot. He grasped for the reins and tried to stand to gain control. He pitched forward, slamming into the front of the chariot. He looked behind and saw Lamoni's chariot coming fast, but the horse was running wild, and the king wasn't inside. Ammon pulled hard on the reins, and finally his horse slowed enough that he could jump out of the chariot.

His knees buckled as he hit the ground. The sword flew from his hand on impact, and Ammon rolled several times. The horse was running again, dragging the chariot. A plume of dust choked Ammon as he scrambled to his feet, narrowly avoiding two horses that came charging past with no riders on them. The third chariot flew past; the guard driving it looked as if he were about to fall off.

Ammon stared after it for a second, then the pain of his injuries distracted him. One of his ankles throbbed, and his shoulder ached, the heat spreading along his arm. A long scrape to his elbow started to bleed.

He half ran, half limped to pick up his sword, then he loped to the tree line. Once inside the shadow of the trees, he assessed the road. Two guards lay in the middle of the road—that would explain the riderless horses.

An arrow stuck out of the chest of one man. The other guard was writhing on the ground, an arrow protruding from his arm. The other guards had split up, canvassing the edges of the forest, their swords drawn.

Ammon looked for Lamoni but couldn't see him. He must have escaped his chariot, but where had he gone? Ammon kept his sword aloft as he moved in and out of the trees, making his way closer to the target of the first arrow. At least four arrows had been shot relatively close together, so that meant there was more than one attacker.

His pulse pounded in his ears, perspiration breaking out all over his body. *If anything happens to the king* . . . then Ammon saw him. On the other side of the road, the king's turquoise cape was unmistakable as it peeked from behind a set of trees.

Take off your cape! Ammon wanted to shout. Everything was quiet, too quiet. He imagined he could hear the breathing of the guards and the panic thumping in the king's heart.

Ammon removed his sling from his waistband and loaded a rock into it. He crouched so he was mostly concealed. Keeping his focus on the king, he willed him not to run, not to make any move that would expose him. Ammon kept his eyes trained on the king, ready to interfere if needed.

The guards finished their cursory search, and one finally attended to the guard with the arrow in his arm. A rumbling sound grew closer. The third chariot came back, driven by a dust-covered guard. He pulled to a stop, and they loaded the wounded guard onto the chariot.

"King Lamoni," one of the guards hissed.

Ammon stared at the king, hoping he'd stay hidden, at least for a while longer. It was too soon to feel safe again.

The guards spread out again, searching for the king this time. When a couple of the men neared Ammon, he heard one whisper, "What if he was abducted?"

Ammon rose from his crouched position. The two men turned, and he motioned for them to be quiet. They crept closer.

"Pack up and prepare to leave," Ammon whispered. "Act as if you can't find Lamoni. Don't go too far. I know where he is, and I'll keep him covered. I'll signal when it's safe."

They moved quietly among the other guards, passing on the message.

Lamoni had seen Ammon from across the road. He was staring right at him, having left his cover of trees. Ammon raised his hand and put his finger to his lips, then he motioned for the king to remove his brightly colored cape. Lamoni pulled off his cape and disappeared again.

Ammon waited until the guards were out of sight, then he started to creep back along the tree line. He moved quietly, keeping his breathing inaudible. He gripped the sword in his hand and used it to move branches out of the way. His mind turned over the possibilities of the attackers—who they were, whether they were enemies to the king. *Or are they enemies to me? Is it Zaman? Would he go this far?*

Ammon stilled, pausing to hear if there was any movement. He wondered if the border guards were a part of this and if they had followed the party along the road.

He crept closer to the road, knowing he had to get to the king in order to truly protect him. *Unless I'm the target.* He'd have to cross the road, exposing himself to any attackers. There was only one way to find out if he was the target.

Ammon pushed off from the ground and sprinted across the road. He dove toward a group of bushes and landed on the other side with no arrows pummeling him. He crouched behind a thick bush, listening for any approaching sounds.

The wind picked up slightly, creating a rustling overhead. Ammon wiped the perspiration from his face and took a slow breath. Then he rose, the scrapes on his arm stinging from the dive into the bushes. He ignored the persistent pain as he crept toward the king's hiding place. When Ammon reached him, the fear on Lamoni's face relaxed.

Ammon stopped a few paces from the king and motioned for him to wait. The two men waited for several minutes, listening. Either the attackers were gone or they were very patient.

"Let's go," Ammon mouthed.

Lamoni slowly rose, and as soon as his head came into view, Ammon heard something behind them. Sharp awareness swept through Ammon, and his first instinct was to protect the king. He slammed into Lamoni, driving him to the ground.

Ammon's body jerked violently in response to a searing pain in the back of his shoulder. Without looking, he knew it was an arrow.

"I've been hit," he gasped. He scooted off the king, staying close on the ground. "Break it off."

Lamoni's eyes widened, but he worked quickly. Keeping low, he positioned himself to snap the arrow. "Ready?" he whispered.

Ammon nodded, clenching his fists together and squeezing his eyes shut in anticipation.

It was over in a second, but the pain was deep and concentrated. Ammon gritted his teeth to keep from crying out as the pain intensified.

When it started to lessen, he opened his eyes again. He'd broken out in a fresh sheen of perspiration.

The king was already binding the wound with a strip torn from his kilt. "Can you get up?"

"Yes." Ammon forced his breathing to remain steady so the nausea wouldn't overtake him.

"Finished," the king said, worry in his face. "How will we get out of here? We've got to get you to a healer right away."

"Stay as low as possible. You go first, and I'll follow and cover." With his right hand, Ammon used the king's shoulder as a support to get on his knees. They crawled several paces first then stood up in a crouch and started to run.

Another arrow then shouting and running behind them.

"Go!" Ammon cried out, not worrying about hiding behind trees and bushes now. They zigzagged through the jungle, heading in the direction of the city. Lamoni was surprisingly fast. Ammon was barely able to keep up, his shoulder feeling as if it were on fire.

The attackers were losing some ground, but Ammon and the king kept pressing ahead. The terrain began to look familiar, and Ammon realized they were nearing the place where he'd defended the king's flocks. And now he was defending the king himself.

"Sebus," the king said, recognizing the territory as well. Soon the trees would thin and open into the rocky meadow that surrounded the lake. "Where can we hide?"

"Over the next ridge, let's drop down and take cover. If we can't lose them, we'll have to face them." Ammon's breathing came harder as the pain in his shoulder radiated through his chest.

The king plunged on, and they scurried up the ridge, weaving in and out of the trees. They were growing dangerously sparse, and as they crested the top of the hill, Ammon caught a glimpse of the waters of Sebus.

They took a hard right and half slid down the hillside. Ammon nearly cried out as he jarred his arm, sending jolts of fire through his shoulder. "We've got to take cover now," he said, trying to stay focused above the pain.

They scrambled into a set of bushes, grabbing clumps of dirt and covering their bodies then lying still. Every movement sent another jolt of pain through his body, but now wasn't the time to check his wound.

When the attackers crested the hill at a labored run, Ammon finally got a view of who'd been chasing them.

He recognized a couple of the men from the band of rebels he'd fought at the waters of Sebus. Dedan was with them, but no Zaman; although, it was clear he was behind this attack—and who the real target was.

Next to him, the king growled, "I'll have them executed for treason."

"They're after me, not you," Ammon whispered.

"You're under my protection, and an attack on you is an attack on my family." Lamoni gripped his sword and sat up, making ready to rise.

"No," Ammon said, moving next to the king. "Don't risk it—when they leave, we'll return to the palace, and you can issue warrants for their arrest. I don't want you getting injured, or worse, on my behalf."

Lamoni resisted for a second then relented and settled back into his spot. The movement caught Dedan's attention.

"Too late," Lamoni whispered.

"Leave me," Ammon whispered back.

"Never."

Ammon grimaced. "Leave and find the guards. These men know you've already identified them. They'll only try to scare me." Still, the king hesitated, so Ammon added, "I've fought three times as many men—the Lord will protect me, but the city needs their king to lead them; they need you safe at the palace."

When the king didn't budge, Ammon shot out, "Now!"

Taking hold of his sword, Ammon stood, battling against the nausea rising in his stomach. The group of men walked swiftly toward them, their gazes glancing about as if to look for others.

"Leave me," Ammon said again, hoping he'd be able to stay upright until the king was out of sight, but the king didn't move. "I can't have your blood on my hands."

"Nor I yours," Lamoni said.

Dedan and his men were only a few paces away now. They stopped, and Ammon met Dedan's gaze openly.

"You would dare to threaten your king?" Ammon said, propping his sword on the ground so he could lean on it.

"We're not here to harm the king," Dedan said, his tone defiant.

"Where's Zaman?" Ammon asked.

Dedan flinched. "He's trying to correct your evil doings."

"I've done nothing without the blessing of the king and queen," Ammon said, perspiration running along his face. He hoped Dedan wouldn't notice how much pain he was in.

"You've tricked them," Dedan growled.

The king stepped forward. "There is no trickery here."

Dedan took another step back. His gaze went from the king to Ammon. "We respectfully ask you to leave our land in peace."

"An arrow in the shoulder is 'respectfully' asking me to leave?" Ammon clenched his jaw as another wave of nausea hit him.

Dedan paled as he seemed to scramble for an answer. "We're a strong people, able to make our own decisions, and we don't need a Nephite telling us how to live." Though he stood ramrod straight, Ammon noticed him trembling beneath his stiff exterior.

The king jumped in with a reply. "My people will become a free people. You will have the liberty of worshiping according to your own desires."

Dedan stared at the king, his eyes wide. Ammon sensed he hadn't expected this sort of invitation.

"No one is being forced to be baptized," Lamoni continued. "The queen and I have chosen to be baptized. Everyone else may choose for themselves."

Dedan offered a slow nod, his gaze staying on the king. "Many people in the land feel you've chosen a Nephite over your own people."

"I will explain otherwise—tonight!" the king declared. As he spoke, the sound of horse hooves grew closer. The guards had located them. Relief washed through Ammon as the guards rode up. Not that Ammon wasn't willing to meet Dedan in a battle, but there would be no battle if Ammon collapsed on the first lunge.

Dedan took several steps back along with his men, fear plain on their faces.

The guards surrounded them quickly. A look of defeat crossed Dedan's face.

"Take them away," the king told the guards. "Then send a message to all the people in the land. At sundown, I'll be in the market square with new declarations for the land of Ishmael."

Ammon's mind grew hazy as he watched the guards lead Dedan and the other men away. *Where was Zaman?* Dedan had taken the easy way out—if Zaman had been with them, Ammon was sure he would have shot an arrow more true. *He'd have hit my heart.* His hand slipped on the hilt, and he almost stumbled. He righted himself, taking several deep breaths. He blinked and focused on the king. Lamoni was looking at him, saying something, but Ammon couldn't hear. Again, his hand slipped, and this time he didn't catch himself.

CHAPTER 22

Elena stayed curled up on her mat in the priestess room, a bitter taste in her mouth from the wine she'd just purged from her stomach. The room was empty now, but she knew they'd all be back before nightfall. The routine was the same every day—early morning washing rituals, rotating visits to the priests' circle where the other women took turns performing fertility rituals, preparation of the food left as offerings by the public, simple meals, care of the temple idols, evening prayers . . . Elena wrapped her trembling arms about her body.

Her arms were marked now, just as the other women's. The pain had been intense and the fear even greater that she'd fainted on the altar. When she'd awakened, it was over, and her arms were bandaged. The swelling had gone down for the most part now, though they were still tender. Yet, that was only preparation for the final initiation. She'd been told that once the markings were healed and she was cleansed of the blood, she'd enter the final initiation into the order of the priestesses—the fertility rite.

She exhaled, her breath coming out as a shudder of despair. Abish had been right—about all of it. The priestesses might be celibate in the eyes of the public, but inside the temple walls, they were nothing more than prostitutes. Sunray had tried to explain the importance of the fertility ritual—that the priests were blessing the whole of harvest through their sacred reenactments.

But Sunray's words only formed a hard rock in Elena's stomach.

The priestess continued to ply her with the strong wine, and each time, Elena was able to drink a little less, keeping her mind sharp for the most part. She'd pled illness. The women had been patient and understanding so far, but she'd heard them talking at night when they thought she was asleep.

Time was running out. Her initiation had to take place seven days from the time she'd entered the temple. *And today was the sixth day.*

The young priest with the heavy-lidded eyes had entered the chamber the past two nights as the others were at their worship service. He'd spoken to her, tried to convince her that she needed to forget her old life. Each night he'd left with a promise that he'd return again. The seventh day would be the final time, and there would be no more delaying after that.

The priest would arrive at any moment. Every sound made Elena flinch. He'd told her to call him Harvest. She knew it wasn't his real name, and she even wondered in her more lucid moments who he really was. What his life had been like before . . .

The door clicked open and without turning her head, Elena knew it was him. She closed her eyes quickly, hoping he'd assume she was asleep.

His bare footsteps were practically soundless as he walked toward her. She could almost see his hand reaching down to tilt her cup, to make sure she'd drunk all of the wine.

She startled when he touched her shoulder. He'd never tried to touch her before but had just spoken in whispered words about her destiny as a priestess. She opened her eyes and saw the priest's smiling face, his heavy lids lifted.

He'd removed his priest hat, and his shorn head gleamed in the lamplight. "Did I wake you, River?"

Don't call me that, Elena was about to answer then remembered she was supposed to be under the effect of the wine. Instead, she nodded. His hand remained on her shoulder, burning an imprint that she feared would never come off—just like the markings on her arms.

Her stomach turned over, and she swallowed against her scratchy throat. She wondered how fast this priest could run and if she could make it out the door and down the hall before him. But she hadn't discovered a way out yet. She constantly feared that if she did run and they caught her, they would put her in the dark cell again.

"River," the priest said, his gaze on her.

My name isn't River. The thought struck her again, but her mouth seemed too numb to speak. Perhaps she hadn't expelled enough of the wine. Sunray had declared that her new name would be *River*—since she was so restless. "Like the swirling waters," Sunray had said, her smile ironic.

"River, this is day six," the priest said as he leaned closer, his voice meant to be soothing, but it only made the nausea in her stomach sharpen. "Are you ready to become a full priestess tonight? You have no need to fear me, I promise." His hand stroked her shoulder. "You know I'll be gentle."

She tightened her arms about her; he'd said the same thing the night before. She winced at the throbbing that flared up in her arms. The day after the markings had been carved into her skin, she'd tried to wash them away, but they'd only inflamed and burned more. The markings were permanent. Her eyes smarted at the thought of anyone seeing her arms now. She'd never be able to hide the marks—not from Abish, not from Ammon. They'd know what she'd become from first sight, assuming she could ever leave the temple.

Perhaps it was better that she never leave the temple and just accept her new life.

No, Elena thought. *I'd rather die than make the choices a priestess does.*

She finally looked at the priest and studied his expression, the depth of his eyes, to see if there was true compassion in them. There had to be exceptions. There had to be other women who'd come to the temple by mistake or by force and had changed their minds. *The priests and priestesses aren't barbaric, are they?*

"Harvest," Elena whispered, pushing up on one elbow. "I need you to listen to me."

A radiant smile transformed his face, and guilt rushed through Elena. Then she reminded herself of what he *truly hoped for*, what he thought she might be saying.

His hand moved down her arm, lightly brushing the swollen cuts, then his hand stopped at her wrist. His long fingers wrapped around it possessively. Elena forced panic from her voice as she spoke slowly, trying to give the impression that the wine had done its deed. "I have beautiful jewelry that my mother left me. My father has capes that are fit for royalty."

The priest's eyes narrowed. He might be young, but he wasn't a fool. She hoped her ruse was working.

Elena pressed on before she lost her courage. "I promise to bring these to you for the temple, to honor the maize god, to supply you with comforts in your service here." She moved her wrist slightly, and when the priest's grip loosened, she held his hand.

He looked at their clasped hands, surprise then pleasure reflecting on his face.

"Harvest," she said his name again, and he practically purred. "Please help me return to my family. My father . . . is ill . . . and I'm the only one to care for him. My brother will marry soon and be busy with his new family." It wasn't exactly true, unless Zaman and Abish did marry eventually. And she was certain her father missed her—that might be called an illness. Elena kept her gaze on the priest, hoping for any semblance of mercy.

His hand moved against hers, threading their fingers together. Then he pulled her hand toward him until it hovered next to his lips. When he spoke, his warm breath brushed against her skin. She fought back a spike of nausea.

"You are so young, so innocent," the priest said. "Sunray warned me about your desire to return home." His gaze bore into hers. "It will pass, I promise. Especially when we unite, you will finally understand your duty and realize how foolish you sound right now." His gaze hardened at the last words.

She tried to pull her hand away, but his grip increased, sending threads of pain into her arm.

"River, I know who your family is. They've turned you over to the temple, and you are now the maize god's. All of your previous wealth is no longer yours to claim. You are not the woman you used to be." He released her hand but placed his palms on each side of her face. "Elena is dead. Everyone has forgotten her." His gaze traveled the length of each arm. "You have been renewed. You belong to the maize god now. And I am here to represent him."

Elena's heart pounded, and she clenched her jaw, fighting back the panic.

His hand moved beneath her chin, lifting her face toward his. "The maize god commands you to come to the harvest in the name of your people and to ensure the preservation of your family." His fingers pressed against her face, and his other hand snaked around the back of her head.

"We *will* unite," the priest said, his breath hot against her skin. "Tomorrow is your last chance to comply . . . cooperatively . . . For after that, there will be no mercy."

Something snapped inside her mind, and she moved back, wriggling out of his grasp. His hands clamped down on her arms, and he pulled her against him. He was not much bigger than she, but his strength was far superior.

"No, please," she cried out.

His words filtered through her hair as he pressed his lips against the side of her head. "We *will* unite in the name of the maize god. The balance of the city is too fragile for a priestess to abandon her duty. We will all pay the consequences should you choose to disobey." His mouth hovered right next to her ear. "It's my job to make sure you obey. I've made my oath, and I will not break it."

Elena shuddered as he clutched her, one of his hands moving along her back. She pushed against him hard, surprising him enough that she was able to scramble out of his grasp. She rose and hurried to the table with an oil lamp. He nearly lost his balance but recovered and leapt after her.

She snatched the oil lamp from the table, but he'd already reached her, anger blazing in his eyes. One of his hands gripped her arm, and the oil lamp clattered to the table. He forced her to face him, one hand clawing at the front of her tunic. His other hand was on her neck, his fingers digging into her flesh. "You are fortunate I am an honorable priest," he hissed.

Footsteps sounded outside. The priest leaned close. "Tomorrow, my sweet." Then he was gone, exiting the room seconds before the priestesses entered.

No one looked at her as she stood trembling, oil lamp in her hand and robe torn. It was as if they knew what the priest had been about to do but didn't care. *What about these women? Had they been forced into submission? Had they been drugged with wine until they forgot their old lives? How can anyone* choose *this?*

Dismay settled over her as the priestesses continued to ignore her and readied themselves for bed. *How can they pretend nothing is amiss?*

Elena placed the oil lamp, which had gone out, back on the table. With shaking hands, she tied the gaping hole in her tunic together with the edges of the cloth. Sunray walked about the room blowing out all of the oil lamps except for one, leaving Elena in near darkness.

The women settled in for the night, each on their own pallet, each maintaining silence. Elena took a deep breath and straightened her shoulders. Then she walked to her bedroll and knelt down.

She clasped her hands together and bowed her head, not to an idol in the room or a nature goddess or god but before the true Lord. She bowed her head and silently prayed, not caring if the other women saw her actions. Her words were awkward, stilted, and new, but her heart was full of grief as she prayed that she'd be made free.

* * *

Ammon dragged his eyes open then immediately shut them again. The light was too bright. He felt as if his eyes had been swollen shut, and he tried to remember if he had been in another fight.

"He's awake," a voice said, and Ammon recognized Kumen's tone.

I'm in the hut with Kumen again—but why is it so bright? He concentrated and forced his eyes open a slit, barely letting the light filter in. It was Kumen all right. The lopsided smile, the crooked front teeth.

"Ammon," Kumen said.

He opened his eyes wider. It wasn't so painful this time but still very bright. "Why am I asleep in broad daylight?" he asked, surprised at how scratchy his voice sounded. It was as if he hadn't spoken in a long time.

Disjointed thoughts jolted through him as the memories surfaced. Running with the king through the forest. A threat. He looked at Kumen, who hovered above. "The king?"

"He's on his way."

"So, he's not . . ." Ammon swallowed against the burning in his throat.

Confusion crossed Kumen's face, then it cleared. "Don't you remember what happened?"

"I'm not . . . sure." Ammon tried to turn his head, but the ache in his neck stopped him. "Was I in a fight?"

Kumen smiled. "Something like that. Here," he said, raising a water skin to Ammon's mouth. "Drink."

Ammon took several clumsy gulps, with most of the water trickling down his face. He tried to rise again, but the pain increased.

"Don't try to move," Kumen said, putting a hand on Ammon's chest. "You're likely to be dizzy."

Ammon's eyes were now adjusted to the brightness of the room, and he realized they were in the palace. No other home had such luxurious murals on the wall or fine linen hanging over a raised platform bed.

More flashes of memory hit Ammon. The runaway chariots, one arrow narrowly missing him, another that struck his shoulder, Dedan. *But then what happened?* He didn't remember Dedan fighting him. "What happened to me?" Ammon said.

"The arrow wound in your shoulder—you lost a lot of blood, then it festered. You've been feverish for three days."

"Three days?" Ammon tried to comprehend the passage of time. "I— what about those men who attacked us?"

"In prison."

"Yes, indeed," another voice cut in. Lamoni swept into the room, a broad smile on his face. "When word reached me that you'd awakened, I came as soon as possible."

At the sight of the king alive and well, gratitude filled Ammon. His mind was clearing more by the minute.

"The men are in prison, and a search is out for Moriah's son, Zaman."

Ammon closed his eyes briefly. "You spoke to Moriah?"

"No," the king said. "The man is nowhere to be found."

Ammon opened his eyes. "What do you mean?"

"He's gone. The homestead has been deserted," Lamoni said. "I have a guard stationed there to alert me if anyone tries to return."

Lamoni turned and walked to the window, stepping into the direct sunlight. "It seems there's a secret organization out there. Led, no doubt, by Zaman and Pahrun."

Ammon's stomach churned. He knew all about secret organizations.

"They're traveling about and preaching against your teachings," the king said, facing Ammon. "They're trying to destroy our newly established Church."

Ammon inhaled sharply; he also knew all about the path of destroying the Church. "We need to stop it."

"We will." The king's gaze moved past Ammon to an unseen spot behind him. "We have scouts looking for their hiding places and spies trying to infiltrate their secret meetings."

Pushing up on his elbows, Ammon winced at the pain in his shoulder. It had been bandaged tightly.

"Ammon—" Kumen began.

"Help me up," Ammon said with a growl.

Kumen pulled him to a sitting position, and Ammon took a couple of deep breaths, trying to keep the pain and dizziness at bay. "What about Moriah's daughter?"

"I assume she's with her father, wherever they're hiding out," Lamoni said.

"We must stop him," Ammon said. "The Church is new, and the converts will be torn between their new convictions and the pull of tradition."

"Agreed," King Lamoni said. "We have plans in place for several synagogues and have already started building them. We were waiting for you to wake up before calling together the congregations to warn them."

Kumen jumped in. "The more people we can baptize, the better."

Ammon looked from the king to Kumen. "We only baptize those who truly want to covenant with the Lord. I'll not turn this into a competition." He looked at the king. "Call the congregations together. We'll meet right away."

"But you're still weak," Kumen interrupted.

"Then, my friend," Ammon said, swinging his legs over the side of the bed, "you'll have to bring me a walking stick."

Someone cried out in the hallway.

"Who goes there?" King Lamoni spun toward the door.

A guard entered. "A woman—the queen's servant is demanding to speak to Ammon."

"Send her in," the king said.

Abish entered. Her face was flushed, tears bright in her eyes. She rushed to Ammon and knelt before him.

"She was taken from her home," Abish said in a rush. "It happened a few nights after you left. There was no time to prepare, and I have been awaiting your return and awakening."

Ammon stared at her, not sure what she meant at first, but as she continued to spit out words, dread coursed through him.

She gripped her hands together. "I'm not sure which temple, but I think I've narrowed it down to three. I've been asking—"

"Wait," Ammon said, his voice louder than he intended. "Abish," he began more quietly, "you're speaking of Elena? She's been taken to a temple?"

Abish nodded, fresh tears falling on her cheeks. "I wanted to tell you as soon as you returned, but they said you were unconscious."

He put a hand on her shoulder. "Tell me everything you know."

She started to tremble. "Her brother and father are nowhere to be found, but I know they did it. They took her to the temple. Do you know what will happen to her there?" Her voice fell to a whisper. "What has likely already happened to her?"

Ammon shook his head slowly, although he had a good idea.

The king walked to Abish's side, staring at her intently. "Moriah's daughter is in one of the temples?"

"Yes."

The king looked from Abish to Ammon, understanding growing in his expression. "And you know Moriah's daughter and care about her?"

Ammon could only nod, upset that he'd spent three days ill and helpless.

The king was silent for a moment, as if he drew the final connections between Zaman's rage at the Church and Ammon. "If this woman has been sent to the temple, she will become a priestess," the king said in a hollow voice. "She'll be sanctioned and preserved for the gods. Once a woman becomes a priestess, she's unfit for public life. She becomes . . ." He glanced at Ammon. "The property of the temple and of the priests."

The room was silent. No one moved. No one spoke.

Finally, the king said, "I'm sorry, Ammon. Even if we were to find this woman and even if she were taken there against her will, it's been too long. A day or two might have been time enough, but the final ceremonies must take place before seven cycles of the sun."

Ammon's eyes burned as he stared at Abish. *Is it too late to save her?* "When was she taken?"

"Three nights after you and the king left for Middoni."

"Six days ago," Kumen whispered. He met Ammon's gaze, but there was no hope in it.

"The king's right," Abish said. "It's been too long. Today is the seventh day. The sanctification will take place today at the very latest. But it's probably already happened."

"We can force the priests to let her go," Ammon said.

Abish hung her head. "Even if we could, even if the king ordered it, she would not be the same woman."

Heat pulsed through Ammon, churning into anger. "She'll remain pure in God's eyes. I don't care what she's been through—she'll always be the same woman to me."

Abish lifted her head, eyes rimmed in red. "She'll be marked with symbols all over her arms, possibly all over her body. She'll be ashamed to come out in public and try to live a normal life. And she'll . . ." She hesitated. "She'll be a used woman. The priests will include her in their fertility rituals."

Ammon's heart thudded in his throat, in his ears, trying to drown out Abish's words, trying to believe it couldn't be true—not about Elena. He'd never felt so helpless, so hurt, so angry that he hadn't protected her. He had to find her. And no matter what she'd been through, she needed to know that he loved her and his feelings would never change. Regardless of what had happened, he wouldn't let her remain in the temple.

Moriah broke his promise. Anger pulsed deeper through Ammon at the realization.

CHAPTER 23

If ye will obey my voice indeed, and keep my covenant, then ye shall be a
peculiar treasure unto me above all people: for all the earth is mine.
—Exodus 19:5

The crowd had amassed into the hundreds by the time Ammon and the king took their places on the platform. The noise died down as the people recognized that the meeting was about to begin.

Ammon clenched his teeth together as a wave of dizziness passed through him. *Not now*, he thought. *I need to speak to these people—strengthen and comfort them. Please, Lord*, he silently prayed, *grant me health so that I may minister unto your flock.*

Kumen sat next to Ammon, watching him furtively. The king's healer was also on the platform, his gaze tracking Ammon's movements. For now, he'd sit and wait until the king was finished with his instructions to the people.

As the king walked forward on the platform, the crowd hushed completely. All eyes were focused, all ears eager to hear.

"Welcome, my people." Lamoni raised his hand in the air. "I want you all to know that Ammon, my former servant, is recovering well from his injury. We were attacked just inside the borders of the land. The rebels were caught and imprisoned."

A low murmuring of approval rippled through the crowd.

The king glanced at Ammon then continued. "We're still searching for the leaders of the rebels. If you know their whereabouts, we expect you to come forward. You will be rewarded. I also want you to know that Ammon is no longer my servant. He is a leader in our community now, and I have made him the head of the Church."

Conversation erupted until the king raised his hands again for silence. "On the way to the land of Middoni, I met my father, the high king. He gave me freedom to rule over the land of Ishmael according to my will. We are free from his edicts and any previous oppressions."

The people clapped in agreement.

"Therefore," the king said, waiting for the clapping to quiet, "you're now completely under my rule, and you're a free people to worship how you see fit. I will not tell you which god to worship or which synagogue to attend. The choice is yours."

Lamoni smiled as the clapping began.

"You're granted the liberty of worshiping the Lord God," he called out over the noise. "You may join the Church that Ammon leads. Or you may continue in the traditions of your fathers. There will be no persecutions among you against any man who might worship differently. You are free to become baptized, or you are free to turn away."

The king pointed at Ammon, who stood and bowed. "We're building synagogues for those who join the Lord's Church so that the people might assemble themselves together and worship. Ammon has been given the charge to carry the message to every person, but it is up to you to accept or reject it."

He motioned for Ammon to join him at the front of the podium. "This man saved my life. This man protected the king's property and asked for nothing in return. I trust him with everything I have. I know his message is true. Please give him his earned respect."

Ammon stepped forward to a clapping congregation. Unbelievers were mixed in with the Church members, and he prayed that his message would soften many hearts. His legs felt weak as he stood before the crowd, but he knew the Lord would give him strength. Gazing over the crowd, he noticed many familiar faces of people who had become dear to him.

"The Lord has given us commandments to live by so that we might become a righteous people," Ammon began. As he spoke, he kept a look out for Abish, who had left soon after sharing her information. She was on a quest to discover which temple Elena had been taken to.

The only reason Ammon could stand here was that he knew Abish was searching for Elena. He had put his faith in the Lord that He'd direct Abish's path. The Lord had given His blessing that Ammon could marry Elena—she would be rescued. His injuries had delayed that rescue, but even if she came back a changed woman, he would accept her with open arms. *Please, Lord*, he prayed in his mind. *Help deliver Thy message to this people. Bless Abish in her journey and preserve Elena.*

Ammon preached for about an hour. There were some groups who left, but most stayed to hear him teach. "I'm not here to judge you or to tell you that I have been the best example. In the land of Zarahemla, I turned against the Lord and tried to destroy His Church. I was rebuked most severely. In fact, the Lord sent an angel to stop the path of destruction that my brethren and I were on.

"I share my experience because I know that those who repent and exercise faith will bring forth good works." He stopped for a moment as Kumen handed him a water skin to drink from. "I was given mercy, and you will be given mercy if you are penitent. Pray unto the Lord continually, without ceasing. He will reveal His mysteries to you. Only through the Lord will souls be brought unto repentance.

"Righteous people turn away from delighting in the shedding of blood, spending time in the grossest iniquity, and entering into all manner of transgressions," Ammon said. "The commandments given by the Lord give us a way to avoid these damning transgressions."

As he taught the people about the commandments, there was a small disturbance in the back of the congregation. Abish was pushing her way through, hurrying toward the platform. Ammon finished recounting the commandments as she reached him.

He crouched down to hear her. "What is it?"

Her face was flushed, her hair pulled free of its usual neat plaits. "I think I've found her."

Hope jolted through him. "Are you sure?"

She bit her lip then held up her hand. Dangling from her fingers was a thin leather strap.

On the strap was a ring.

Ammon's heart stilled as he stared at the familiar ring. The one given to him by his father in what seemed another lifetime. The one Ammon had given to Elena with his promise.

"I found it in the marketplace," Abish said. "It was being sold by a representative from the Maize Temple."

"Wait here," Ammon said.

She stayed by the side of the platform, clenching the necklace in her hand.

Soon the king dismissed the congregation and turned Ammon. "Come with me, and bring Abish."

Ammon, Kumen, and Abish followed the king and his guards. Ammon leaned on Kumen for support as they kept up with the king's brisk pace. Once inside the palace, they walked along a narrow corridor that opened into a small room. It had a few cushions, a single table, and a high window.

"Wait in the hall," the king directed the guards, then he closed the door. Turning, he held out his hand.

Abish seemed to understand, and she opened her fist to reveal the necklace. She handed it over to the king.

He held the ring up to the light, then he looked at Ammon. "You gave this to Moriah's daughter?"

"Yes," Ammon said, the necklace bringing to surface a myriad of emotions. She should still be wearing it—not be enslaved inside the temple.

"You're planning to marry her?" the king asked.

"Yes," Ammon said in a quiet voice, his heart aching anew.

The king rubbed his forehead. "This complicates the matter."

Ammon stiffened. "How so?"

"If I demand her release, and the two of you eventually marry, it will seem that I've lied to the people."

"How can that be?" Ammon said.

"I just promised the people they're free to worship how they please," the king said, absently turning over the ring in his palm. "I told them I wouldn't interfere in their worship. If I demand the return of Moriah's daughter—I am interfering. I don't know if she went willingly—"

"She didn't," Ammon said.

"No," Abish said. "She would have never gone willingly."

The king's gaze narrowed as he looked at Abish then Ammon. "Do you know that for certain?"

Ammon glanced at Abish's pale face then back to the king. "Yes," he whispered.

"Let's assume she was taken against her will, and let's assume she wants to come back to you and marries you," the king said in a hesitant voice. "It will be breaking all traditions. No priestess has ever married. To have her break with tradition will appear as if I'm exercising control over the priests' and priestesses' freedom of worship."

"Even if she was taken against her will?" Ammon said, incredulous.

"If her father gave his permission, it's considered her wish too, and it will hold up in any Lamanite court since this happened last week," the king said. "If I had only given the new edict earlier—but it was not in my power until my father freed me to do so."

Ammon blew out a breath. "I see." He turned away from the king, trying to gain control of his emotions.

"I'm sorry, Ammon," Lamoni said in a pain-filled voice. "I'll request an audience with the high priest of the Maize Temple. Perhaps we can find out the details."

Ammon looked over at Kumen—whose dark eyes were burning with the same indignation Ammon felt.

The king swung open the door and ordered one of the guards to bring the high priest to the palace.

When the guard left, the room was silent again until the king said, "All we can do now is wait."

"And pray," Abish said in a small voice. She stifled a sob by clamping a hand over her mouth. Ammon crossed to her and put an arm around her shoulders as she quietly cried. He closed his eyes and silently prayed. Again.

* * *

Elena hadn't slept the night before, anxiety keeping her all too aware that she was just hours away from Harvest forcing her to become a true priestess. Or minutes. The priestesses had been gone all day and had made it a point to tell her they'd be gone well into the evening.

That morning, she'd remained curled up on her pallet as the women awakened one by one and prepared for the morning rituals. Sunray had come to check on her before leaving the room. She placed a cool hand on Elena's forehead. "You are not well?"

Elena said nothing.

"You must accept your new life, River. It will be easier if you let the happiness inside." She smiled, but Elena could hardly look at the woman. "I am so happy here. I love my new sisters, and we're treated like queens by the priests." She moved her hand along Elena's hairline. "The sooner you embrace the temple, the sooner you can begin your glorious destiny." She set a cup of wine in front of her. "If you drink, it will be easier. If not, Harvest will have other ways."

Elena stared at the cup of wine from across the room. It had remained untouched by her pallet all day. Her mind was numb, not from wine but from hunger and fatigue. Though she'd spent days locked in this room, it was as if all of her strength had left her at the temple door.

She looked down at her arms and removed the linen bandages. Her skin was nearly healed now, and the markings were distinct against her fair skin. Maize stalks twisting with flowers—flowers representing the blessing of fertility, stalks representing the connection of heaven to earth.

Elena drew her thin robe about her as if it would add some sort of protection. A shudder ran through her body as she imagined the approaching priest and his entrance into the room. She'd have nowhere to hide, and he had proven to be stronger than she.

As the moments passed, her panic increased, her silent prayers becoming more fervent. She touched the door knob with a trembling hand. It was bolted from the outside, just like the other times she tried it. She'd have to wait for the appearance of the priest. The wait wasn't long. When she heard his soft footsteps padding closer, she was ready, oil lamp in hand and determination in every part of her. She would not submit to this evil; she would rather die defending her virtue than become part of something so horrible and evil as this so-called religion.

As the door opened, she swung the lamp at his head, making contact with a terrific thud. The impact echoed through her arms, sending shots of pain through the newly healed skin. As the priest staggered backwards in surprise, Elena shoved him and leapt through the doorway.

In the hall, she turned left, in the opposite direction she'd been taken the other day. She had no idea where the exit was, but she hoped to find a place to at least hide and beg for the Lord to help her.

She ran, turning a corner then another, fully expecting someone to be chasing her, shouting after her. But there was nothing.

Her heart pounded against her chest, and she tried to curb her breathing to keep as quiet as possible. She stopped before a set of stairs that went upward. She glanced around quickly; there were no doors in this corridor but only a narrow space between the wall and the steps. She squeezed into it and crouched, staying hidden in the shadows and waiting.

She almost didn't hear him, not until she saw the color of his robe. The light brown cloth peeked over the steps that climbed above her hiding spot. Her body went cold all over; tiny bumps of skin raised on her arms and neck. The cloth swayed ever so slightly above her. He wasn't moving.

She couldn't hear his breathing, hadn't heard his footsteps. *Could he see her? Hear her?*

Elena held her breath, her body starting to ache from holding still. The cloth disappeared, and she thought she heard a faint shuffle as he moved upward. For another minute, she didn't move, although she let her breath out ever so slowly. She closed her eyes in relief, adding another prayer.

She didn't see the hand that reached down and grabbed her hair.

Elena screamed, but she couldn't move. Harvest somehow managed to block her exit, one hand gripping her hair, the other plunging a thorn into her shoulder. His eyes glistened as he stared at her with a victorious smile on his face.

She opened her mouth to scream again, but the priest slammed her head back into the wall. Pain exploded instantly, followed by darkness. She was vaguely aware of being dragged from her hiding place before she remembered no more.

* * *

The setting sun had splashed orange and yellow across the sky before word came from the high priest of the Maize Temple. He wasn't coming. Not today.

"He's not coming for two more days?" Ammon said, staring at the king after the messenger left. "Doesn't he know you are the king?"

"It's as I thought." Lamoni sat with heavy dejection as he sat on his throne. "Every priest in the land knows of my declaration. They'll test it to the extreme."

Kumen, Ammon, and Abish stood before the king in the throne room, each of them lost in their own thoughts. Ammon twisted the necklace he'd tied around his neck, the one Elena should be wearing.

"Two days will be too late," Abish said in a quiet voice.

Her words pierced Ammon's heart; they were absolutely true. Even now, it might be too late for Elena to be spared the humiliation of a fertility ritual, but waiting any longer would only make her exposure worse. His gaze locked with Kumen's. The king might not be able to take any direct action, but Ammon had to find a way. He looked at the king, who was gazing past them all, his face troubled.

"What if we find her father?" Ammon said. "And he makes the request for the release?"

The king's face brightened, and he leaned forward. "That might work . . ." His expression clouded again. "You'll be walking into the rebel's lair, though—Moriah is likely hiding with Zaman. And Pahrun can be fearsome." His eyes filled with concern. "They want you dead, Ammon."

"I know," Ammon said. "I'll take several men to help me."

The king shook his head. "The more I think about it, the more dangerous I realize it is. Let the scouts who are out right now bring them in." He clasped his hands together, his mouth drawn in a serious line. "I'm sorry. I wish there were no delay, but it's too dangerous for you to seek him on your own, even if you do have guards with you."

"I'll take the risk," Ammon said.

The king lifted a brow. "It's against my advice."

"Do you forbid it?"

"No," the king said in a quiet voice. "But how will you find him when the scouts have not?"

"I'll issue a challenge to Moriah," Ammon said. "Knowing Zaman, it will be too hard to resist. Zaman will come with his father."

The king was on his feet. "I don't recommend this. Zaman fights without honor—you could be killed."

"The Lord will protect me," Ammon said.

"Will He protect you if you're a complete fool?" the king shouted, his face red.

Ammon hung his head, breathing in deeply. When he raised it, Lamoni was still standing, his hands clenched into fists at his side.

"I'm not afraid," Ammon said.

"I am," the king said. "For *you*. I thought you told me the Lord sent you here to preach."

"He also told me that Elena should be my wife."

The king's fists opened, and he sat down on the throne, his face still red. "Then do it." His voice was hoarse. "Deliver your challenge."

"I'll report back as soon as I can," Ammon said.

The king clenched his jaw and turned to the court scribe. "Let it be known that Ammon is challenging Moriah to meet him—" He looked at Ammon.

"In the market square at dawn," Ammon filled in.

"In the market square at dawn," the king continued, "to barter for the release of Moriah's daughter from the Maize Temple."

Ammon nodded with satisfaction then, without another word, left the throne room. Kumen followed him. They were halfway down the corridor before Ammon realized Abish was following them as well.

He turned as she caught up with them.

"I'm coming to the market square in the morning," Abish said, her eyes flashing with determination. "I know Zaman as well as anyone. Perhaps he'll be more reasonable if I'm there."

"No," Ammon and Kumen said at the same time.

"Please." Abish's hands shot out and gripped each of their arms. "I can't bear to think of anything happening to Elena. She's like a sister to me. Zaman and I—he was very angry the last time I saw him, but perhaps with the passage of time . . ."

"Abish," Ammon said in a gentle voice, prying her hand off his arm. "We don't even know where they're hiding. It might take hours for them to get the message. It may not be in time. If he doesn't appear, then I'm going to hunt him down. If he does come, he and his men will come to fight—to kill. They've become traitors to the king, and they'll not hesitate to harm anyone who's in their way. Someone like you will be used to their full advantage."

"So I would be too much responsibility?" she said.

Ammon nodded.

Abish looked over at Kumen, her gaze pleading. "Elena is like my family—surely you understand I'd do anything to help her."

The three stood in silence for a moment. Then Ammon removed a dagger that was tied at his waist and handed it over to Abish. She beamed with pleasure. "Thank you," she said.

"Don't hesitate to use it," Ammon said. "We'll meet on the palace steps before dawn."

Abish hurried away, hiding the dagger in her robe.

CHAPTER 24

Blessed are all they that put their trust in him.
—Psalm 2:12

Ammon woke with a start less than an hour later, his body soaked in perspiration. He'd nearly collapsed in the corridor after Abish left, and Kumen helped him to bed. But now he'd seen Elena in a dream. She'd been huddled in a corner of a dark room, crying.

He turned in bed, his shoulder throbbing anew, and he was sure he probably needed a new bandage. Kumen was spread out on a rug on the floor, snoring. Ammon couldn't wait any longer. It was fully dark now. Dawn suddenly seemed too far away—it might be too late. Elena needed him now.

He rose from the platform bed and swung his legs to the ground. The movement woke Kumen.

"What's wrong?" Kumen asked.

"I'm going to the Maize Temple."

Kumen was wide awake now, and he scrambled to his feet as Ammon took a long drink from a water skin. Then he walked to the door.

There was no argument, no pleading from Kumen, simply, "I'm coming with you."

A guard posted outside Ammon's room straightened as they exited. He made a move to follow, but Ammon held up his hand. "I have Kumen with me. If I'm not back by first light, I'll be in the market square."

Confusion crossed the guard's expression, but he nodded and remained at his post.

Ammon's shoulder ached, and his body felt weak as they hurried through the dark streets, but the ache in his heart was stronger. The market square was busy with evening vendors who used torchlights to attract the late customers. They passed cooking fires and aromas of family suppers being prepared. He heard the screech of children as they played their games inside their homes.

The Maize Temple was one of the larger temples in the land, situated on top of a hill outside the main town.

"Will there be guards?" Ammon asked as they hurried as fast as his energy could spare.

"Yes," Kumen said. "There will be more than one entrance though. Perhaps they are not all guarded."

Ammon knew he couldn't depend on that. His hand rested on one of the daggers strapped to his waist. He hoped he wouldn't have to use it, hoped there was a better way. But the high priest's answer to the king made it clear that they would not be giving up Elena easily.

The image of a helpless Elena returned again and again to Ammon's mind, propelling him beyond his strength. They avoided the main steps of the temple and instead cut through the trees and brush that led up the hillside. Near the top of the hill, a guard was posted at the front temple entrance. Ammon's throat tightened as he assessed the long, steep steps that descended down the hill—someone could be pushed down those in a fight.

Kumen motioned for Ammon to follow him. They continued around the temple, looking for another entrance. They found a low doorway on the side, and Ammon paused. There was no guard there, but it was likely locked.

They crept to the doorway, but his assumption had been correct; the door was locked. Ammon pressed his good shoulder against the door, gauging how thick the wood was. When he was satisfied, he braced himself with both hands against the sides and, before Kumen could protest, kicked the door in. It splintered. Ammon kicked again, and the door gave way, hanging to one side. He pushed through, walking blindly into the dark interior, Kumen right behind him.

"I can't see a thing," Kumen whispered.

"Shh," Ammon said. "Just move as fast as you can until we bump into someone."

They were in a narrow corridor that led both ways, both equally dark. As they moved as fast as they dared, a light shone behind them. "Wait," Ammon whispered.

He turned to face the growing light. Around the bend, a man appeared, his long face illuminated by the torch. "Who's there?" the man called out, trying to sound gruff, but his high-pitched voice was far from harsh.

Ammon said nothing, just waited for the man to grow closer. Suddenly, he leapt toward the man and grabbed him. In a flurry of scuffling, he had the man captured, holding him at knifepoint.

Kumen stooped to pick up the fallen torch. He held it high overhead, lighting the corridor.

"Are you a priest?" Ammon asked, one arm wrapped around the man's neck, the other holding a dagger to his face.

"Yes," the man choked out. "We have no silver. The people bring animals as offerings."

"I'm not looking for silver," Ammon growled. "Show us the Nephite woman who was brought seven days ago."

"There's n-no Nephite woman here," the priest stammered.

Ammon increased the pressure, and the priest started to gag.

"We know she's here, and we know she was brought against her will." The priest struggled against Ammon. *"Where is she?"*

The priest's body went limp, and he gasped, "In the circle."

Whatever the circle was, it couldn't be good. "Show us."

"Impossible," the priest said. He twisted in Ammon's grasp, but he pressed the blade of his dagger against the man's cheek, and the priest finally stilled. "It's forbidden. No one outside the order is allowed inside."

"Then bring her to us," Ammon said.

"The ritual cannot be interrupted, or the gods will—"

Ammon yanked the priest's arm backward, and he cried out.

"You broke my arm," the priest gasped.

"Not yet," Ammon said, increasing the pressure.

The man cried out in agony.

"You don't want to alert too many people," Ammon said, "or I'll have to use this dagger."

"All right," the priest whimpered. "I'll show you the place, but no one can enter until after—"

"Go. Now!" Ammon demanded.

He pushed the priest forward as they moved along the narrow corridor. It opened up into a wider hallway lit with the occasional torchlight. The hallway turned in a circular fashion as it sloped downward. They reached a flight of stairs, which they quickly descended. At the bottom, an eerie sound reached Ammon's ears—a mixture between chanting and praying. All of the voices were male.

The skin on his neck bristled as he imagined what might be happening to Elena at that very moment. "Hurry," he commanded.

The trembling priest led them to a low door that was more of a half door. Ammon shoved the priest at Kumen, who immediately took possession of him, then Ammon kicked in the door. By the time it fell, the priest was sobbing with wretched cries.

Ammon stepped into a room that was brilliantly lit with at least a dozen torches, filled with the smoky haze of burning incense. It took a second to focus on what was going on through the haze.

A large altar stood at the center of the room, surrounded by priests who were staring at him, jaws slack with shock. Several women were in the room too, wearing white robes and sheer veils over their faces. The priests didn't have on robes as the one outside did but wore colorful kilts, looking as if they were dressed for a festival.

But it was what lay on the altar that drew his attention immediately. Even with her face turned away, Ammon recognized Elena. Her eyes were closed, and her hair had been plaited and threaded with ribbon. She wore a white robe, her arms bare, revealing black designs on them. She seemed unnaturally still. Horror and disgust collided in Ammon. He didn't know if she was unconscious or if they had done something to her or were about to, but he had to get her away.

"If anyone moves or tries to stop me, your friend will bleed to death on this floor," Ammon said as Kumen forced the other priest into the room.

Several of the people gasped as they stared at their fellow captured priest.

Ammon was at the altar in three strides, using his dagger to slice the ropes that bound Elena. He tried not to think too much about her condition as he freed her wrists and ankles. Her eyes were closed, and she didn't move as he lifted her.

Heat pulsed through the muscles in his shoulder, but he ignored it. He turned and carried Elena out of the stifling room. "Bring the priest with us," Ammon said to Kumen.

The air in the hallway brought a small reprieve as they traveled back the way they'd come. "Elena," Ammon whispered as he carried her. Her skin was warm against his, and he felt the steady pulse of her heart against his chest. She was alive.

Once outside the temple, Kumen released the priest, and they hurried into the trees. As they scuttled down the hill in and out of patches of moonlight, Kumen said, "How will we explain this to the king? Everyone knows who you are."

Ammon knew the king would be upset, but holding Elena in his arms flooded him with joy. She was breathing; she was alive. That's all that mattered. Her hair spilled over his arm, and all he wanted to do was kneel down and bury his face in it.

He wasn't worried about the temple guards chasing after him; they'd find another way to seek repercussions.

The walk back to the palace was long, but Ammon didn't mind. People came out of their homes to stare at him carrying a woman through the streets. At one point, Kumen took Elena from Ammon, as much as Ammon was reluctant to let her go. "You're going to collapse," Kumen said, hefting her into his arms.

When they reached the palace, Ammon was carrying her again. He took her straight to his room and laid her on the bed. "Go find Abish," he said.

Ammon knelt by Elena's form while Kumen left to find Abish. The oil lamp in the room cast shadows on the walls. He grasped her hand and pressed his lips against it. "You're here, you're really here."

Her eyes fluttered opened then shut.

"Elena?"

A soft moan came from her lips. He stared at her closed eyes, willing them to open. He touched her cheek. Her head moved slightly, then her eyes opened again. She stared at him without a word.

"How do you feel?" he asked.

Her lips parted, and Ammon heard the rush of air from her exhale.

"Ammon?" she said, her voice just above a whisper.

"I'm here," he said, moving his fingers through her hair.

"I must be dreaming," she said, staring at him. Her eyes closed again.

"Elena?" He leaned over her, listening for her breath. It was steady but faint.

The door opened, and Kumen entered with Abish behind him. Abish rushed to the bed and gasped. "When Kumen told me—I didn't dare believe it." She covered her mouth with her hands. "Is she all right?"

"She opened her eyes and spoke then fell asleep again," Ammon said, unable to take his eyes from Elena's face.

"Let me examine her," Abish said.

Ammon took a long look at Elena. "I'll be right outside." His body trembled as he stood, and he knew the exhaustion had caught up with him. In the hallway, he leaned against the wall and sank to the floor.

"You need rest," Kumen said.

Ammon only nodded. His heart and strength were in that room. He tried not to think of what Abish might discover about how Elena was treated. Touching the necklace at his throat, he wrapped his fingers around the ring. It no longer belonged to him, just as his heart no longer belonged to him. He untied the leather then closed his eyes and waited for Abish's call.

Sometime later, a woman's voice woke Ammon. He blinked his eyes open, realizing he'd fallen asleep sitting up. Abish had come into the hallway and was speaking with Kumen.

"How is she?" Ammon asked.

Abish turned with a tremulous smile. "She's unharmed, for the most part. She did not go through the full sanctification process."

Ammon exhaled in relief. "What about her arms?"

"The markings may fade with time but are most likely permanent," she said.

"They will always be a reminder," he said.

"Yes," Abish said. "But you saved her just in time."

A weight lifted from Ammon's shoulders, though he knew there would be consequences of breaking into the temple and threatening the priests. "Is she awake?"

Abish nodded. "She's asked for you."

He stood then leaned against the wall as the dizziness returned. Kumen hurried to grab his arm. "I'll be fine," Ammon said after a moment. He entered the room where a couple more oil lamps had been lit, making the space brighter.

Elena's eyes were closed, but as he crossed to her, she opened them. Ammon wasn't sure what reception he'd receive, so he was grateful Abish and Kumen had stayed in the hallway to offer them some privacy.

Elena watched him walk toward her then lifted her hand as he sat beside her. He took it and pressed her cool palm to his lips.

"How are you feeling?" he asked.

She blinked several times, and a tear trailed down her face.

Ammon reached out and absorbed it with his fingers. Then he leaned over and kissed her cheek. She wrapped her arms around him, lifting up from the bed to cling to him. As he held her, she trembled, and he wished he could stop it.

"I didn't know if I'd ever see you again," she said at last. "I prayed night and day." Her voice broke. "I've never wanted anything more in my life."

His arms tightened about her. "You're safe now."

She drew away, and Ammon reluctantly released her.

"My brother . . ." Her voice choked off.

"You don't have to tell me now. I know it's painful. I know your brother and father took you against your will," he said, reaching out to smooth her hair.

Elena stopped his hand with hers, clasping his. "It wasn't my father—he didn't know. If he did, Zaman wouldn't have had to abduct me in the middle of the night. My father would have formally presented me at the temple."

Ammon stared at her, not wanting to press, but he had to know. He'd issued a challenge to her father. "Zaman abducted you in the middle of the night?"

"Zaman and two others. I think one was Dedan; I'm not sure about the other man." She took a shaky breath. "My father didn't know—at least in the beginning."

Ammon exhaled, releasing her hand and standing up. "I issued a challenge to your father." He could feel her eyes on him. "We meet at dawn." He turned to look at her, regret seeping through him. "I assumed he'd broken his pledge to me. I assumed he was in league with your brother."

Elena's face was pale, her cheeks hollow as she took a careful breath. "My father may not have known about it in the beginning, but he did nothing to free me once he found out."

Ammon walked around the bed and gazed out the narrow window. There was little to see—thick clouds had covered the moon. "We don't know that," he said in a quiet voice, mostly to himself. He wondered silently if Moriah had gone with Zaman of his own free will or if he was as much a victim as Elena. It was hard to imagine that a father would be so cruel to his daughter—yet it was as hard to comprehend Zaman's actions toward Elena.

Not so hard to imagine, Ammon thought as the breath left him. *I was once so cold, so hardhearted, so willing to compromise everything dear to me.*

"I don't care anymore," Elena said, sitting up in bed. A flush covered her cheeks. "Whether my father knew or didn't know . . . whether he helped or didn't . . . they've both betrayed me." A tear escaped her eye, but her tone remained firm. She brushed it away and climbed out of bed, wrapping her arms about her torso.

Ammon winced at the sight of her marked arms—angry red welts still covered them.

"I'll find a way to support myself," Elena said, her words coming out in a rush, "and they'll have no say about my life. I can become independent. I don't care what the people will think." Her stance was defiant, her voice growing in strength. "Let them gossip and predict—"

"Elena," Ammon cut in and took several steps toward her until he was on the same side of the bed as she. "I'll take care of you."

She closed her eyes and turned away. "You pity me now."

"I know I have next to nothing, but the king has declared I'm no longer a servant." He waited for her response, but she kept her back turned. "Of course, I'll always serve him and these people, like I promised. But I'll find a way to provide you a home."

Her voice was quiet when she spoke. "You received your answer from the Lord?"

He took another two steps until he was standing right behind her. "I did." He expected her to turn around with joy on her face and embrace him. But she didn't move. For a long moment, all he could hear was her breathing.

Taking off his leather necklace with the ring, he held it out to her. "This ring belongs to you."

"Where did you find it?" she asked in a faint voice.

"Abish discovered it for sale in the marketplace. That's how we found out which temple you'd been taken to."

Elena finally turned around; there was no joy on her pale, drawn face. She didn't touch the necklace but looked down at her folded arms. "I've changed, Ammon."

"I don't care about the markings."

"It's not just about the markings," she said, lifting her eyes to him. "I've changed inside." She ran her fingers down his arm, barely touching him, as if she were afraid to get too close. "When I was in the temple," she whispered, looking away again, "I prayed for deliverance. I prayed that the priests would leave me alone. I prayed that I'd see you again." She brought a hand to her mouth as she closed her eyes.

Ammon waited. It was painful to wait, but he needed her to be truthful—no matter how much it hurt him.

"I was delivered, and the priests didn't harm me that way." She opened her eyes but didn't look at him. "You stopped them."

Ammon reached for her, but she moved away.

"But I was marked, Ammon. No matter how you feel about me or how the Lord said you can take me to wife, I will always carry the markings. The people will see me as a deserter of the Maize Temple. I will be ostracized from society and seen as a woman who rejected the sacred duty of a priestess." She took a deep breath and stretched out her arms. "These markings will never disappear and will always stand between me and any man."

"No," Ammon said, grasping her hand and pulling her toward him. He touched her shoulder, her hair, her cheek. "They will never be between us."

"You don't understand," she whispered. "It's not how *you* see the markings but how the people see them. I am what I am now, and I have no choice but to accept it. I'll forgive my father and brother . . . someday . . . but for now, I need to be completely free of them—of everyone. I am a marked woman now, unfit for marriage. I need to find a way to support myself. I need to be strong for *myself*." She touched his face, resting her palm against his cheek.

He leaned down, resting his forehead against hers. "Elena, the Lord will soften the hearts of the people."

Tears coursed along her cheeks as she took a shaky breath. "The people are too established in their ideas. The only way to spare you the judgment is for me *not* to marry you. Don't you see? Everyone will see the marks on my arm and know that I left the temple, and the priests will tell people that you forced me out. If you married me, they'd see you as breaking their traditions, controlling their right to worship, defying a father and brother to have *your* way, possibly forcing me to be baptized."

"No. I'd explain everything—"

"My brother has already done that in his own words. He's poisoned many against you already—against the king. If we marry, they'll see it as solidifying what Zaman has told them." Her hand rested on his shoulder.

"A wedge will be driven between the Church members and the rebels. They'll use it against us. And I'll never be able to cover up the fact that I was a temple priestess in all but the final rite. Tension will escalate."

"The truth will be heard and believed," Ammon said.

"Only by those who *wish* to believe it." She pulled away from Ammon. "If you give me up, then there is no power behind Zaman's claims. His influence will fade, and he'll be seen as a radical. His followers will soften their hearts and be willing to listen." Her gaze held his. "The ripple effect will be amazing. Many more will convert; many more souls will be saved because of our one sacrifice."

She took the necklace he held in his hand. She reached up and tied it around his neck. "I can't accept your ring," she whispered. She lowered her hands and moved away from him, wrapping her arms about herself again. "You'll see this is the best way. Go to the challenge at dawn. Tell my father and brother that you've freed me from the temple and that I will not marry and I will not be baptized yet, but I will be my own woman. All that I ask is that they leave me in peace."

CHAPTER 25

Thus saith the Lord God of Israel, That which thou
hast prayed to me . . . I have heard.
—2 Kings 19:20

The clouds had thickened during the night, and the only evidence of the approaching dawn was the dull gray light. Ammon stood in the center of the square, his sword in one hand.

King Lamoni, Kumen, Abish, and several guards stood at one end of the square. Dozens of people had gathered, all to watch the events transpire, but none would interfere. Ammon would face this alone. *With the help of the Lord.* He'd been praying ever since he'd left Elena's presence that somehow, someway, her heart would be changed, that the Lord's promise he'd felt would be fulfilled, but his heart was heavy and his body ached.

He'd taken off the necklace she'd tried to give back to him and had left it on the bed while her back was still turned. He told her he loved her and that the ring only belonged to her—that he'd never give it to another woman. She hadn't looked at him, hadn't said another word, which was why he was praying for a miracle. He knew that with God all things were possible. But he also knew that Elena had made her choice. And it would take a miracle to change her mind. If her brother or father confessed their wrongdoings, that might just be the miracle he needed.

Ammon clenched his jaw as the air softened and the sky began to lighten overhead. If Moriah didn't come this morning, there would be another day—that Ammon was sure of.

He felt the change in the air before he heard or saw anything. Zaman was coming. Ammon's stomach knotted as he turned to see Zaman approach, flanked by a dozen men, Pahrun among them.

They wore only loincloths, their bodies unwashed, perspiration on their faces and torsos. Zaman had new markings carved into his body. Ammon thought of the markings on Elena's arms—ones that were done involuntarily. Zaman's unhealed marks stood out like blisters across his chest and forearms, plainer on his light skin than those on his dark-skinned brethren.

Ammon felt as if he'd just opened a door to let evil in. He met Zaman's eyes. There was no mercy in them. No softening. The hatred in his gaze was blacker than ash. Ammon held his breath and wrenched his gaze from Zaman, searching for Moriah. The older man traveled at the back of the group, nearly hidden, his gaze averted. But his torso was free of the deep markings of his son's.

A sliver of hope touched Ammon's heart. *O Lord*, he prayed, *please direct my words and my actions.*

Zaman had his sword drawn, and the sun chose that moment to break through the clouds on the horizon, flashing against the obsidian. His face twisted into a cruel smile.

Heart thudding, Ammon wondered if Zaman would come at him with his men. It would be eleven to one. Ammon had given the king strict instructions not to interfere, no matter what. He wondered now if he'd been mistaken.

Zaman's band stopped a few paces from Ammon, but Zaman continued walking straight at him. He sported an ugly, partially healed gash on his arm where Ammon had injured him before.

His hand gripped his sword, ready to defend should Zaman take a swing.

The man said nothing at first, but walked around Ammon as if he were preying on an animal. Then he stopped in front of Ammon. "I see the arrow missed its target."

"Perhaps Dedan needs a bit more training."

Zaman scoffed. "Perhaps he missed on purpose."

"Why would he do that?"

Zaman didn't answer, but his eyes flickered. "You dare challenge my father, an old man?"

Ammon let out the breath he'd been holding. "He broke a promise."

"He kept his promise," Zaman growled. "We put her in the safest place in the land. Away from you."

Heat made its way through Ammon. He looked past Zaman to Moriah, who met Ammon's gaze for an instant then looked away. "You took her from her home," Ammon said, his focus back on Zaman. "You took her from her father. You took her from everything she knows and left her as chattel." He stepped forward, closing the distance between him and Zaman, so close that Ammon could smell the man's foul odor. Zaman flinched but didn't move away.

"Do you know what they did to her?" Ammon said in a low voice.

Zaman's nostrils flared. "She's a priestess now, revered above all women in the land. She'll spend her days worshiping the true god, the maize god."

"No," Ammon said, his eyes narrowing. "They carved her arms. They tied her to an altar so that the priests might have their way with her."

Zaman's face darkened. "The priestess rites are sacred, and they bless all of civilization with posterity."

"Take your revenge on *me*. Not your sister. She was barely alive when I found her. They poisoned her in order to force her to do things against her will."

"Elena's out of the temple?" Moriah cried out. He pushed through the group of men and stumbled forward. It was then that Ammon noticed how weak the man looked, as if he were a broken man. His former robustness had faded, his eyes wild and desperate.

"Yes," Ammon said in a quieter voice. "She's in a safe place."

Moriah's shoulders sagged in relief. "Tell her . . . tell her I'm sorry—"

"Father!" Zaman shouted. He shoved the old man away, and Pahrun took a firm hold on Moriah, pulling him back into the group.

Zaman's expression was furious when he turned back to Ammon. "I see you've brought many witnesses—how like you. In our first fight you pretended reluctance. But I now see your true character—that you delight in bloodshed just as I do. You want a show? Let's give them a show." Zaman brought his sword around in one swift movement.

Ammon was slow to react, his attention on Moriah. Ammon barely deflected Zaman's sword before it could touch him.

A woman screamed as Zaman came at Ammon with full fury, and it took everything Ammon had to fight him off. Even in his weakened condition, he was able to match the man's strength. The wilderness hadn't been good to this man—the lack of regular meals had probably weakened him as well.

But what Zaman lacked in stamina, he made up for in intensity. Every lunge, every swing of the sword was meant to kill. There was no mercy in his eyes, no doubt that this would end with one of them dead.

Zaman dove for Ammon's legs, tripping him. As Ammon rolled, Zaman's sword came down hard on Ammon's sword, wrenching it out of his grasp.

He scrambled to his feet and lunged for his sword before Zaman could get to it. In a second, Ammon was on his back, raising his sword to meet the next downward strike. Zaman's other hand pressed against Ammon's injured shoulder, sending fiery pain through it. His vision blurred.

He wrenched beneath Zaman's clutch, still holding his sword aloft. With both legs, he kicked Zaman off balance. Ammon was on top of Zaman in an instant. He dropped his sword and wrapped his left hand around Zaman's neck. With his right hand, he withdrew one of his daggers and forced it against Zaman's chest.

Zaman's eyes widened as Ammon's pressure around his neck increased. Ammon pressed the dagger until it broke Zaman's skin. His eyes bulged as his hands clawed at Ammon's grip. But he remained firm, and finally Zaman's hands went limp as his face went from red to white.

Ammon leaned close and whispered, "The only reason I spare your life is because you're her brother. If you were not, I'd run you through." He loosened his grip, and the color flooded back to Zaman's face.

He turned his head and coughed, gulping air as if he'd been held under water. After the gasping subsided, he looked at Ammon and spat in his face.

Ammon didn't move. "You might curse me, but you've broken her heart."

"Get him out of here!" the king's voice filled the square. "Let it be known that Zaman, son of Moriah, will never be welcomed in the land of Ishmael again!"

Ammon moved off of Zaman, becoming aware of the burning pulse in his shoulder that had now spread through the rest of his body. By sheer will, he remained upright.

Zaman moved slowly until he was on his feet, shaking with anger. "I leave this land with pleasure—I leave it to those who wish to live as fools." He looked past Ammon to the king. "I have issued my warning." He turned slowly to his group of men. "Let's go."

The men joined his side—all but Moriah.

"Father?" Zaman said.

Moriah shook his head. "I can't leave her."

"She is nothing to us now. By rejecting the temple, she has made her choice," Zaman said.

"So have I," Moriah said.

"Father, this is a mistake."

"No," Moriah said in a hoarse voice. "I know what I am doing. And I have to make a confession in case I never see you again." He lowered his head for a moment. When he looked up again, tears shone on his face. "I believe, my son. I believe in the miracles I saw in the king's court. I know that Ammon was sent by the Lord."

Zaman's face was dark red as he rushed to his father and gripped his shoulders. "Not you too—Father, you have been tricked!"

"No, son," Moriah said. He sank to his knees, his trembling hands clasped together. "O Lord, forgive me of my sins."

Zaman stared at him in horror.

"O blessed God, have mercy on my son!" Moriah cried out. "Deliver his soul unto repentance."

Zaman backed away, disbelief on his face.

Moriah fell to the ground, his arms stretched in front of him as he continued to pray.

"No!" Zaman screamed. "I'd rather have you dead than possessed of the devil." He charged toward his father, but Ammon leapt in front of him, sword ready.

Abish screamed and ran forward. She grabbed Zaman's arm. "Don't hurt your father."

Zaman stopped, confusion and desperation on his face as he stared at Abish. The king moved to Ammon's side, his own dagger drawn.

"Zaman," Abish said, her voice pleading. "Don't do this. Think of your sister. You've already lost one parent."

He shook his head, his gaze hardening as he focused on Abish. "You've betrayed me most of all."

"There's been no betrayal, Zaman. Only truth. I pray that you will see it," she said.

Zaman took a couple of steps backward, his face growing dark. "You're nothing to me, woman. You've been bewitched. I no longer know you." He turned and plowed into his group of rebels. They parted as he ran across the square, and then they followed after him.

* * *

Elena's dreams alternated between the shorn head of the priest and the swaying white-robed figures of the priestesses surrounding the altar. Terror sliced through her as she wrenched at the ropes. Her hands flailed, and she realized there were no more ropes. *Where am I? Has it already happened? Has Harvest completed the fertility rite?*

She tried not to sob, but the cries escaped her anyway. Someone was touching her, touching her hair, her face, speaking her name, her *real* name.

Her eyes flew open, and for a second she thought it was the priest staring down at her. But the eyes were different, the hair, the shape of his head.

Father.

"Elena," he cried out. He pulled her into his arms and buried his face in her neck.

"Father," she said, clutching him as he sobbed. Elena's own tears mingled with his. "What is it? What's happened?"

"Oh, my daughter. My dear, dear daughter." Moriah pulled away and cradled her face. "I was so wrong. Can you forgive me?"

Elena's voice wavered as she spoke. "Of course, Father."

Her father sank on the bed next to her, clasping her hands, his body shaking with sobs. "I'm sorry I didn't protect you better; I wasn't there to stop Zaman. I didn't know they'd taken you, but I acted like a coward when I found out." His words tumbled out so fast that Elena could barely keep up.

"But I told him—I told your brother the truth," he said. "I want to be baptized. I want to become a member of the Lord's true church." His voice trembled. "In front of everyone at the square, I admitted my wrongdoing and pledged my devotion to the Lord. I told the people I sent you to the temple against your will and that I denied the truth of Ammon's teachings."

Elena gasped. She clung to the sleeves of his robe. "What did Zaman say?"

"He left us. The king banned him from the land." He pulled away, touching her cheek tenderly as tears dripped down his own face. "He wanted to kill Ammon and destroy the Church. But now Zaman's left the city by order of the king, and you're safe. I'll never abandon you again."

A glimmer of hope rose in Elena like a ray of sunshine in the dawn. "With your public confession, the people will know that I wasn't forced to worship a certain way," Elena said. "They'll know that I wanted to leave the temple, that I am now free to make my own choices."

"Although there will always be those who will find a way to bring down the Church," her father said. "I am ashamed to say that I was one of them."

Elena grasped her father's hand. "What happened to change your mind, Father? How did you come to know the truth?"

"It was in the forest, when I was living with Zaman. They were so vengeful, so full of hatred, that it made me ill. Something didn't feel right.

I spent many sleepless hours secretly praying." His voice caught. "And something whispered to me—it could have only been the Lord's Spirit— that Ammon spoke the truth."

He squeezed Elena's hand. "'You must know there will always be opposition against those who try to follow the Lord, whether it's you or me or Ammon." His gaze moved past her.

It was then that Elena noticed someone else in the room. Ammon stood near the door, watching them. His eyes were rimmed in red as if he'd been crying. His tunic was torn, and several scratches stood out on his face and arms.

"Did my brother hurt you?" Elena asked Ammon, her voice cracking.

He shook his head slightly, his eyes never leaving hers.

"Elena," her father's voice cut in gently. "I give both of you my blessing."

She barely heard her father over the hammering of her heart. It was as if she and Ammon were the only ones in the room. She now realized that whether or not she married Ammon, there would be those fighting against the Church, spreading falsehoods, and tearing apart goodness. It wouldn't be because of her.

Her throat felt tight as she looked at Ammon. With all that she had lost—her homeland, her mother, and now her brother—she couldn't lose one more person.

Her hand moved to the necklace at her throat, the one she'd put on after Ammon had left, the one she'd held onto as she had cried herself into an exhausted sleep.

Ammon noticed the gesture. "I see you're wearing my ring again."

"You did say it belonged to no other, no matter my decision."

One side of Ammon's mouth lifted. "I did say that. And it's still true."

"Does that mean you forgive me for changing my mind?" Elena asked, fresh tears springing to her eyes.

Ammon's face broke out into a grin. "Always."

CHAPTER 26

The Lord will be the hope of his people, and the strength of the children.
—Joel 3:16

Ammon drew Elena's hand in his, holding it securely, never wanting to let go. It had been three weeks since he'd rescued her from the Maize Temple. "We'll dedicate this synagogue tomorrow. We expect hundreds of people to come since it's the first completed church. The other synagogues will follow shortly."

Elena squeezed his hand and leaned her head against his chest as her other arm came around his waist. "It's a beautiful building. So peaceful." She sighed. "Opposite of the feeling I had in the Maize Temple."

Ammon wrapped a protective arm about her. In less than a month, they'd become man and wife. Until then, their time together would be limited, so he'd brought her for a look at the new synagogue before his long schedule of upcoming dedications began. The sun's last rays filtered through the high windows, casting a warm glow throughout the building. It was a simple design, the interior plain compared to the elaborate temples. Rugs adorned the floors, and the cushions that had been donated were stacked against the walls. A platform had been erected at the front of the space so the preaching could be better heard.

It was a wonder that tomorrow this building would be filled to capacity. The Lord had truly blessed him in the land of Ishmael. He had spent the last three weeks teaching the people on a daily basis, exhorting them to righteousness. A lump formed in his throat as he thought of the people's response and how many of them were zealous in keeping the commandments of God. He had hoped and prayed for success when he'd journeyed to this land but had never dreamed he'd find such favor with the king or such willing people who wanted to learn the gospel—or find a woman like Elena to marry.

He was grateful that Elena and her father were both safe now, free to worship as they pleased. They'd moved back into their home, and the king had assigned guards day and night to watch over their home in case Zaman decided to return.

Elena nestled against Ammon, and he tightened his hold as they gazed at the synagogue while the last bits of daylight faded. He wished they didn't have to separate each night. But soon they'd be married, and he wouldn't have to say good-bye anymore.

He kissed the top of her head. "Are you ready?"

"Yes," she said, drawing back and lifting up her face toward his.

He took her face in both hands and kissed her softly. When she pulled him closer, he drew back and chuckled. He released her and smiled at her flushed face, although it likely matched the color of his. "Your father's waiting."

She closed her eyes with a sigh. "I know." When she opened her eyes again, her smile was brilliant. Her hand slipped into his. "Let's go."

They exited the synagogue and stepped into the last hints of twilight. The warmth of the day still lingered, and Ammon knew it would be a perfect evening for baptisms.

Elena kept hold of his hand, something she hadn't done in public before. She had also stopped wearing her usual scarf over her head, although she kept her sleeves long to cover her marked arms.

They walked along the main road that led toward the palace. Ammon greeted those who passed. A couple of children ran up to him, tugging at his kilt and talking excitedly about the new synagogue.

When the children ran past, laughing and calling back farewells, Elena turned her face upward. "They love you already."

"The Spirit has softened their hearts."

"It's not just that," Elena said with a laugh. "*You* are highly lovable."

"Are you trying to tell me something?"

"I think you already know it."

Ammon smiled as they left the main road and stepped onto the path that led to the river. In the seclusion of the trees, he stopped her. "*What do I already know?*"

"That you're lovable."

He looked up at the sky. "And?" he prompted.

"That I love you!"

"Much better," he said, his gaze back on her. She was so different from when he first met her—yet still the same. "But if you keep talking like this, we'll be late, very late."

She moved closer. "They'll understand."

"How did I become so fortunate?" Ammon whispered.

Elena's hands slipped behind his neck. "I'm the one who's fortunate. Look at what you've brought to our land, to our people." Her voice wavered, and she blinked rapidly. "You've saved souls, Ammon. There's no repayment for that."

He pulled her into his arms. "I wish my parents could meet you," he said, his voice thick.

"What will they think of their prince's choice?"

He ran his fingers through her hair. "They would fall in love instantly."

"Are you trying to tell me something?" she whispered.

"That I'm the most fortunate man on earth. That you'll always have my heart." Ammon lowered his voice. "That I love you more every minute."

Elena buried her face against his chest, and they stood together as the darkness gathered around them. Then, as the new moon rose, they walked hand in hand toward the river.

Torchlights lined the shore, at least a dozen of them.

Ammon was surprised at the gathered crowd. There would only be two baptisms tonight—Elena's and her father's.

King Lamoni stepped forward to greet and congratulate Elena. Moriah watched the reception with a wide smile on his face. Then Abish and Kumen came next to embrace Elena.

Ammon was grateful to see Abish brighten when she was around Kumen. He was becoming a good friend to her and a comfort since the tragedy of Zaman's departure.

After the welcome, Ammon turned to the gathering. He couldn't contain the joy in his voice. "Who would like to be first?"

Moriah pointed at his daughter, and she shook her head with a smile. "Father is first," she said.

Moriah shrugged, a grin on his face. He followed Ammon into the cool water. When they reached the middle of the river, Ammon stopped and turned to Moriah.

"Are you ready?" Ammon asked.

"Yes," Moriah said, his voice reverent.

Ammon clasped Moriah's wrist and began the prayer. After Ammon plunged Moriah into the water, the man came up with a shout.

Moriah embraced him fiercely. "Thank you, Ammon. Thank you for everything—for your sacrifice, your service to our people, your devotion, and your love for my daughter."

"I've never been happier," Ammon said, now soaked. The two men drew apart, both their eyes wet with tears. Ammon walked Moriah to the shore and watched as he embraced his daughter and the others who were waiting.

Then Ammon held out his hand to Elena. She stepped forward and took it, the dry touch of her hand warming his cold, wet hand. Together they walked into the swirling river until they were waist deep. "Is the water all right?" he asked.

Elena smiled, her eyes bright with unshed tears. "It's perfect."

"Just hold onto me," Ammon said.

"Always."

CHAPTER NOTES

CHAPTER 1

Scriptures referenced: Alma 17:9–11, 13, 17–18

Book of Mormon scholar S. Kent Brown estimates that the sons of Mosiah left Zarahemla in 94 BC to begin their missionary work in Lamanite lands (*Voices from the Dust*, 218).

In Alma 17:7, we learn that Ammon and his fellow missionaries took all types of weapons with them on their journey to teach the Lamanites, including swords, spears, bows, arrows, and slings. According to historian Matthew Roper, ancient Mesoamerican *macuahuitl* swords "consisted of a long, flat piece of hardwood with grooves along the side into which were set and glued sharp fragments of flint or obsidian" (*Journal of Book of Mormon Studies*, "Swords and 'Cimeters' in the Book of Mormon," 8:1, 1999, 36). Short knives or daggers were also quite common and were known as "short swords" or "fighting knives" (38). Roper quotes ethno-historian Brian Hayden in "that obsidian-edged macanas were used predominately by the elite . . . plain wood blades were used by peasant fighters" (38).

CHAPTER 2

Scriptures referenced: Alma 20:1

In Alma 20:8, we learn that King Lamoni's father is the "king over all the land." This means that Lamoni's father (called Laman in the novel) was the high king, the king over all the Lamanite territories with jurisdiction over the lesser kings. In other words, King Lamoni was "subservient" to his father's commands and wishes (John A. Tvedtnes, http://maxwellinstitute. byu.edu, Provo, Utah: Maxwell Institute, "Book of Mormon Tribal Affiliation and Military Castes," 4).

In this novel, I've named Lamoni's father, the high king, Laman. Scholar John L. Sorenson says that Laman might have been a "title of office, in the same manner that Nephite kings bore the title 'Nephi'" (http://maxwellinstitute.byu.edu, Provo, Utah: Maxwell Institute, "Peoples of the Book of Mormon," 2). In other words, "Laman" is possibly a name that the high king takes upon himself when he reaches the Lamanite throne. Although, Sorenson clarifies that since we are told in Alma 17:21 that Lamoni is described as a descendant of Ishmael—which means his father had the same ancestry—it's plausible that Lamoni's father may have carried the "Laman" title (ibid).

CHAPTER 3

Scriptures referenced: Alma 17:21–23

Interestingly enough, when King Lamoni asks if Ammon desires to dwell among the Lamanites and Ammon responds in the affirmative (Alma 17:23), King Lamoni takes him at his word with no further questions asked. Perhaps it's due to that fact that an oath, which it appears Ammon has made, is as binding as life itself. Hugh Nibley explains that an oath, such as the one Zoram made to Nephi (1 Nephi 4:35, 37), is "most sacred and inviolable" (*Lehi in the Desert*, 103). Although Ammon did not use the binding terms such as "on my life" or "as the Lord liveth" (ibid), it seems that his oath was solid enough for King Lamoni to place absolute trust in Ammon.

Fruit was eaten in season throughout Mesoamerica. According to Sorenson, there were no known methods for preserving fruit. The most common fruits eaten were guava and a type of cherry. Other crops that made up the daily diet included beans, corn, squash, potatoes, chili peppers, avocados, and tomatoes (*Images of Ancient America*, 36).

CHAPTER 4

In *Images of Ancient America*, Sorenson outlines the social strata, or class structure, among the Mesoamericans. At the top of the so-called pyramid are the rulers, kings, or overlords. Second come the magistrates, priests, and military officers. Third in class structure come the shamans, or medics, traders, servants, and soldiers. Fourth, at the bottom of society, are the slaves, sacrificial victims, and prisoners of war (81).

Chapter 6

Trees are an established sacred symbol in Mesoamerican culture, especially the ceiba tree. The Mesoamericans considered the ceiba as the center of the universe, and temple complexes were positioned around the tree. The ceiba is also used for its cottonlike fiber, called *kapok*, that can be used for stuffing bedding and making upholstery.

Chapter 7

When Ammon arrived in the land of Ishmael, he had great cause to call repentance unto the Lamanites. He bided his time, but some of the abominations that were taking place included autosacrificing (blood-letting), or human sacrificing, as a ritual to give back life to the gods who created the sky and earth (*The Maya*, 13; *Images*, 142).

Sorenson supposes that human sacrifice might be a part of the "abominations" that Nephi prophesied of in 1 Nephi 12:23 (*Images*, 142). Sacrifices of this nature were conducted by the priests for individual people or the community as a whole. In Alma 34:11, Alma might have been alluding to the blood sacrifices that took place in the form of self-mutilation: "There is not any man that can sacrifice his own blood which will atone for . . . sins" (*Images*, 209).

The goddess Chak Chel was considered the wife of supreme god Itzamanaaj. Chak Chel was also called "Lady Rainbow" and was the goddess of childbirth, medicine, and weaving. In some areas, she was known as the moon goddess (*The Maya*, 216).

Chapter 8

In the Book of Mormon, "mourning for the dead was characterized by extreme weeping, wailing, prayer, fasting, and possibly self-sacrifice of blood" (*Images*, 156).

Mesoamericans primarily worshipped multiple deities in the form of human gods or animal gods. They believed deity lived in a sort of heaven, with various levels of three, seven, and thirteen. Sorenson explains that "people had a special relationship, in name and loyalty, with a particular god" (*Images*, 138). In Enos 1:20, we learn that the Lamanite people were steeped in idolatry. Sorenson says that almost from the beginning, the Lamanites "had idols, and presumably, beliefs and practices related to gods other than the God of Israel" (140). Various gods, both with powers of good and evil, are referenced throughout the Book of Mormon, including "demons" (Hel. 13:37), "idol gods" (Mormon 4:14), and "sorceries, and witchcrafts, and magics" (Mormon 1:19) (ibid).

CHAPTER 9

In the Mesoamerican culture, a shaman was revered as a person who "has received a calling from supernatural powers to be an intermediary between them and common mortals" (*Images*, 136). Priest-cults went hand in hand with shamanism, where priests were considered to have similar powers. Sorenson clarifies that "offerings were commonly made . . . to deities who were thought to control" such things as crop growth and animal health, and "every step in life . . . is ceremonialized: being pregnant, giving birth, courting, borrowing and repaying money . . . being buried, etc." (ibid).

CHAPTER 10

Scriptures referenced: Alma 17:26–39; 18:9

There is some debate whether horses were used among the Nephites and Lamanites. In this book, I've included the horses and chariots as part of the story as dictated in Alma 20:6, although Nibley clarifies that horses weren't necessarily ridden during this time period but used to pull carts. In addition, it seems that only kings possessed horses, so it wasn't something that the Lamanites had casual access to (*Teachings*, 297).

CHAPTER 11

Scriptures referenced: Alma 18:1–43; 19:6

CHAPTER 12

Scripture referenced: Mosiah 27:11

CHAPTER 13

Scriptures referenced: Alma 19:1–14

CHAPTER 14

Scriptures referenced: Alma 18:36; 19:19–20, 22–36

Extended visions seem to be repeated throughout the Book of Mormon. Just as Alma the Younger had a three-day vision in which he was "born of the Spirit" (Mosiah 27:24), King Lamoni has a several-day-long vision. He is "laid upon his bed for the space of two days and two nights" (Alma 18:43). On the third morning, just as Ammon prophesies, the king arises and blesses the name of God (Alma 19:12). Smaller visions and manifestations of the Spirit occur after the king revives and then sinks to the ground again with his queen, Ammon, and several servants (v. 17).

In Mosiah 18:11, people clap their hands for joy when Alma tells them that they will be baptized. It seems that this is still a part of the Guatemalan culture today. Joseph L. Allen said that when he was traveling through Guatemala, a native Quiche-Mayan woman was their tour guide in a church and a museum. When she became excited, she'd clap her hands and laugh (*Sacred Sites*, 38).

CHAPTER 15

Scriptures referenced: Mosiah 18:12–14

CHAPTER 16

Quetzel birds were highly prized among the ancient Maya people. These people believed the bird would not survive captivity, so after plucking the tail feathers, they would set the bird free to grow new ones. Quetzel feathers were also used in royalty headdresses and capes. It's also the current national bird in Guatemala (www.wildernessclassroom.com, see "Quetzal").

CHAPTER 17

Scriptures referenced: Alma 29:34–36; see also Alma 18:29–30, 34, 36, 39; 19:34; 20:1–3

"On my life" is one of the forms of taking an oath. In biblical and Book of Mormon times, uttering an oath upon someone's life was serious in nature. It was a promise not to be broken, and when one declared something "on my life," it was upheld. Just as when Ammon pledges an oath to King Lamoni, leaving Lamoni no room for doubt, the oath that the character of Zaman makes in this chapter is grave indeed (*Lehi in the Desert*, 103).

Chapter 18

Scriptures referenced: Alma 20:4, 6–22, 24–27

On the journey to the land of Middoni, Lamoni and Ammon cross paths with Lamoni's father, the high king. We learn in Alma 20:9 that Lamoni missed an important feast on a "great day" made for his father's sons and his people. Similar to Ancient Jerusalem's feast of the Passover, this feast was one not to miss. Nibley explains that the king would have already felt slighted by his son for missing the great feast, so to see his son traveling with a Nephite as a friend was an even greater insult (*Teachings*, 311).

When Lamoni defies his father in Alma 20:15 by saying, "I will not slay Ammon, neither will I return to the land of Ishmael," Nibley explains that "he defied his father openly, and to defy the king openly is treason" (*Teachings of the Book of Mormon: Part Two*, 312). This explains why the high king was so angry with his son Lamoni and "drew his sword that he might smite him to the earth" (Alma 20:16).

Nibley also explains the sudden turn of events when the high king offers "half of the kingdom" (Alma 20:23). The tables are turned when Ammon gains the upper hand in the attack from the high king. Nibley says that "the person who has the gun has all the power." The gun is now in Ammon's hand, so to speak, and suddenly the king is ready to promise Ammon anything. The king has lost the battle, which means that, technically, Ammon can take all—or take the king's life. Knowing this, the high king bargains for his life and offers Ammon a compromise (*Teachings*, 312–13).

Scholar John A. Tvedtnes clarifies that Lamoni's father "granted his son autonomy in his kingdom" over the land of Ishmael ("Book of Mormon Tribal Affiliation and Military Castes," 4). This was a great honor and meant that Lamoni could now make important decisions, which were manifested when he started building synagogues throughout his land (Alma 21:20) and giving his people freedom of worship (v. 22).

CHAPTER 19

Scriptures referenced: Alma 1:3–17; 21:1–14, 22:12

Antiomno, king of Middoni, was apparently a friend to Lamoni since Lamoni was eager to help Ammon retrieve his brethren through the connection (Alma 20:4). Antiomno, like Lamoni, was also a lesser king and answered to the high king, Lamoni's father. Tvedtnes points out that Aaron and his fellow missionaries may have converted seven cities in the Lamanite territory (Alma 23:8–13, 15). But those cities didn't include Middoni under King Antiomno's rule or "the cities of the Amalekites and Amulonites and the Lamanites living in the same region . . . which comprised the lands of Amulon, Helam, Jerusalem, and nearby areas" ("Book of Mormon Tribal Affiliation and Military Castes," 4).

On an interesting note, we learn that Aaron taught from scriptures when he was preaching to the Nephites. In Alma 21:9, we read that "Aaron began to open the scriptures unto them concerning the coming of Christ." Does this mean that Aaron carried a copy of the scriptures with him—perhaps written on vellum? Also, in Alma 22:12, "Aaron . . . began from the creation of Adam, reading the scriptures unto the king," which possibly indicates that Aaron had something physically in hand to read from.

CHAPTER 20

Sorenson explains that hallucinogens were used in Mesoamerica by priests and/or nobility. Mushrooms or, on a more general level, tobacco was used for sacred purposes. Priests also implemented fasting, where they'd only eat once a day for several days, months, or years at a time (*Images*, 151).

CHAPTER 21

Scriptures referenced: Psalm 5; Alma 21:22

The prayers of the Nephites may have been patterned after those found in Psalms 4 and 5. The pattern of opening the prayer with "O God" or "O Lord" is consistent, followed by questions, then praises, love, and gratitude given to the Lord.

Chapter 22

When Ammon reminds his brethren of why they decided to become missionaries, he refers to the Lamanites as people "whose days have been spent in the grossest iniquity" (Alma 26:24). There are many similarities in the worship practices of ancient Israel, which Lehi and Nephi would have been familiar with, and those in Mesoamerica. During the reign of King Zedekiah, immorality was in full force in not only the society but in the religious venues, which included idolatry and various forms of immorality, such as sacred prostitution. This may have been one of Ammon's duties— to preach against such immoralities as temple prostitution (see "1 Kings– Malachi," *Old Testament Student Manual*, 235–37).

Chapter 23

Scriptures referenced: Alma 21:19–23; 26:17–22, 24

In the ancient Old World, as well as in Mesoamerican civilization, Sorenson says that "spiritual concerns were mainly a social, not an individual, matter." The tendency toward family and tribal unity in religion was so strong that it's no wonder that individuals who decided to change their religious view were ostracized (*Images*, 136).

Chapter 24

Burning incense was not only a ritual used by the Nephite and Lamanite ancestors but was also done during rituals by the Mayan people (*The Maya*, 244). Ancient Mayans highly valued *pom*, "the resin of the copal tree, which was used as incense—so holy was this that one native source describes it as the 'odor of the center of heaven'" (206).

Chapter 26

Scripture referenced: Alma 21:23

SELECTED BIBLIOGRAPHY

Allen, Joseph L. *Sacred Sites: Searching for Book of Mormon Lands*. American Fork, Utah: Covenant Communications, 2003.

Brown, S. Kent. *Voices from the Dust*. American Fork, Utah: Covenant Communications, 2004.

Coe, Michael D. *The Maya: Seventh Edition*. New York: Thames & Hudson, 2005.

Nibley, Hugh. *Teachings of the Book of Mormon: Part Two*. Provo, Utah: FARMS, 2004.

Nibley, Hugh. "Lehi in the Desert," *Lehi in the Desert/The World of the Jaredites/There Were Jaredites* [The Collected Works of Hugh Nibley, vol. 5]. Salt Lake City: Deseret Book, and Provo, Utah: FARMS, 1988.

Old Testament: 1 Kings–Malachi. Religion 302 Student Manual. Salt Lake City: The Church of Jesus Christ of Latter-day Saints, 1982.

Roper, Matthew. "Swords and 'Cimeters' in the Book of Mormon," *Journal of Book of Mormon Studies* 8:1, 1999.

Sorenson, John L. *Images of Ancient America: Visualizing the Book of Mormon*. Provo, Utah: FARMS, 1998.

Tvedtnes, John A. "Book of Mormon Tribal Affiliation and Military Castes." Provo, Utah: Maxwell Institute. http://maxwellinstitute.byu.edu.

ABOUT THE AUTHOR

Heather B. Moore is the Best of State and two-time Whitney Award–winning author of the Out of Jerusalem series and *Abinadi, Alma, Alma the Younger,* and *Ammon.* She is also the author of the nonfiction work *Women of the Book of Mormon: Insights & Inspirations.* Visit Heather's website at www.hbmoore. com.